New Yor...

NA...

"Singh ...
level ca...

"The a...

Nights
Night Shift
WITHDRAWN

$7.99
ocn876668357
Berkley mass-ma   11/26/2014

#1 *New York Times* Bestselling Author

ILONA ANDREWS

"Ilona Andrews's books are guaranteed good reads."
—Patricia Briggs, #1 *New York Times* bestselling author

"[A] vividly drawn, kick-butt series."   —*Monsters and Critics*

National Bestselling Author

LISA SHEARIN

"Lisa Shearin always delivers a great story."
—Ilona Andrews, #1 *New York Times* bestselling author

"Shearin weaves a web of magic with a dash of romance
that thoroughly snares the reader. She's definitely an author
to watch!"   —Anya Bast, *New York Times* bestselling author

NIGHT SHIFT

NALINI SINGH
ILONA ANDREWS
LISA SHEARIN
MILLA VANE

BERKLEY BOOKS, NEW YORK

THE BERKLEY PUBLISHING GROUP
Published by the Penguin Group
Penguin Group (USA) LLC
375 Hudson Street, New York, New York 10014

USA • Canada • UK • Ireland • Australia • New Zealand • India • South Africa • China

penguin.com

A Penguin Random House Company

NIGHT SHIFT

A Berkley Book / published by arrangement with the authors

For information, address: The Berkley Publishing Group,
a division of Penguin Group (USA) LLC,
375 Hudson Street, New York, New York 10014.

ISBN: 978-0-425-27392-0

PUBLISHING HISTORY
Berkley mass-market edition / December 2014

PRINTED IN THE UNITED STATES OF AMERICA

10 9 8 7 6 5 4 3 2 1

Cover art by Tony Mauro.
Cover design by Rita Frangie.
Interior text design by Laura K. Corless.

CONTENTS

SECRETS AT MIDNIGHT

NALINI SINGH

CHAPTER 1

Bastien Smith knew he'd been suckered. By his own mother no less. The only thing that *might* make it bearable was if Sage had been suckered, too. "Tell me you didn't know," he said to his younger brother through gritted teeth, both of them propping up the wall nearest the door and an escape they couldn't make.

Eyes narrowing, Sage folded his arms. "Are you accusing me of breaking the bro code?"

Bastien shoved a hand through his hair, the dark red strands no doubt a mess by now. "Sorry." It was only right he apologize after suspecting Sage of something so heinous, even if it had resulted from sheer exhausted frustration. "Mom told me she needed help setting up."

"Technically, she did." Sage nodded toward the heavy dining table their mother had asked the two of them to shift into the large living area of the home where they'd both grown up. It fit, plenty of space around it for their mother's guests to mingle, only because Bastien and Sage had first hauled the usual living room furniture into other rooms of the house.

It hadn't taken long, both of them happy to help their mom prepare for the "book club luncheon" she'd been looking forward to all week. What she'd neglected to mention was that all her book club buddies were bringing along their nubile daughters, nieces, neighbors, and any other random young female they could corral into this excruciating exercise.

Normally, Bastien would've groaned, then sucked it up. He loved his mother, would never hurt her. But normally, he wasn't strung out from two solid weeks of sleepless nights . . . because he didn't want just any woman. He wanted *her*, the woman he knew in his gut was his mate, but who, against all known laws of changeling mating, he couldn't *find*.

He'd first tasted the scent of his elusive lover on a street in Chinatown fourteen days, eight hours, and seventeen minutes ago, the scent igniting a possessiveness in him that was as feral as it was joyous. Yes, he'd thought, *yes*, and turned to follow the scent that spoke to him in a way nothing else ever had . . . only for it to dissipate into intangible mist even his changeling-acute senses couldn't pierce.

Refusing to believe he'd lost her, he'd spent hours searching the area, day fading into darkest midnight, until he'd finally had to go home empty-handed, his soul craving the touch of hers. The leopard inside his skin had clawed him awake only hours later, certain she was just beyond his reach, hurt and in pain. Torn apart at the idea that he wasn't there when his mate needed him, he'd immediately gone out again.

Dawn had come on a smudge of light that grew steadily brighter, bringing with it hundreds of people of every size and shape and hue, but not her.

The rest of the world might be in the grip of a tense silence as they waited to see if the days-old historic change in the lives of the Psy, the psychic race that shared the planet with changelings and humans, would spill out into new violence, but Bastien cared only about finding her.

He'd repeated the pattern from that first night every night since, prowling the empty and fog-shrouded city streets in his leopard form long after its other residents found their beds. He'd discarded thousands of trails, sensed myriad secrets, and three or four times, he'd caught the wild, sweet, utterly unique and just as intoxicating scent that was hers, but it never lasted. Not as a scent should last. It faded out with impossible abruptness in the middle of a narrow pathway between buildings, or halfway down a flight of stairs—places where she couldn't have gone anywhere unless she had wings.

The idea that she might be an aerial changeling, perhaps part of the falcon wing with which Bastien's pack had an alliance, would've been an answer that gave him a way to find her, but there was a feline undertone to her scent that told him he was stalking a fellow cat changeling.

One who was there one instant, gone the next.

Always when the changeling scent ended, he caught a softer one below it that also awakened his most primal instincts. Despite the fact he knew a changeling male couldn't have that kind of a visceral reaction to two different women, he'd followed that scent, too—only it was too gentle, too easily lost among the bitter odors of coffee and spice outside a restaurant, or the overpowering aromas that poured from a beauty parlor, the city a kaleidoscope to his senses.

In truth, *both* scents were less intense than they should be. The only reason he could track the feline one longer was that it had a bitingly primal edge to it that made it stand out even amid the other changeling scents in the city.

It was starting to drive him to madness.

"I didn't even get a bite of the brownies." Sage's mournful voice broke into his thoughts, his brother's gaze on the table groaning with food on the other side of the wall of female flesh. "I was just about to grab one when they began arriving, and I tried to bolt out the back door."

So had Bastien. Only to be stopped by their mother's firm order to stay.

"Why is it"—Bastien folded his arms, mirroring his brother's stance—"that though we're the ones ostensibly doing the choosing, this feels like a two-man meat market?"

Sage bared his teeth at a tall human blonde who turned his way, her body angled in invitation. She hurriedly glanced in another direction, and Sage smirked . . . until he found himself on the receiving end of a patented maternal glare, Lia Smith's petite body as stiff as a general's.

Smirk wilting, he pushed off the wall, a big, tough leopard changeling with his metaphorical tail between his legs. "Crap, I have to go make nice now, or I might as well say good-bye to ever again tasting one of Mom's brownies." Shoulders hunched, he shot Bastien a pleading look. "Don't abandon me, man."

Bastien turned into a rock, feet glued to the floor and arms still folded. "Hell no. And don't even think of bringing up the bro code," he added when Sage went as if to open his mouth. "I've had to suffer through far more of these than you."

As he watched his brother thrust his hands into the pockets of his jeans and slink off to join the lovely, perfumed mass of women who might as well have been a tank of ravenous sharks, Bastien fought the urge to simply shove open the door and leave. No matter how raw and trapped he felt right now, he knew his mother was only trying to help, because though he hadn't said anything to her, Lia Smith knew her children.

She'd clearly sensed he was unhappy, even made the connection that it had to do with his single status. How could he explain the impossible to his mom? A changeling male *never* lost the scent of his mate once he'd caught it. He should've been able to stalk her through fire and hail, snow and rain, much less down city streets.

"Sweetheart." His mother's hand on his arm, the scent of her familiar and of home. "Come into the kitchen. I need you to grab some glasses from the top cabinet."

He followed her without argument, avoiding even the glancing touch of other women. His leopard was in no mood to be touched by any unmated female but the one he couldn't find; Bastien wasn't certain he'd be able to control the urge to snarl if one of the women in the room dared attempt even minor skin privileges. Better to make certain the situation didn't arise.

"I know which ones," he said once he and his mom had reached the thankful emptiness of the kitchen. Opening the cabinet, he easily grabbed the spare set his mother would've had to use her step stool to access.

"Thank you, baby boy."

Bastien didn't protest her address. He'd long ago accepted the fact that no matter his age or maturity or position in the pack hierarchy, he'd always be her cub. Now, she cupped his face with gentle hands, her eyes searching his, the brown of her irises ringed by a rich yellow-green as her leopard rose to the surface of her mind. "I made a mistake today, didn't I?"

Swamped by a wave of love for the woman who'd kissed countless scraped knees for him when he'd been a child, he closed his hands over her wrists. "Ignore me. I'm just in a bad mood."

"No." She straightened the collar of the white shirt he wore over black pants, having intended to go into the office to catch up on work after helping move the furniture. "Something's wrong, and I've made it worse. I know I shouldn't interfere"—a rueful cast to her expression—"but I love you all so much I can't help myself."

"I know." Never had he questioned his parents' love for him and his siblings, that love the foundation on which his life was built. It was why he hadn't walked out when Lia ordered him and Sage to stay; hurting her would make neither the animal nor the human part of him feel good.

"Do you want to talk about it?"

"No, not yet." He drew her into a tight hug, his leopard rubbing against his skin, akin to how he'd rubbed against Lia's side as a cub when they'd both been in their leopard forms. "I have to handle this myself."

Squeezing him with fierce affection, Lia drew back and brushed his hair off his forehead, Bastien leaning down instinctively to make it easier for her. "Go on," she whispered with a conspiratorial smile, "you can escape out the back."

"Oh good," Vera Robbins said from the kitchen doorway, having appeared just as Lia spoke. "You can give me a ride, young Bastien."

Bastien barely refrained from groaning. The elder was a vigorous and energetic hundred and twenty-five, a woman noted for her warmth and wisdom. She also delighted in reveling in Bastien's past as a "ladies' man." Bastien didn't deny he'd indulged in skin privileges enthusiastically in his early twenties, but so did most leopard changelings at that age, their sexuality an integral aspect of their nature.

Vera would be shocked to hear he hadn't taken a lover in eight months, and now the only lover he wanted was an illusion he couldn't track. "Happy to," he said, because while he wasn't sure he could handle Vera's teasing in his current frame of mind, refusing her was simply not on the cards. She was pack—more, she was a former soldier who'd put her life on the line to protect that pack more than once.

Vera had earned the right to demand whatever the hell she damn well pleased.

Kissing his mom good-bye on the cheek, he escorted Vera to the sleek black car that was his own and got her settled in before he went around to take the driver's seat.

"What a nice car." Vera stroked the soft black leather-synth of her seat. "Though not what I'd expect from a healthy young dominant in his prime." A raised eyebrow. "I was looking forward to a ride on that jetcycle of yours."

Grinning despite himself, he put the gleaming beauty of his car on hoverdrive and guided it silently out of the forested area around his parents' home deep in DarkRiver's Yosemite territory. "I'll bring it by next week, take you for a spin."

"Hmph." She tapped her cane on the floor. "You could've at least made sure this car was red."

"I have enough red in my life," he said, referring to the dark shade of his hair.

That made the older changeling throw back her head and laugh, the sound big and open. "I suppose you're too big to fit in those zippy sports cars."

Bastien had sat in one once; he'd lasted exactly two seconds before the claustrophobia had him wanting to rip the damn thing to shreds with his claws.

"All shoulders and muscle," Vera said before he could respond. "Strong thighs, too."

"Are you hitting on me, Vera?"

"You can only dream, young Bastien." Another burst of laughter, before she poked him in the arm. "Why aren't you mated or with a long-term lover? We both know you have no trouble attracting women."

The question grated against his insides. "Does no one respect my private life?"

"You're in a pack. Of course not," was the rapid response, one he couldn't argue with. "Now answer me. I'm a hundred and twenty-five—I don't have time to dillydally."

"No one can pass Mercy's tests," he said, wanting Vera off the painful and currently maddening subject of mating.

"That sister of yours has a good head on her shoulders."

Noticing Vera tug her shawl around her shoulders, he quietly turned up the heat.

"So," the elder said a moment later, "she's overprotective, is she?"

Bastien thought of the infamous "kitten defurring tools" with which Mercy had scared off the last woman he'd been seeing—after first convincing his date Bastien ate live kittens for breakfast. She'd even put a "kitten cage" in one of his cupboards, the better to horrify his date. Bastien had already known he and the woman in question weren't the right fit, so the fact she'd believed Mercy's ridiculous story had simply been the last nail in the coffin. "If it's the right girl," he said, "it won't matter."

Vera's smile caused her face to seam with the lines of a life generously and fully lived. "Yes," was all she said, before settling back into her seat.

A half hour later—having been forced to insult his panther of a car by keeping it to a crawling speed that didn't make Vera threaten to whack him with her cane—Bastien parked in front of a single-floor dwelling not far from the home of the pack healer. Walking around to open Vera's door, he didn't make the mistake of offering her a helping hand. The elder would bloody him for the insult.

His nape prickled a second later, a wild, intoxicating scent with a softer undertone making his nostrils flare and his pulse slam against his skin: *her* scent, *all of it*, the soft and the sharply primal, not two women but one.

Too stunned—too *happy*—to wonder how or why his mate's scent had split in two on the streets, Bastien's leopard sat up, muscles quivering and head cocked in absolute attention. All this time, he'd been searching the city, but she was *here*.

Hand clenching on the edge of the car door, he turned to look back down the drive.

A slamming punch to the heart, a kick to the gut, a sense of absolute rightness.

It was as if he'd been seeing the world through a misty fog until this moment of piercing clarity. And what he saw was a small, curvy woman with masses of honey-colored hair and big hazel eyes set against skin of a darker honey.

A cat, he thought at once; he'd been right, she was a cat. Then the feline scent whispered away as inexplicably as it'd done on the streets, and all he could taste was the lush, sweet scent of a human female he wanted to lick up from head to toe. Cat or human, one thing was clear: She was his.

"Kirby, honey. What good timing."

Kirby. Her name is Kirby.

Shutting the door and curling his fingers into his palms to conceal the claws that had sliced out as his leopard reacted to her, he waited for Kirby to reach them instead of pouncing like he wanted to do with every single cell in his body.

Patience, he counseled the more primitive half of his nature, and forced his claws to retract. The leopard growled within him but assented to the human's will—because scaring her away was not on the agenda. No, he'd coax, charm, and pet her into his life, into his arms.

Bastien Michael Smith had found his mate, and he was keeping her.

VIVID green eyes watched her with an unwavering focus that raised the tiny hairs on Kirby's arms and made her stomach go tight, a strange breathlessness in her chest. She didn't recognize the tall, muscled male with skin tanned a beautiful gold, but he had to be part of the DarkRiver leopard pack—there was something feline about the way he stood, a stealthy predator at rest. She had the insane urge to go up to him, touch him, *curl naked against him, skin to skin*.

The uncharacteristic nature of the forceful, sensual compulsion snapped her back to her senses, and all at once, she was aware of Vera looking at her with a distinctly quizzical expression on her face. Not sure how long she'd been standing stock-still staring at the stranger, Kirby held up a small white box in her arms and said, "I baked yesterday." Her pulse thudded hard and fast, her words huskier than they should've been. "I thought I'd drop off half the cake for you, since I know you like black forest."

"I like black forest, too." A deep male voice that brushed over her senses like the most luxuriant fur, the lips that had shaped the words curved in a teasing smile, until she could almost believe she'd imagined the feral intensity of him when he'd first looked at her.

Tapping her cane on the ground, Vera looked up into that

green-eyed face that had twisted Kirby's insides into a tangled snarl. "I suppose you want some?"

"Yes, please." Hands behind his back, expression as innocent as a five-year-old's.

Snorting, Vera jerked her head at Kirby. "This is Bastien. Don't let him charm you—next thing you know, you'll be naked."

Kirby's face filled with heat, the rush of blood so loud in her ears that she almost missed Bastien's protests. Ignoring them both, Vera walked toward her door at a spry pace, a grace to her movements even at this age that made it clear she was changeling. Not able to look Bastien in the face when her own was no doubt the color of an overripe tomato, Kirby began to follow the other woman . . . and realized she'd acquired a six-foot-plus shadow.

"I feel I have to defend myself," he murmured, the words a purr of sound against her ears.

Cat, very definitely a cat. A big, gorgeous, stalking cat. "Really?" she managed to say, goose bumps rising over her skin at his proximity, the scent of clean, fresh soap and warm-blooded male in her every breath. "You don't like making women naked?" It was a response driven by some heretofore hidden part of her that told her to show him her claws, despite the fact she was human, didn't *have* claws. No matter if it felt as if the sharply curved tips were shoving against her skin.

CHAPTER 2

A pause.

Kirby had the feeling she'd surprised the leopard at her side, but he recovered quickly. "Oh, I do." His voice had dropped, acquired a rougher edge that threw her stomach into a dangerous free fall. "However, and despite Vera's refusal to believe me, I'm very particular about who I make naked now that I'm no longer a hormone-driven teenager. Of course, when I was a teenager, a naked woman would've ended things rather abruptly, physically speaking."

Skin burning again when it had just settled, Kirby nonetheless refused to back down. "I hope your ability to stand . . . firm"—*Was she really saying this?*—"against temptation has improved with time?" She'd never flirted in such a sinfully sexual way, hadn't known she could.

A hand on her lower back, the touch searing her through her cardigan and the camisole she wore beneath, and his breath warm against her earlobe as he bent close to say, "You have no idea, little cat."

Fighting the shiver that threatened, she walked into Vera's house and to the kitchen, where she placed the cake on the counter and said, "I'll make the coffee," before either Bastien or Vera could make the offer themselves.

The routine task gave her something to do, though if she'd thought it'd help her ignore Bastien, that proved a futile effort. Sprawled in a chair opposite Vera at the kitchen table, he was saying something that had his packmate laughing.

"Why are you dressed up so spiffy?" Vera asked once her laughter had faded, lifting her fashionable but unnecessary cane to tap Bastien's forearm. "Was it for the girl selection?"

Bastien dropped his head in his hands, the stunning dark red of his hair catching the sunlight pouring through the kitchen windows, all of which overlooked woods filled with verdant green firs. His white shirt was pulled taut over his shoulders in this position, his strength apparent. "I thought Mom needed a few minutes' help moving furniture for a book club lunch," he growled when he raised his head. "If I'd known it was about matchmaking, I'd have worn my rattiest jeans and a stained T-shirt."

Ears straining to catch every snarly word, Kirby found the cups as the coffee began to perk.

"Your mother loves you." Vera glared at Bastien. "You're in fine form, prime of your life, you should find a girl before you get old and crinkly."

"Gee, thanks, Vera." A masculine mutter as he leaned back again, one arm braced lazily against the back of his chair, his big body loose limbed, very much a cat at rest. "I was hoping I had a few more years yet."

Vera's response was a grin bright and full of anticipation. "I'll enjoy watching you fall, Bastien Smith. I bet she wraps you around her finger."

A shrug, those deliciously broad shoulders catching Kirby's attention again. "Of course she will." Impossible as it was, it felt as if his voice was pitched to stroke over her senses. "What would be the point otherwise?"

Vera's smile turned affectionate. "I'm glad to see you understand that." Glancing up as Kirby brought across the tray holding the coffee, Vera's expression softened. "And you, Kirby?" She tugged Kirby into a seat. "Have you found someone yet?"

"I've only been in the city two weeks," she said, conscious of Bastien going preternaturally still for a single, taut moment, the green of his eyes no longer human, before he rose to get the cake.

"From the accent," he said, "I'm guessing . . . Georgia?"

Kirby nodded, happy he'd changed the subject, but Vera wasn't done.

"Two weeks, schmoo weeks. It's never too early to start looking." The older woman's eyes glinted, flicking from Kirby to Bastien. "You two would make pretty cubs together."

Kirby wanted to die. Dig a hole, jump inside, bury herself for good measure.

Bastien on the other hand—now standing between her and Vera—served up the cake without missing a beat, his body heat lapping against her like a tactile caress. "Undoubtedly," he said, "but not if you terrify Kirby away with warnings about the likelihood of ending up naked while with me."

Kirby responded in pure self-defense, driven by that strangeness in her that said she couldn't permit him to overwhelm her. Not now, not ever. She might not be a dominant, but it was critical he didn't see her as weak. The tips of her fingers stung on that fierce thought, the pain sharp, biting. Putting down the coffee cup that was clearly hotter than she'd realized, she said, "That likelihood is getting less and less with every word you speak."

Laughing, Vera slapped her thigh. Bastien retook his seat with a meek expression belied by the fact he'd shifted his chair so that his thigh pressed against Kirby's own. It incited an escalation in her clawing awareness of him, her skin prickling in a way that felt as if it came from inside and out both. Almost as if she had a leopard under her skin, too, one that was rubbing up against it in an effort to get closer to this gorgeous cat who made her nerve endings go haywire.

Shaking off the curious sensation, she focused on his conversation with Vera. Intelligent, witty, a little bit wicked, Bastien was the kind of man who'd never have trouble attracting a woman. Kirby was far from immune. If she was brutally honest, she'd never reacted to anyone as strongly as she'd done to Bastien.

That violent wave of need, of *want* at the start, followed by an increasing desire to know more about him, know everything . . . it was profoundly unsettling. As was the tearing disappointment that had her nails digging into her palms and her eyes threatening to burn when he glanced at his watch and said, "I better get into the office. With the instability caused by the Psy political situation, I have to keep an extra-sharp eye on things."

"All work and no play." Vera shook her head as Kirby stared deliberately into her half-empty coffee cup in an effort to hide her disturbing reaction, her skin flushing alternately hot then cold. "Be careful you don't become a dull boy."

"I thought I was making women naked on a regular basis?" Rising with that quip, Bastien went around to kiss Vera on the cheek. "Can I give you a ride somewhere, Kirby?" he asked, his hand on the back of her chair.

Scared by how much she wanted to lean back, rub her cheek against his arm, tug him down to her mouth, she shook her head.

"Don't be silly," Vera said. "You haven't got a car."

Her fingers flexed, the tingling in her fingertips increasing in strength. "It's no trouble to catch the—"

Bastien's breath whispered hot and silken over her ear, his face a caress away from her own. "I promise I don't bite." It was a dare.

Kirby had stopped accepting stupid dares as a teenager, but a primal defiance rose up inside her at his words. It swamped the near-panic that had gripped her at the realization that he was about to leave, totally overwhelmed the sense of self-preservation that said she needed to put some distance between them so she could think.

"I deal with five-year-olds every day," she said, his jaw brushing across her temple when she turned her head slightly. The contact made her want to shudder, ask for more. Swallowing down the wrenching need that was too powerful to make any kind of rational sense, she somehow managed to keep her tone even as she added, "You're a pussycat by comparison."

"Careful, Bastien." Vera's smile was wide. "Kirby's got a brain."

Pulling back Kirby's chair so she could get up, though he remained close enough to touch, Bastien said, "I like women with brains."

A snort. "Oh? I thought certain other attributes had priority."

"'Bye, Vera." Bastien began to walk backward out of the kitchen, waggling his fingers at the older woman—who, from her smile, was clearly charmed by the packmate she'd been teasing.

When Kirby picked up her purse and joined him, he turned to face the correct way, then placed his hand on her lower back again. The contact renewed the odd sensation of fur rubbing against the inside of her skin, made her toes curl even as her breasts ached.

Kirby knew she should pull away—and not only because of her increasingly out-of-control response to him. Thanks to a changeling friend in junior high, she understood the concept of skin privileges: the right to touch, in and out of the pack, different layers of contact acceptable for different situations. A male's hand on a female's lower back was an intimate act in human society, even more so in the changeling world.

If she did nothing about Bastien claiming the right, he'd take it as silent acquiescence to his pursuit. If she said no, he'd back off immediately, DarkRiver a pack that adhered to strict and disciplined codes of behavior. Kirby knew that because Vera had told her after pointing out that Kirby was a young, single woman living in changeling-heavy territory and thus had a good chance of coming into contact with interested males.

"If it's a predator, leopard or wolf, be blunt," the older woman had said. "Subtle doesn't work when they get set on a woman. But no male in either DarkRiver or SnowDancer will go where he's been specifically uninvited."

So Kirby didn't have the excuse of ignorance. But she didn't pull away, didn't tell Bastien to stop touching her. Because regardless of her worry at the ungovernable nature of her reactions, his big body beside her, the pressure of his hand, it felt good . . . better than anything had felt in a long, long time.

The sensation of warm rightness was potent enough to cut through the cold knot that had been part of her for as long as she could remember, a heavy lump centered in her chest that hurt deep in the night and made her cry inexplicable tears. These days, she cried in silence, woke to find her face wet. As a child, she'd screamed awake, her throat raw and terror in her blood.

"Hey." Bastien's hand circling gently on her back. "Everything okay?"

Nodding, she slid into the expensive black car that told her whatever Bastien did, he was very successful at it, and watched him walk around to get into the driver's seat. Bracing his arm along the back of her seat, he waited until she met his gaze.

"If you don't want to be here," he said quietly, "or if you feel uncomfortable with me, tell me." The leopard looked at her out of his eyes. "Do you want to leave?"

"No." Her answer was driven by instinct, the moment pregnant with a meaning she couldn't consciously grasp. "Memories," she found herself saying to the beautiful male who'd been a stranger an hour ago. "I remembered something that made me sad."

Bastien reached out to tuck her hair behind her ear, his fingertips brushing the curve of it to shimmer sensation through every inch of her. "Do you often remember?"

She shook her head as the prickling in her skin eased—to be replaced by a greedy desire for more. "No." The dream-crying had faded to nonexistence in the later part of her childhood, only to return with a vengeance when she relocated to San Francisco. "I think it must be from the stress of moving to a new place."

Bastien went as if to play with another strand of her hair, then glanced at Vera's cottage. "She'll accuse us of necking in her drive if we don't get going."

The dry words made her laugh, the sadness fading, and she knew he'd done it on purpose, this leopard she didn't know . . . and yet did in her very bones.

Starting up the car, his grin devastating, he said, "Which way?"

Kirby gave him her address, then realized she'd never asked his original destination. "Will it be out of your way?" She should've offered to get out at the transit stop, but she couldn't make herself say it.

One hand confident on the wheel as they pulled out, Bastien reached across to run the knuckles of his free hand over her cheek. "You could never be out of my way, Kirby."

Every inch of her melted at that rough caress of sound. "Vera is right. You're dangerous."

"Who, me? I just deal with stocks and bonds all day."

Fascinated by him, compelled to know everything, she

angled herself in the seat so she could look at his profile, the hard line of his jaw cleanly shaven. "Really?" she asked.

He nodded. "I'm in charge of DarkRiver's financial assets."

Kirby thought of what she'd read in the papers about the pack and how it was effectively one of the biggest corporations in the city, a corporation in robust financial health, and knew she'd been right. Bastien was very good at his job. "Do you have other clients as well?"

"A few small ones. Why, do you want to invest?" A raised eyebrow. "We could definitely come to an agreement about my fees," he added with a smile that invited her to play.

Kirby wanted to trace that smile, kiss it into her own mouth. "Kindergarten teachers don't make enough to invest."

An interested look before he returned his attention to the road. "Which kindergarten?"

"The one near DarkRiver's city headquarters in Chinatown." As a result, she had as many changeling students as human, and had spent the past month learning how to handle children who didn't yet have full control over their shifting.

"The other day," she told him, the memory a delight, "I couldn't find a student until my assistant teacher pointed out that he was in cub form on a tree branch above the swing." Kirby had eventually coaxed the boy, who'd apparently had a fight with a friend, to jump into her arms. "They didn't cover that in my training."

Bastien turned onto the main road back to San Francisco. "You should talk to Annie," he said. "She teaches seven-year-olds I think, including a lot of changeling kids, could probably give you some pointers."

"Would she mind?" Kirby loved her new position and wanted to do a good job; she wasn't too proud to ask for help from more experienced teachers.

"No, she's a sweetheart. I'll get her number from the pack directory, tell her to give you a call." His lips curved again. "Of course, that means you have to give me your number."

"Or I could ask Vera for Annie's contact details," she teased, the compulsion to touch him so aggressive that she had to fold her arms to keep from reaching out. Still, a wild, unknown part of her lunged at him, as if it would shove out of her very skin.

"Oh, that's just mean." Scowl darkening his features, he

reached across to tug at her hair. "Did you meet Vera at the kindergarten?"

"Two of her grandchildren attend and she comes in as a volunteer a couple of times a week." The other woman had, for reasons of her own, taken Kirby under her wing at their first meeting, becoming her first friend in this city. "Do you always work on Sundays?"

"Only when necessary." Settling into his seat as they hit the highway, he said, "Tell me more stories about the kids you teach."

Smiling, Kirby did, then Bastien told her about his pack, about the forests he loved, asked her what it had been like to live in Georgia. The time passed in a heartbeat, until she blinked in surprise at realizing they were almost to her apartment.

"I—" She hissed out a breath.

"Kirby?" Bastien's gaze snapped to her, returned to the road a second later. "I'll pull over."

"No, it's nothing." Wincing, she rubbed her abdomen, the stabbing sensation already subsiding, as it had the other three times she'd felt it since moving to San Francisco. "I've been eating too much pier fast food," she admitted, scrunching up her nose.

It was all so new and different: the water, the seagulls, the rich clam chowder served in a sourdough bowl that she'd had twice already this week, including for lunch today. "I just have to get back on the straight and narrow and I'll be fine."

Bastien frowned. "We'll go to a clinic, just in case."

Shaking her head, she indicated a parking space in front of the three-story building in Chinatown where she'd found an affordable apartment courtesy of the fact it was the size of a shoebox. She didn't mind. What mattered was that it was within walking distance of the kindergarten and in the heart of the city, meaning she never experienced the icy kiss of absolute aloneness. "I don't feel sick really." It was a sharp, vicious pain when it struck, but then it faded, which was why she kept talking herself into more pier food.

Having parked the car, Bastien touched the back of his hand to her forehead. "No fever at least." He took a card from the wallet he'd thrown into a holder when he entered the car.

"This is my number. Call me if you feel worse. I'll drop by on my way home to check in on you."

Used to taking care of herself, she said, "You don't have to." The comment went directly against the huge part of her that wanted to crawl into his lap and ask him not to leave, her skin aching for his.

"Kirby, I'm a dominant predatory changeling male," he said, as if that explained everything, his tone suddenly unbending. "I also have a mother who'd box my ears if I left you alone in this situation, not to mention what Vera would do to me." A deep smile that creased his cheeks. "Have pity."

Kirby didn't have to argue with herself to answer. No, the battle was to maintain some kind of control over a body and a mind that were rocketing out of her control. "All right," she said, stomach fluttering in a way that had nothing to do with pain. "Do you work from the DarkRiver building?"

Stepping out, he opened the passenger door for her and waited until she was on her feet before leaning back against the car to say, "No. My team and I have a dedicated space in the Financial District."

Only a few minutes away, the madness in her whispered.

"I'll be there till about seven." Rising to his full height, Bastien curved his hand around the side of her neck for a moment. "I'll come by right after." He brushed his thumb over her pulse. "Yes?"

Throat dry, she nodded. "Yes."

His gaze dropped to her lips and for a second she thought he'd kiss her, but then he drew back his hand, the green of his eyes leopard-wild. "Rest." A rough command. "I'll see you in a few hours."

Heart a staccato drumbeat against her ribs, she watched him prowl around to get into the driver's seat. Cat, definitely a cat.

CHAPTER 3

Bastien loved numbers, loved the high-stakes energy of the financial world—but thanks to his family and his pack, he also had a solid, stable head on his shoulders. It was what made him so good at what he did.

Most of DarkRiver's investments were medium to high yield, low-risk, which meant that if carefully managed, as Bastien managed them, the pack was immune to market fluctuations. However, and with his alpha's knowledge and authorization, he also had a small percentage in extremely high-yield, extremely high-risk investments that kept their portfolio from stagnating.

Over the years since he'd taken charge of that portfolio, he'd increased DarkRiver's financial assets exponentially, and he had no intention of stopping that trajectory. So yeah, he liked his job, liked that what he did helped maintain and support his pack, but today, the hours couldn't pass fast enough. His leopard snarled inside his mind, wanting to go to Kirby, and it took all of his human willpower not to give in, not to find her, bite down on her neck, *mark* her.

Shoving a hand through his hair, he grabbed a bottle of cold water in a futile attempt to cool things down. He could be as possessive as any predatory changeling, but he'd never felt such a feral need to brand a woman. Not that his response to her was exactly a surprise.

Kirby, after all, was his mate.

It didn't always happen this hard, this fast. Mercy and her mate, Riley, had known one another for years before the mating dance slapped them both sideways. But for some, it happened in that first, stunning instant of contact.

The knowing was visceral, as if he'd sensed the other half of himself, her presence intoxicating to his senses.

The soft and the wild, the two scents that were both hers.

He frowned. The feline whisper to Kirby's scent hadn't made another appearance the entire time he'd spent with her and that was impossible for a changeling, so she was definitely human. *His* human. Leopard and man, both parts of him smiled, figuring he'd have plenty of time to work out the complex mystery of her scent.

Had she been changeling, he'd have—No, he'd have done exactly the same things he planned to do to win his sexy little human mate. He'd court her, seduce her, pleasure her . . . and by the time she realized what was happening, she'd already be his. The last thing he could afford to do was come on so strong that he scared her.

With that thought in mind, he rolled up his sleeves and focused on figures that today seemed as dry and as boring as dust, in spite of the financial turmoil caused by the recent political shift among the Psy. That's what a lot of people didn't understand—the psychic race might've been standoffish to a large degree until recently, but all three races—human, changeling and Psy—were connected on a global level; civil war in one sphere affected them all.

Sometimes, it was subtle, as with the market fluctuations, other times overt.

Bastien's mouth set in a grim line as he considered the toxic bomb discovered ten days prior in the city's central skytrain station.

"But that," he muttered, "isn't what you need to be thinking about right now. Get to work so you can spend as much time as possible with Kirby in the coming week."

He did exactly that, was ready for a break when his phone

rang a couple of hours later, Grey's number on the display. "What do you want, shrimp?"

"Do you want to come over tonight?" his younger brother asked. "Sage and I are getting pizza and watching the basketball game."

"Thanks, but not tonight."

"Better offer?"

"Way better." His entire body grew taut at the thought of Kirby; if she no longer felt ill, he had every intention of talking his way into staying. God, he wanted to pet her, hold her, nuzzle his face into the curve of her neck and draw in that intriguing scent that made no sense.

If, however, she was still sick, he'd coax her into going to a clinic. And if Kirby proved stubborn about it, he'd pick her up and take her. She could be mad at him later—*after* the doctors checked her out. Bastien did not mess around when it came to looking after the people who mattered to him.

"Not one of the women from the luncheon?" Grey's voice broke into his thoughts, his brother's surprise open. "I thought Sage said you snuck out early—he's cranky about that, by the way."

"She's no one you two know." He wasn't ready to share Kirby with his family or his pack yet. Not only did he want her all to himself until he was drunk on her, he didn't want to risk her being overwhelmed by the Smith clan or his affectionately nosy packmates. "I'll see you later this week. And tell Sage he can be cranky when he's been ambushed by a setup as many times as I have."

"When should I start worrying?"

"Not for a few years yet." Hanging up after a bit more back and forth with his brother, he knuckled down to work again.

There were three more calls, two from packmates who needed advice about personal financial matters, the third from his father. Michael Smith had obviously been talking to his mate, and was checking up on his son. Happy to answer his father honestly, Bastien told him he was fine. Hell, he was ecstatic.

That visceral excitement had intensified to fever pitch by the time he left the office.

Kirby sounded sweetly delighted when she answered the

intercom and cleared him into her building, her accent redolent of mint juleps and magnolia trees. Deciding he was going to kiss her on that lush mouth of hers as soon as possible, licking and tasting and indulging, he took the steps to her apartment three at a time, making it there just as she opened the door.

A slight gasp, followed by a shy smile that made him want to bite, her pretty honey-colored hair in a ponytail that bared the delicate skin of her nape. "That was fast."

Leopard stretching under his skin at her proximity, he allowed himself to tug on a curling tendril of hair that had come loose from the tie. "I bring gifts to bribe my way inside." He held up the bag from a family-run restaurant one block over. "Chicken noodle soup. Good for whatever ails you. And if you're feeling better . . ." He showed her the frozen yogurt he had fantasies of feeding her spoonful by spoonful, and yeah, maybe he wanted to lick it from her skin for his own dessert, but he *was* a cat. Kirby couldn't be too surprised if he gave in to temptation.

"So?" he teased gently when she didn't step back, her caressing gaze on his shoulders, his chest. It was all he could do not to cup her jaw, claim a hot, deep kiss, tell her she could touch him anytime she wanted.

Cheeks coloring, she invited him into the tiny space that would've normally made his leopard stir-crazy. "I feel fine," she said. "I had a couple of twinges right after you left, but then nothing."

From the scent and look of her, her skin glowing, she didn't appear ill. Yet once again, he caught a hint of that other scent, wild and inexplicable, that confused his leopard. "Have you been spending a lot of time around another cat lately?" he asked, though the scent was too integrated into her body to be anything other than her own.

Yet the way she moved, everything else about her, was human.

Kirby tilted her head to the side, lines forming between the rich, unusual hazel of her eyes, flecks of green intermingled with near yellow. "No, why?"

"I thought I caught a scent." Except there was nothing in the air now except Kirby's warm softness overlaid by a peach accent that probably came from her body lotion.

Of course, thinking about Kirby rubbing lotion over her naked flesh probably wasn't the best of ideas right now. "Might be one of your neighbors," he said to put her at ease, while his mind worried over the puzzle of it.

"Maybe." She bit down on her lower lip, and he wanted to growl that that was his job.

Yeah, he was having trouble controlling both the animal and the man.

"I haven't met all my neighbors yet." Smile holding a quiet shyness again, she smoothed a nonexistent wrinkle on the front of her fitted sea green T-shirt. "I'm not very brave with strangers." A soft confession.

Bastien's need for her segued into a violent tenderness, and right then, all he wanted to do was hold her. Just hold her. "I think you're braver than you know," he murmured, folding his arms to leash the instinct. "It's not every woman who packs up and moves across the country on her own." She'd come to him, whether she knew it or not, and it wasn't a gift he'd ever forget. "I'm damn glad you did, little cat."

Skin flushing a delicate pink, she turned to put the dessert in the freezer, the black fabric of her yoga pants stretching across her curves. "We should eat before the soup gets cold."

BASTIEN took the seat right next to Kirby when it was time to eat, his arm along the back of her chair and his eyes on her profile. Flustered, she said, "You're staring." Like he wanted to take a big greedy bite out of her, his eyes an impossibly vivid and primal green shade that told her it wasn't only the human part of him that watched her.

"Hmm." A rumbling sound that made her want to press her hand to his chest, feel the vibration of it. "Eat." He picked up her spoon, dipped it into the soup, brought it to her lips. "I want you healthy for all the debauched things I plan to talk you into later tonight."

The rough warmth of his other hand curving around her nape stole the words on her tongue. All her life, she'd ached for contact with another living being, hungered to touch and be touched. The lack of tactile contact in her life *hurt*. As a child in the foster care system, she'd had few choices; it should've been different for the adult she'd become, but despite her need, Kirby couldn't imagine being with someone without bonds of affection, of care. However, building those bonds was incredibly difficult for her after a lifetime of not belonging to anyone.

Then had come Bastien.

"Hey." The spoon clinking back into the bowl, knuckles running over her cheek. "I didn't mean to make you uncomfortable."

That voice, a low, deep purr that stroked over her skin. "You didn't," she answered, her own voice husky. "I'm just not used to . . ." Being so wanted. No one in her life had ever pursued her as Bastien was doing, ever cared enough to get her soup when she was sick, much less touch her with any kind of tenderness.

"To a bad-mannered cat?" he said, the thumb of the hand he had around her nape stroking over her pulse point. "I bring you soup then don't let you eat it." The heat of him a dark kiss, he picked up the spoon again. "Let me make up for it."

Stomach fluttering at the coaxing words, she parted her lips to say what, she didn't know, and he slipped the spoon inside. And somehow—Kirby wasn't sure quite how—she ended up in his lap, one of his hands splayed on her lower back, his shoulders heavy with muscle under her arm and his thighs rock hard below her.

When she belatedly realized where she was and made to get off, he playfully threatened to sulk . . . then fed her more soup. All the while verbally petting her with affectionate, sexy words that made her feel intoxicatingly sensual, a beautiful woman.

"You haven't eaten," she said afterward, warm and full and aroused on the innermost level.

He nipped at her lower lip in a startling contact that nonetheless wasn't unwelcome, his thighs shifting under her body as one of his hands squeezed the curve of her hip. "I plan to nibble on you."

Her skin prickling with that strange, near-painful awareness, and her heart a throbbing drum, Kirby brushed her fingers over his jaw. She knew then that she was about to invite this gorgeous, charming leopard into her bed after a single day's acquaintance. Her need for him was deeper than simple sexual desire, however. Some long-dormant part of her, anguished and in pain, whispered that Bastien alone could assuage the terrible emptiness inside her.

It felt as if she'd been waiting for him her entire life.

Such a dangerous thought. And still, she wasn't going to step back, wasn't going to be rational about this. "Will—" Agony tearing through her abdomen, she doubled over with a shocked cry, her vision blurring.

"Right." Face grim, Bastien rose with her in his arms and headed for the door. "You're going to see a doctor, no damn argument."

In too much pain to respond, her insides shredded open by clawing blades that cut and tore, she curled into the protective strength of his body. It was a quick ride to the nearest twenty-four-hour clinic, but the pain faded rapidly in those fleeting minutes, to the point that though she felt bruised from the inside out by the time they arrived, she was otherwise fine.

Mystified, the Medical Psy on duty did a number of scans using his ability to see through the skin; he even requested a second opinion from a human colleague. Neither had any answers. "Do you want to remain overnight?" the M-Psy asked. "In case the pain reoccurs."

Kirby was shaking her head before the medic finished speaking.

"I hate hospitals," she said to Bastien when he frowned. "I'll feel better at home." Regardless of the fact she'd never needed intrusive medical attention of the kind that could explain her dislike, it was a gut-wrenching one, close to a phobia if she was honest. The smell of a certain disinfectant seemingly used in all medical facilities made her want to retch. Even now, her bruised muscles cramped, stomach twisting. "I won't be able to rest here."

Bastien squeezed her hand and only then did she realize she had a death grip on him. "All right." He didn't speak again until the doctor had prescribed some painkillers and they were in the car on their way back to her apartment.

"You call me if it happens again." An order.

Shifting in the passenger seat to face him, she curled her tingling fingertips into her palms. "You're being pushy and bossy."

"I get that way when I'm worried about someone I care for." It was near to a growl, his hands white-knuckled on the steering wheel. "You will tell me?"

Shaken by the blunt statement of care, she said, "Yes," her irritability spiraling without warning into a joy so piercing that it terrified. God, she was falling too hard, too fast, her emotional equilibrium nonexistent around the changeling in the driver's seat.

A serrated pain in her chest, three knives drawn through the *inside* of her skin.

CHAPTER 4

Bastien glanced at her at once, though she hadn't made a sound. "You're hurting." His fingers brushed over her cheek before he turned his attention back to the road, his tension apparent in the roughness of his voice. "We'll be home soon."

Kirby's throat thickened. He was so wonderful. How was she supposed to protect her already battered heart? "I don't know what's wrong with me," she said, scared in a way that sent her pulse stammering.

This time when Bastien reached out, it was to gently squeeze her nape. "We'll figure it out."

He kept the warm strength of his hand on the sensitive, vulnerable skin until he had to remove it to maneuver the car into a parking spot half a block down from her apartment building. "Wait there."

Scowling—just because she understood his protectiveness, even adored it, didn't mean she was about to allow him to boss her around—she pushed the passenger-side door open right as he reached her. She looked up . . . to find herself the focus of leopard-green eyes that glowed in the darkness. "I can walk," she said, even as her breath caught at the sheer, wild beauty of him.

He refused to budge from in front of her. "You're barefoot."

"*Bastien*"—she wished she could growl, too—"you are not carrying me again." She was an independent adult female and it was *critical* Bastien see her that way, not as a weakling he had to cosset. "Move," she said, and when he simply folded his arms, she gave in to the strange, overwhelming urge to bare her teeth at him, the sound that emerged from her throat perilously close to a snarl.

"Now you're trying to get me into bed." His grin transformed her near-feral annoyance into a sense of happiness so strong it didn't seem possible it could exist . . . happiness because he was hers.

Eyes still night-glow, Bastien unfolded his arms. "I'll give you a piggyback ride. Come on." Turning to get into position, he shot her an "I dare you" look over his shoulder that made her want to nip at his mouth, draw in the scent at the crook of his neck.

He was playing with her, she thought all at once, delighted.

Unable to resist, she stood on the edge of the car door frame and wrapped her arms around his neck. He hoisted her up with effortless ease, muscled arms locked under her butt. Burying her nose surreptitiously in his neck, she cooperated when he turned and asked her to push the door shut with her foot, the car locking automatically.

Then he strode down the street while she grew drunk on the exhilarating soap and skin and maleness of his scent, and battled the urge to use her teeth, to bite down hard. So he'd be marked. So everyone would know he was hers. Then she'd tear off his clothing with her bare hands, kiss and touch and lick, embedding her scent into his skin, ensuring that even after one mark faded, the other would remain.

Skin flushing at the untamed possessiveness of her thoughts, she nonetheless held on tight, her bones melting at the feel of his strong, hard body moving against her own. When an older couple strolling by smiled at them, she smiled in return, feeling truly young for the first time in her life.

The world might be in a state of turmoil as a result of the recent Psy civil war, but Kirby's much smaller world was filled with a joy she'd never known.

"How's the service?" Bastien asked a few seconds later.

"Passable."

"Careful." It was a growled warning, a squeak escaping her throat as he pretended to drop her. "You don't want to make the driver mad."

Oh, I adore you.

Her need for him an ache deep within, Kirby surrendered and nuzzled his neck. While she was free with reassuring hugs when it came to the children she taught, it was hard for her to show affection in her personal life. No one had ever welcomed it from her. Bastien did. Angling his neck in a silent request for more, he made a sound that vibrated against her upper body.

An ear-to-ear smile broke out over her face. "You purr!"

"Maybe."

Delighted with everything about him—including the protective bossiness that had made her snarl—she held on as he ran up the steps to the door of her building. She'd expected him to take the elevator once they were inside, but he jogged up the three levels to her place without breaking a sweat or losing his breath. It was a stunning display of strength, throwing the deceptiveness of his usual lazy prowl into stark focus.

Kirby couldn't help but imagine how he'd move against her . . . *in* her, in a far more intimate setting, all power and strength and healthy golden skin rubbing over her own.

Butterflies in her stomach, her lower body molten.

"Hey, now." A rumbling wave of sound against the taut tips of her nipples. "Don't be thinking those things tonight. You're going to rest."

Cheeks burning, she pressed her palm to the scanner beside the apartment door. "How did you . . . ?"

"I'm changeling, little cat," he reminded her. "I can scent you"—a deep inhale—"and you're delicious."

Certain she'd die of mortification, she wiggled off his body the instant they were inside. "That's so unfair," she said, not meeting his gaze.

Wrapping one arm around her waist, he hauled her flush against him, the thick heat of his arousal pushing aggressively against her belly through their clothing. "How's that?" Pure wickedness in his smile. "Fair enough?"

Kirby went to respond, found her mouth claimed in a kiss

sumptuous and lazy, Bastien's tongue stroking slow and hot over her own. As if he had all the time in the world to kiss her, as if he was savoring the taste of her.

Making a complaining sound in the back of her throat when he broke contact, she rose on tiptoe, hands fisted in the dark red silk of his hair. He groaned, his mouth opening over her own and his palms skimming down her sides, their second kiss as opulent as the first, both their chests heaving by the time he raised his head again.

But this time, he pressed his index finger against her kiss-damp mouth when she sought to initiate another. "No tempting me." A stern expression, but his body pounded for her, his skin hot. "I am not taking advantage of a sick woman."

Kissing his throat since she couldn't reach his mouth without his cooperation, she licked up the taste of him. "I'm fine."

Another masculine groan, his hand clenching in her hair before he tugged her away, those night-glow eyes slamming passionately into her own. "When we go wild between the sheets," he said roughly, "I want you healthy and strong enough that I can bite"—a little nip of her lower lip that made her quiver—"pet"—his free hand stroking down her side—"and take you all night, then come back for seconds."

Narrowing her eyes, she gripped at his shirt, her heartbeat nowhere near steady after that sensual recitation. "You're terrible."

Smile feline in its satisfaction, and so, so bad for her self-control, he nudged her toward her bedroom. "Brush your teeth and get into your pajamas."

Her lips quirked, the heat tangling with a raw wave of affection. "I'll go as soon as I lock the door behind you, I promise."

"No need." Folding his arms, he leaned back against that door. "I'm sleeping on your couch."

Kirby blinked. "Bastien—"

The hard glint back in his eyes, he shook his head. "Only way I'll leave is if you call someone else to stay over. You shouldn't be alone after what happened."

She'd wanted him to stay, but not because he thought he had to babysit her. Thrusting a hand through her hair, messing up her ponytail, she said, "I've been alone before when I've been sick." Every single time since she hit legal adulthood. Even before that, any "company" she'd had had been perfunctory at best. "I—"

"Have you ever before been in that much pain?" Bastien's growl raised every tiny hair on her body. "You doubled over. I could feel you shivering in my arms from the shock."

Not capable of lying to him, she admitted the truth. "No. Never anything that violent." It had *hurt*, as if something was trying to claw its way out from inside her.

"So I stay."

"I guess if you do something dastardly," she muttered, wondering who he was to her, this occasionally infuriating leopard male she already trusted down to the bone, "Vera will hound you forever."

Sliding his hands into his pockets, muscles no longer bunched up, he shuddered. "You have an evil streak."

Her mouth cracked open in a huge yawn halfway through her laugh, and all at once, she was exhausted. As if she'd been running a race of which she had no knowledge.

When Bastien took her shoulders and turned her toward the bedroom, she went, crawling straight into bed without bothering to change. She was aware of Bastien turning off her bedside lamp, tugging the blankets over her . . . then nothing.

CONCERNED by Kirby's rapid descent into deep sleep, Bastien watched over her for several minutes, leaving only after he was certain her breathing was smooth and her scent clean of any signs of sickness. Once in the postage-stamp-size living area—which his leopard tolerated only because it meant Kirby was always in close proximity—he directed a jaundiced glance at her tiny two-seater couch.

Hell, no.

It took less than a minute to strip and shift into his leopard form. Padding around the room, he settled into his new skin before curling up on the carpet. Hopefully Kirby wouldn't freak if she woke in the night and saw him before he could shift back. The leopard huffed in response to the thought— Kirby might be a little shy now and then, but she had grit.

Her snarl earlier had been beautiful.

Yawning on that proud, pleased thought, he lay his head on his front paws and catnapped, rising regularly to pad into the bedroom to check up on the small woman who lay curled up under three thick blankets. It made the human inside the cat smile, think of how he'd enfold her in his arms at night once she was his, so she'd snuggle into him for warmth.

It was sometime in the morning that his ears picked up rustling noises from the bedroom. He entered to find Kirby twisting and turning, her skin shiny with perspiration and the blankets shoved to the bottom of the bed, the sheets themselves pulled off the mattress to tangle around her arms and legs.

Shifting in a joyous agony of pleasure and pain, his body dissolving into shattered light before re-forming into his human form, he crouched down beside the bed and checked her temperature.

Hot.

Too hot for a human.

About to attempt to wake her so he could determine if she simply had a fever, or if it might be something more serious, he barely escaped being hit by her hand as she flung it out in her sleep. Closing his own hand instinctively around her slender wrist, careful to moderate his strength so he didn't hurt her, he frowned at the rapid pace of her pulse. It thudded against her skin in a violent drumbeat.

"Kir—" Her name froze on his lips as he truly *saw* what it was he held in his grasp.

A small, feminine hand, the skin flushed with heat . . . and the tips clawed. Neat little claws, adorable in contrast to his, but very definitely not human. His leopard prowled to the surface of his mind, sniffing at her. She still smelled luscious and intoxicating and human, except for that maddening, wild undertone that tugged at his senses until he could *almost* identify it . . . right before it slithered out of his grasp.

One thing he'd caught though—she was unquestionably a cat of some kind.

"Kirby," he said softly, too softly for human ears, his tone near sub-vocal.

Thick lashes fluttered, then rose . . . as the claws sheathed themselves back into her skin, with no sign they'd ever been there. "Bastien?" A sleepy murmur, her skin starting to cool, her heartbeat steadying. "Hurts."

Protective instincts already violently aroused, his words came out harsh, near to a true growl. "Where, baby?"

"Hurts so much." Her eyes closed, her breath hitching. "Touch . . ."

She was asleep again, but not at rest, her crying quiet, heartbreaking. Unable to bear it, he got into bed with her and wrapped her in his arms, his need to alleviate her pain such that he forgot he was naked. Kirby didn't startle awake. Turning immediately into his chest, she tucked up her arms between them, rubbed her cheek against his skin, her own streaked with silent tears.

Touch, she'd said, so that was what he did, petting and stroking her into a calmer state, the sigh she released a benediction. His mate, he realized on a wave of rage that had his own claws slicing out to brush her skin, was touch-starved. A lack of physical affection was painful for humans, but it was agonizing for pack-minded changelings.

"Never again," he promised in a fierce whisper, and, claws retracted, slid one hand just under her T-shirt so it lay against her skin, curving his other over her nape.

It made her release a soft moan before she seemed to slip into a peaceful, deep sleep, the strange, inexplicable undertone in her scent once more dull and hidden. It took time for his anger to abate, but when it did, he had to face the cold, hard facts: Either Kirby was lying about being human rather than changeling or she didn't know.

The latter should've been impossible. Dorian, one of the DarkRiver sentinels, had been latent until approximately a year and a half ago, but though he hadn't been able to shift into his leopard form, the other man had always known of that leopard. He'd smelled like a cat, had the hearing of a cat, the instincts of one. Not only that, but his movements in human form had immediately marked him out as a feline changeling.

Kirby, on the other hand, smelled wholly—if oddly delicately—human the majority of the time, and while she was as sensual and as affectionate as any DarkRiver changeling underneath her shyness, there was nothing inherently feline about her physical presence. If she knew, she was the best actress he'd ever seen, but even the most gifted actress couldn't mask her scent to that extent, not from a fellow changeling.

Notwithstanding any of that, one thing was clear: Bastien had to inform his alpha.

The idea of exposing Kirby made his leopard snarl, his arms locking around her trusting form, but Bastien knew he had no choice. If he didn't tell Lucas and another member of DarkRiver detected Kirby's secret, she'd face harsh punishment for breaching the iron-clad rule that stated no adult predatory changeling could cross over into another's territory without permission, except in cases of imminent risk.

Bastien's scent on her should keep her safe. Lucas wouldn't mete out the penalty without first contacting him, but Kirby would be terrified in the meantime. And, given that they weren't yet lovers, he couldn't be certain his scent would hold on her skin.

No way in hell would he risk it. Lucas had to know.

Bastien would deal with any consequences.

"You're mine, little cat," he murmured, brushing his lips over her temple, "and I'm not letting go." Not now. Not ever.

CHAPTER 5

Bastien got up before Kirby, and was fully dressed when she rose happy and energetic. It soothed man and leopard both to see her that way, and he made sure to sneak in a playful kiss, his body wrapped around hers, before he drove her the short distance to the kindergarten.

Never would his mate hunger for touch again.

Cheeks still flushed, she surprised him by leaning across from the passenger seat to claim his mouth in an affectionate good-bye once they reached her workplace. "Will I see you tonight?" She fiddled with the belt of the dark green dress coat she wore over a kindergarten-appropriate outfit of jeans and a white shirt with elbow-length sleeves.

He wanted to tell her he was her mate, would always be there for her, but her life was already complicated—Kirby needed him to be her rock right now, not use her vulnerability to shove her into the passionate intensity of the mating bond. "Unless you plan to seduce another helpless male," he said with a teasing smile.

Making a face at him, she got out, then leaned down to smile through the open window. "I can't wait to see you again."

Her courage in saying what was in her heart further enslaved him. Forcing himself to leave once she entered the cheerful little building that would soon fill with children's voices, he went to his apartment only long enough to shower and change. Ten minutes later, he was dressed in jeans paired with a dark gray T-shirt, and on the phone with his assistant, issuing instructions about what needed to be done in his absence.

Then—staying on the phone using the car's wireless capabilities—he drove not to DarkRiver's Chinatown HQ but to the green sprawl of the pack's Yosemite territory. According to Lucas's admin assistant, the DarkRiver alpha was working from home today. Bastien's own assistant continued to touch base with him throughout the drive, but even as he fielded the queries, part of his mind was on the conversation he'd had with Kirby over breakfast.

"Do you have any changeling ancestry?"

Kirby's laughter had been as sunny as the morning light pouring through the narrow window at one end of her kitchen. "No, plain old human as far as I know." An open smile that kicked him right in the heart. "Do you mind?"

"I'd think you were perfect even if you were an ice-cold Psy."

Bastien would stake his life on the fact that there'd been no deceit in her then, or at any time prior. As far as Kirby was concerned, she was human. Except, that was simply *not possible*. A changeling's animal was as integral to his or her life as the human half of their nature—Bastien couldn't be human as he couldn't be leopard.

He was changeling, accustomed to the feel of his leopard stretching lazily beneath his skin when he wore this form, and to thinking with a man's mind if necessary while in cat form. The idea that Kirby could've separated the two somehow, stifling her animal side . . . it not only made no sense, it should've been physiologically impossible according to all known laws of science and nature.

Yet her scent argued otherwise. He'd finally realized why he'd had such trouble tracking her—it was because Kirby's scent wasn't integrated as it should be. The feline part was too primal for a changeling, not balanced by the human aspect, while the human part was too gentle without the feline edge to it. Kirby didn't have the natural depth to her scent a human would have, because she *wasn't* human, her scent meant to be a combination of the two sides of her nature.

"Bas." His assistant's voice interrupted his turbulent thoughts. "I just got the report on those shares."

"Go." Wrenching his attention to the topic at hand, he listened, then gave further instructions, after which he switched to speak to another colleague, before handling a minor issue for an elder in the pack.

The work was welcome; it kept his mind from going around in circles.

He was back in contact with his assistant by the time he parked the vehicle in Yosemite, directing the younger male to make several small financial maneuvers designed to benefit the pack. That done, he gave a "do not disturb" order and stuffed his phone into the front left pocket of his jeans before stretching out into a run, the alpha pair's aerie in a part of the forest inaccessible to vehicles.

Though he ran in human form, he gave up control of his body to the leopard. It loved the freedom of the forest, loved feeling the wind ripple through its coat, the carpet of forest debris soft and quiet beneath the pads of its paws. That leopard, however, was also very strategy minded and enjoyed what Bastien did for the pack—to the cat, the financial stuff appeared akin to a game, a hunt.

Seeing a young soldier on patrol on the extended perimeter around Lucas's aerie, he halted, the human half of his nature rising to the surface once more. "Luc in?"

The tall auburn-haired male nodded, grin bright. "He's on babysitting detail."

"Thanks."

Ten minutes later, he found Lucas sitting at a small table set below the sprawling canopy of a forest giant, the dwelling cradled in its branches concealed by dense foliage. The cabin the alpha had built when his mate's pregnancy became too advanced for her to climb the rope ladder to the aerie was gone, no trace of it on the forest floor.

Lucas had a tablet computer on his lap, a sleek phone set to one side of the table, and what looked like a set of marked-up contracts on the other. Right then, however, his attention was on the baby girl who lay happily on her back on the blue-and-green picnic blanket beside the table, kicking her legs in the air.

As Bastien watched, Luc set aside the tablet to go down to the blanket. Tickling Naya gently on the bottoms of tiny feet covered by the sunny yellow fabric of her footsie pants, he pushed up her fluffy white sweater to blow a raspberry against her stomach, his hair the same rich black as his cub's.

Naya's giggles floated on the air, her delight infectious.

"She doesn't bite, Bas." An amused glance.

"I was taking a photo for Mom." Sliding away his phone, he sprawled on the blanket on his back, and—with a glance at Lucas—picked Naya up to place her on his chest. She batted at him with baby fists, her smile sweet and innocent. Catching those soft hands, he pretended to bite and growl, which made her convulse in laughter in the way only babies could.

"And the patented Smith charm strikes again." The dry comment had barely left Lucas's mouth when his phone beeped.

Grabbing it from the table without leaving his seated position on the picnic blanket, he spent a couple of minutes discussing a timetable change relating to a construction project for which Bastien was handling the finances. When he hung up, it was to give Bastien his full attention. "What is it?" The question of an alpha to a member of his pack, not one man to another.

His leopard immediately aware of the difference, Bastien rose to a sitting position, too, and placed Naya carefully on her back on the blanket, where she grabbed her daddy's hand to gum at his fingers. "There might be a situation." It was difficult to speak past his protectiveness where Kirby was concerned, but he forced himself to lay it all out.

Panther-green eyes watched him without interrupting until he was done. "You're convinced she doesn't know?"

"She's not a liar, Luc." Of that, both parts of his nature were in snarling agreement. "Whatever this is, it's not a case of her attempting to sneak into our territory."

"All right." Lucas leaned down to lightly tap his daughter on the tip of her nose in what was clearly a game between them, Naya's tiny hands trying to catch his finger; each miss made her laugh that open, bright laugh, and try again. "Stay on top of it and keep me posted."

Bastien blinked. "Just like that?" Given the volatile political climate, the entire pack on alert for signs of aggression from any corner, he'd expected more of an inquisition.

Lucas's lips curved. "I can scent blood—you've cut your palms with your claws, you've been fighting so hard not to go for my throat because I questioned you about your Kirby."

Bastien stared at his palms, having not realized what he'd done.

"And," Lucas continued, allowing his daughter to catch his finger to her gleeful cry, "since you're one of the most stable, centered members of the pack, your loyalty beyond question, it's pretty damn obvious she isn't just a friend or a casual lover."

"She's mine," Bastien answered simply.

Lucas picked Naya up to cradle her against his chest, pressing a kiss to the top of her head. "No alpha worth his salt gets between another leopard and his woman." Steady eye contact, alpha to packmate, dominant to dominant. "You're no green boy, Bas. I trust your judgment."

That, Bastien thought, was why Lucas was alpha. It wasn't only about brute strength, but about the intelligence to know his people, and the heart to have faith in them. "I know you have to inform the senior people in the pack about her being in the territory"—ensuring Kirby's safety—"but do you mind if I tell Mercy?" His sister and her mate were currently out of state, touching base with the falcons.

"Why don't you talk to her when she and Riley return from Arizona?" Lucas glanced down as his cub yawned, the smile on the DarkRiver alpha's face gentler than Bastien had ever before seen. "I'd think about talking to Dorian, too, soon as possible."

The blond sentinel, Bastien had already figured out, was the only one who'd been through anything that might be analogous to Kirby's situation. "I was planning to call him from the car." Reaching out, he touched Naya's fisted hand where it lay against Lucas's heart and the baby curled her delicate fingers around his. "How do you bear it, Luc?" he murmured, his own heart raw with emotion for this small new packmate. "She's so vulnerable, so fragile."

Lucas's panther looked out at Bastien through a human face. "Would you die to protect her?"

"That's not even a question." Bastien would bleed for any of his packmates, but the smallest, most vulnerable had a special place in all their hearts.

"That's how I bear it," Lucas said. "By reminding myself that every man, woman, and juvenile in this pack would fight to their last breath to protect her from harm." A soothing rumble in his chest as Naya made a tiny sound, the leopard speaking to its cub. "We're family, Bas, and family stands together. Whatever's going on with your Kirby, we'll figure it out."

The words centered him, calmed his leopard. No matter what, Kirby was no longer alone. She had him—and she had the strength of DarkRiver behind her.

BASTIEN had just hit the edge of the city, having spent a good forty minutes talking to Dorian about what it had been like to shift after a lifetime of being latent, when he received another call. "Kirby?" he said, having programmed her number into his phone.

"Bastien." A shuddering breath. "I—c-can you come get me? I've taken the rest of the day off, arranged a substitute."

"I'll be there in ten minutes."

He pulled up to find Kirby waiting a few meters up from the kindergarten. "I'm sorry," she said as soon as he got out of the driver's seat. "I didn't know who else to call." Her eyes huge, she swallowed. "You must've been doing something important."

"Shh." Enfolding her trembling body in his arms, he ran his hand firmly up and down her back, making sure to touch the bare skin of her nape with each stroke. "I'm glad you called me."

He could've held her forever, but he was conscious that though quiet, this was a public spot. More important, it was near Kirby's place of work. "Come on, little cat. We'll go somewhere private to talk."

Once he had her in the car, he turned up the heater full blast and drove them a short distance to a city park dotted with comparatively small evergreens, around which meandered a walking path. Today, it was empty, the grass a deep jewel green under sunlight. Bastien got out as soon as they arrived, viscerally aware of Kirby's continued distress, and sensing she'd do better out in the open.

Kirby didn't argue when he drew her into the park, wrapping one of his arms around her shoulders so he could cuddle her close. "Tell me what's wrong."

Stopping, she turned into him beside the straight trunk of a young pine. "Something strange is happening to me." The words were utterly inadequate to express the raging chaos within her, but they were all Kirby had.

"Go on."

Bastien's steady gaze, his deep voice, his touch—oh, how she loved the way he touched her so readily—it gave her an anchor as she described her strange madness. "I was in the back room getting a drink of water for one of the children," she began, still unable to make sense of it, "and all at once, I could hear every single child in the main room. Not just a blur of voices, but specific voices, each word crystal clear."

Rubbing her hands over her face, she tucked back the strands of hair that had escaped her ponytail. "I dismissed it as a weird acoustic effect when it faded after a few seconds," she said, her heart beginning to race again as it had then. "Then I walked out with the water . . . and into an avalanche of scent. I couldn't breathe, felt as if I'd suffocate under the weight of it."

Eyes intent, Bastien ran his free hand up and down her arm, his other one still strong and warm around her shoulders, but didn't interrupt.

"I dropped the water"—thank God it had been a plas cup meant for little hands—"and it went all over the carpet. The scents disappeared almost at the same time, but I knew I couldn't stay, risk the children when I couldn't predict what might happen next."

Hugging her arms around herself, she asked the question that had been tormenting her since. "Is it all in my head?" She couldn't forget the fact the doctors at the clinic had found absolutely nothing wrong with her. "I could be having some type of a psychotic breakdown."

Bastien gripped her chin. "You are not going crazy."

Kirby stilled, caught by the unadulterated certainty of his tone, as if he knew something she didn't. "Bastien?"

"Not here." He scanned the park, and she knew he'd noted the three elderly people who'd arrived in the past few minutes. "We'll go to my apartment. It's not the best place for this discussion, but our forested territory isn't close enough."

Kirby held her tongue until they were back in the car, her cheeks burning with an emotion that had her gritting her teeth. "If you knew something, why didn't you say so?" The words came out curt, her anger at him for lying to her—even by omission—smashing up against bewildered hurt.

Hands clenching on the steering wheel, Bastien began to drive. "Because whatever this is," he said, his voice gravel, "it's nothing simple."

Kirby wanted to snarl at him for that nonanswer.

CHAPTER 6

"We'll be at the apartment in minutes," Bastien said into the tense silence.

Not in the mood to make conversation, Kirby nonetheless found herself captive to her endless curiosity about Bastien. "I didn't think a leopard changeling would like an apartment." He'd done his best to hide it, but he'd been edgy in hers.

"I don't. That's why I bought such a ridiculously expensive place."

Kirby understood why the apartment had been so expensive the instant she stepped into it. Aside from a small private enclosure at the back, there were no internal walls in the space that had to cover half a floor. The entire front wall was crystal clear reinforced glass, the floors a gleaming honey-colored wood.

Above, and to her right was a loft-style space that had to house a bed, while the left part of the central area held an arrangement of sofas and large floor cushions that looked decadently comfortable, an open kitchen on the other side.

The entire place was drenched in light.

"Beautiful," she whispered.

The lines of stress easing from his expression—and why did that make her heart ache, make her want to kiss him, even as she continued to fight the more primitive urge to bite him—he clasped her hand. Sighing silently at the contact that felt deeply right, she allowed him to tug her toward the wall of glass, and to the door cleverly concealed within it.

There was a generous balcony beyond, with a view of the Bay, the water sparkling like shattered sapphires under the sunshine. Gripping the railing, the metal digging into her palms, she stared at him. "You're *rich*. Really, really rich."

Leaning back against the railing, arms propped on either side, he shrugged. "I'm good at making money, been investing my own income since I was a juvenile. Does it make a difference to you?" Green eyes glinting at her from beneath half-lowered lashes.

Kirby fought the urge to bare her teeth at him. What was wrong with her lately? The thought had barely formed when she moved faster than she'd believed she could. Tugging down his head with a hand fisted in his hair, she nipped sharply at his jaw. "Don't make me even more mad than I am already."

His grin creased his cheeks, his arms locking around her waist. "Bite me again." At her narrow-eyed look, he nuzzled the side of her face before saying, "Truth is, I'd rather be at my aerie." The leopard paced behind his eyes, its presence so strong that Kirby could almost see it.

Almost touch the gold and black of its fur.

"The days I can work from there," Bastien continued, "I let my brothers, other packmates who want a night in the city, use this place, so we get our worth out of it."

It betrayed so much of how he saw the world that he so naturally said "our" for a place that, to many other men, would've been a status symbol. For Bastien, she realized, it was his pack, his family, who were important, who mattered. She hurt with wanting the same—never had she fit in, always the constant outsider. And now . . .

"Please tell me what you know," she said quietly, fear a metallic taste in the back of her mouth, a shivering rasp over her skin.

His expression stripped of any hint of humor, Bastien picked up one of her hands, a hand Kirby hadn't realized she'd clenched by her side. "Open for me, little cat."

As the blood rushed back into the strained-white flesh, he ran a single finger across the tips. "Do your fingertips ever tingle?"

Heart slamming hard against her ribs and mouth dry, she nodded. "Just recently." She stared at her own fingers. "It's not painful, but it prickles."

Bastien continued to hold her hand, stroking his thumb absently over her skin. "In the weekend, the pain you felt"—wild green eyes capturing her own—"if I said it felt like something was trying to claw its way out, would I be right?"

Unable to accept what he was asking her to believe, she shook her head, broke the searing intimacy of the eye contact. "It can't be. I'm human."

Bastien cupped her jaw, turned her face back to him, the brush of his skin over her own almost succeeding in calming the skittering panic within. "Tell me about your parents."

"I—" Her blood went cold. "My parents died when I was a toddler," she whispered, the brutality of her history something she preferred to forget . . . a history that led to one inescapable conclusion, but for the impossibility of it. "The care services would hardly mistake a changeling child for human."

"Not necessarily. Changelings don't shift till around one year of age."

"That's how old I was when it happened." She forced herself to recall the small number of facts that had seeped into her memory over the years, in spite of her refusal to access her own records. "My birth date is unknown but, according to one of my social workers, I was examined by a pediatrician and judged to be approximately twelve months old. If I hadn't yet shifted, I should've soon after I was found."

"Yes." Bastien frowned. "How did you lose your parents?"

"In a fire." She didn't know much more than the basic details of that fire, her anger at her unknown parents for abandoning her a raw wound that had never healed. "I was found on the street dressed in one-piece pajamas covered in soot, the bottoms of my feet burned and bloody.

"It was clear I'd come from a nearby house that had gone up in flames, but while the police did discover the remains of an adult male and female who must've been my parents"—she swallowed—"for some reason, those remains were never identified."

"Ah, hell." Bastien's exclamation was rough. "You experienced a severely traumatic event around the same time that you were meant to complete your first shift," he said, tucking her close. "It must've fundamentally altered your development."

It sounded right . . . yet wrong. "No," she whispered, a cold chill in her blood. "What if I *did* shift for the first time that day? So happy, so excited. Then . . . then a bad thing happened."

Bastien stepped back, took her face in his hands again. "Do you remember?"

"No." All she had were lingering echoes of emotion. "But I know that's what happened." Could almost see it. "Wouldn't a baby think the two events were connected—the shift and the fire?" Pain twisted her heart. "The human half blamed the animal, and the animal blamed itself."

"And," Bastien said harshly, "you had no one who understood what was going on inside you. No packmate to comfort you, reassure you it wasn't your fault." He kissed her cheeks, her jaw, her lips.

Finding strength in the affection, she told him the rest. "The only reason anyone knew my first name was that it was stitched into my pajamas." Her last name, Rosario, had apparently been the name of the street where she'd been found. "That's the only other piece of information I have."

"Your adoptive parents might—"

"I was raised in care." Kirby didn't like to think of the seventeen long, agonizingly lonely years she'd spent in the system, but if the truth to her present lay in her past, then she had to find the will. "I had terrible, screaming nightmares as a child." A sympathetic social worker had given her that information after she grew old enough to wonder why she didn't have a family when other infants and toddlers were quickly adopted.

"I kept being chosen for adoption, then returned." Like a broken machine being sent back to the warehouse for a refund. "They finally stopped trying to place me when I was six and I spent three years in state institutions for troubled children before the nightmares faded"—as far as the world was concerned at least—"and I was cleared for the foster care system."

Bastien's claws threatened to release. He wanted to break something, shred those who had wounded his mate when she'd been a small, vulnerable cub unable to fight for herself.

"I remember, you know," she said quietly, her eyes on the ground. "Being taken by people who said they wanted me, feeling happy and hopeful, and then being brought back because I wasn't good enough."

"Bastards." So angry he was trembling, he closed his hand around the side of her neck and pressed his lips to her temple.

Kirby lifted her hand to his hair, petting him in gentle strokes. "It wasn't so bad, being in care. I wasn't abused or anything."

Bastien's leopard growled within at that unwitting indictment on her childhood. "You're fucking amazing, you know that?" He pressed his forehead to hers, his rage cut with violent pride.

"No, I'm a coward." Breaking away in a jerking movement, she paced to the end of the balcony and back. "I tell myself I'm still angry at my parents for leaving me, that that's why I've never requested my records. The truth is, I'm afraid."

Her eyes shone wet, her shoulders knotted. "Because if I read those records, then I can't avoid the truth any longer, can't pretend that maybe I'm not alone, that one day someone will come for me." She dashed away her tears. "I'm twenty-four years old and I'm still hoping. How stupid is that?"

"You don't get to do that." Bastien pulled her stiff body into his arms, his fury at what had been done to her a vicious storm within. "You don't get to hurt yourself, and you never ever get to call yourself stupid."

She thumped fisted hands against his side. "Why? Who're you to give me that order?"

Bastien didn't even think about it—his mate was hurting and needed reassurance. "I'm yours," he said bluntly, wrapping his hand around her ponytail and tugging back her head so he could look into those beautiful, pain-filled hazel eyes. "You are *not* alone. Do you understand?" There was nothing in his life more certain than what he felt for her, and it was no longer simply about the primal pull of the mating bond. It was about Kirby. Sweet, strong, sometimes snarly Kirby. "I will always be here for you."

Her breathing erratic, Kirby didn't respond to his declaration. Instead, she tugged her hair free and said, "I'll e-mail the records request today." She refused to meet his gaze, her own obstinately on the glittering water in the distance. "It'll probably take a few days for the files to come in."

Bastien gritted his teeth to hold back the leopard's anger as she surreptitiously wiped away the tracks her tears had left on her face. It wasn't Kirby's fault she didn't believe him—no doubt all those prospective adoptive parents had promised her forever, too. But he wasn't his mother's most stubborn boy for nothing.

Kirby would soon discover that when Bastien Michael Smith made a promise, he kept it.

FEELING bruised on the inside, Kirby didn't argue against Bastien's nudge back into the warmth of the apartment, but when he made her a cup of sweet tea and ordered she drink it, she put her hands on her hips. "Stop growling at me!" She might be shaky, horribly tempted to believe in his every promise, but she was not and never would be, a pushover.

"I am not growling at you," he growled, thumping down the mug of tea on the counter.

Of course the hot liquid splashed all over his hand. Grabbing his wrist when he hissed and pulled back, she stuck it under the cold water tap. "Don't move," she snapped when he went to pull it away, shooting him a glare as he growled again, the sound vibrating against her skin. "You're worse than my students."

No warning, no nothing, he just leaned down and nipped the tip of her ear sharply with his teeth. "Bastien!" Jumping, she let go of his wrist long enough for him to wrap his arm around her, trapping her between his weight and the sink.

Her entire body sang at the proximity of his, hard and hot and deliciously overwhelming against her back, but her worry about him kept her focused. Taking his wrist again, she put it under the tap. "It's a bit red."

He nuzzled at her, licked out at her skin.

Kirby couldn't control her shiver. "Cat."

A smile against her skin. "I like the taste of you." Another lick, his free hand braced against the sink to block any escape.

Kirby didn't want to escape this muscled masculine trap. "So," she said, trying to keep her brain in gear, "I have some changeling blood—"

"No, it's more than that." He kissed her nape, making her toes curl, and she thought that, perhaps, this gorgeous man was attempting to distract her from the pain of the childhood loss that had so badly scarred her.

Eyes burning, she turned and pressed her lips to his jaw.

Rubbing his cheek against hers, he continued to speak. "Changeling genes are dominant, at least when it comes to shifting. A full or half-changeling child always shifts—and your scent tells me you fall into that category. Even if you're latent, you should know what you are."

"So I'm some kind of freak," Kirby muttered. "Great."

Bastien's snarl raised every hair on her body. "What did I tell you about hurting yourself?" With that furious comment in a voice that barely sounded human, he broke her hold, turned off the tap, and spun her to face him.

Kirby stood her ground, recognizing the predator in him, but dead certain he would never hurt her. That certainty held even when he placed his hands on her hips, his claws slicing out to lie against the fabric of her coat.

"You're not a freak. You're Kirby." His tone dared her to disagree.

Skin uncomfortably aflame all at once, she dropped her hands to the belt of her coat and undid it, shrugging off the thick fabric to throw it aside. Bastien's hands went right back to where they'd been, strong and dangerous over denim and cotton.

"Sexy, smart, beautiful Kirby." It was a purr of sound.

And then he kissed her.

One hand unraveling her ponytail, the other sliding under her shirt to lie on the curve of her waist, his skin rougher than her own, and his mouth enslaving hers.

She felt his claws, but he didn't so much as scratch her as he tasted her like she was his favorite dessert. With tiny bites and long, slow licks that demanded she join in. When she did, stroking her tongue against his, he purred, the vibration shivering through her entire body to make her wonder what it would be like if they were both naked.

"Bastien." Her nipples tight little points, she gripped his shoulders, exquisitely aware of him shifting one big hand to her butt to help her attain the right angle to rub against the rigid temptation of his cock, her claws kneading his—

Shoving away with a tiny scream, she stared at her hands. "Oh God." The claws retracted almost before she was sure she'd seen them. "I—"

Bastien put his hands on either side of Kirby's body, once more trapping her against the counter and keeping her within touching distance. "Yes," he said. "You just semi-shifted." And, because he hated to see her so lost, so scared, he nipped her ear again. Hard enough to sting.

"Argh!" Gripping his hair, she tugged his face down to her own. "Stop that or I will *really* bite you."

There she was, his tough Kirby who'd built a life for herself through sheer grit and determination. "Promise?" His cat batted playfully at her, wanting out of Bastien's human skin so she could play with him in reality. *Soon*, he promised the leopard.

"You're—" Releasing him after a hard, infuriated kiss that made his chest rumble in another purr, she said, "I think I better take leave from work until this is all sorted out."

Bastien nodded.

"I'm so new I'll lose my job if I don't go back within a week." Her temper faded into a sadness that had him wrapping his arms around her. "I really liked this job."

Protective as he was, Bastien wanted to fix everything for her, but he knew Kirby wouldn't thank him for it. "My sister tells me that's the top kindergarten in the city." Mercy's mate had apparently already begun to scope things out, even though it would be six months yet before their babies were even born. "They wouldn't have hired you if you weren't the best—you'll find another position when you're ready."

A small nod against his chest. "My rent's paid up for the next two weeks at least."

That statement, Bastien couldn't let pass, because as Kirby needed to have pride in her work, he needed to care for her. Shifting so he could look at her face, he said, "You don't ever have to worry about a place to live." He'd hidden his intentions at the start so as not to rush her, but after hearing of what she'd gone through as a child, he wanted her to know she was *wanted, adored.* "Right now, we need to go to the aerie." The natural surroundings would put her animal more at ease.

Small white teeth sank down into her lower lip. "I hardly

know you," she whispered, but made no move to pull away, instead petting his chest with small, absent strokes, as if to soften the impact of her words.

"Some people"—he closed his hand over hers—"we know in a heartbeat." Leopard and man both looked into the unusual hazel of her eyes and saw their future. "Others, we'll never know, even if we speak to them for a thousand years."

Blinking rapidly, Kirby buried herself against his chest. "I'm so scared, Bastien." Her voice trembled.

"I'm with you every step of the way, little cat." He held her close, the side of his face pressed against the softness of her hair. "We'll do this together."

CHAPTER 7

Chest tight, Kirby made the records request on their way to her apartment to pick up what she'd need for a few days at the aerie. When Bastien reached across to run his knuckles over her cheek, she leaned into the touch, so painfully happy that he was in her life.

Some people, we know in a heartbeat.

He was right, and despite her fear at the violent depth of their fledgling connection, at how much it would hurt if he changed his mind and rejected her, she wasn't going to back away. Bastien was too important, too wonderful, and she wanted him to be hers, only hers, the possessive thoughts at once shy and wild.

When he suggested they stop at the fresh goods market on their way out of the city, she gladly fell in with the idea. "I think doing something mundane will be good right about now."

Forty-five minutes and a quick snack at the attached café later, the wicked cat next to her was coaxing her into surrendering to the lure of a slice of organic carrot cake with cream-cheese icing, when she heard, "Bas!"

Startled, she looked up from the tempting display to see a man with rich brown hair and hazel eyes darker than her own prowling toward them. Despite the difference in coloring, the Smith familial stamp was unmistakable.

"Sage." Bastien scowled. "What the hell are you doing here?"

"Mom messaged, asked if I could grab a few things for her, drop them off on the way home." Sage's words may have been for Bastien, but his eyes never moved off Kirby. "I'm the good-looking brother," he said with a smile so charming, it was adorable. "Sage."

Kirby liked him at once, comfortable in a way she rarely was with strangers . . . but of course, he was Bastien's brother, and she trusted Bastien down to the bone. "Kirby."

"Cake, huh?" Sage rubbed his jaw, blew out a breath. "I'd go for the double chocolate with vanilla frosting myself."

Throwing an arm around her shoulders, Bastien said, "Stop flirting, you're terrible at it," to his brother, but she could tell it was only pretend, the two men obviously friends as well as family.

FIFTEEN minutes after they'd run into Sage, Bastien closed the fresh groceries in the trunk of the car and pointed a finger at his brother. "Don't tell Mercy, Herb."

Sage rocked back on his heels, a glint in his eye. "Worried she'll scare away your girl, *Frenchie*?"

"I don't think Kirby's the scaring-away type, are you, little cat?" Proud of the woman who was his own, he cupped her cheek, ran his thumb over her lower lip.

Coloring, she nonetheless pressed a kiss to his palm. "If I was," she pointed out, "all your growling would've done it already."

Bastien saw Sage's eyes go leopard at that instant and knew his brother had realized exactly what was at stake. Not that he wouldn't tell Mercy and Grey anyway—but he wouldn't mention it beyond that tight circle. Not yet, not until Bastien was ready. He and his siblings might rag on one another, but they'd never mess with something so important.

Leaning close to Kirby, Sage whispered, "Ask him about the infamous kitten defurring episode."

"Remind me to strangle you later." Bastien opened the

passenger door for Kirby, saw his brother's smirk turn into a grin when Kirby waved at him after getting into the car, her eyes sparkling.

"Frenchie, huh?" she said, once they were on their way again, the laughter in her tone welcome.

"I really need to strangle him. Surely, my folks wouldn't notice one less son."

Shoulders shaking, Kirby turned in her seat to face him. "You're close."

"Yep, all four of us are pretty tight-knit." Every one of his memories of childhood included one or the other of his siblings. "Not that we didn't fight like feral wolves sometimes," he told her. "In one notorious incident, Grey, who was only a tiny cub at the time, got mad at Sage and clamped his teeth on the tip of Sage's tail."

Kirby's smile lit up her whole face. "What happened?"

Wanting to kiss her breathless, he said, "Stubborn bastard refused to let go, despite Mercy and me trying our hardest." The memory made his leopard huff with laughter. "When Sage tried to shake him off, he just dug his claws into the earth and growled in the back of his throat. We finally had to admit defeat and call in the Power of Mom."

Kirby's laughter filled the car. "Tell me more."

He went to do just that when his phone rang. "Sorry. Probably work."

To his relief, Kirby didn't seem to mind the fact that he had to be in contact with the office for most of the trip, her eyes on the scenery. Still, he didn't like her so quiet, her fingers twined to strained whiteness around one another.

"What music do you like?" he asked between calls.

"Cheery, chirpy pop."

Wincing, he pulled up a station that delivered exactly that. "You owe me."

"Come on"—she turned in her seat to face him once more—"it's not that bad."

"I'm sorry? I can't hear you past the sugar blocking my eardrums."

She mock punched him and his leopard purred. He wanted to luxuriate in her touch, wanted to demand the most intimate, most private skin privileges, but while he delighted in skin-to-skin contact with her, he wouldn't push her to consummate their relationship. If he woke to see regret in Kirby's eyes, it would fucking break him. No, when they took that step, he needed his mate with him all the way, confident and passionate and demanding in her own right.

"It's not a long walk from here," he said some time later, parking in a nominated area within the pack's forested territory. "We have to be careful of the natural vegetation."

Having been twisting her neck to look every which way as they drove in, Kirby stepped out to spin around happily on the spongy carpet created of fallen leaves and pine needles. "I want to explore everything!"

Her unhidden delight eased any concern he might've had about her being comfortable in the rich green wilderness that sang to his changeling soul. Slinging the duffel with her stuff over his shoulder, he clasped her hand in his, eager to have her in his home. "I'll run back for the groceries." He couldn't wait to show her all his favorite spots in the forest, his leopard as excited as a cub.

When a lynx with thick golden-brown fur wandered over just as they were about to reach the aerie, Kirby froze on a wondering gasp. "Is that . . ."

"Not a changeling." Crouching down, he ran his hand over the creature's back, its tufted ears standing straight up. "But, he's a friend of mine."

Kirby came down beside him, one of her hands braced on his thigh in the sweetest torture. "Will he allow me to pet him?" Wistful need.

"Here." Taking hold of her hand after she settled on her knees, he held it out to the lynx's nose. "Don't feel bad if he decides against you," Bastien said, wanting her to enjoy her first brush with the area's natural wildlife. "The damn beast took six months to deign me acceptable."

Except the lynx took one sniff at Kirby and jumped up to place his front paws on her thighs. "Bastien, oh, he's beautiful." Face suffused with joy, Kirby began to stroke the cat.

Bastien considered the intriguing tableau. Regardless of species, none of the wild creatures were this friendly to anyone outside the pack. Of course, Kirby had such neat little claws . . . yeah, they could've been of a lynx.

Settling with his back against a tree, legs out in front of him, he watched her pet the utterly lazy, spoilt creature now sprawled in her lap. That lynx was going to follow her around every time she was in the area, he thought with an affectionate grin for his wild counterpart. Bastien would likely find it on the branches outside their aerie, waiting for her.

Well done, cat, he thought a little ruefully, his own leopard yet deprived of her touch.

KIRBY and Bastien finally reached their destination a half hour from that meeting, the lynx having left them ten minutes earlier with an affectionate brush of his body against Kirby's legs. Now, Kirby watched Bastien climb up to the aerie hidden in the arms of a massive tree, one so big, she couldn't take it all in.

This world intoxicated her with its magnificence, the way Bastien moved in it, his muscles fluid, a primal song. He'd climbed the tree using his claws, yet had left only faint marks on the trunk that would soon close over, not a single gouge to be seen. Just one more sign that he wasn't an intruder here, but an accepted part of this incredible ecosystem, one who respected the land that nurtured him.

"Rope ladder coming down!" he called out after disappearing behind the leaves with her duffel.

"Thank—" She screamed as Bastien jumped from his high perch . . . to land with the pouncing grace of the cat he was, his powerful body ending up in a crouch.

"Sorry if I scared you." A sheepish look. "I forget it looks dangerous."

"No." Kirby waved the hand she'd thrown out in a futile attempt to stop him. "I'm used to changelings jumping out of trees," she said through her still-thumping heart. "Most of them are five years old, and the trees are only a hundred times shorter than this one, but same principle." In truth, he'd been magnificent, a fact she could appreciate now that she wasn't swamped in terror.

His smile creased his cheeks, his green eyes backlit with an untamed glow. "A smartass. I like it." Tugging at her so she fell against his chest, he ran his hands boldly down to her butt, squeezed. "I like this ass even better. Makes me want to bite."

Kirby's entire body went molten, but she wasn't about to let him get away with teasing her so outrageously without repercussions. Hauling him close with one hand on his nape, the other in his hair, she claimed a hot, tangled kiss from this man who made her forget she wasn't experienced, her actions driven by naked instinct. A second later, she was backed up against the nearest tree trunk, his hands petting and molding her flesh as their mouths engaged in erotic battle.

Moaning, she returned kiss for kiss, touch for touch, delectably conscious of the hard push of his arousal against her abdomen. He was so big, so strong, his touch a drug to her senses. Gasping a breath between kisses, she returned to their private war, hooking her legs around his waist when he hitched her up.

A snarl, his mouth tearing away from her own, though there was no danger that she could see, no reason to stop. The lightning heat of his glare had her narrowing her eyes, her fingertips prickling. "What?"

"What? *What*?" He closed one clawed hand very carefully around her throat. "I'm trying to be a good guy by not seducing you when you've had one hell of a shock, and what do you do but kiss me all sexy and aroused and wet." Growled-out words. "How the hell am I supposed to keep from devouring you?"

Kirby wanted to pounce on him for that blunt declaration. "I don't feel vulnerable or taken advantage of," she assured him, petting his beautiful chest through his T-shirt.

His snarl rumbled against her breasts.

"In fact," she murmured, looking at him through half-lowered lashes, "why don't *I* take advantage of you?" The idea of having his naked body as her personal playground made her breath catch—surely she'd figure things out as she went along, especially since she had a partner who made no bones about wanting her.

"I'll be gentle." She didn't know where this sexual confidence was coming from, but it felt so, so good to play with Bastien. "Promise." Kissing his throat, she ran her hands over his shoulders.

Mine. It was a feral thought, should've scared her. It didn't. No, it made her want to purr as Bastien had begun to do.

Having already learned it was his weak spot, she continued to kiss his throat, the taste of him her own personal aphrodisiac.

This is how he should react to me, said the awakening wildness within her, possessive and sensual and with no time for the rules of civilized behavior. *This is how it should be between us.*

"Grr." Pulling her mouth from his throat, Bastien snapped his teeth at her, making her jump . . . before her nipples went achingly tight, her body honey slick in welcome.

Bastien's nostrils flared. *"No."*

"No?" Muscles clenching around an emptiness she knew only he could fill, Kirby poked him in the chest. "Don't you try to tell me you know best."

He leaned in with his hands braced on the trunk on either side of her head, stubborn male will and feline temper. "When you're bruised and hurt inside, I damn well will."

She bared her own teeth at him. "Who made that rule?"

"I did." A nip of her kiss-swollen lower lip.

She growled low in her throat, wanting to claw him. Not to hurt. Never to hurt. Just so he'd know she wasn't helpless, was a worthy playmate.

Bastien hissed out a breath, his lips curving. "Hello, little cat."

In front of him, Kirby snatched back the hands she'd had on his chest, staring once more at the curved tips of her claws. The most stunning change though, was one she couldn't see; her eyes had turned a pale, pale gold with a vivid black pupil.

Tapping a claw, Bastien grinned. "Cute."

A dangerous pause. "Cute?" Placing one hand back on his chest, she dug those pretty claws in enough that he felt it. "Want to take that back?"

"Hell, no." Not when it got her claws on him. Not able to resist in spite of his attempt at good behavior, he kissed her again, rocking his painfully aroused body into the inviting softness of hers.

Melting, she rubbed up against him, her claws going up to prick at his shoulders as she kneaded. His cock threatened to explode and embarrass him at that unambiguous sign of welcome. Cupping her jaw, he indulged himself in another deep, raw kiss before putting at least a meter between him and his mate—who'd drawn his blood just enough for it to be foreplay.

Face flushing, she reached down to undo her coat and throw it aside. "I'm all hot," she said, her breasts pushing against the shirt she had on underneath.

Bastien thought for a second that she intended to win their sensual battle by baring herself to the skin—and yeah, who was he kidding, he'd never last if Kirby pressed her naked curves against him—but then she tugged at her collar, said, "I'm really hot." Kicking off her shoes, she tore off her socks. "Bastien, why is it so *hot*?" It was a plea, her eyes flicking from gold to hazel and back again. "I can't breathe."

And he realized they'd run out of time.

CHAPTER 8

Thinking back rapidly to what Dorian had told him, he said, "Kirby, look at me," putting every ounce of his dominance in his voice. No matter the nature of the creature that lived within Kirby, it wasn't as dominant as Bastien's leopard. That knowledge was instinctive, a survival mechanism built into every changeling, predatory or not.

Whimpering, Kirby met his gaze, unable to refuse the order. It was why he'd never given her any such order in their time together thus far, and never would in their ordinary life. He didn't ever want his mate to obey him simply because her animal saw him as the more dominant, would tear himself to shreds before he stole her free will.

Today, however, she was frightened, panicking, the fear a shivering darkness in her eyes; both parts of her nature needed him to take charge. And though he was unprepared for such a violent and sudden shift, having expected to have time to ease her into it with the pack healer's help, no way in hell was he going to allow anything to go wrong.

"Give in," he ordered, Dorian's advice about the need for Kirby to trust the trapped creature within resonating in his mind. *"Give in*, Kirby."

Crying out, Kirby went to her knees, pressing a fisted hand to her abdomen. Her eyes were huge and wet when she looked up. "Bastien, it's clawing at me!"

She was, he realized, too confused to understand him, her focus shot. Going down in front of her, he put his hands on either side of her head, anchoring her in the instant. "No, it just wants out." He kept his tone firm, steady. "It isn't trying to hurt you."

When her breathing went shallow, perspiration breaking out over her skin in a fine shimmer, he locked his eyes with hers. "Stop fighting, Kirby," he said, once more using his dominance to force her to concentrate. "Accept your animal. That's all it wants."

Her face disappeared under his touch and he felt the plush kiss of fur before she was back, terror in every jagged breath, her eyes cycling between human and cat too hard, too fast. "No, no, something bad . . . something bad is happening!"

Partial shifts could be held on purpose, but it took considerable skill. This was dangerous, parts of her going in and out—because her arm had just done the same thing. "*Kirby,*" he growled, too afraid for her to temper his voice. "Listen to me. Nothing bad is happening." It had been a child's cry that had come out of her mouth, of the cub she'd been when her world went up in flames. "This is a good thing, a beautiful thing."

Another scream, a trickle of blood from her nose.

No, no, no. Shifting should never be this horrible pain. "You can't fight it, baby. If you do, you'll rip yourself apart." He controlled the urge to yell, conscious that might scare the animal within her, make her devolve further. "Trust in the shift. Let it happen."

She shook her head, skin clammy and claws digging into his wrists in feral desperation. "I won't be able to come back." Piercing terror, her legs shifting in and out to leave her fighting for balance.

"You will." He steadied her. "You *will.*"

This time when she cried out, her skin bubbled with pinpricks of blood, as if her body was being turned inside out. Frantic, the human part of him turned to the leopard, found an answer in the animal's linear thinking. "I'll shift first," he said, shaking her wrists enough to capture her attention. "Your cat will follow mine." It was a gamble, one that relied on the level of her trust in him. "I'm more dominant."

"Cat?" Dazed golden irises met his.

"Yes." The fact she'd no doubt assume he meant she was a leopard, too, would work in his favor. "Your cat will do what I say." At least until his Kirby found her confidence again.

Her clawed hands dropped to dig into the fallen leaves, her body shaking hard enough that her teeth clattered. "I'm so afraid."

"Don't be." Cupping her face, he kissed her, hoping the tactile reassurance would allow her to hear him. "It's not an intruder, baby. It's just another part of you."

ANOTHER part of me.

A part she'd forgotten and kept trapped for a lifetime.

Of course it hurt. It—they—hurt so much.

"I'll be able to come back?" she sobbed, drowning in shame at having done this horrifying thing . . . and then her mind shifted and she felt so ashamed at having left her human half alone all this time . . . before the human part of her was looking out at Bastien once again.

"Yes." Absolute confidence in Bastien's voice, no room for argument. "Now, just think of your cat and become your other self." He dissolved into a million particles of shattering light, his clothes disintegrating off him, and then there was a big, heavily muscled leopard in front of her, its forehead gently bumping her own.

Heart thundering at the proximity of a creature so dangerous and extraordinary, she felt a need, such terrible need to be the same, to run, to look at the world through eyes far more keen than the human ones that were all she could use now. It hurt to be shut away, to be tied up, to be only half. Why was she doing this to them? It was time to run, to play, to be together . . . to be with him.

Frighteningly aware her thoughts weren't exactly human, Kirby attempted to wrench back control. Searing pain in her rib cage, claws raking her bloody.

Bastien snarled in a violent fury of sound.

And the pain stopped.

Your cat will follow mine.

Scared still, she held the primal green gaze of the leopard who had made her a promise, and *trusted*.

It was agony but it wasn't pain. It was a stunning, dazzling ecstasy and it tore her up then put her back together. Afterward, she wobbled, her body's center of gravity dramatically altered. Her view, too, had changed, become low—she was staring at the black spotted golden chest of the leopard in front of her.

Small, thought the cat that was her, tipping up its head to look at the larger predator. When he butted his face against her own, she felt happy . . . then shy, ducking her head . . . to see that her fur was a thick silvery gray with hidden bits of black. Lifting up a paw that seemed too big for a small cat, she looked at it quizzically, but then the leopard nuzzled at her and she dropped the paw, too happy to be with him to worry about why her fur was the wrong color.

He recognizes me!

It was a joyous thought. Even though she'd been hiding for so long, scared and guilty and afraid, he knew her. She'd fought the ugly fear to wake up because she'd found him, needed him to see her, accept her, claim her.

The other half of her had been brave all this time; now she had to be brave.

The leopard nipped at her ears. She jumped with a startled yowl. When the leopard huffed in laughter, she decided to pounce, show him she could play, too. Except her body went the wrong way and she ended up tumbled to the side. Prowling over, the leopard nudged her back up on all four paws, then put one of his own paws very carefully in front of the other. Again and again.

She didn't understand why he was moving so slowly when he was strong and graceful. She wanted to see him run, wanted to run with him, the wind rippling through their fur.

Head tilted to the side, she continued to watch his strange behavior, and because she didn't want him to move too far away, put her paws forward like he'd done. And she didn't fall, was walking! *Oh! Oh!* Now she understood, now she knew he was teaching her.

Adoring him even more, she brushed her tail over his . . . but fell short. About to angle her head to look back, see what was wrong with her tail, she felt his twine around her own. Shy again, she looked down, her attention caught once more by her strange silver-colored paws. Lifting one up, she stared at it carefully, retracting and releasing her claws, spreading her toes. *Big paw. Small cat.* Still a cat.

Satisfied, she put it down and leaned her body against his, the warm beat of his heart a steady pulse against her fur.

When he walked again, she walked with him, his tail twining and untwining around her own, her body brushing his. He took her to a place that wasn't too far, but had many scents. It confused her. Until he showed her how to pick one and track it, then nipped at her ear again when she tried to do too many things at once.

This time, she swiped at his leg with her claws to remind him she wasn't weak.

Growling at the swipe, he bared his teeth.

She bared her own back at him.

And the leopard bent down to look into her eyes. Staring back, she reached up with a clawed paw and patted his face. He nipped at her nose, not in rebuke this time, but in affection. Happy, so *happy*, she butted her head against his and then they played, wild and free and without fear.

BASTIEN shifted into human form, and carefully lifted up the gorgeous Canadian lynx who was Kirby into his arms. She'd fallen asleep after two hours of play and exploration, her small body vibrant with energy. Now, she didn't stir as he judged the distance to the aerie and took a running start, managing to climb up to the balcony outside it even though he only had the use of his feet and one hand.

Retracting his claws, he carried Kirby inside the open-plan space and placed her on his bed. His scent would comfort her in her sleep, because while the human half of Kirby hadn't yet figured out what he was to her, the lynx knew. That lynx had fur of an astonishingly lush silvery gray marked with tiny patches of black on the legs. The black appeared again in the adorable tufts on her pointed ears and the end of her short tail.

"God, you are so beautiful, human or cat."

Indulging himself with several luxuriant strokes through her fur, he finally forced himself to get up and pull on some jeans. Then, certain Kirby would sleep for a while yet, he jumped down and ran to the car to grab the groceries. His mate would be starving when she woke, the shift burning energy like wildfire, not to mention the way they'd explored together.

Keeping an eye on her as he prepared the meal, he wasn't the least surprised when she shifted spontaneously in her sleep, a lusciously curved nude woman now on his bed, her skin flawless honey.

He groaned. "I should be up for sainthood." Finding a blanket, he covered her sleeping body . . . and smiled at her drowsy murmur of his name before she snuggled down again.

A few minutes later, he called Lucas to update him on Kirby's shift and species, then requested his alpha reach out through DarkRiver's network of allies and friends to see if anyone knew of a lynx pack that had lost a Canadian lynx child approximately twenty-three years ago. He couldn't assume Kirby had come from Canada, however, as there were American packs that included Canadian lynx. A number had even emigrated to join packs in Europe's colder climes.

While wild lynx tended to be solitary, or stick to very small groups, changeling lynx had been influenced by the human half of their nature—akin to other feline changelings—to create larger, tightly bonded packs. Someone *had* to be missing a child, though the fact that Kirby had never been claimed argued against that.

Bastien hoped he was wrong. His mate had been alone so long—he wanted her to have a family, a pack. He was ready to offer his own in a heartbeat, but he also knew she'd have questions about her past, her existence as a lynx that he and his packmates wouldn't be able to answer.

"Bastien?"

Having been stirring the protein-rich stew he'd made for her, he turned to find Kirby sitting up in bed, blanket wrapped around her body. Warm and soft with sleep, she was so perfect his heart ached. "There you are, little cat." Turning off the cooker, he went to the bed and, taking a seat, cuddled her into his lap.

A yawn, her nose warm as she nuzzled at his throat. "I really am. A little cat."

"You're a Canadian lynx," he said, his leopard rolling around in the sweet and wild taste of her, her two different scents now gorgeously combined into a single strong and unique thread. "Cute tufted ears and all."

She froze, a dark shadow passing over her face. "A lynx?"

"Hey." Fisting his hand in her hair, he rubbed his nose over her own. "What's the matter?"

"C-can we still be together?" Kirby forced herself to ask, the idea of losing Bastien making her cat—*a lynx!*—hiss and snarl. "If I'm a lynx?" Not that it mattered; she would fight for him until her claws were bloody and her body broken. He was *hers*.

"Did I ever tell you about Mercy's mate?" Bastien said with a slow smile that made her abdomen clench.

"Yes. His name is Riley."

"He's a wolf."

Kirby's cat sat up inside her, shook its head. Kirby felt like doing the same. "A wolf?"

"Yeah, that's what my brothers and I said." A scowl. "Planned to beat him up for it, too, but he adores Mercy so we tolerate him."

Kirby saw right through the bluster. "You really like him," she said, joy bubbling through her.

"Maybe." A playful bite of her jaw, his teeth grazing her skin. "Grr—"

Laughing from deep in his chest when she slapped a hand over her mouth, he drew away that hand to drop a tender kiss to the center of her palm. "You need to eat, my ferocious lynx," he said, but seemed powerless to stop himself from dipping his head and running his lips up the sensitive line of her throat.

She arched into the caress.

"You're all pretty skin and curves and luscious heat." A wet kiss to the point just above her pulse; it made her shudder and curl her hand around his nape.

"I want to push off this blanket"—another kiss—"and spend all night exploring every delicious inch of you."

CHAPTER 9

An hour later, dressed in one of Bastien's shirts and a pair of panties from her overnight bag, Kirby finished eating and decided she could cheerfully murder the man beside her. Despite his aroused body and erotic kisses, he'd made it clear he had no intention of going any further, regardless of her repeated assurances that he would in no way be taking advantage of her.

"I feel gloriously, vividly alive," she said as he fed her a thin slice of ripe pear, the dark, masculine scent of him making her breasts swell, her cat rubbing up against her skin in an effort to get closer to him. "It's as if I've only been half-awake this entire time."

She let him slide a second slice of succulent fruit between her lips, a drop of juice dripping down her chin. Bastien leaned over from where he was sprawled in the chair next to her own, still wearing just those well-loved jeans that hung distractingly low on his hips, and licked it off. Her breasts strained further, the place between her thighs damp. When his eyes went to half-mast, night-glow green glinting at her as his chest rose in a deep inhale, she had to fight to withhold a whimper.

"I'm going to do bad, bad things to you in a minute," she

threatened when she could speak, toes curling at his unrepentant smile.

"Open that pretty mouth." He painted her lips with another juicy slice, then, pupils dilated, watched her act on his request oh-so-slow.

Kirby swallowed the first bite he offered, came back for the last of the slice, licking her tongue over his skin to get every bit of the juice. Neither woman nor cat was impressed when he withdrew his hand.

"Go a little higher," he purred . . . and only then did she realize she'd cut through denim with her claws, was digging into the skin of his thigh.

Skin pulsing as her blood rushed to it, she retracted them. "I'm so sorry." Control was obviously a learned skill. "Did I hurt you?"

"Want to kiss it better?"

Kirby's eyes dipped to the erection straining the zipper of his jeans and, heart kicking, she decided to take the dare. But she hadn't even lowered her head an inch before he halted her with a kiss that tasted of ripe, juicy pear and Bastien.

Moaning, she melted into it, her entire body humming in anticipation. She'd been waiting for him so, so long and now she ached. "Bastien!" An infuriated cry, his lips no longer on her own.

"What's the rush?" He fed her another bite. "I want to play."

Swallowing the fruit, she decided his idea of play might make her certifiable. She'd about decided to pounce on him and damn the consequences, when the solar-powered comm built into the wall chimed an incoming call.

Bastien turned lazily to glance at the code . . . and was on his feet with feline quickness. "Emergency code," he said, answering the call.

Out of view of the camera where she sat at the table, Kirby was still able to see the scared girl on the viewscreen—a girl, who, it turned out, had crashed her car and needed a ride home.

"I broke the rules," she admitted, voice trembling, "and went to a new club on my own. There's no one else around."

Kirby glimpsed the dark street behind the teenager, felt her stomach knot.

Bastien, however, didn't lose his calm. First, he made

certain the girl wasn't injured, then got the exact details of her location. "I'll have someone there ASAP." He was already pulling out his phone as he spoke. "Will the car need to be towed?"

"Yes."

In the next few minutes, Kirby heard Bastien arrange a rescue with a man named Teijan, as well as a tow, all the while reassuring his anxious young packmate. He kept her on the comm line until she was safely picked up by a handsome, dark-eyed man in a crisp black-on-black suit.

"Thanks," Bastien said to the other male. "Sorry to interrupt your date."

"No problem—it was going downhill anyway." A lithe shrug. "I'll get your misbehaving cub home."

Call ended, Bastien finally sat back down.

Feeding him a slice of pear, Kirby said, "Is she a relative?" She was curious to know everything about him but wary of pushing too hard, even though her newly awakened cat rolled its eyes and said she was being silly. It was hard for her to trust instincts that had been dormant for a lifetime.

Bastien coaxed her into straddling his lap before saying, "Not blood, but she's pack, and pack's family." A simple statement that encapsulated so much. "I'm one of the emergency contacts for her year group." He pretended to bite her fingers when she fed him a second slice. "I also happen to be the one least likely to tear her a new one during the assist—I wait till after."

She went to pick up another piece of fruit from the plate to find he'd already snagged the last slice. "So," she said, the feel of his thighs beneath her a slow seduction, "you have the right to discipline younger packmates? I thought that was up to the alpha."

"We all take responsibility for the cubs." He touched her lower lip with the slice in his hand, coating it with juice before licking the stickiness off in a very feline way, all flicks and licks. "This time, the offense is bad enough that she'll be brought up before the maternal females." He shuddered. "I've been there, and it's not a comfortable place to be."

Kirby had so many questions, about these "maternals," about life in a pack, and when Bastien didn't seem annoyed or tired by them, she kept asking, kept learning.

"Will I have to be part of your pack now?" She'd fallen in love with DarkRiver through his words—to be part of such a close-knit "family" . . . she couldn't imagine it.

Bastien went motionless, his focus acute and eyes human—yet she could feel the cat brushing up against her. "Normally, no," he said. "You're lynx, and from outside the territory."

Disappointment crushed the hopeful joy in her heart. "Oh."

Seeing the way Kirby's shoulders slumped, the light going out of her eyes, Bastien's blood roared with a renewed wave of rage, his fury directed at the people who'd taught her to expect abandonment. He fought the anger with brutal force of will, because that wasn't what his mate needed right now. "If, however"—he held her gaze, made sure she was listening—"you *want* to join, you can become pack. You just have to ask Lucas and take the oath."

It wasn't that simple, of course, but he'd make sure that for Kirby, it would be. The fact was, she'd be welcomed automatically into the pack as soon as they mated—but damn if he'd use her hunger to belong to rush her into the bond. He needed her to choose him, the leopard far too adoring of her to accept anything else.

"I'll sponsor you," he said, strangling his own need and focusing only on hers, the protective, possessive heart of him unable to see her hurting in any way. "First you have to promise you're not a spy out to do dastardly deeds."

Her smile branded his heart. "You're wonderful."

Leopard arching under the verbal petting, he said, "We'll also have to discuss the fact you may one day find your lynx pack and want to be with them." Shifting packs was nothing a changeling did easily, but Kirby's situation called for flexibility.

"I can't imagine it." A wondering murmur, her claws kneading at his shoulders.

She had no fucking idea what it did to him to see her so comfortable with herself in his company. Deciding he'd better get up before he acted on his most primitive instincts where she was concerned, he took them both to their feet. Then, as they cleared the table, he luxuriated in the feel of her padding around in his space. Small and sexy and smelling of him, she was perfect.

When he tugged playfully at her ear after she came to hug him, she shivered, then blushed. Grinning, he nibbled at the tip of one ear. "So, my lynx likes her ears touched." The discovery delighted both parts of his nature.

"It's weird." But she purred against him when he repeated the caress.

God, he was going to have so much fun with her in bed— fun his body wanted *now*. Gritting his teeth, he reminded himself she'd been through a hell of a lot in the past thirty-six hours, and snuggled her close. "Want to watch a movie and make out?"

"No." A glare out of eyes gone translucent gold. "Not when you're all talk, no action."

"You are so in trouble." Adoring her for making no effort to mask her desire, he stalked her backward to the large floor cushions in front of the comm screen. "Big trouble."

"I'm quaking in my boots." With that sassy comment, and though a blush shaded her cheeks, she slid one small hand over his erection.

Bastien lost it.

Her breasts were crushed against his chest the next instant, as he took her mouth in a kiss so sexual it burned, her nipples hard points he wanted to touch, to taste. Raising one hand, he went to close it over a plump mound when his leopard raked its claws through his gut in a harsh reminder of what was at stake.

Breaking the kiss so suddenly it left them both off balance, he cupped her face, spoke before she could. "I don't ever want you to regret being with me," he said, hiding nothing of what he felt for her. "I never want you to question the first night we spend together, wonder if your choice was driven by shock or fear." Agony seared him at the mere thought of it. "That would fucking break my heart, Kirby."

Kirby had been falling for Bastien since the second they met, but at that instant she tumbled head over heels. He was *hers* and he was wonderful. Retracting the claws that had sliced out when he so abruptly broke contact, she petted his chest. "I would never regret being with you."

Only Bastien would do for her, no one else. She didn't need experience to know that what they had was special, a gift. "But"—she pressed two fingers over his lips when he parted them as if to speak, fierce emotion threatening to choke her—"I can see how a protective, stubborn leopard might think tonight might not be the best time to get naked and have a really, *really* good time."

He growled deep in his chest.

Scrunching up her nose at him, she said, "I promise to protect your virtue." That was when she realized he'd given her the sexual reins, this strong, dominant male, who, instinct told her, liked to take the lead. How could she do anything but adore him? "I'll settle for first base."

Green eyes gone night-glow met her own. "I'm constantly being suckered by the women in my life," he muttered, and when she raised her eyebrows, added, "To think I took you for shy."

Grinning, she nuzzled a kiss to his throat. "Instead of a movie, maybe we could talk about your family?" she suggested, still diffident about asking for emotional intimacy.

It took him less than fifteen minutes to have her in hysterics with tales of his "feral" childhood. When he started in on Mercy's inspired ideas to run off women she didn't think were good enough for her brothers—including the "infamous" kitten defurring incident—Kirby gulped. "I guess I better prepare myself."

Bastien scowled where he lay on a large floor cushion, muscular arms crossed behind his head. "I was planning to tell her soon, but—"

"Don't worry about leaving me alone for a few hours," she interrupted before she could stop herself, shifting to her knees on her own cushion. Bastien's family was a core part of his life and she needed to know they'd accept her. If they didn't . . . "I—I want you to tell her."

Scowl even heavier at her blurted-out statement, Bastien hauled her down to sprawl on his chest. "I was going to say Sage is going to blab anyway, so it can wait."

Kirby nodded but clearly didn't do a good job of hiding her nerves because, eyes narrowed, he continued to speak. "If I had my way, I'd have introduced you to the whole damn lot of them the instant after we met." The unadulterated pride in his tone made her eyes burn. "I just didn't want to scare you with the lunatic asylum straightaway."

Kirby's laugh was shaky, a little wet. "Really?"

Bastien stroked her hair off her face. "Really." Damn the people who'd taught his mate she wasn't good enough, the scars so deep even her lynx's knowledge of their bond couldn't keep them from breaking open. Only constant love and affection would achieve that goal. Bastien had every intention of showering Kirby in both. It would be his pleasure and his privilege.

"The second my mother knows about you," he warned, "she's going to start knitting booties for her grandchildren—and she'll call you up, ask which patterns you prefer. Mercy's barely three months along and she's already in possession of enough booties for a football team. One with teeny tiny players."

Kirby's shoulders trembled as she struggled to keep a straight face. "No?"

"Oh, yes. Be afraid, be very afraid."

A firm shake of her head. "I already like your family."

"They'll love you—after they make you run the gauntlet. Because you know, you could be a devious wench out to break my heart." He thought about Mercy, decided another warning was in order. "My sister is *really* overprotective. Show no fear."

Kirby bared her teeth. "Bring on the kitten defurring tools."

"That's my lynx."

CHAPTER 10

—————

After a night of exquisite torture holding Kirby's warm, curvy body against his own without it going any further, Bastien spent the day coaching her on how to shift at will, as well as how to handle senses that had become far more acute now that her lynx was out of hibernation.

With the mating bond not yet set in stone, he was brutally possessive of her, but suggested they call in Dorian for a couple of hours. "Dorian learned to move in cat form as an adult," he told Kirby; "so he'll be able to explain things better." The other male was also already mated, thus less apt to set off Bastien's aggressive instincts, instincts he couldn't fully control this far into the mating dance.

Kirby agreed to the instruction, but she was wary with Dorian.

However, and in spite of his violent dominance, the white-blond sentinel proved a patient teacher who had Kirby smiling at him by the time the session ended. "Thank you," she said. "I'm so glad Bastien asked you to come over."

Dorian didn't respond to the heartfelt words with an affectionate touch, as Bastien knew he normally would have; the sentinel had no doubt picked up on Bastien's precarious equilibrium. "You're doing me a favor," the other male said instead. "Finally *I* get to teach someone."

He thrust a hand through his hair. "You have no idea the razzing I took from the others when I fell on my ass my first few hunts." A scowl directed at Bastien. "Bas here sent me a nice sensitive card with a leopard in diapers on the front."

Kirby's mouth dropped open. "Bastien, you didn't."

Cuddling her close, he rubbed his jaw along her temple. "Sheesh, Kirby, it's not like I could hug him and say motivational bullshit."

Dorian's snarl was belied by the amusement in his vivid blue eyes. They both knew the razzing had been affectionate, the entire pack overjoyed at his ability to shift.

"I'll see you both later," the sentinel said now. "I promised my mate and son an after-school drive to get ice cream."

It wasn't long after Dorian's departure that Kirby's phone rang, the records request she'd filed answered not by social services, but by a detective who'd been on the job at the time of the fire. "I never forgot you," Detective Shona Bay said, the intensity of her dark gaze apparent even through the small screen. "You were so tiny, so shocked. I carried you to the hospital myself, your poor little feet were in such bad shape."

Then, as Bastien held Kirby, the detective told her why the victims had never been identified. "Your family was just passing through. Came in on the train, rented the vacation house with cash for a week. No paper trail outside the home, and everything in it went up in smoke when an electrical fault caused a fatal overload early that morning."

"The owner?" Bastien couldn't believe he—or she—hadn't remembered the names of the people to whom they'd rented a home.

The detective rubbed her hands over her face. "I went looking the first day, had a bad feeling it may have been a cash rental, given his habit of them." Lips twisting, she said, "Turned out he'd had a fall while doing maintenance on another one of his properties two days earlier, took a serious bump to the head. Ended up recovering totally, except for some short-term memory loss."

Bastien didn't need the detective to spell it out to realize the time span of that memory loss had included the landlord's meeting with a small lynx family. Luck had not been on the side of his little cat that long-ago day in Georgia, he thought, holding her tighter as her hand flexed and fisted convulsively against his back, her arm wrapped around him.

"Far as we could figure," the detective continued, eyes on Kirby, "you must've squeezed outside through a pet door your parents probably didn't expect you to fit through." Shaking her head, she said, "Your palms were burned, too, soot and tears on your face."

"Were you able to recover anything?" Bastien smoothed his hand down Kirby's spine, able to feel the fine tremors shaking her frame. "The smallest piece could help Kirby trace her family."

"I found a photo that looked like it was taken in a maternity suite of two adults with a baby," the detective said. "Posted it everywhere I could think of, used it to search through missing persons files for years, but I made a mistake." Her shoulders slumped. "I searched only through the missing tagged human, figured it had to be right since you were human."

Kirby, his strong Kirby with her courageous heart, shook her head. "You had no way of knowing." Taking a deep breath, she said, "The photo . . . do you still have it? Even a copy in a database?"

Shona Bay blew out a breath. "We had a major server meltdown ten years back that affected a lot of systems, so I can't promise. I'm sorry." The other woman tapped a finger on her desk. "I'm going to hunt for the physical file and the original photograph, but given the time that's passed, there's a good chance it's already been destroyed."

Kirby nodded, holding it together until the detective signed off. Then she screamed, thumping her fists against Bastien's chest. "It's not fair! I just want to know who I am! I just want to know!"

Aware she couldn't hear him right now, Bastien simply kept her safe while she worked out her rage and sorrow, then held her skin to skin all night, his own fury a wild thing inside him. He wanted to fix this for her, make it better, but there was nothing he could do but be with her as she built a new life for herself out of the ashes of the old.

IN the three days that followed, Bastien grew even prouder of Kirby's strength. She came back fighting, determined not to let the dead end of the records search stop her from living her life. "I made it this far alone," she said, then touched her fingers shyly to his jaw. "Now I have you. No excuses for not going forward."

Owned utterly, he took her to meet Lucas so she'd know she had the DarkRiver alpha's sanction to join the pack. She handled the meeting with a sweet self-assurance that had Lucas giving her an approving look and a gentle kiss that was more than simple acceptance; it was the welcome of a predatory changeling alpha pleased with this new member of his pack.

Smug and happy because she was his, Bastien showed Kirby more about being changeling, watched over her during another session with Dorian, taught her about pack life, and introduced her to a lynx family that lived in the territory. The Bakers were a mature couple, with a grown son and a younger daughter, but Enid and Kirby clicked at once.

As a result, she felt comfortable enough to go off on exploratory trips in the forest with the older woman, Bastien and Kirby both aware Enid had much to teach her about her unique lynx senses. Bastien remained violently proud of his mate for her courage, but he had to fight his protectiveness each time she disappeared into the trees. He refused, however, to stifle her confidence or damage her new friendship by insisting on accompanying the women.

Instead, he spent the time working via a comm link to the office . . . and worrying, conscious of how new Kirby was to her animal form, her reaction times slow. The forest was their home, but it had its dangers, and she didn't yet know them all.

Now, late afternoon on the third day, she tugged him down with her hands gripping his hair and nipped at his lower lip. "Go to dinner with your brothers." It was a passionate order, her brow dark. "Otherwise you'll pace a hole in the floor, and I won't be able to concentrate for thinking about you."

Seeing the truth of the latter in the pale gold of eyes gone lynx and hating that he was causing her anxiety, he forced himself to do as she asked. Somehow, he even managed to fool Sage and Grey into thinking he was on an even keel as the three of them unanimously decided to invite themselves to dinner at Mercy and Riley's, the couple having returned from Arizona the previous night.

"We'll take upside-down pineapple cake as a bribe," Grey said with mischievous feline cunning. "Mercy can't resist it."

Bastien wasn't the least surprised to discover his sister already knew he was seeing someone—though Sage had apparently kept quiet till then. The normality of his siblings' ensuing ribbing helped the time pass, soothed the ragged edges inside him. He especially got a kick out of telling Mercy to do her worst; his lynx, he thought with snarling confidence, could handle it.

Back at the aerie just after nine thirty, he didn't panic when he found it empty, despite the fact the plan had been for the two women to return by nine. Following Kirby's scent—as vivid to him as if it was his own—he found her a short distance away, having a grand old time playing a game with three non-changeling lynx.

Bounding up to him the instant he appeared, she looked at him in wild welcome. And since Bastien had no resistance where Kirby was concerned, he stripped and shifted . . . to find himself pounced on, his mate in a playful mood that translated into her human form when they shifted back twenty minutes later.

Purring in his arms in bed, her skin flushed, Kirby kissed him with luscious slowness. "Why are we torturing ourselves again?"

"I have no fucking idea." His chest heaved up and down, his leopard's fur brushing against the inside of his skin.

Kirby ran her fingers over his kiss-wet lips. "I want you."

At that instant, he couldn't think of any rational reason not to take her, brand her. So when the comm panel chimed, he ignored it—until he realized it was his alpha's code. Groaning, he left the erotic warmth of Kirby's arms to answer the call, audio only.

What Lucas had to say changed the tenor of the entire

night. "We've had word from a lynx pack in Calgary that's been searching for a small family unit that disappeared twenty-three years ago."

Kirby began to tremble, hope a tremulous whisper inside her.

Striding over to cradle her in his lap, Bastien asked the question she couldn't form. "What did they say?"

"One of their members decided on a largely solitary existence when he turned eighteen," Lucas replied. "He stayed in erratic touch with the pack—sometimes nothing more than a scribbled postcard after a year."

His lynx nature, Kirby understood, must've been very strong.

"A year and a half after they'd last heard from him," Lucas continued, "he contacted them to say he'd fallen for and mated with a human woman, had a baby girl, and intended to head home with his mate and cub in a month. No one ever arrived, and neither did the photos he'd promised of his new family."

Blood cold, Kirby found her voice. "Why was I . . ." She couldn't say it, couldn't ask why the pack hadn't come for her.

"They couldn't find you."

"What?" Bastien growled. "They lost a *child*?"

"The last message just said the family was on the road, roaming their way home." Lucas's voice held taut frustration. "It meant the pack had no idea where to look when Kirby and her parents didn't arrive. They dispatched trackers, sent out requests to countless local and international agencies, asking for news on a family composed of an adult male lynx, a human female, and a female lynx cub."

"But I never shifted." Kirby ran a shaking hand through her hair, her thoughts in splinters. "W-what happens now?"

"You look very much like the elder who contacted me," Lucas told her, "so there's not much doubt in my mind about the familial relationship. Still, I'd suggest a DNA test to confirm it, and quickly. Your grandma doesn't strike me as a patient lady. She's ready to claim her cub and your grandpa is willing to fight us all for you."

Kirby's lower lip quivered as Lucas signed off, her throat thick. "I have a grandma and a grandpa."

Bastien wrapped her in the solid safety of his arms. "Yeah, and they sound just as tough as their grandchild."

Kirby began to cry in earnest. She had a family, and they hadn't thrown her away. They wanted her, had searched for her all these years. It altered the foundations of her existence.

THE DNA test was done by Dorian's scientist mate, and a mere twenty-four hours following Lucas's call, Kirby walked into the living room of DarkRiver's healer. To come face-to-face with an older woman who had eyes of pale lynx-gold set in a face that echoed Kirby's as strongly as Bastien's echoed his brothers. She took one look at Kirby and enclosed her in an embrace so fierce, Kirby could barely breathe.

But it was all right, Kirby holding on just as hard. Then she was being hugged by a man of medium height with snow-white hair who had tears in his eyes and called her "my cub's cub," a hundred, a thousand words spoken over one another as they tried to catch up on a lifetime.

"My son," her grandmother said an hour later, the three of them walking alone in the woods behind the healer's home, "he was a strong, wild one, and he *loved* you." Her hands touched Kirby's cheeks. "Don't ever doubt that."

Throat scraped raw from the emotional storm that had passed, Kirby nodded, asked, "My mother's name, can you tell me?"

"No, kitten, I'm so sorry," her grandmother said, squeezing her hand. "The silly boy, he was so possessive—called her his mate in the message he sent." Old sorrow in her gaze, before the pale gold filled with determination. "But now that we have *your* name, we should be able to use it in concert with our son's to trace your mother."

It might take time, Kirby realized on a crashing wave of hope, but it was very, very doable. Kirby's birth must've been registered somewhere. Those records would exist. Even if not, there had to be travel records, or a rental agreement, a co-signed loan . . . Taking a shaky breath she hugged both her grandparents in turn. "Thank you for searching for me."

"We will *always* be there for you." Her grandfather held her close with one arm around her shoulders, while his mate stroked Kirby's hair back with gentle hands and said, "We have something for you."

It was a gift beyond price.

"A recording of my father's last message home," she said to Bastien that night. "Will you watch with me?" She couldn't imagine sharing this painful, beautiful instant with anyone but her green-eyed leopard, strong and protective and her rock.

"I'd be honored." Slotting in the data-crystal, he wrapped his arms around her from behind and they watched the comm screen fill with the image of a handsome blond man with unusual green and yellow-flecked hazel eyes that lit up when he spoke of his mate and child.

"I can't wait for you to meet my beautiful mate." His pride poured out of the screen. "She's small and human, but fierce as any lynx. And our cub? A gorgeous, wild thing." Love filled his expression. "You'd laugh to see me, Mom. I'm gaga over my girls, can't bear to be parted from them. We've explored the world together, but our baby will be shifting soon, and we want her to be able to play as a lynx with her cousins, grow up surrounded by pack like I did."

Pushing a hand through his hair, he pressed two fingers to his mouth, then onto the screen. "We're roaming the long way home, but we'll be there soon. Then you can tell me what a fool I was for thinking I'd never want to bond with anyone." Laughing, his self-deprecating smile contagious. "I love you both. See you in a month."

Kirby cried again in Bastien's arms, for all that had been lost, for the fact she'd never meet her mother and father, and for the joy of having found her grandparents, of knowing she had never been unwanted.

She was Kirby.

She was changeling.

She was a lynx.

She adored a certain possessive red-haired leopard.

She had family. She had friends. Her life was full to overflowing.

CHAPTER 11

The next two days were both strange and wonderful for Kirby. First came an envelope from Detective Shona Bay. In it was a note scrawled in blue ink:

Turns out I never returned your file to Records after the last time I checked it out. Bad behavior on my part, but it means it wasn't destroyed as per protocol. I'm glad I can give you this at least. I only wish I could've done more.

—Shona

Below the note was the original photograph found in the fire-ravaged home, of the man Kirby had already seen on the message, a tiny baby swaddled in a white blanket, and a woman with shiny light brown hair and an enormous smile, her eyes turned lovingly toward the child in her arms.

Joy blazed from the image, and it was enough to heal the last of the ragged wounds in Kirby's soul. "I have her face now," she whispered to Bastien, the two of them sitting on the edge of the aerie balcony, her wild lynx friend curled up by her side. "I can see with my own eyes that she loved me, that they both loved me. One day, I'll discover her name, but until then"—tears smeared her vision, turned her voice husky—"I'll just call her Mom."

Enfolding her in his arms, Bastien said, "I dared call Mom by her name once when I was a cub. It did not end well for young Bastien."

Kirby laughed, the sound wet. "I think my mom would've been the same. My dad, too." It felt good to say that, to acknowledge the two loving people who'd brought her into this life.

Her grandparents cried when she gave them a copy of the photograph, then asked her to stay with them in the guest aerie they'd been assigned on DarkRiver land. She hated being separated from Bastien—in this, she was her father's daughter, she thought, her throat thick—but hungry to get to know more about her family, she acquiesced.

However, when her grandmother asked her to come to Canada, join their pack, she didn't hesitate to shake her head. "I want to visit, meet my aunts, my cousins, spend more time with you, but my place is here." With Bastien, his name branded on her heart so deep, she knew nothing would ever erase it.

Mate. The lynx swiped a claw inside her mind, a little exasperated at the human half's thickheadedness. *Mate!*

Oh!

Champagne in her bloodstream, her joy effervescent, Kirby had to force herself to stay in place rather than running to pounce on Bastien. Enid had been explaining the more intimate facts of changeling life to her during their time together, things a parent would normally teach his or her growing cub. Kirby had been reticent with her questions at first, but Enid was so matter-of-fact about it, having already brought up a son, her daughter apt to be as curious when she grew older, that there was no awkwardness.

One of the things Enid had spoken to her about was the wonder of the soul-deep connection that was the mating bond. So Kirby understood the precious gift of it.

More, she *felt* the beauty of it deep within.

Once, she would've worried that Bastien hadn't initiated the bond because he wasn't sure he wanted her for life. To think that now would be an insult to her leopard, strong and loyal and so insanely protective that she knew they were going to butt heads about it on a regular basis. She couldn't wait.

"What?" Her grandmother scowled at her. "Your far-too-charming leopard refuses to relocate to our territory?"

Kirby knew full well her "far-too-charming leopard" would do anything to make her happy. She felt the same about him. And Bastien's bonds to his family, his pack, had grown over a lifetime, would hurt to rip out, while hers were just budding. Care for his heart was the most important, but not the only reason for her decision.

Closing her hand over her grandmother's, she said, "This land has become my home." An absolute truth. "I've made friends"—she stroked her fingers through the fur of the wild lynx who'd followed her to the guest aerie—"started to put down roots, been treated as a packmate."

It was her grandfather who placed his hand on her shoulder, squeezed. "I always knew my boy would sire a strong cub. Strong as another lynx I know."

Making a face, her grandmother patted Kirby's hand. "I'm proud of you for building a life for yourself, but I'm greedy to have you in mine, too." A kiss pressed to her forehead, the older woman's eyes narrowed as she said, "I expect you to visit several times a year. Bring your leopard so we can make sure he's treating you right."

In her grandmother's voice, Kirby heard the resonance of old pain, of the agony of waiting for a young family that had never arrived. "I will," she promised. "I'll comm call every few days, too, if you don't mind." Never would she take this gift for granted.

"Mind?" A blinding smile. "I'll look forward to each and every call."

The rest of her grandparents' visit passed by in a happy snapshot of talk and laughter, and yes, more than one teary moment. Returning to Bastien's aerie the afternoon the two left for Calgary, she decided to make dinner while waiting for him to get back from the city. Her skin was tight with anticipation, woman and lynx both in possessive agreement.

It was about damn time Bastien Michael Smith understood that his mate was no longer vulnerable or shocked or in any way unsteady. She'd made her decision and it was a decision that would never, ever change. He was hers and she was keeping him.

So engrossed was she in her plans that she almost missed

the sound of feet hitting the balcony, as if someone had climbed overlimb from another tree. A second later, a stunning woman wearing jeans and a simple white T-shirt stood in the open doorway, her red hair pulled back into a high ponytail and her legs long.

Even if Kirby hadn't seen the photos scattered around the apartment and aerie, she'd have guessed the familial connection in a heartbeat. It wasn't just the hair, she thought, but something about the shape of their eyes, a way they had of holding themselves. "You must be Mercy." Hands a little clammy, she nonetheless smiled, recalling Bastien's words: *Show no fear.* "I'm Kirby. Come in."

"Thanks." Sauntering inside, her walk lazily feline, Mercy took in the meal in progress on the kitchen counter, her body so lithely muscled that her pregnancy—her *multiple* pregnancy, according to Bastien—wasn't obvious at first glance. "What's for dinner?"

Kirby bit the inside of her cheek and decided what the hell. "Fresh kitten cutlets. Want one?"

A hitch in Mercy's step, before she turned and saluted Kirby with two fingers, no hint of a smile on her face. "Touché."

Conscious she wasn't out of the woods, Kirby walked around to finish prepping the cutlets—a prosaic chicken—before washing her hands and putting on a pot of coffee. Mercy said nothing throughout, simply leaned up against a nearby wall, arms folded and eyes watchful. Her dominance was potent, the other woman a senior member of DarkRiver.

"So," Kirby said, unwilling to be intimidated, "pistols at dawn?"

Mercy's eyes gleamed. "Bastien tells me you're a kindergarten teacher."

"Yes." To her joy, she had a job to return to next week, the board having been sympathetic to her unique circumstances. "Maybe I'll teach your pupcubs one day." Bastien had laughingly explained that since no one knew if Mercy's babies would shift into wolf pups or leopard cubs, everyone had taken to calling them pupcubs.

"Maybe."

Yes, Mercy was a tough nut to crack, but Kirby wasn't about to give up, her lynx digging in its claws. "Cream? Sugar?"

"Both. Two sugars." A pause. "The pupcubs like sugar."

Kirby considered whether that tiny tidbit indicated a thaw in Mercy's mood, decided not to be too optimistic. "Here you go. Bastien's blend—much nicer than the instant stuff I used to drink until he spoiled me."

"Bastien does have good taste." Mercy unfolded her arms to accept the cup. "You like his city apartment?"

"Sure, it's stunning, but I love this aerie more." The sound of the tree leaves whispering in the wind, the wild lynx who often dropped by, the scents in the air, and most of all, Bastien's happiness here, it all mingled into a song of homecoming. "I do still have to use the rope ladder to get down," she admitted. "I don't quite trust myself to jump even in cat form."

"You'll get better." Mercy took a sip of the coffee. "Dorian said he spoke to you."

"Yes, he's been incredibly helpful. So has everyone else I've met from the pack."

"We're not always this welcoming with strangers—it's a good thing you knew Bastien beforehand."

Kirby decided to stop fencing. This was too important. "I adore him, Mercy," she said, holding the other woman's gaze even though her lynx knew she risked angering a far more dangerous predator. "I'd adore him if he didn't have a penny to his name or a pack to call his own, or if he lived in a tent." Her chest ached with the fury of her emotions, her breath catching. "He's smart and gorgeous and wonderful and overprotective and stubborn enough to drive me mad and I can't live without him!"

"If you think Bas is stubborn," Mercy drawled, "you haven't seen Grey in action." A slow smile so reminiscent of Bastien's that Kirby missed him unbearably. "You had me at the kitten cutlets."

Bursting out laughing, Kirby set aside her own coffee before she spilled it. "God, your stone face is legendary."

Mercy patted her cheek, her leopard's laughter in her eyes. "Welcome to the family, little sister."

BASTIEN didn't begrudge Kirby the time she was spending with her grandparents, but it had been fucking hard to not have her close. He hadn't even bothered to attempt to deny himself the pleasure of watching over her from a distance the two nights she stayed at the guest aerie.

Yeah, he knew rationally that her grandparents weren't going to hurt her, but caught in the coils of the mating urge, he wasn't exactly thinking with clean logic. If Kirby decided to head to Canada to meet more of her father's pack, he'd damn well be going along. Forget about being civilized and understanding—he *needed* to be with his mate.

It had seemed like the right choice not to push her into intimacy at the start, but now he wished he'd used the passionate heat between them to tie Kirby to him on the physical level at least. What if she began to pull back now that she'd seen all the choices open to her? What if she decided she might prefer to explore her sensuality with a fellow lynx?

The agonizing jealousy inspired by the thought of anyone else touching Kirby, and fed by his raw need to claim her, tore through him as he arrived at the aerie—to find her waiting in lynx form, ready for a run.

Barely controlling his desire to lunge at her, he stripped and shifted. Kirby rubbed up against him, her fur thick and soft, the way she pretended to bite him affectionate. As if she could feel his feral tension, wanted to soothe him . . . as a mate might do. His leopard settling at the petting, though he remained on a brutal edge, he took her on a run to the lower Sierra.

There was no snow yet, but there would be soon enough. Built for that environment, her paws natural snowshoes, his lynx might just outpace him on it. He looked forward to the challenge, to playing with Kirby on her natural turf. Now, however, he was content simply to be with her under the starlit night, the moon a silver spotlight that caressed her fur like a lover.

Arriving home at the midnight hour, the world hushed around them, Bastien shifted back into his human form, while Kirby stayed lynx. She was having trouble getting used to the nudity most changelings grew up accepting as natural. "I could jump up to the aerie, throw down some clothes."

She nodded, tufted ears bobbing.

"Or," he drawled, his gut tight with a need only Kirby could fulfill, "I could stand right here and watch a pretty, sexy woman come out of the shift, then run my hands all over her bitable body."

He expected a yowl of defiance, but the world fractured into light and then a lusciously sensual woman—his mate— was rising from a crouch, honey-colored hair tumbling over her back as she smiled and crooked a finger . . . and the mating bond smashed into him, the connection vibrant and primal and tasting of Kirby.

Stunned, they stared at one another.

Bastien pounced the next instant, his hands on her hips, his lips on hers. Wrapping her arms around him, she opened her mouth and he took full advantage, giving his hands free rein to explore her curves. "You are mine," he growled into her mouth. "Always mine. I love you until I can't breathe." The mating bond might've drawn them together, but it was now entangled with heartbonds as strong.

"You're mine, too." Hand fisting in his hair on that ferocious claim, she moaned and held on tight, her body straining as she rose on tiptoe. When she made a frustrated sound, he hitched her onto his hips and turned to the tree trunk, then paused.

"Bastien?" Kisses along his jaw, her skin silky soft against his.

"Bark will hurt your back," he muttered, nibbling on the tip of her ear because he knew it drove her nuts.

Shivering, she purred, sought his lips for a kiss. He opened his mouth on her own, licked and tasted, but it wasn't enough. He wanted her body under his, wanted to be inside her, her pleasure feeding his. "Up," he said, his breath jagged. "Climb."

She tightened her thighs around him. "No." Nipples rubbing over the hard wall of his chest, she kissed him again, licking just the way he liked. "Here."

He almost gave in, pounded her on the forest floor, was stopped only by the sneaking suspicion that had taken root when he'd realized how touch starved she'd been. "Have you done this before?" he asked, too aroused to be anything but blunt.

"No." She didn't stop tormenting him, her slickness erotic temptation against his abdomen. "I am so ready, Bastien." Her body moving sinuously against his own. "I want to be with you. Only you." Kiss after kiss. "I love you. I love you. I love you."

God, she made him her slave.

Determined to give her a good memory despite his ragged control, he walked to the rope ladder and started hauling them up. She held on but did nothing else to help him, nibbling and kissing at his jaw until he thought he'd go mad. "Behave," he snarled, nipping at her ear but careful not to hurt.

Another shiver, a wicked smile. "No." Another kiss, this one on the mouth.

Swinging up onto the balcony, he somehow found the door, stumbled inside and to the bed. Where he finally, finally, had her curves under the rigid planes of his own body. Pinning her hands above her head with one hand around her wrists, he settled his lower body snug against her damp heat.

It made him groan.

Kirby arched up, sliding her folds over his erect cock.

"Bad lynx." Chest heaving, he snapped his teeth at her.

She snapped back, then arched her neck in invitation. Leaning down, he suckled at the flutter of her pulse. Laving his tongue over the red mark with unhidden possessiveness, he closed one hand over her breast, teased her nipple. "You are so pretty everywhere."

A shy-sweet smile, sparkling pleasure-hazed eyes, her tongue flirting with his until he gripped her jaw to hold her in place for an open-mouthed kiss, wet and hot and a prelude to sex. Legs still locked around him, she opened for him, demanded more, the damp musk of her so intoxicating his claws sliced out to tear the sheets.

"Shit." Retracting them, he pressed his forehead to hers. "Sorry, baby. I'm having trouble holding it togeth—"

Pelvis arching against him, she sucked at his throat as he'd done at hers—possessive and determined—and that was it. All he wanted, *needed*, was Kirby. She was liquid heat and hot honey on his fingers when he touched her between her thighs.

"Bastien!"

If he'd had *any* hope of taking this slow, he lost it on the ripples of her pleasure. Pushing one sweetly curved thigh wider, he waited only until her body had stopped clenching in orgasm before beginning to slide in. She moaned, her claws digging just enough into his shoulders that it felt amazing.

"Tell me if it hurts," he grit out, because not for anything would he hurt his Kirby.

Kisses on his throat, a purr in the back of hers. "It feels sooooo good."

Shuddering, he withdrew after that first shallow penetration and slid back in, reining in his instinct to thrust; she was so tautly stretched around him, so small. But she was also lusciously aroused, her unhidden desire threatening to erase the last, faint glimmers of his control.

It was excruciating.

It was beautiful.

Then at last, he was buried to the hilt and they were kissing.

Hand tightening on her thigh, the taste of her in his every sense, he withdrew, pushed back in slowly.

Once. Twice. "Fuck!"

Spine locking, he came in a violent rush, his face buried in the curve of his mate's neck. His utter lack of control would've been embarrassing . . . except that he felt her gasp as she came again, her body clamping down possessively on his cock.

Male pride restored, Bastien collapsed on her. Her fingers petted his hair, her arms and legs imprisoned his very happy body, her words a husky whisper. "Can we do that again? I really, really, *really* liked it."

Bastien grinned. "Hell, yeah."

EPILOGUE

Kirby glared at Bastien as he led her out in front of a lovely home set deep in the forest the next day. "Is this your parents' house?"

"Yep."

She dug her heels in. "I'm about to meet your mom and dad and you couldn't have warned me?" Her old jeans and faded T-shirt would hardly make the best first impression, not to mention the leaves she no doubt had in her hair from playfully wrestling with her mate not long ago. "We're leaving right now so I can change."

Bastien tugged her forward instead, insouciant. "Don't worry, little cat. They're going to see what I see."

Kirby wasn't so certain, but the door was already opening to reveal a small woman with hair of rich dark gold. "Bastien? Why are you lurking out—" A dazzling smile broke out on her face. "Well," she said, walking over to take Kirby into her arms, "there you are."

The maternal warmth of the touch, the words, erased any nerves Kirby might have had. And when Lia Smith said, "I'm so happy to welcome another daughter to this family," she knew she was going to adore Bastien's mother just as much as she loved Lia's son.

"Hey, Frenchie!" Sage poked his head out the door, the sun hitting the brown of his hair to reveal hidden strands of red. "Did you bring any baguettes?"

"Why don't you go season something, Herb?"

Kirby's shoulders shook as Lia Smith glared at each man in turn. "I gave you both beautiful names. Use them."

"Yes, Mom."

Kirby didn't stop smiling the entire time she was in the Smith house, was the same when she spoke to her grandparents on the comm later that night. "Our future babies are going to be utterly spoiled," she said to her mate afterward, delighted at the idea.

"In case you missed it," Bastien muttered, "they're also going to be demons."

Kirby laughed, pleased with the idea of her own little red-headed demons. "If Mercy and Riley are having pupcubs," she mused, "what will we have?"

"Lynxpards?"

"Doesn't have the same ring to it."

"Hmm." A long pause before Bastien began to laugh so hard he almost fell off the bed. "We'll have little birbys, that's what we'll have."

She slapped his chest. "Don't you dare say that in front of your brothers or we'll never hear the end of it."

Of course he let it slip and of course the future birbys became part of the family lexicon. Sitting around the table being teased about it for the umpteenth time two months later, her visiting grandparents laughing as hard as the Smiths, Kirby knew she'd want it no other way. "I think we should visit Vera tomorrow and take her a great big cake."

Bastien smiled. "Yeah. I think we should. She gave us the best gift, didn't she?"

"Yes."

MAGIC
STEALS

ILONA ANDREWS

already short and skinny. The see-through thing would swallow me. Besides, that outfit was a baby-doll outfit. Looking cute and sweet was the last thing I wanted to do, because tonight Jim Shrapshire and I had a date.

Jim Shrapshire ran Clan Cat, one of the seven clans in Atlanta's Shapeshifter Pack. A werejaguar, he normally served as the Pack's Chief of Security. Jim wasn't just a badass. He was a badass who wrote a book for badasses on how to be a badder badass. Which is why, when Curran, the Beastlord and the ruler of the Pack, had to go on an expedition to the Mediterranean, he left Jim in charge of fifteen hundred shapeshifters. Curran had been gone for about a month and Jim was keeping the Pack together with iron claws. He was the smartest man I ever met. He was scary, funny, had muscles in places I had no idea muscles existed, and for some weird reason he liked me.

At least I thought he liked me. Things were complicated. As the alpha of Clan Cat, he was in charge of me and he'd been really careful not to take advantage of it. We'd been trying to date, except that Jim was busy and I was busy, too, so we barely managed a date every two to three weeks. When we did connect, we talked about everything under the sun and we made out. He let me set the pace. I decided how far we went and the first few times we got together, we didn't go very far.

Kissing Jim was my definition of nirvana, but some small part of me never believed he was really there for me. Jim needed his equal: a powerful, aggressive, and sexy woman. He got me, Dali, a skinny vegetarian girl who had to wear glasses with lenses as thick as Coke bottle bottoms, threw up when she smelled blood, and was about as useful in a fight as a fifth leg on a donkey. To top it all off, my own mother, who loved me more than the whole world, wouldn't describe me as pretty. She told people that I was smart, brave, and educated. Unfortunately none of it helped me right now, because tonight I wanted to be sexy. I wanted to seduce Jim.

I had the whole thing planned. I bought the wine. I cooked a big meal. I even made him a steak. I cooked it last in a separate pan to make sure no meat juices got onto my gnocchi. I may have gagged a few times from the smell and I had to use two forks to move it around because I didn't want to touch it, but I was pretty sure it was cooked correctly. I chose this outfit, because the model wearing it in the ad looked exactly the way I wanted to be: she was tall, with double-D breasts, plump butt, tiny waist, and she had the kind of face that would make men turn to look at her. The lingerie was great on her.

I glanced back at my reflection. I wanted to knock him off his feet, not make him fall down laughing. If I hadn't already put mascara on, I would have cried.

None of it might matter anyway. It was twenty minutes past eight o'clock. Jim was late. Maybe he got held up. Maybe he changed his mind on this whole dating thing.

The doorbell rang.

Ah! I spun around the bathroom, grabbed my blue silk kimono, slipped into it, and ran down the stairs.

The doorbell chimed again. I checked the peephole. My heart skipped a beat. Jim!

I swung the door open. He stood on my doorstep, tall, dark, and so hot, it made me weak in the knees. I'd been crushing on him for years and every time I saw him, my breath still caught. His scent washed over me, the sandalwood, light musk, and creamy vanilla of his deodorant; the hint of citrus and spearmint in his shampoo; and the fragrance of his skin, a complicated mix of tangy sweat and slightly harsh male smell, blending into a multi-layered chorus that sang, "Jim" to me. All of my smart words disappeared and I turned into a half-wit.

"Hey!" Oh, great. Hay is for horses.

"Hi." He shouldered his way into the house. He wore dark jeans, a black T-shirt, and a leather jacket over it. Jim usually wore black. His skin was a dark, rich brown, his black hair cut short, leaving his masculine face open.

He leaned forward. I stood on my toes and brushed a kiss on his lips. He didn't kiss me back. Something was wrong.

"I've got a bottle of Cabernet Franc," I said. Jim cooked like a chef and liked wine. The man at the wine store told me this was an award-winning wine. "From Tiger Mountain Winery."

He nodded. I didn't even get a smirk.

What if he were breaking up with me?

"I'll go get it." My voice turned squeaky. "Go ahead and sit down."

I went into the kitchen, got the two wineglasses, and poured the deep red wine into the glasses. He couldn't possibly be breaking up with me.

I grabbed the glasses and went into the living room.

Jim was asleep on my couch.

Oh no. Last time I found him asleep in my house, a spider creature had been feeding on his soul. Not again.

I shoved the glasses onto the side table, grabbed his shoulders, and shook. "Jim! Jim, talk to me."

He blinked and opened his beautiful dark eyes. They were glazed over as if he weren't fully there.

"Are you okay? What's wrong?"

He peered at me. "I was challenged."

In the Pack, personal challenges decided leadership. They meant a fight to the death. There was no mercy. "Who?"

"Roger Mountain," he said.

Roger Mountain was a panther, vicious and ruthless. Jim was alive, so he had to have killed Roger, but I had seen Roger fight before. He tore his opponents into pieces.

"How bad?" I asked.

"Not that bad."

"Jim?"

He raised the side of his T-shirt. His entire torso was dark. It took me a second to realize that it was one continuous bruise. Oh you silly idiot man. "Have medmages seen this?" The Pack had its own hospital and our medmages were some of the best.

"Sure."

"What did they say?"

"They said it was fine."

"I'm going to hit you with a wine bottle," I growled. "What did they really say?"

"I spoke to Nasrin. She said bed rest for twenty-four hours."

Of course, she recommended bed rest. The fight had to have drained Jim down to nothing, and changing shape took a lot of energy, especially now. Magic flooded our world in waves. When magic was up, spells worked and transforming was easier and still, if a normal shapeshifter changed form twice in twenty-four hours, Lyc-V, the shapeshifter virus, would shut your body down for a nap. I was exempt from this rule, because while I carried the virus, my magic was mystical in origin, but Jim's wasn't. With technology in control, a fight behind him, and two shape-changings, Jim should've been in bed, not here.

"So, instead of resting you shifted out of warrior form and drove here?" He couldn't have been that reckless. He could've fallen asleep at the wheel.

Jim yawned. "I didn't want to miss it." He smiled at me. "You look really pretty."

Oh you stupid dummy.

"I'm just going to sit here for a second," he said and closed his eyes.

Jim was six feet tall. My couch was tiny. If he fell asleep here, he wouldn't be able to walk in the morning. "Nasrin said bed rest, not couch rest." I wedged my shoulder under his armpit. "Come on. We're going upstairs to the bedroom."

His eyes lit up for half a second. "Well, if you insist . . ."

"I insist." I pulled him upright. I was a vegetarian weretiger, but I was still a shapeshifter. I could've carried him up the stairs except I didn't think he would let me. "Come on."

We walked up the stairs and I deposited him on the bed. I loved huge soft beds, and this one was a queen with a mattress topper so thick I had to hop to get onto it. Jim landed on it and sank in. I reached for his boots, but he sat up. "I've got it."

His boots hit the floor. He lay back and closed his eyes. I slipped into the closet and pulled off my lingerie. I didn't want him to see me in it. If he did, he might think that I had a plan for the evening and was upset because it collapsed. I didn't care about the plan. I just wanted him to be okay. I threw on a pair of plain cotton panties and a white tank top, came out, and slipped into the bed next to him.

Magic rolled over us in an invisible wave. All of the electric lights went out and the feylantern in the bathroom stirred into life, glowing with gentle blue. My magic flowed through me. Excellent. He would heal faster during a magic wave.

"Sorry I ruined the date," Jim murmured.

I snuggled up to him, my hand on his chest, careful not to press too hard. "You didn't. This is perfect."

KNOCK-KNOCK-KNOCK.

I opened my eyes. I was lying in my bed. I inhaled deep and smelled Jim. His scent was all around me, the clean, citrus-spiced smell that drove me crazy. His arm was across my waist, his body hot against my side.

Jim was in my bed and he was holding me. I smiled.

Knock-knock-knock.

Someone was knocking on my front door. That was fine. They could keep knocking. I would just keep lying here, in my soft bed, wrapped in Jim. Mmmm . . .

"Dali! Open the door."

Mom.

I jerked upright in my bed. Jim leaped straight up and landed on his feet, his arms raised, his body tense, ready to pounce. "What?"

"My mother is here!" I jumped to the floor, jerked a pair of shorts from under my bed, and hopped on one foot trying to put them on.

He exhaled. "I thought it was an emergency."

"It is an emergency," I hissed in a theatrical whisper. "Stay here! Don't make any noise."

"Dali," he started.

I grabbed a pillow and threw it at him. "Shush!"

He blinked. I grabbed my kimono, tossed it over me, shut the door to my bedroom, and ran down the stairs, holding on to the rail for dear life so I wouldn't trip. The last thing I needed was my mother finding out I had Jim in my bedroom. There would be no end of shock and questions and then she would want to know if we had set the date for the wedding yet and when are the grandchildren coming. I didn't even know if Jim was serious.

I jumped the last seven steps, tied my kimono, and reached for the door.

The wineglasses. Oh shoot. I raced into the kitchen, grabbed the two wineglasses, dumped the wine down the sink, stuck them into the nearest cabinet, emptied the vegetarian curry soup into the sink, threw the butternut squash gnocchi into the trash, tossed the steak I made for Jim after it and shoved it deep into the garbage can in case my mother decided to throw something away. I washed my hands, ran for the door, and opened it.

My mother raised her hands. She was holding her bag in one and a box of donuts in the other. She was about an exact copy of me except thirty years older. We were both short and tiny and when we spoke, we waved our hands around too much. A woman about my age stood next to her. She had dark hair, big eyes, and a cute heart-shaped face. Iluh Indrayani. Like me, she was born in the U.S., but both of her parents had come from Indonesia, from the island of Bali. Her mother knew my mother and we met a few times, but never really talked.

Something bad had happened. The only time my mother brought visitors to my house who weren't family was when some sort of magical emergency had taken place.

"You left me on the doorstep for half an hour," my mother huffed.

"I was asleep." I held the door open. "Come in."

They walked inside, my mother in the lead. Iluh gave me an apologetic look. "So sorry to bother you on a Saturday."

"That's okay," I told her.

We sat in the kitchen.

"Would you like something to drink?" I asked.

My mother waved her hands. "You talk. I'll make coffee."

Above us something thudded. I froze.

My mother stared at the ceiling. "Did you hear that?"

"Hear what?" I asked, my eyes wide. I would kill Jim. He could sit completely motionless for hours when on stakeouts. I'd seen him do it. He had to be dropping things on purpose.

Thud!

"That!" My mother turned predatory like a raptor. "What was that?"

Lie, think of something quick, lie, lie . . . "I've got a cat."

"What kind of a cat?" My mother's eyes narrowed.

"A big one."

"I want to see," Mom said. "Bring him down."

"He's a stray and a little wild. He's probably hiding. I probably won't even be able to find him now."

"How long have you had him?"

"A few days." The more I lied, the deeper I sank. My mother had a brain like a supercomputer. She missed nothing.

Mom pointed a teaspoon at me. "Is he neutered?"

Oh my gods. "Not yet."

"You need to neuter him. Otherwise he'll spray all over the house. The stench is awful. And when he isn't out catting around, little female cats in heat will show up and wail under the windows."

Kill me, please. "He is a nice cat. He's not like that."

"It's instinct, Dali. Before you know it, you'll be running a feline whorehouse."

"Mother!"

My mom waved the spoon and went back to making coffee.

I turned to Iluh. She gave me a sympathetic glance that said, "Been there, endured that, got the good daughter T-shirt for it."

"What can I do for you?" I asked.

Iluh folded her hands on her lap. "My grandmother is missing."

"Eyang Ida?"

Iluh nodded.

I remembered Ida Indrayani. She was nice lady in her late sixties with a friendly warm smile. She still worked as a hair-dresser. The family didn't really need the money but Eyang Ida, Grandmother Ida, as she was usually called, liked to be social.

"How long has she been missing?"

"Since last night," Iluh said. "She was supposed to come to my birthday party in the evening but didn't show up. Sutan, he's my husband, and I stopped by her house on the way back from the restaurant. The lights were off. We knocked on the door, but she didn't answer. We thought maybe she'd fallen asleep again. Her hearing isn't the best now, and once she falls asleep, it's hard to wake her up. My parents keep wanting her to move in with them, but she won't do it. We went back to her house first thing in the morning, but she wasn't there. She hadn't opened her shop either, and that's when we knew something was really wrong. My mother has a spare key so she unlocked the door. My grandmother was gone and there was blood on the back porch."

Not good. "How much blood?"

Iluh swallowed. "Just a smudge."

"Show her," my mom said.

Iluh reached into her canvas bag. "We found this next to the blood."

She pulled a Ziploc bag out of her purse. Inside it were three coarse black hairs. About nine inches long, they looked like something you would pull out of a horse's mane.

"We tried going to the police, but they said we had to wait forty-eight hours before she can be declared missing."

I opened the bag and took a sniff. Ugh. An acrid, bitter, dry kind of stench, mixed with a sickening trace of rotting blood. I shook the hairs out on the table and carefully touched one. Magic nipped my finger. The hair turned white and broke apart, as if burned from the inside out. Bad magic. Familiar bad magic.

Iluh gasped.

"I told you," my mother said with pride in her voice. "My daughter is the White Tiger. She can banish evil."

"Not all evil," I said, and pushed a sticky-note pad toward Iluh. "Could you write your grandmother's address down for me? I'll go visit the house."

Iluh scribbled it down and got a key out of her purse. "Here is the spare key." She wrote down another address. "This is my parents' house. I'll be over there today. Is there anything I can do? Do you want me to come with you?"

"No." She would just get in the way.

"Do I need to pay you?"

My mother froze in the kitchen, mortally offended.

People often confused ethnicity and cultural upbringing. Just because someone looks Japanese or Indian, doesn't mean they have strong cultural ties to their country of origin. Cultural identity was more than skin deep. Because of the nature of my magic, I was known to many Indonesians in Atlanta, and learning about the culture and myths of my parents wasn't only a part of my heritage, it was part of what made me better at what I did. Iluh chose to have less ties to Indonesian families. Culturally she was more mainstream. You can't be offended by someone who simply didn't know how things worked.

"You don't have to pay me," I explained gently. "I do this because it's my obligation to the community. Generations ago my family was given the gift of this magic so we could help others. It's my duty and I'm happy to do it."

Iluh swallowed. "I'm so sorry."

"No, no, I'm sorry you felt uncomfortable. Please don't worry about it."

"Thank you," she said. "Please find her. She is my only grandmother."

"I'll do what I can," I told her.

I walked Iluh out to the door. When I returned, my mother crossed her arms. "Pay? What, like you're some kind of maid?"

"Let it go, Mom. She just didn't know."

"She should know. That's my point. Are you going over there?"

"Yes. Let me just get dressed."

"Good," my mother said. "I'll make you dinner while you're gone. That way when you come back, there will be something to eat."

No! "Thank you so much, but I'm okay."

"Dali!" My mother opened the refrigerator. "There is nothing in here, except rice. You might have to purify a house today. You don't even have cakes for the offering."

There was nothing in there because I was planning to store leftovers from Jim's and my dinner. Jim, who was currently hiding upstairs and whom I had to sneak out of here. "I was going to go grocery shopping today. And I'll steal some of your donuts for the offering." I had apples in the fridge and my garden was in bloom. That would be plenty for the offering.

"I'll make you something to eat. Look at you, you're skin and bones."

"Mother, I'm perfectly fine. I'm twenty-seven years old."

"Yes, you are. Your sink smells funny, your refrigerator is empty, and your trash is overflowing. And!" My mother pulled two dirty wineglasses out of the cabinet.

How did she even know? It was like she had radar.

"What is this? Have you been drinking?"

Help me.

"Drinking alone? That is not healthy for you. Look, you couldn't even bother to wash the glass. You just got another one and then stuck the dirty one in there. That's what alcoholics do."

"I'm a shapeshifter, Mom. I can't get drunk even if I tried." Technically I could. If I drank an entire bottle of whiskey, I would be buzzed for about twenty minutes or so, and then my body would metabolize the last of the alcohol and I would be sober as a baby.

"Drinking, not eating, messing with stray cats." My mother shook her head. "You know what you need? You need to meet a nice man. You need to get married and have lots of healthy children . . ."

I put my hands over my face.

Something thudded above us again.

"That's it." My mother marched to the stairs. "I'm going to see this cat."

"You'll scare him!" I chased her up the stairs. "Mother!"

My mother opened the door to my bedroom. It stood empty.

"Puss, puss . . ." My mother bent down and glanced under the bed. *"Puss, puss . . .* Does your cat speak Indonesian?"

Actually he does. He learned it just for me.

"I told you, he's hiding." Maybe he went out the window.

The door to the closet stood open. The tomato red lingerie I had left on the carpet was missing.

"Kitty, kitty, *puss, puss . . ."*

Jim was still here. I could smell him. I edged into the closet and raised my head. Jim stood above the door, legs propped up on the top shelves of the closet, his back pressed against the wall. The stupid lingerie hung from his fingers.

I wished I could fall through the floor.

Jim shook the lingerie at me and raised his dark eyebrows.

My mother turned around. "Why are you blushing?"

I had to get her out of my bedroom. "I really have to go and look for Eyang Ida," I said. "I'm going to get dressed now."

My mother looked at me.

"May I have some privacy?"

"Fine." She shook her head and went out of the room. I heard her walk down the stairs, locked the bedroom door, sagged against it, and let out my breath.

Jim stalked out of the closet, moving completely soundlessly across the carpet and leaned against the door next to me.

"How much did that thing cost?" he whispered.

"Never mind," I whispered back at him. "You did that on purpose."

"Did what?"

"Dropped things. Are you a jaguar or an elephant?"

"I'm a stray cat, apparently. And your mother wants to neuter me."

"She wouldn't want to neuter you if you stayed quiet." Neutering was the last thing he had to worry about. If she found him, she'd be overjoyed and run out of the house so we could get busy making grandchildren.

He grabbed me and picked me up. His eyes sparked with an amused light.

"What are you doing?" I whispered. "I'm mad at—"

His mouth closed on mine. His lips brushed me, teasing, coaxing, and I melted, opening my mouth. He brushed a single sensual lick across my tongue and I shivered. His scent swirled around me, amber and musk, and tangy sweet citrus, carrying me away to a secret place, where there was only Jim, my hot, crazy Jim, with his strong arms locked around me. His kiss grew intense, passionate, then possessive. Every stroke of his tongue said, "I want you." I wrapped my legs about his hips and let him kiss me. Our tongues mingled, as we shared the same breath. He had no idea how beautiful he made me feel when he kissed me like this.

"Dali! What's taking so long?"

I broke away from him.

He shook his head, his arms wrapped around me. "No."

"I have to go."

"No, you don't."

I wiggled and felt him. He was hard and ready for action.

"Jim, let me go. We can't make out now."

He nodded. "Yes, we can."

"My mother is downstairs."

He didn't seem impressed.

"It's that red thing, isn't it?" I whispered.

"No, actually it was your little tank top and panties as you jumped out of bed this morning. Or specifically what was in them."

"Dali?" my mother called.

I slumped onto him. "She isn't going to let it go."

"Which car are you taking?" he asked.

"Pooki."

He set me down on the carpet. "I'll catch up with you."

Before I could say anything, Jim opened the window and jumped out of it. I sighed, yelled, "Coming, Mom!" and went to get dressed.

POOKI was my Plymouth Prowler. When you're barely one hundred pounds and other shapeshifters make fun of you behind your back because you're the only tiger who eats grass in the entire state, you have to do something to prove that you're not a wimp. My thing was cars. I raced them. Unfortunately being half-blind meant I crashed a lot, but being a shapeshifter meant I walked away from most of it, so the risk balanced itself out. Jim kept forbidding me to race, as the alpha of Clan Cat. I kept disobeying him. Some things just had to be done. When I raced, I felt powerful and strong. I felt awesome. I couldn't give that up no matter how many times I had mangled my cars.

Normally Pooki occupied a treasured spot in my garage, but a friend asked me to take care of his Corvette. He didn't live in the best neighborhood and he was paranoid about his baby being stolen while he was out of town. So right now the Corvette chilled in the garage next to Rambo, my '93 Mustang, and Pooki had to suffer the indignity of being parked in the driveway. I looked around. No sign of Jim. Hmm.

I unlocked Pooki, got in, and began to chant under my breath. The magic was in full swing and it took fifteen minutes to get the water engine running. Pooki had two engines, a gasoline one and the enchanted water one. Internal combustion engines refused to combust during magic, which made no scientific sense, because gasoline fumes still burned in open air. But trying to measure magic by Newtonian laws of physics and Gibbs's thermodynamics was pointless. It didn't just disobey those laws. Magic had no idea they existed.

The engine purred. I waited for an extra second, hoping Jim would jump into the car out of nowhere, but nothing happened. His scent was still on me. I sighed, backed out of the driveway, and drove down the street.

It was too much to hope for a whole day together. The Pack was keeping him busy.

I pulled up to the stop sign. The passenger door opened and Jim slid into the seat next to me. I clicked the locks closed. Ha-ha! He was trapped.

"I'm going to try to find Eyang Ida. She's a nice old lady, who disappeared from her house and some sort of bad magic is involved."

He nodded. "Can I come along?"

"Yes. Put your seat belt on."

"I should drive," he said.

I laughed.

"Dali," he said, dropping into his "I'm a Serious Alpha Man" tone. "I've seen you drive."

"Nobody drives Pooki but me. You know this. Seat belt."

Jim clicked the seat belt in place and braced himself.

I stepped on the gas. We took the next turn at thirty miles per hour. Pooki didn't quite careen, but he thought about it. Jim swore.

I laughed a little bit. "The magic is up. The fastest it will go is forty-five."

Jim braced himself with his legs. If he were in his jaguar form, his fur would be standing up and all of his claws would be out, sunk into the upholstery.

We passed a crumbling wreck of an office building, jutting to the sky, its insides looted long ago by enterprising neighbors. Magic hated the by-products of technology, including pavement, computers, and tall buildings. Anything taller than three or four stories, unless it was built by hand and protected with spells, crumbled into dust. Atlanta's entire downtown lay in ruins, and buildings still crashed without warning here and there. Most Atlantans didn't care. Repeated exposure to fear-inducing stimuli creates familiarity, which in turn greatly reduces anxiety. We had acclimated to the chaos and technology. Falling buildings and monsters no longer terrified us. I wasn't that afraid of monsters in the first place. I was one.

"When are you going to tell your mother about us?" Jim asked.

Never.

"You do realize that she met me, right?"

I made a hurrumph noise. That was all I could manage.

"I'm too old to be hiding in closets," he said.

"You wouldn't have to hide in a closet if you didn't keep knocking things over."

"What's the deal?" he asked me.

Girls like me didn't get guys like Jim. And if they did, they couldn't keep them. Jim was everything an alpha of a Clan should be: powerful, ferocious, and ruthless. Clan Cat wasn't the easiest clan to deal with. We all liked our independence and we chafed at authority, but we listened to Jim. He'd earned it. He ruled like an alpha, he fought like an alpha, and he was built like an alpha, too, broad shoulders, strong arms, great chest, a six-pack. You looked at him and thought, "Wow." You looked at me . . . I was everything an alpha of a Clan wasn't: physically weak, with an aversion to blood, and bad eyesight that even Lyc-V couldn't fix, because it was tied to my magic. If I had transformed into some deadly combat beast, I might have gotten a pass. But my ferocious tiger image was only fur-deep. I would fight if my life was threatened, but to be an alpha, you had to live for combat.

Not that Jim was some sort of murder junkie. He went physical only as a last resort and when he fought, he went about it with a methodical precision, brutal and lightning fast. I loved that about him. He was so competent, it was scary sometimes, and I admired that he was so good at something he had to do. But I had also seen him in combat long enough to recognize the excitement in his eyes when he struck and the quiet moment of satisfaction when his opponent fell dead to the ground. Jim didn't look for a fight, but when one found him, he enjoyed winning.

The shapeshifters were all about physicality and appearances. It was so unfair, I used to cry about it when I was a teenager. To top it all off, I did magic. Not only the tiger purifying magic, but actual, spell-based magic. I wrote curses in calligraphy. They didn't always work. The shapeshifters mistrusted magic. They were magic and they had very little need for it. It just added to my overall uncoolness.

In shapeshifter society, an alpha couple acted as a unit. They upheld the laws together, they made decisions together and when they were challenged, they answered challenges together. In a challenge, I wouldn't be an asset to Jim. I would be a vulnerability. So all of this magical fairy-tale thing that was happening, his scent in my car, his big body in my bed, and our stolen secret dates, was temporary. Soon Jim would wake up and smell the reality. He would leave me and that would rip my heart out. When that happened, and it was a when not an if, I wanted to nurse my wounds in peace. I didn't want pity from my mother, my family, or the Pack. I got pitied enough as it was.

I didn't even want to think about it. I just wanted to enjoy the magic while it lasted.

"Dali!"

I realized we were heading straight for a pothole, swerved, and hit the bulging asphalt, where a tree root had burrowed under the pavement. Pooki went airborne. My stomach tried to fall out of me. The Plymouth landed on the asphalt.

"Whee!" I grinned at Jim.

He put his hand over his face.

"It's not that bad!"

"Dali, are you ashamed of introducing me to your mother?"

"No!"

"Is it because we are planning on having sex before the wedding?"

"No. My mother is from Indonesia, but she's been in the United States for a long time." Not to mention that she would be so overjoyed that I was having sex in the first place, she would probably call all of our relatives and tell them about it. They'd throw a party to celebrate.

"Then why do I have to hide?"

Think of something quick . . . "You know, this introducing thing goes both ways. You haven't introduced me to your family either."

He nodded. "Okay. We're having a barbeque this Sunday. You're welcome to come."

I opened my mouth. Nothing came out. A barbeque with

Jim's family? With his mother, his sisters, and his cousins . . .
Oh no.

Jim reached over, put his fingers under my chin, and
pushed my jaw up to close my mouth. "The way you're driving, you'll bite your tongue off."

I was smart. With all of that brain power I had to manage
some sort of smart way to escape. "I can't just show up
unannounced."

"I already told them that I would ask you, so they know
you might be coming."

"Oh so you just assumed I would show up?"

"No, but I thought there might be a possibility that you
wouldn't turn me down."

He just refused to be ruffled and he was so logical about it.
It was hard to argue with logic.

I made another turn. We'd swung into an older neighborhood. Magic destroyed tall buildings, breaking them down
into dust, but it also fed tree growth. The people-friendly
trees, red maples, yellow poplars, red and white oaks, which
usually grew in carefully managed spaces to shade the front
lawns, had shot upward, spreading their thick limbs over the
road and their massive roots under it, bulging the asphalt in
waves. The street looked like a beach with the tide coming in.

"Dali, I need to know if we're on for this barbeque."

"Driving on this road is just awful. They should do something about this."

"Dali," Jim growled.

"Yes, I will come to the barbeque, fine!"

He shook his head.

"Thank you for inviting me," I said.

"You're welcome."

I pulled up before a small yellow house and turned off the
engine. "This is it."

The house sat in front of us, a typical one-story ranch-style
home, its walls bright with cheerful chicken yellow paint. A
neat front yard, recently mowed, stretched to the front door,
shadowed by an old redbud tree. A dozen bird feeders and wind
chimes, some plain, some with shiny colored-glass ornaments,
hung from tree branches. It looked so neat and bright, just the
way you would imagine a grandmother's house should be.

I really hoped nothing bad had happened to Eyang Ida.

"Roll down your window," I asked.

He did. The air drifted in, baked in the relentless heat of Atlanta's summer. I closed my eyes and concentrated. In my mind, the cheery front wall of the house fell forward. Inside foul magic waited, rotten and terrible. It dripped from the furniture, slid down the walls in thick, dark drops, and coated floorboards with its slime. Every house has a heart, the echoes of its owner's presence, and simple magic that turns a building into a home. The heart of this house was rotten to the core. Something had fed upon it and now it was dying.

Fear raised the tiny hairs on the back of my neck. This was bad. This was so bad.

The ugly magic noticed me. Hundreds of mouths appeared all over the slime, dark slits armed with sharp, black teeth. The slime stretched toward me, trying to take a bite. It felt familiar. This was Indonesian black magic. Things were out of balance here, way out of balance.

I opened my eyes. The house appeared so welcoming from the outside. Just you wait, you nasty thing. You have no idea who you're trying to eat. I don't know what you're doing in this house, but I will purge you out. You don't get to defile the home of someone I know.

"What is it?" Jim asked.

"Eyang Ida is a nice lady," I told him, my voice tight with anger. "Something evil is squatting in her house and feeding on it. I'm going to get it out. This is going to get creepy fast. Do you want to stay in the car?"

Jim looked at me, his face completely flat.

"Jim?"

He leaned toward me and said in a quiet, scary voice, "I don't stay in a car."

Well of course. That would be ridiculous. Big Alpha Man does not stay in car. Big Alpha Man roar and beat manly chest. He'd locked his teeth. Jim was an incredibly smart man. That's why I fell for him so hard. He was also incredibly stubborn.

I sighed. "Look, this is something I do. If you come with me, you have to do it on my terms. I'm going to do some magic and you will have to go along with it and not act like it's stupid."

"It's your show."

Say what you want about Jim, he always treated my magic with a healthy dose of respect. My calligraphy didn't always work, but my Balinese magic was a different story. He had never seen that side of me before.

I popped the trunk open and got out of the car. Two chests sat in the trunk, the small one with my calligraphy supplies and the large one with all of my Balinese items. A box of donuts sat on top of the bigger chest. Jim's eyes lit up. He reached for the box and I slapped his hand lightly. "No. Offering."

I opened the large chest, pulled out a necklace of iron wood beads with a large black amulet hanging from it. A stylized lion, bright red with details painted in gold gleamed on the amulet. The lion had large round black eyes half covered by bright red lids, a wide nose with two round nostrils, two wide ears, and a huge open mouth filled with bright white teeth.

"Barong Bali," I told Jim, as I put the necklace over his neck. "King of spirits and sworn enemy of Rangda, the Demon Queen."

Jim studied the amulet. "So how often do you do things like this?"

"About once every couple of weeks," I said. "There is usually something untoward going on."

"And it's an insult to offer you money for it?"

"The legend says that a long, long time ago on the island of Bali, there lived an evil sorcerer. He was a terrible man who summoned demons, cast curses, and stole children and young pretty men and women to drain them of their blood so he could use it in his dark rituals. A man called Ketut had had enough and he asked Barong Bali for the strength to destroy the sorcerer. Barong Bali spoke to Ketut and told him that he would grant him powers to banish evil, but in return if any villagers came to Ketut for help against the dark magic, neither he nor his family could turn them away. Ketut agreed and Barong Bali made him into Barong Macan, the Tiger Barong. Ketut defeated the sorcerer and his descendants have guarded the balance between evil and good ever since."

"Do you think it's true?" Jim asked.

"I don't know. But I'm a tiger, I have the power to banish bad magic, and people come to me for help."

"Are you afraid that if you started charging for the services, you would be tempted to prioritize?"

I glanced at him in surprise. Wow. Nailed it. "Yes. Right now rich and poor are equal to me. I get no compensation either way, except for the satisfaction of restoring the balance and doing my job well. I'd like to keep it that way."

"There should be some reward for this," he said.

"People leave gifts," I told him. "Sometimes money, sometimes food. Mostly on my doorstep or with my mother. I never know who they are from but I appreciate it always."

I opened the large chest and took out the statue of Barong Bali. It was about a foot tall, but size didn't matter. "Please put him under the tree."

Eyang Ida had loved the tree. It grew with her as she aged, and I could feel traces of her in the tree's branches. The tree's spirit loved her. It would help us.

Jim set the statue by the tree roots. I slipped my shoes and socks off and took my offering out of the chest. I had made it in the house before I left. Jim regarded the banana leaf twisted into a small basket, the elaborate palm leaf tray, and the arrangement of flowers and fruit, and raised his eyebrows. I added a donut to it, took it to the statue, knelt, and placed it at Barong Bali's feet. Jim knelt next to me.

I sat still, sinking into meditation, and let my magic permeate the lawn. It flowed through the soil, touched the tree roots, and spiraled up the trunk into its leaves. A subtle change came over the magic emanating from the tree. The spirits noticed Jim and pondered his connection to me. If there was enough of a bond, they would recognize it. Trouble was, I wasn't sure if there was enough of a bond.

"So is the sugar-glazed donut a traditional Indonesian offering?" he asked.

Smart-ass. "No, the traditional offering calls for cakes. In this case I'm offering something that I like very much. The effort in making canang, the offering, is what counts."

"Why don't you just do your sticky-note thing?"

The last time we went into a house corrupted by magic, I had written protection kanji on a sticky note and stuck it to his chest.

"Because this dark magic is of Indonesian origin. I'm

much stronger at my native magic than I am at writing curses on pieces of paper."

The spirits still weren't sure. I couldn't just leave him on the lawn here. He would beat his chest and follow me into the house. I had to show them why he was important.

"Jim?"

"Yes?" he said.

"I need help."

"I'm here," he said.

"I need you to think about why you first asked me out. Like really think about it."

"I asked you out because—"

I raised my hand. "No, please don't tell me." I was too scared to find out. "Just think about it."

"Okay."

I knew exactly why I had a crush on Jim. It wasn't just one thing, it was the whole thing. He was one of the smartest men I've ever met. When Curran painted himself into a corner, he went to Jim and trusted him to think of a way out of it. He looked . . . Well, he was hot. Unbearably hot, like the kind of man you might see in a magazine or on TV. There was this raw masculinity about him, a kind of mix of male confidence and power. He was so unlike me. I was small and slight, and he was large and corded with muscle. I liked that duality, the contrast between me and him. It turned me on and I watched him when he wasn't looking. I knew the way he held his head, the angle of his shoulders, the way he walked, unhurried and sure. In a crowd of identically dressed men, I would instantly know my Jim.

But what made me fall in love with him wasn't his smarts, his looks, or even the fact that he was lethal. All that was great, but that alone wasn't enough. So I opened my heart and let the spirits look within. My life was often chaotic. I got scared. I lost my temper. I freaked out. I was never sure if my curse magic would work or not. I was helpless without my glasses and that scared me, too. But Jim . . . Jim could take a single step into my chaos and suddenly my problems sorted themselves out. He tackled them one by one with his calm logic and then he would turn to me and say, "You can do this." And I realized that he was right and I could. He believed in me.

A warm feeling spread through my bare feet and streamed

through me, all the way into my fingertips until they were tingling.

"Something's happening," Jim said, his voice calm.

"Let it happen."

Jim sat very still. Muscles tensed and gathered on his frame, as if he were about to pounce. The spirits were touching him and he clearly didn't like it. Apparently "let it happen" meant "get ready to kill."

The amulet on his chest shuddered. The Barong Bali's eyes snapped open with a metallic click. The spirits recognized our bond and granted their protection to him. Of course it also meant that Jim would see things through my eyes now. It would be a bit of a shock.

"The spirits granted you the gift of sight," I said. "Now you can see the world as I see it. It's only temporary. If you take off the amulet, you will become magic blind again. Also it will likely stop as soon as this magic wave is over." I rose to my feet. "We're going to enter the house now. You might see some really weird stuff. Don't freak out."

He gave me another flat Jim look.

We walked to the door. I put the key in, turned it, and swung the door open. The house lay before us, dark and cold. A faint stench of carrion drifted through the air. Jim shifted his stance, falling into that loose, ready pose that meant he was ready for something to leap on him and try to rip his neck open. I put my hands together, closed my eyes, and let my power roll in a wave from me.

Jim snarled.

I opened my eyes. Viscous, fetid magic dripped from the walls all around us, sliding along the panels, translucent and dappled with blotches of darkness.

"What the hell is this?" he growled.

"This is you dipping a toe into my world. Stay close, Jim."

The walls near the door were lighter, the foul magic patina thinner, but at the end of the hallway, the magic grew thick. I could see the open kitchen window from where I stood, and the dark slime pouring through the frame into the house. Whatever it was came from the backyard.

Small fang-studded mouths formed in the slimy magic,

stretching toward me. Jim jerked his knife out. It was huge, dark grey, with a curved tip and serrated metal teeth near the handle.

I took a deep breath and raised my hands, my movements slow and graceful, hands bent back, fingers wide apart, trembling.

The evil magic paused, unsure.

In my head the bamboo flutes sang, with the metallic sounds of the xylophone setting the beat. I opened my eyes wide, bent my knees, my toes up off the floor, and turned. Magic pulsed from my body. The slime around us evaporated, as if burned off by an invisible fire. Bright sunlight spread in a wave, rolling over the walls, floor, and ceiling purging the rot. It cleared the hallway, the living room, the kitchen, and slid over the window frame. The dark slime dropped out of sight.

Weird.

"Holy shit," Jim said.

I frowned. "This is wrong."

"What do you mean wrong? That was fucking unbelievable."

"Usually when a house is this corrupted, the magic is deeply rooted. It should've taken more than two dance steps to clear it. I don't understand this. There is so much corruption, but it's all really shallow."

I marched to the kitchen and opened the door to the back porch. The backyard opened onto a stretch of woods. A wrought iron fence separated the grass from the trees, a narrow gate ajar. The foul magic hovered between the trees, coating the bark, dripping, and waiting. It felt me and slithered deeper into the woods.

Where are you going? Don't run. We're just starting.

I crossed the grass, walked through the open gate, and kept going into the forest, Jim right behind me. The magic streamed away from me. I chased it down a path between the massive oaks. The same scent I had smelled on the coarse hair in my kitchen filled my nostrils: dry, acrid, bitter scent. Almost there.

The path ducked under the canopy of braided tree limbs bound together by kudzu. I followed it, moving fast through the natural tunnel of leaves and branches. The green tunnel opened into a clearing. A massive tree must've fallen here and taken a neighbor or two with it. Three giant trunks lay on the grass. The surrounding trees and kudzu laid claim to the light, greedy for every stray photon, and the leaves filled the space high above us, turning the sunlight watery and green. The air smelled wrong, tainted with decay. It was like being in the bottom of a really deep, scum-infested well.

Eyang Ida sat on the trunk. Her skin had a sickly grey tint, her eyes glassy and opened wide. She stared right at me, but I didn't think she could see me. The magic swirled around her, so thick, it was almost opaque black.

I stopped. Jim paused behind me.

"Is that her?"

"It's her." I raised my hand to stop him if he tried to go to her, but he didn't move. He really did trust me. I had asked him to stay close and he followed my lead.

Ferns rustled to the left of me and a creature stepped into my view. About ten inches tall, it looked like a tiny human, with dark brown skin, two legs and two arms. Long, coarse hair fell from its head all the way past its toes, dragging a couple of inches on the ground like a dark mantle. It stared at me with two amber eyes, each with a slit, dark pupil like the eyes of a blue temple viper, then it opened the wide slit of its mouth, showing two white fangs, and hissed.

"What is that?" Jim asked.

"A jenglot," I said. Just like I thought. This was one of the traditional Indonesian horrors. Except that judging by the amount of magic in that house, there had to be more of them. A lot more. "It's vampiric."

Another jenglot crawled out onto the trunk. A third pair of eyes ignited in the hollow of a tree.

"It and its family stole Eyang Ida out of her house," I said. "They will feed on her blood's essence and when there is no more essence left, she'll become one of them."

The woods came alive with dozens of eyes. Big tribe, at least fifty creatures. I had expected fifteen, maybe twenty. But fifty? Fifty was bad.

"Are they hard to kill?"

"Yes. They are hardy. Setting them on fire helps."

"There are a lot of them," Jim said.

"Yes."

"You might need some help . . ." Jim's voice was very calm. He weighed our odds. The numbers weren't in our favor.

With a soft whisper, a creature slithered onto Eyang Ida's lap. If it had legs, this jenglot would stand at least a foot tall, with hair twice as long, but it had no legs. Instead it had a snake's tail, long and brown, like the body of a spitting cobra. The royal jenglot.

The jenglots rustled through the greenery, circling us. They would swarm us in a moment.

Normally when I changed shape, for a minute or two, I had no idea where I was or why I was there, but in this case, with Jim next to me, I had to take a chance.

I took off my glasses and handed them to Jim. "Here, hold this for a second."

He raised his eyebrows and took my glasses.

I let go. The world swirled into a thousand blurry lights in every color of the rainbow. Ooh, so pretty. Pretty little color bubbles.

A familiar scent swirled around me, captivating. Ooh, Jim. Jim. He was here, with me! Jim . . .

What is that smell?

Ugh. Nasty, disgusting scent. Unclean. Ew.

A jenglot! There was a jenglot coiling on Eyang Ida's lap. Gross. Wait, what was Eyang Ida doing here? Where was I?

The Queen Jenglot raised her head, opened her mouth, and hissed at me, the black magic behind her flaring like demonic wings.

What? Outrageous. The nerve. Who did she think I was?

I stomped my huge white paw onto the ground and roared. The sound of my voice rolled like the toll of a giant's gong, deafening, and my magic followed it like a blast wave. It touched the closest jenglot. The ugly creature hissed in panic, broke into pieces, as if instantly turned to ash, and disintegrated. All around me, jenglots vanished, breaking into ash and melting into thin air. The Queen Jenglot hissed, flailing. Its magic tried to fight me, but my roar swallowed it like a raging forest fire swallowed a puddle. The Queen vanished.

The disturbing stench disappeared. The woods exhaled, liberated of the evil taint, but Eyang Ida didn't move. She was still bound. Not for long.

I padded to Eyang Ida on my big soft paws and curled by her feet, my left front paw on my right. Hold on. I will free you, too.

I faced Jim and let my magic spread from me. Flowers pushed through the moss at my feet, blooming into tiny yellow and white blossoms. A blue butterfly floated next to me, bouncing on soft wings. A white one joined it, then another and another . . .

Jim stared at me, his jaw hanging open.

My magic slid up the tree trunks. The oaks above us groaned, their branches moved, compelled by my power, and a ray of sunlight, pure and warm, fell on the old woman's face. Eyang Ida took a deep breath and blinked.

Jim dropped my glasses into the moss.

THE problem with being a shapeshifter is that you can never keep your clothes on, which is why I always carried a spare outfit in my car. So when we pulled up in front of Eyang Ida's son's house and Jim carried the fragile old lady to the front door, I was able to knock with my modesty intact.

The door swung open and Wayan, Eyang Ida's son, saw his mother. He grabbed her from Jim and ran inside. The family swarmed us and pulled us into the house. The air washed over us, bringing with it aromas from the kitchen: tumeric, garlic, onion, ginger, lemongrass, cinnamon, and the roast duck. Bebek Betutu was cooking somewhere nearby.

Everyone was talking at once. What happened, why, does she need to go to the hospital? I answered as fast as I could. She was attacked by black magic; she will be okay; no, the hospital isn't needed, just bed rest and lots of love from her family; no, thank you, I wasn't hungry . . . After the first twenty minutes, the storm of questions and excitement died down and Iluh got through to us.

"Thank you for saving my grandmother!"

The relief on her face was so obvious, I hated to shatter it. "It's not over yet."

Iluh's face fell. "What do you mean?"

"I need to talk to you," I told her.

A couple of minutes later Jim, Iluh, her mother Komang, and I sat in the wicker chairs on the back porch, away from the family's buzz. Iluh and Komang looked alike: both pretty, graceful, and tall. Komang held a degree in chemical engineering. My mother and she had come to Atlanta as part of the same corporate expansion just after the Shift.

I faced Komang and spoke in English for Jim's benefit. "This is Jim. He is . . ."

Oh gods what should I call him . . . If I introduced him as my boyfriend, it would get back to my mother.

"We work together," Jim said.

Nice save.

"And we're dating."

Damn it!

Komang raised her eyebrows. "Congratulations!"

Argh! I almost slapped my face with my hand.

"Won't it cause an issue at your workplace?" Iluh asked.

"It won't." Jim gave them a smile. "I'm the boss."

I glared at him. *What the hell are you so happy about?* He grinned at me and patted my hand with his.

I turned to the two women. "Your mother was attacked by jenglots."

Komang blinked at me. "A jenglot? How bizarre. She was always afraid of them. She saw one when she was a child. It wasn't real, just something a taxidermist made out of some horsehair and a dead monkey, but it terrified her. She had nightmares about it for years."

There was no such thing as coincidence when it came to magic. "Usually when a jenglot tribe appears, it begins with a Queen. She enchants a person and begins to feed. When the magic essence of the person is exhausted, he or she becomes a jenglot. The jenglot magic begins to poison the area. One by one the tribe grows. A typical tribe is about five to eight members. More than twenty, and the tribe becomes a swarm. We saw at least fifty jenglots around your mother."

"Fifty?" Komang opened her eyes wide.

"Yes," Jim said.

"A swarm of this size would have to steal a person every

week," I said. "There is no way fifty people vanished in Eyang Ida's neighborhood and nobody noticed. Not only that, but because jenglot magic is so toxic, it poisons the area around their nest. It is difficult to purge. The purification in Eyang Ida's house took very little effort."

"What are you trying to say?" Iluh asked.

"Someone summoned the jenglot swarm. I think someone deliberately targeted your grandmother."

The two women looked at each other.

"But why?" Komang asked.

"Eyang Ida has no enemies," Iluh said.

"No personal grudges?" I asked. "No irate neighbors? Nobody jealous or mad at her? Any frenemies?"

Komang glanced at Iluh. "Frenemy?"

"A fake person who pretends to be nice but secretly hates you," Iluh said. "I don't think so."

Komang shook her head. "No, she would've told me."

"It doesn't have to be someone with a grudge." Jim leaned back in his chair. "Most homicides are committed for three reasons: sex, revenge, or profit."

"We can rule out sex," Komang said. "My mother was happily married for over fifty years. My father died two years ago and she isn't looking for romance."

"Revenge is probably not a factor either," I said. "Your mother was universally loved and respected."

"That leaves us with profit," Jim said.

"She had a life insurance policy," Iluh said.

Komang drew herself back. "Are you suggesting . . ."

Uh-oh. "It's not connected to the life insurance," I said quickly. "You need a body for the life insurance, and if everything had gone as planned, Eyang Ida would've become a jenglot. She would be declared missing and the family would have to wait years before she would be officially listed as deceased."

"What other things of value did she have?" Jim asked.

"Well, there is the house," Komang said. "You've seen it. It's not something I would expect anyone to kill her over. People don't murder each other for thirty-year-old three bedroom, two baths. Her car is safe and runs well, but it's not expensive."

"Any artifacts?" I asked. "Cultural items? Sometimes people don't realize they own things that hold valuable magic."

Komang sighed. "She collects My Little Pony toys."

Iluh nodded. "You should've gone to the bedroom. She has shelves of those. She thinks they are pretty. She sculpts them out of modeling clay and paints them."

That's something I would've never guessed.

Iluh bit her lip.

Jim focused on her. "You thought of something."

She exhaled. "It's probably nothing. Eyang Ida owns part of the building where her salon is located. A few months ago a law firm contacted her asking if she would sell it."

"I remember that," Komang said. "We've looked over the proposal. She owned that place for years, so she turned them down."

Jim turned alert, like a shark sensing a drop of blood in the water. "Did they say on whose behalf?"

"No." Komang frowned. "I think the client remained anonymous."

"Do you remember which law firm?" I asked.

"Abbot and something," Komang said.

"Abbot, Sadlowski, and Shirley!" Iluh said, her face lighting up. "I remember because if you put all the capitals together you get—"

I giggled. Iluh giggled back.

Komang gave Iluh a disappointed mother look.

"They should've rearranged their names," Iluh said.

"It's a place to start," Jim said.

I drove through the quiet streets to Eyang Ida's salon. It was the best place to start. We could go after the law firm, but no lawyer worth his or her salt would divulge the name of their client if the client wished to remain anonymous. Right now, with the attempt on Eyang Ida's life having failed, was the best time to snoop around and see if anyone was unsettled by it.

Jim sat in the seat next to me. It was the strangest thing. His face was relaxed, his pose lazy. Jim had only two modes: menacing and waiting to menace. He usually worked so hard on being scary, he intimidated people while he was asleep.

I slowed down, just to keep him languid a little longer. The way he sat now, draped over the seat, made me think of him lying on a blanket on the grass under the peach trees. Just lying there, quietly napping, with the sun on his face. I could lie next to him, read a book, and bring us some iced tea when we got thirsty . . . In another universe.

"What was the plan, telling Komang that we're dating?" I demanded.

"Just keeping the record straight," Jim said.

"You just told my mother's BFF that I have a boyfriend. I'm going to get a call from her."

"You can handle one phone call," he said.

"And then the phone calls from my uncle and my aunt, and my cousin and my other cousin, and my once-removed cousin's second daughter, and my roommate from college whom I haven't seen in four years . . ."

Jim smiled.

"It's not funny."

"If you called them all together and made one big announcement, it would save you some trouble," he said.

Ha. Ha. Oh so funny. "Is that why you're inviting me to the barbeque? So you can knock it out?"

"They already know," he said.

Great. Magic alone knew what he told them about me.

We pulled up in front of a long rectangular building. Built with sturdy red brick, it faired the magic well—the walls seemed mostly intact and the roof was in good repair. Five businesses occupied the building. First, Ida's Hair Place, closed and dark, the door intact; then Vasil's European Deli; followed by Family Chiropractic and Wellness Center; F&R Courier Service; and Eleventh Planet, a comic book store.

"Why offer to buy just one business?" I thought out loud. "That would make no sense."

"Exactly," Jim said.

"There is nothing super great about this location. The street has some traffic but it's not really busy."

"And the parking lot is more than half empty," Jim added.

That was true. Two cars waited by the comic book shop, a horse tied to the chiropractor's pole shifted from foot to foot, a large truck sat by Vasil's Deli, and a bunch of bicycles rested in the bike racks by the courier service. I concentrated. I felt nothing mystical or magical about this location. It was thoroughly . . . average.

"Whoever this person is would have to either make the offer for all of the businesses—" Jim started.

"Or be one of the business owners in the building looking to expand," I finished. "I feel an urge to shop."

"As an attentive boyfriend and your caring alpha, I fully support you in it."

Every time he said he was my boyfriend, I had to fight the need to go, "Wheeeee! He said he was my boyfriend!"

We got out of the car and walked toward Eyang Ida's salon. Walking next to him always made me notice how large he was. He loomed above me, almost a foot taller than I was. He was walking next to me, wasn't he? How did that even happen?

"Jim, why are you here?" I asked.

"Do you want me to be somewhere else?" he asked.

"No!" Poor half-blind Dali, sounding so desperate. "I meant that you have the Pack to run and here you are with me. You're almost never with me." Okay, now I'd gone from desperate to pathetic.

"I know," he said. "But you are Pack. This is Pack business. The rest of the Pack will hold on for one weekend. They know where to find me."

"I don't believe you."

We were almost to the door.

Jim stopped. I looked at his face. His eyes were warm and I stopped with my foot up in the air. His eyes were never warm. Merciless, guarded, hard, yes, but not warm. Not like this.

"I want to know what you do," he said quietly. "I want to hang out with you and spend time with you. I like us being together."

I almost melted right there. And then guilt mugged me. I've been avoiding the Keep. I could've gone and spent time with him. He was busy and probably miserable and I've been selfish and worrying about who would think what. That wasn't me.

I reached over, ducked under his arm, rubbed my head against him, and smiled. He squeezed me to him, the tips of his fingers lightly sliding over my skin. Oh my gods, he did the cat thing. It made me want to pull his clothes off just so I could touch more of him.

We stopped by the door and sniffed in unison.

Hmm, let's see, Eyang Ida, car fumes, a half dozen scents of soaps and shampoos, five different people scents, all about a day old—must've been her customers . . . Nothing fresh except Iluh's scent deposited a few hours ago. She must've came to the salon to check on Eyang Ida.

"You think she could've done it?" Jim asked.

"Iluh?" I turned it over in my head. "No. I think she loves her grandmother. But also Iluh doesn't have strong ties to the community. Jenglots don't exactly slither around in the street. They are unique to Indonesia. She might have known of them but not where to get them or who could summon them."

"Do you know who could summon them?" he asked.

"And that right there is the thing." I frowned at him. "Most people from Bali do a little bit of magic. Every time you make an offering, you do magic. It's not uncommon for people to occasionally sacrifice things. But jenglots are tied to black magic. A typical witch doctor might make a jenglot like a voodoo doll, and then feed it magic and blood and hope it would come to life and do his bidding. Or they might buy an aborted fetus, embalm it, and make a tuyul out of it."

Jim blinked.

"It's a thing," I told him. "But anyway, I would know. I am the chosen of Barong. I'm the White Tiger, a force for good, and I guard the balance. When a black magician does something like create a jenglot or unleash a tuyul, it creates an imbalance and I correct it. It would be the same if I tried to use my power for something unnatural, like stave off a normal illness in my relative. I could save them for a time, but a chosen of Rangda, the Demon Queen, would appear and undo what I had done. The balance must be maintained. Right now there is no champion of Rangda in the community. He went to live with his daughter in Orlando, because he is elderly and she is worried about his health. And if there was a new one, he or she would come and talk to me. It would be my business to know about them and their business to know about me."

"You would talk?" Jim asked.

I nodded. "We would both be guardians of balance. Do you remember that Russian, the one who is the priest of the God of All Evil?"

"Roman?" Jim asked. "Yes. Nice guy."

I spread my arms. "It's like that. I could have a nice, civil meal with the chosen of Rangda. Not that we would like each other and some of them do go nuts and become aggressive in her name, but it's about balance. Summoning fifty jenglots, that's not balance. That's some crazy shit, that's what that is."

We stopped by the deli. It looked dark. The paper sign read: CLOSED. I tried the handle. Locked. Hmm. If Vasil was being eaten by jenglots, too, there was something seriously bad going on.

We moved on to the Family Chiropractic and Wellness Center.

"Are you going to menace them?" I asked. "Because if you are, they won't talk to me, so you can just wait outside."

Jim gave me a flat look and held the door open for me. I walked into a quiet reception area. The walls were painted a soothing mint green and large metal flowers decorated the wall. The air smeller faintly of rose geranium and lavender. Someone must've been warming some oils. A man in his thirties smiled at me from behind the counter. "May I help you?"

"Hi." Jim approached the counter, his hand out. I looked at his face and my jaw dropped. Jim, the "punch through solid wall to get to the bad guy" Alpha, was gone. He looked . . . friendly. Concerned but friendly. Like he lived in a suburb and invited neighbors over for cookouts friendly.

Jim was shaking the man's hand. "My name is Jim Shrapshire. This is my colleague, Dali. Her relative owns a salon two doors down from you."

"Pleasure to meet you. I'm Cole Waller. We noticed Ms. Indrayani wasn't here today. Is she alright?"

I picked my jaw off the floor and made my mouth move. "She isn't feeling good this morning."

Concern touched his face. It seemed genuine. "Sorry to hear that. I hope it's nothing serious."

To tell him or not to tell him? If I didn't tell them, and this was connected to the property, they could be in danger.

"I'm afraid it is. Someone used magic to target her."

"Seriously?" The man turned back and yelled, "Amanda!"

A blond woman emerged from the depths of the office. "Yes?"

"This is my wife, Amanda. She's the chiropractor." The

man came out from behind the counter and stood next to his wife. "Someone tried to hurt that nice lady who owns the salon."

Amanda blinked. "Ms. Indrayani? Oh my God, what happened? Is she okay?"

"She's fine for now," Jim said, his face concerned. "We believe someone targeted her because they want this property. Have you received any buyout offers?"

Cole frowned. "Yes. Yes, we have."

He walked back behind the desk, opened a filing cabinet, riffled through the files hanging on the metal racks, and produced a piece of paper. I glanced at it. Abbot, Sadlowski, and Shirley letterhead, letter, enclosed offer to purchase. Dated two months ago.

"Did you agree to sell?" Jim asked.

"We thought about it," Cole said. "The price was generous."

"But this place is our own. It's about five minutes from our house. We have an established client list," Amanda said. "And our son's school is only ten minutes from here. The bus drops him off two hundred feet down the street. It's so nice. He walks here, gets a snack, does his homework and then we go home together. If we moved, he would have to be dropped off near our home and with the phones not working during magic, we wouldn't even know if he made it or not. My older brother died on his way from school. He was run over . . ."

"We said no," Cole finished for her and hugged her gently.

"Do you have any idea who the buyer is?" Jim asked.

Cole shook his head. "Got to be someone in the building. I've talked to some people, but nobody admitted it. The thing is, they're offering two hundred and fifty grand. If it's one of the owners and the other four got the same offer that makes it a cool million for the building. I can't imagine any of us pulling together that kind of money. There is Vasil, who runs the deli. He works six days a week and half day on Sunday. Then there is the courier place next door. Never see more than three couriers there. The guy who runs it, Steve Graham, is some sort of fitness nut. Runs marathons and complains about how in the future magic is going to make everyone fat. Makes his couriers ride bicycles."

"Dotes on his daughter," Amanda said.

"Yes, he talks about her all the time."

"The Eleventh Planet is run by two college kids," Amanda said. "They host card games and have a tip jar on the counter. I'd be surprised if they have two nickels to rub together."

"The thing I don't understand is why," Cole said. "The building's kind of old and the location is great for us, but it's not exactly Central Market Lane."

"Have you noticed anything unusual?" I asked. "Strange behavior from the other owners, odd magic?"

"Unusual?" Amanda shook her head. "Well, Vasil isn't here today. I suppose that's unusual. He's usually here like clockwork. A very nice man."

"Do you think they'll come after us?" Cole asked.

"It's a possibility," Jim said.

Amanda sighed. Her shoulders drooped. "God, if it's not one thing, it's the other. You know, even with all of the things that go on, I never worried about magic. I mostly worry about traffic accidents."

Cole put his arm around his wife again.

I handed him a card with my name and phone number. "If something strange does happen, please call me."

STEVEN Graham turned out to be a spare man in his forties. He looked like a bicycle enthusiast, his body toned, his frame narrow, and his movements economical, as he stood behind a counter, the wall behind him lined with sample box sizes and price stickers. The lone courier remaining in the office, on other hand, looked more like a doorman in some nightclub. Big, broad shoulders, chest slabbed with muscle. He gave Jim an I'm-a-bigger-man stare. Jim looked at him for a moment. The courier crossed his arms on his chest. Ha-ha.

When we were young, we could hide behind tables and chairs when threatened. But once we reached five, that behavior wasn't acceptable anymore, so we folded our arms on our chest, forming a barrier and protecting vital organs. Judging by the courier's clenched teeth and fists, he was building one hell of a barrier between himself and Jim. *That's right. My Jim is scary. It won't help you, anyway.*

"Shipping or notice?" Steven Graham asked.

"Neither," I said, while the courier and Jim looked at each other. The place smelled like packing supplies: cardboard and glue. Plastic tape had become too expensive a while ago and now the boxes were sealed with homemade paper tape dipped in glue made by blending cornstarch with boiling water. That's exactly what I smelled, and tons of it.

"I'm a relative of Ida Indrayani, who owns the salon in this building. She was magically attacked, and we're looking into who might be responsible."

Steve took a step back. "Is she okay?"

"She's fine for now," Jim said.

"What the hell is this world coming to?" Steve shook his head. "Was it a sexual assault?"

What? "No," I said. "It was a magical assault."

"I keep telling my daughter, you have got to carry Mace. There are perverts and murderers in this world, but what are you going to do? You can't send children to school in a tank. What happened to basic human kindness? You know, the good things." Steve waved at the courier. "You can stop scowling, Robbie. Excuse him. We got robbed a year ago. He's my security. He's here to look scary."

"And if things get serious?" Jim asked.

Robbie flexed his chest at him. Oh you silly, silly man.

"Stop that." Steve waved at him.

"We're were wondering if you received any offers to sell this property," I said.

"As a matter of fact, I have. Some lunatic offered me a lot of money for it." Steve shrugged. "I would've taken it, too. My kid wants to go to TCU. Forty grand per year. *For-ty.* I wrote them back, but I never got a reply. I think it was a bogus offer. The amount of money was outrageous for these premises."

"If you received a notice, you may be a target as well," Jim said.

"Well, that's just great. Fantastic." Steve shook his head. "Because it's not enough my people get assaulted on the street, now this, too. One of my guys was riding by a fence last month and it sprouted teeth and tried to eat him. Ruined his back wheel."

"Do you have any idea who might be wanting this building or why?"

Steve shrugged. "Who knows? Sicko idiots are every-where. This is what happens when people stop living right. You know, you've got to be eating clean. You've got to take care of your body. It's about your carbon and magical foot-print. I've been here eight years. I'm the oldest business in the building and I've got to tell you, it's nothing special."

"Thank you for your time."

"Sure, sure." Steve pulled a card from the holder and offered it to us. "Think of us if you need to ship something."

We went outside. "Sexual assault?" I raised my eyebrows.

"He has a daughter. He's probably constantly worried she'll get assaulted," Jim said.

We strolled down to Eleventh Planet.

"You've made a weird face," Jim said.

"I was picturing that guy inside the shop on a bicycle. I can't do it. But I can picture him with a club in his hand just fine."

"Imagine that," Jim said.

"Speaking of weird faces, you smiled in the chiropractor's office!"

Jim shook his head. "I don't remember that."

"I saw it! I was there. It happened, Jim."

His eyebrows furrowed. His face turned so grim, that if he attempted to smile, it would probably crack and shatter into pieces. "You must be mistaken."

"Jim!"

He smiled at me. It was a brilliant, dazzling smile. It almost knocked me off my feet. Usually when Jim showed his teeth to people, he did it because he was about to kill them.

"Before I became Chief of Security, I worked for Wende-lin. You remember her?"

I did. Wendelin wasn't someone you'd forget. When she joined the Pack, she decided to call herself Wendelin Fuchs, which stood for Wendelin Fox, just like I chose to call myself Harimau. With my eyesight and aversion for blood, I knew I would be in for a rough road, so I chose my last name because every time I said it, it reminded me that I was a tiger. Wendelin chose hers because she wanted to mislead people. She turned into a wolf, ruthless, cunning, and so scary, even Mahon, the alpha of Clan Heavy who turned into a giant Kodiak, made the effort to avoid her. I had no idea Jim had worked for her. When

I met him, he was beta of Clan Cat and as far as I knew, that was all he did. When Curran made him the Chief of Security after Wendelin retired, everyone, including me, was surprised.

"For the first three years with her all I did was covert work," Jim said. "Pretend to be someone you're not. Go to the right place at the right time, listen, talk to people, be likeable and be convincing. It wasn't my favorite part of the job, but I've learned to be what people expect me to be. People expect the Chief of Security to be a scary hardass, so I give them that. Werecats expect their alpha to show teeth every time someone steps out of line, so I give them that, too."

My heart sank. "Does this mean that if I expect caring boyfriend Jim, you'll give me that?"

"No," he said. "You just get me the way I am, which means you're screwed. I'm mostly an asshole."

I put my hand on the door handle of Eleventh Planet. "Can you do a comic geek?"

"What will I get if I do it?"

"What do you want?"

"Make me dinner tonight," he said.

Dinner. Offering food was a special thing to the shape-shifters. Our animal counterparts showed affection with food. It said so many things without words. I care about you. I will share what I have with you. I will protect you. And sometimes it said I love you. I'd made him dinner before, but the way he said it now sent little shivers down my back. I forced my voice to sound casual. "You've got a deal."

THE owners of the comic shop were college kids. We only met one, Brune Wayne, a short blond guy in his early twenties, who spent way too much time at the gym, waved his arms when he talked and immediately explained to us that he was named after his grandfather and lamented that he was only one letter away from being Batman. His partner in crime, Christian Leander, was helping his parents with some furniture today. The comic book shop was just like all the other comic book shops in Atlanta. With computers gone, paper books and comics once again became a viable form of entertainment, and the shop was doing good business.

Jim knew way more about comics than I had expected. He and Brune had clicked and Brune showed us around, talking nonstop. It was too bad about the nice old lady, and they did get a letter but they thought it was a prank, because nobody would pay crazy money like that, so they threw it in the trash. And these are hand-painted miniatures. A local guy makes them. Look, they are magic. The dragon's eyes glow. Isn't that like the coolest thing?

By the time we got out of there, my ears were ringing and I had so many comic book titles and superhero names stuck in my hair, I'd need to shampoo twice to get it all out. But one thing was clear. Brune didn't have a mean bone in his body.

Frustration nagged at me. Anyone who could summon a whole swarm of jenglots was dangerous and wasn't afraid to kill. So far all we had were possible victims. Pulling off that kind of magic took dedication and years of practice. None of them felt that powerful, magically, and none of them seemed to have the kind of money hiring someone of that power would require, not to mention dropping a million on buying up this property.

We had to make progress and soon, because he or she would try to finish what they started. I couldn't face going back to the Indrayani family and telling them, "So sorry your beloved grandma is dead because I was too stupid to figure out who was responsible."

"Look," Jim said.

A car pulled up to Vasil's Deli. A man got out. He was in his fifties, with salt-and-pepper hair. He walked up to the deli's door, keys in hand. His fingers were shaking. His face was pale, his eyes bloodshot. He dropped the keys, crouched to pick them up, finally managing to get one in the lock, opened the door, and stepped inside.

Jim and I walked toward the deli. The CLOSED sign had been flipped to OPEN. The man was sitting in a chair, slumped over the counter, nodding off. Jim opened the door and I saw it, the dark furry cloud of magic, wrapped around the man, hanging off his back like a revolting liquid sack bristling with boar quills. Thin, slimy strands crossed his neck, garroting his throat, and stretched across his face, trying to worm their way to his nose and his eyes.

I jumped onto the counter and grabbed his hands. The magic hissed at me. The liquid sack on the man's back broke and a nest of black furry snakes erupted, wriggling toward me, each armed with a dark beak where the mouth should've been. Jim cleared the counter and sliced through the phantom snakes with his knife. His blade passed through them. They didn't even notice.

I pushed with my magic. The beaks struck at me, gouging bloody wounds in my arms. I pushed harder, trying to purge the awful darkness. It persisted, tightening around the man. I strained. The magic slithered back, retreating from his face but clenching to his back.

The man opened his blue eyes and looked at me.

"Mr. Vasil?" I asked.

"It's Mr. Dobrev," he said quietly. "Vasil is my given name." He looked at my hands holding his. "Don't let go."

"I won't," I promised.

"Dali, talk to me," Jim said, his face grim.

"You see the magic?" I asked.

"Yes."

"Right now I'm holding it back, but this is all I can do. If I let go, it will swallow him again."

"Why is this happening to me?" Mr. Dobrev asked.

"We don't know," I said. "When did it start?"

"Two nights ago. At first it was just a heaviness, then a headache. I went to bed early. I thought I had caught the flu. Then she came."

"Who is she?" I asked.

He leaned to me. His voice shook. "The hag."

"Tell me more," I said. "Tell me about the hag."

His face went slack. He had big, rough hands, the kind strong men who work with their hands a lot get, and his calloused fingers were trembling. He was terrified. "I opened my eyes. The bedroom was dark. I felt this oppressive weight on my chest, so heavy. Like a car. My bones should've cracked and I don't know why they didn't. And then I saw her. She was sitting on my chest. She was . . ." He gulped the air. "Thin . . . like a skeleton. Long, matted grey hair, black fur on her arms, and fingers with talons, like a bird. Long talons, just like in the painting."

"What painting?"

"A painting I saw . . . long ago. She sat on top of me and stared. I couldn't call out to my son. I couldn't move. I couldn't even wriggle my toes. We stayed like this for hours. I finally fell asleep and woke up tired. So tired. Last night she came again. I could barely move this morning. I think she's trying to kill me."

Jim looked at me.

"The old hag syndrome," I said. Most of my magical expertise was tied to what Westerners considered Far East, but I had some education about European myths. You can't live in the U.S. and not be exposed to it. "Before the Shift, people thought it had to do with deep sleep paralysis, which occurs when the brain transitions from rapid eye movement phase to wakefulness. Sometimes mental wires get crossed and the brain partially wakes up but the body remains paralyzed, as if we are still asleep. It feels like a great weight is pinning you down and you are frozen. Before the scientific age, people thought it happened because of demons, incubi and succubi, or sometimes, old hags. If the legends are true, she'll feed on him until he is dead and I don't have the power to purge her like this."

"We're going to have to kill the hag," Jim guessed.

That's why I loved him. He was smart and quick.

"Mr. Dobrev," I said. "I need you to fall asleep."

He shuddered like a leaf. "No."

"It's the only way. We will be right here. When she comes, we'll take care of her."

"No."

"You will wake up, Mr. Dobrev. You don't know me, but trust me, you will wake up. Go to sleep now, while you still have some strength left."

He looked into my eyes and let go of my fingers.

"Take a deep breath," I told him, trying to sound confident. "It will be okay. It will be fine."

The dark magic rolled over him. Mr. Dobrev took a long shuddering breath. He looked like he was drowning.

"It's okay," I murmured. "It's okay. I'm here. I won't go anywhere."

"Please," he said. "Why me? Why . . ."

I felt so terrible for him. He was so scared. But it was the only way. "Let it happen," I murmured.

Gradually his eyes lost their light and turned glassy. He blinked, then blinked again, leaned back in his chair, and closed his eyes.

"If the myths are true, she has to become corporeal to kill him," I said. "When that happens, we have to get her first."

Jim pulled a second knife from the sheath on his hip.

We waited. The shop was quiet around us.

"I don't get it," I said. "It has to be connected to Eyang Ida. That's just too big of a coincidence. But jenglots and the old hag are literally from opposite sides of the planet. No magic user should be able to summon both."

"We need to look into that law firm," Jim said.

"He did say he saw the hag in a painting before?" I asked.

"Yes."

It meant something. We sat and waited.

I had no idea how much time had passed. It had to be close to an hour. Jim brought my cursing kit to me and I sat with it, my ink, brush, and papers ready, staring at the deli meat cuts behind the glass under the counter. I was hungry. The rest of the shop was filled with shelves crowded with canned goods, Slavic-themed snacks and every fruit and vegetable that could be pickled. I really wanted to try some, but taking without permission was stealing.

A few minutes after Mr. Dobrev's breathing had evened out, the furry magic began to crawl ever so slowly, shifting from his back onto his chest, and finally now it sat right under his neck, a big ugly blob that took up all of him all the way to the waist.

The roar of a water engine came from the outside. I glanced through the glass storefront. A yellow school bus rolled down the street.

The sack on Mr. Dobrev's chest trembled.

I leaned forward.

A ripple shifted the fur. Another. It looked like a tennis ball rolling under some revolting blanket.

I pulled a paper out and began writing a curse. The curse

had to be fresh, so I would finish it the second before I actually slapped it on her. I paused with my brush in the air. One stroke left.

Outside a boy, about ten or eleven, turned the corner and walked toward the building. Must be Cole and Amanda's son.

A thin black talon broke the surface of the fur. Something was about to come out.

The air in the middle of the street wavered, as if suddenly a cloud of vapor had escaped from underground and got caught in a dust devil. What in the world . . .

The air turned, twisted, and shaped itself into a car. What the hell? I've never heard of a magic car appearing out of thin air . . .

My brain blazed through the evidence, making a connection. *My older brother died on his way from school,* Amanda's voice said in my head. *He was run over* . . . Oh my gods.

The car turned solid. Its engine revved. There was nobody behind the wheel.

"Jim!" I pointed at the boy. "Save him!"

He whipped around, saw the car, the boy, and leaped right through the window into the street, shards of glass flying everywhere.

A knobby elbow pushed its way out of the sack, followed by a bony hand, each finger armed with a two-inch, black talon. The hag was coming.

Jim dashed across the parking lot. The car, a huge '69 Dodge Charger, snarled like a living thing, racing straight for the boy. Jim sprinted, so, so fast . . . *Please make it, honey. Please!*

The head of the hag emerged, one baleful pale eye then the other, a crooked long nose and wide slash of a mouth filled with shark teeth.

The muscle car was almost on the boy. Jim was ten feet away.

Please, please, please don't get killed.

Jim swept the boy off his feet and the car rammed him and smashed into a pole.

It hit him. Oh gods, the Charger hit him. Something inside me broke. I froze in agonizing horror.

The hag crawled out of the magic and perched on Mr.

Dobrev's chest, clutching at him with her long, creepy toes. She was my size but emaciated, bony, her meager flesh stretched too tight over her frame, while her skin sagged in loose folds and wrinkles.

The car revved its engine. It was still there. It didn't disappear and that meant its target was still alive.

Jim leaped over the Charger's hood, the boy in his arms, landed, and sprinted to us.

The hag reached for Mr. Dobrev's throat. I painted the last stroke on the curse and slapped it on her back. "Poisoned daggers!"

Three daggers pierced the hag, one after the other, sticking out of her back.

The Charger reversed and chased after Jim.

The hag screeched like a giant gull, spat at me, and kept going. It didn't work.

I grabbed a new paper, wrote another curse, and threw it at her. The curse of twenty-seven binding scrolls had worked for me before. The hag clawed at the paper. It pulsed with green. Strips of paper shot out and fell harmlessly to the floor. They should've tied her in knots. Damn it!

The car was feet behind Jim. Please make it! Please!

The hag clawed at Mr. Dobrev's neck.

I grabbed a pickle jar and hurled it at her head. It bounced off her skull with a meaty whack. She howled.

"Get off him!" I snarled.

Jim leaped through the broken window. The Charger rammed the opening, right behind him, and stopped, its engine roaring, wedged between the wall and the wooden frame. Stuck!

I grabbed another jar and jumped on the counter. The hag screeched in my face and I pounded her with the jar. "Get off him, you bitch!"

The Charger snarled. The metal of its doors bent under pressure. The car was forcing its way in.

The jar broke in my hand. The pickle juice washed over the hag. She clawed me, too fast to dodge. Her talons raked my arms, searing me like red-hot knives. I screamed. She let go and I saw the bones of my arms through the bloody gashes.

Jim released the boy. The child scrambled to the back of the store. Jim leaped to the Charger and hammered on the car's hood, trying to knock the vehicle back. The Charger roared. Jim planted his feet, gripped the hood, and strained. The muscles on his arms bulged. I'd seen Jim lift a normal car before, but the Charger didn't move.

I punched the hag in the head, putting all my shapeshifter strength into it. She wasn't getting Mr. Dobrev as long as I breathed. The hag clawed at me again, screaming, slicing my shoulders, her hands like blades. I kept punching her, but it wasn't doing me any good.

Jim's feet slid back. A moment and the car would be through.

It was a car. I knew cars and Jim knew hand-to-hand combat. "Switch!" I screamed.

Jim glanced at me, let go of the car's hood and leaped onto the counter. His knife flashed and the hag's right hand fell off.

I dashed out of the store, jerked a mirror off Pooki's driver side, and ran back in. The Charger was halfway in, its wheels spinning. I wrote the curse, slapped the paper onto the hood, and planted Pooki's mirror on it.

Magic crackled like fireworks.

The car's hood buckled, as if an invisible giant punched it with a fist. Its left front wheel fell off. Its hood bubbled up, as if another punch had landed. The windshield cracked. Something inside the car crunched with a sickening metallic snap. Water shot out through the hole in the hood. The roof of the car caved in. Both passenger and driver doors fell off. The headlights exploded. With another crunch, the entire vehicle shuddered and collapsed into a heap, looking like something with colossal teeth had chewed it for a while and spat it out.

Jim stopped next to me. He was carrying the hag's head by her hair. We looked at each other, both bloody and cut up, and looked back at the car. Jim raised his eyebrows.

"The curse of transference," I said. "This is everything I've ever done to Pooki. Except all at the same time."

Jim looked at the ruined car. His eyes widened. He struggled to say something.

"Jim?"

He unhinged his jaw. "No more racing."

◆ ◆ ◆

BEING a shapeshifter had its disadvantages. For one, smells ordinary to normal people drove you nuts. If you burned something in the kitchen, you didn't just open the windows, you had to open the entire house and go outside. It meant the dynamics within the shapeshifter packs and clans were unlike those of a human society. And by the way, most of those dynamics were bullshit. Yes, we did take some of the traits of our animal counterparts: cats had a strong independent streak, bouda—the werehyena—females tended to be dominant, and wolves exhibited a strong OCD tendency, which helped them survive in the wild by tracking and then running game over long distances. But the entire pack hierarchy was actually much closer to the dominance hierarchy of wild primate groups, which made sense considering that the human part of us was in control. And of course, the most important disadvantage was loupism. In moments of extreme stress, Lyc-V, the virus responsible for our powers, "bloomed" within our bodies in great numbers. Sometimes the bloom triggered a catastrophic response and drove a shapeshifter into insanity. An insane shapeshifter was called loup and there was no coming back from that road. Loupism was a constant specter hanging over us.

But right now, as I poured water over my arms to wash away the blood, I was grateful for every single cell of Lyc-V in my body. My gashes were knitting themselves closed. If you watched close enough, you would see muscle fibers slide in the wounds. It was incredibly gross.

Amanda was sitting on the floor, holding her son and rocking back and forth. The boy looked like he wanted to escape, but he must've sensed that his mother was deeply upset and so he sat quietly and let her clench him to her. Cole hovered over them, holding a baseball bat and wearing that tense, keyed-up expression on his face men sometimes get when they are terrified for their families and not sure where the danger was coming from. Right now if a butterfly happened to float past Cole on fuzzy wings, he would probably pound it into dust with his bat.

Mr. Dobrev was staring at the hag's head Jim left sitting on the counter. He'd walked around the store for a minute or two, surveying the damage, and then come back to the head and stared.

"Mr. Dobrev," I called. "She's dead."

"I know." He turned to me. "I can't believe it."

"You said you saw her in a painting before?"

"When I was a boy. She looked exactly like that."

I was right. I was completely right. Good. Good, good, good, I hated not knowing what I was dealing with.

Jim stepped through the door, pale-faced Brune behind him.

"Where is Steven?" I asked.

"He grabbed a bicycle and went to his daughter's school to check on her," Brune said.

Well, I could certainly understand that.

Jim came over to me. I poured water from a bottle onto a rag Mr. Dobrev had given me and gently cleaned the blood from his face.

"You okay?" he asked quietly.

"I'm okay," I told him.

For a tiny moment we were all alone in the shop, caught in a moment when nobody else mattered, and I smiled just for Jim. And then reality came back.

"We thought it was spell based or talent based," I said. "It's not. It's curse based, Jim."

He waited. Oh. I probably made no sense. Sometimes my brain went too fast for my mouth.

"Most magic is very specific. For example, someone capable of summoning jenglots would have to be a practitioner of Indonesian black magic. He couldn't also be an expert in Japanese magic or Comanche magic, for example, because to reach that level of expertise, he had to devote himself to Balinese magic completely. You can't be a master of all trades. Makes sense?"

He nodded. "Yes."

"So when I saw jenglots, I assumed that they had been summoned by a person skilled in spells or a person with a special summoning talent. But then we ran across the hag. The hag made no sense. She is of European origin. We knew it was connected to Eyang Ida, because it would be just too big of a coincidence otherwise."

"Logically, that means two different magic users are involved," Jim said.

"That's what I thought, but then I saw the car. I don't know of anyone who can summon killer cars. It's not a mythological being. That's something out of horror fiction. Then I remembered that first, Eyang Ida was afraid of jenglots because she saw a fake one as a child, then Mr. Dobrev told us that he had seen a hag in a painting, and then . . ."

"Amanda said her brother was killed by a car on his way from school," Jim said. "I thought about that."

"This magic isn't spell based or talent based. It's curse based. I know curses. They work like computer programs used to: they have a rigid structure. If a set of conditions is met, the curse does something. If it isn't met, the curse lies dormant. For example, let's say I am targeting a person whose left leg has been amputated. I could curse that doorway so any creature missing a leg would get gonorrhea."

Jim raised his hand. "Wait. Can you actually do that?"

I waved my hands at him. "That's not the point."

"No, that's the kind of information I need to know."

"Okay, probably I could."

Jim's expression went blank. "Remind me not to piss you off."

"Jim, will you stop worrying about me cursing you with gonorrhea? You can't get it anyway; you're a shapeshifter. Anyway, under the conditions of that curse, any one-legged person would come through and get the plague. If a three-legged cat came through, it would also get the plague."

"Can cats be affected by human gonorrhea?"

"Not necessarily, but the curse would still try to infect the cat. If I wanted to make a curse more specific, I would define it as 'any creature with only one leg,' which would spare the three-legged cat. Even more specific: any man with one leg. There is a limit to how specific you can get. Back to our current situation. I believe someone has cursed these people to fall prey to their worst fear. I am not sure exactly how this curse was structured, but I think it manifests the irrational fears they had since childhood. The curse relies on them to supply it with the details of their worst fears. Eyang Ida was afraid of jenglots, so she got a giant swarm. Dobrev was afraid of a hag, so it gave him a hag. And when it came to Amanda's fears, it made a living car. That's what Amanda saw in her mind when she worried about her son."

"Makes sense," Jim said. "But wouldn't that take a lot of magic?"

"Yes and no. Cursing is a pay-to-play magic. If there is a curse, there must be a sacrifice. My curses don't always work, because the price I pay is small: special paper, special ink, special brush and the years I spent learning calligraphy. This"—I raised my index fingers and made a circle, encompassing the ruined shop—"this would take a real sacrifice. Blood or flesh or something."

Jim frowned. "What's so important about the building that makes it worth that kind of sacrifice?"

He read my mind. "Exactly. I don't know. But whoever this person is, they are committed. This isn't going to stop. There will be more. What is Brune afraid of?"

"Brune!" Jim barked.

The comic book owner stopped. "Yes?"

"When you were a kid, what were you afraid of?"

"Being short."

"You are short," I blurted out.

"Yes, but I'm ripped." Brune flexed behind Jim. "So I'm okay."

I had no idea how being short could kill you. My body still hurt all over as if someone had put me through a meat grinder and thinking about it made my head hurt.

An imperceptible shift rolled over us, as if the planet somehow turned over in its bed. The magic vanished. The electric lights came on in the shop.

Everyone exhaled.

I dropped Jim off near a Pack safe house. He wanted to take a shower and change clothes. I drove to the meat market and bought another big steak. And then I drove home. I needed to take a shower and make dinner.

Magic always had a price, but in cursing that price was very clearly defined. Pay the right amount of the right commodity—the more precious, the better—and get desired result. And whoever was cursing the store owners knew exactly how far he or she could push it. The curser had cursed for their worst fears to manifest, trusting that the manifestations would kill them. He or she didn't curse them to die. That would've required even greater sacrifice, his life or the life of a loved one. Just any life wouldn't do. A sacrifice had to come at a real cost to the one casting the curse.

All of this made me anxious. We'd stopped three attempts to murder the store owners. That meant three sacrifices wasted. The person would come after us. I had no idea what my worst fear was. Well, no, I knew. My worst fear was that I wasn't good enough. That I wasn't woman enough, sexy enough, hot enough. I'd analyzed myself to death. I had the kind of brain that refused to stay quiet, except when Jim was near. Then it shut up and let me bask in my quiet happiness.

I got home, took a shower, and inspected the kitchen. My mother had been through it. There was cooked rice and a vegetable curry on the stove, and the fridge had been restocked with everything from tofu and cucumbers to apples and watermelon.

I've learned that Jim, like most shapeshifters, didn't care for overly spicy food. He would eat it heroically, but he preferred lighter seasoning. I filled a pot with water, unwrapped the steak and dropped it in.

Blood. Ew. The scent drifted to me from the water. I got a wooden spoon and swished the steak around to get all of the blood and possible contaminants off. I pinned the steak with a spoon and poured the water off, then I got a clean towel, laid it on the counter, slid the steak onto it and patted it dry with the towel. So far so good.

I transferred the steak to a cutting board; got some garlic, squeezed it through a press; added a little tiny bit of pepper, salt, and a little bit of olive oil; smushed it all with a spoon and spread it on the steak.

I could still smell the meat.

And now I reeked of garlic. Hi, Jim, I'm your sexy garlic-smelling date.

I went to the phone to call my mother. My purifying magic came to me from my father's line. But the curses, spells, and the systematic approach, that was all my mother. She saw things clearly, the way I did, and she had more experience.

My answering machine blinked with red. I pushed a button.

"Dali, this is your mother."

Like I wouldn't know.

"Komang called. She says you were there with a man."

I leaned against the island.

"She said the man was very dark and said he was your boyfriend! I want to kno . . ."

I clicked the next message.

"This is your aunt Ayu . . ."

Click.

"Dali!" My cousin Ni Wayan. "My mother told me that you have a boyfriend . . ."

Click.

"Boyfriend? What?"

Click.

Click.

Click.

"Dali," my uncle Aditya said. He was all the way up in North Carolina. The magic has been down for an hour. How did they even get ahold of him this fast? "I am so happy for you."

I pressed Delete All and dialed my mother's number. I didn't know what was sadder, the fact that my family lived to gossip or that all of them were so overjoyed that some male person finally took an interest in me.

She didn't pick up.

I listened to the answering machine come on with a click.

"Hi, Mom. Thank you for the food. I found out what's wrong with Eyang Ida. Please call me back when you get in. I need some advice."

I hung up and looked around the kitchen. I felt so alone all of a sudden. Was this what it would be like when Jim and I broke up?

Sometimes it was best not to get into relationships in the first place. Then you never had to deal with heartache. And we hadn't even had sex yet.

Not that sex always improved relationships or somehow magically fixed them. My first sexual experience wasn't amazing. I was fifteen, my then-boyfriend was sixteen, and it was the first time for both of us. We were both awkward and nervous enough to turn the whole thing into one long fumble. He kept asking me if I liked it and I kept thinking, "If that's all there is to it, wow, that's a letdown." When we finished, he asked me if it was good for me and then he asked if I thought he had a small penis.

We quietly broke up after that. We never talked about it; we just went our separate ways. I've had relationships since. I dated a gorgeous blond guy in college. He was the most handsome man I had ever seen. He turned out to be dumb as a board. He was attracted to me because he bought into the whole mystical sexy Asian girl thing. Combined with my turning into a white tiger, he was sold. The sex was great, but eventually we had to talk. He was disappointed I wasn't Chinese, and I never understood why he thought I would be, because I don't look Chinese at all. He didn't know Indonesia was a country. He couldn't find it on a map even after I showed it to him several times. I told him about Bali and gave him a book with pictures. One night, about two months into our relationship he was laying on the bed next to me and asked me if I would wear a kimono for him like a geisha. And then he asked if we had geishas where I was from. I realized it had to stop.

There had been a couple of guys since, but I always knew they weren't the One. It didn't make me any better at relationships.

I sighed. I was brooding. I didn't like to fail and since my brain ran across a roadblock, it now turned inward in sheer frustration. The One would be here any minute, if the Pack didn't kidnap him to save the world or resolve some life-shattering crisis. He would be starving. I needed to make him that steak.

I had just managed to slide the steak off the pan onto the cutting board when the doorbell rang.

Jim.

I ran to open it.

Jim stood in the doorway. He was wearing black again. Black jeans, black T-shirt, and black boots. The scars on his arms where the hag had sliced him up had healed to narrow light lines. His gaze snagged on me.

I was wearing shorts, a white tank top, and a blue apron with white-yellow flowers. The apron was a bit too long. I realized I was still holding a spatula. There was something in the way Jim looked at me, with a kind of lingering appreciation, that made my heart speed up.

"Come in," I said, my voice squeaky.

"Thank you."

I locked the door behind him. Awkward blind tiger girl is awkward. What else is new?

He stalked into my kitchen. I liked the way he moved, like a massive cat, unhurried, almost lazy, unless something interested him and then he would become all blinding speed and overwhelming power. His scent followed him. He had no idea, but he could make me do all kinds of stupid things just with his scent alone.

He sat on the stool at the counter.

"I made you a steak," I said and poked at it with a spatula. "It's still hot."

"Thank you," he said.

"Don't you want to eat it? I know you're hungry."

"Not right now."

"It will get cold." Here I went through an obstacle course to make him the thing, and he didn't even want it, silly man.

"It's best to let the steak stand a few minutes after cooking."

"Why?" Was it me, or was there a strange almost purring quality to his voice.

"If you cut it right away, all the juices will run out and you'll get a dry piece of meat."

"Ew." I waved my spatula. "Please keep your carnivore details to yourself . . ."

He caught me by my shoulders and leaned close. Oh my gods, things were happening. His lips touched mine, hot and gentle, forging a connection. Suddenly nothing else mattered. I dropped the spatula on the floor, closed my eyes, opened my mouth and let him in. His scent swirled around me, intoxicating, the pressure of his lips on mine deliberate but careful. I lapped at his tongue, my hands stroking the broad width of his shoulders. The muscles were so taut with tension under my fingertips, as if his whole body vibrated with barely contained power. The hint of it sparked an eager need inside me. I wanted him to let go for me. I wanted the real Jim. If I could do that, I could do anything.

His kiss deepened, growing possessive, rougher, turning from a tender invitation to a commanding seduction. Breath caught in my throat. A slow velvet heat spread through me, tightening my nipples. I kissed him back, stroking his tongue with mine and giving him a taste, then pulling back. He kissed me harder. The taste of him sent shivers down my spine. My muscles turned warm and pliant. A soft ache flared between my legs. My head turned dizzy. I had to take a breath. I was losing what little control I had and I wanted so much for it to be good for him.

His arms gripped me, the hard, powerful muscle sliding against my shoulders as he pulled me closer. I pulled back and he let go. We broke apart. I opened my eyes and saw him looking at me and in the depth of his dark irises I saw raw, overwhelming desire.

Oh my gods, I would do anything if he kept looking at me like that.

He wanted me. Oh he wanted me so badly.

I leaned in and nipped his lower lip.

He tipped my head back, his mouth closing on mine, the thrust of his tongue wild and hot. My apron went flying, and then his hands slid under my tank top. His rough thumb caressed my right nipple, sending tiny electric shocks through me. I leaned against that touch, grinding against him, his lust driving me out of my mind. It was all for me. He was excited for me. He was kissing me. His hands gripped my butt and he hoisted me on his hips. The long, hard shaft of him thrust against the aching wetness between my legs. He was hard for me.

I wanted it to be the best sex he ever had.

He tore himself from my mouth. "So beautiful."

Please, Jim, please. Touch me, kiss me, love me . . .

He kissed my neck, nipping the sensitive skin, each pinch of his teeth adding fuel to my fire. I moaned, caught in the whirlwind of sensations, and rode him. I wanted him inside me. I needed to be full of him.

He jumped off the chair, his hands on my butt, caressing me, and I kissed him all the way upstairs. He dropped me on the bed and pulled off his shirt. Muscle corded his frame like steel cables. Excitement dashed through me. His boots and pants came off. He was huge. Oh wow.

He leaned over me and then I had no clothes on. I reached for his neck and pulled him down on top of me. He dipped his head and his mouth closed on one nipple, while his hand stroked the other. The wave of pleasure rolled through me and I arched myself, my hands in his hair. His mouth moved to the other breast. My whole body was keyed up, ready for him, as if I was perched on the edge of a scalding bath and I needed to take a plunge.

He reared above me and I reached for him. My fingers found his hard length and I stroked it. Jim growled. I laughed and wrapped my legs around him. He lowered himself on me, his weight on his arms, his expression wicked and hot, so hot.

"Yes?"

What? Of course it's a yes. "Yes . . ."

He thrust into me, fluid and deep. Pleasure exploded in me and I moaned his name. He built to a smooth, rapid rhythm, sliding inside me, thick and hard, each thrust a burst of ecstasy. I locked my fingers on his back and matched his rhythm. We were one and I was losing myself in the sheer physical bliss of it. He made love to me like I was a goddess. I tried to hold on and stay there with him, but the pleasure crested inside me and dragged me under. I melted into a soft, happy climax. Jim moved faster inside me, pounding, intense, his whole body so rigid, the muscles of his back were trembling under my fingers. His face turned feral. He grunted and I felt him let go inside of me. I wrapped my arms around his neck.

For a while we stayed just like that and then slowly he slid his big body to the side and pulled me to him.

"Mine."

I blinked at him. "What?"

"You're all mine." He grabbed and hoisted me onto him. "Mine, mine, mine."

I laughed and sprawled on top of him.

JIM was a cat. And like all cats, he liked soft places, sleeping, and lying around. We hadn't left the bedroom. We napped, we cuddled, we had sex again and it was glorious. And now we just lay together enjoying each other's company. We were both starving but going downstairs was just too much effort. Outside the sun slowly set. The world was growing dark.

"About the barbecue," I said. "Should I bring something?"

"No, they've got it under control." He was playing with my hair. "I called and told them you would be coming for sure. You'll have to cut them some slack. They've never dealt with anyone like you."

"Anyone like me? Indonesian?" They probably didn't expect him to bring home someone like me. What if they didn't like me?

"No," he said. *"Vegetarian."*

I stared at him for moment.

"It's a barbecue," he said. "We're werecats. Everything is either meat or has meat in it. I explained to them about stuff not touching. They bought a new grill for you, but they can't figure out what to grill on it . . ."

I snorted and laughed.

He grinned back at me. My handsome, smart Jim.

"Just a fair warning: you might end up having corn seasoned in three different ways . . ."

I giggled.

"They're excited," he told me. "You'll have to answer questions. If it gets too much, tell me and I will snarl and make an ass of myself."

"Diversion tactics!"

"That's right. Anything for my beautiful girl."

He said I was beautiful. I smiled.

"I called in a request to the Pack," Jim said. "Let's see if they can dig up anything on that law firm."

The doorbell rang. Who could that be? I slid off the bed and glanced out of the window. My mother, my aunt, Komang, and her daughter stood on my doorstep. Oh no.

"My family is here," I hissed. "Do not make noise."

He laughed at me.

"Jim! I'll strangle you."

"Okay, okay."

I ran into the bathroom to clean up, threw on fresh clothes, and ran down the stairs.

Oh no, the stupid steak again. I dashed into the kitchen,

grabbed the cutting board with the steak, and whirled around. Where to put it? Not the cabinet, Mom would find it. Not in the fridge either, it would contaminate all my groceries . . .

I jerked the wooden cover off the oversize bread basket, stuck the cutting board and the steak in there, pulled it closed, and raced for the door.

My mother raised her hands. "Again?"

"I was sleeping."

"I thought you were chasing after that stray cat you adopted." She walked inside and the other three women followed her.

"You got a cat?" my aunt asked.

"It's a stray," my mother said. "She adopted him."

I sighed, shut the door, and followed them into the kitchen. We sat at the table.

"About that boyfriend . . ." my mother said.

"There is no boyfriend," I said. "It's someone from the Pack. He was helping me and he was just being funny. He's a practical joker."

Komang opened her mouth. Aulia made big eyes at her and Komang closed her lips and sat back.

"Anyway, I found out about jenglots." I explained about the cursing and the property. "This magic user is very dangerous and powerful. It's one thing to summon a mythological horror like a hag. But this person also summoned a living killer car. People believe in old hag syndrome, but most of us would instantly dismiss a killer car as complete nonsense. He or she doesn't require a mythological basis for their summonings. So if someone was afraid of ghosts, this person would conjure a murderous ghost for them even though ghosts do not exist."

"So this person will try to kill grandmother again?" Aulia asked.

"I believe so," I said. "But he or she will come after the comic book guys, the courier shop owner, or me first. This person is clearly targeting everyone in the building and I've made them very angry. They must've sacrificed something personal and now that sacrifice is wasted because of me. They may want to get me out of the way."

My mother frowned. "What is so special about that property?"

"I don't know. I'm checking into it. It is likely that . . ."

Jim walked into the kitchen. He was wearing a white towel around his hips and nothing else. His skin glistened with dampness—he had obviously just taken a shower.

I stared at him in horror.

He nodded to my aunt, my mother, and the two other women. "Ladies."

Then he walked to my silverware drawer, got a fork, took a plate out of my cabinet, walked to the breadbox, speared the steak with his fork, put it on the plate, turned around and walked out.

This did not just happen. It did not happen.

Aulia looked at me with eyes as big as dessert plates and mouthed, "Wow."

All four of them stared at me.

I had to say something. I opened my mouth. "As I was saying, I think the next two targets would be the comic book store guys and the courier shop owner. Their curses are likely already in place. Then me, because I made this person really angry. So Eyang Ida is safe for the time being."

"That's good to hear," Komang said. "Thank you for everything you've done. We will be going now."

She got up. Aulia jumped up as well.

"I am going, too," my aunt said, her voice too high.

I followed them to the door. Aulia was the last one through it. She turned around, pointed up, pretended to flex, gave me a thumbs-up, and fled. I took a deep breath, walked into the kitchen, and sat down.

"I knew," my mother said.

What? "Since when?"

"He came to see me after you saved him from the spider woman."

How did I not know this?

"He said he wanted to date you and he understood if I had a problem with it because he wasn't Indonesian, but that it wouldn't stop him. I told him that you were special and if he wanted to try and win you, he could knock himself out. I told him that prettier men tried and failed."

"What did he say?"

"He said that was fine and you were beautiful enough for

both you and him. And that's when I knew." My mother smiled. "True beauty isn't in how big your breasts are, or how large your eyes are, or how pretty your nose is. All that is temporary. Breasts sag, skin gets wrinkles, waists become wider, and strong backs stoop. I tried to teach you this when you were younger, but I must've done a bad job, because you never learned it. True beauty is in how that person makes you feel. When a man truly loves you, the longer you are together, the more beautiful you will be to him. When he looks at you and you look at him, you won't just see the surface. You will see everything you shared, everything you've been through, and every happy moment you hope for."

Her eyes teared. "Your father died a middle-aged man, balding, with a round belly and when I looked at him, he was more beautiful to me than when we first met and he was twenty and all the girls panted after him." Her voice trembled. "After thirty-two years, we were more than lovers. We were family."

I swiped tears from my eyes.

"You either have that bond or you don't," my mother said. "If the bond isn't there, no matter how pretty the two of you are, you'll go your separate ways. You've changed, sweetheart, since the two of you started going out. You don't lose your temper as often. It used to be one wrong word, and you had all your claws out. He must make you happy. So. If you like him, I like him. If you hate him, I hate him. But I think he loves you and that's all any mother could hope for."

My mother got up and left.

For a while I sat at the table crying and I didn't even know why. About five minutes after the door closed Jim came down from upstairs and put his arms around me. I leaned against him and let him hold me.

MAGIC flooded during the night, but the phone rang anyway. It wasn't for me. It was for Jim. He listened to it for a long time, while I made us breakfast and wondered why I wasn't freaking out about the fact that someone in the Pack clearly knew Jim was spending his nights with me.

"Wait a minute." Jim pulled the phone from his ear. "Dali? I've got a guy at the courthouse. Want to hear what he's found?"

"Yes!" I waved the kitchen towel at him.

"The law firm that sent the letters only exists on paper," Jim said. "It was active about eight years ago but Shirley retired from law practice five years ago and moved away, Sadlowski died shortly after, and Abbot died about a year ago. But the firm still exists as a legal corporation. It's registered with the Georgia Bar Association under John Abbot."

"The one who died?"

"No, different bar number." Jim frowned. "This is where it gets interesting. I also had them check into the building. It's old, pre-Shift. The records are sketchy, but apparently it used to be a strip joint."

"I don't see why it's so valuable." Strip clubs sprang up in Atlanta like mushrooms.

"It was a full-nudity strip club," Jim said.

"And?"

Jim shrugged. "I don't understand what the deal is either. A full-nudity license is more expensive, but that's about it."

"What was the name of the club?" I asked.

Jim repeated the question into the phone. "The Dirty Martini."

"Is the license still active? Can they pull up prior owners?"

"Good idea. Check if that license is still active and see about the last owner," Jim said. "Oh and, Tamra? Check the alcohol permit for me."

"Why alcohol permit?" I asked.

"A place with the name Dirty Martini is likely to serve alcohol." Jim tapped his fingers on the table. He was thinking about something. I could see it in his eyes.

Minutes passed by.

"Okay," Jim said. "Thanks."

He hung up and looked at me.

"Don't keep me in suspense."

"The club owner's name was Chad Toole. He was indicted twelve years ago on money-laundering charges, convicted, and sentenced to thirty years in prison," Jim said. "He died while incarcerated. Guess who represented him?"

"Abbot, Sadlowski, and Shirley?"

He nodded. "You were right. License is still active. The

strip club hasn't been open for eleven years, but apparently John Abbot has paid that license every year."

"That had to cost a fortune."

"Oh it did." Jim nodded.

"So let me get this straight. Chad Toole owns a strip club. He gets in trouble, hires John Abbot to represent him and turns the club over to him as payment for legal services. Chad goes to prison and dies. John Abbot's firm divides the club into five shops and sells it as retail space?"

"Looks that way."

"I am confused. If John Abbot sold the club, what's the point of paying for the permit?" I thought out loud. "Permits are tied to the address. John Abbot must've only sold four shops and held on to one. He still owns a chunk of the original building. That's the only way his permit would be valid."

Jim grinned. "Exactly. There is more. The club also has an up-to-date liquor permit, paid in full again by John Abbot."

He looked at me.

"Why is that significant?" I asked.

"Because it is illegal for a full-nude bar to serve alcohol in Atlanta's city limits. Topless bars can serve it, but the dancers have to wear a G-string."

I crossed my arms. "How do you know that?"

Jim gave me a look. "It's my business to know."

Aha. "So if it's illegal . . ."

"It's not. This law was relaxed after the Shift and then tightened again, but Dirty Martini must've been grandfathered in. It is the only wet full-nudity strip club in Atlanta. In the right hands, it would be a gold mine."

"But the club doesn't exist anymore," I said.

"As long as the permits are on file and the physical location is unchanged, I don't know that the city would care."

I leaned against the island. "Okay. John Abbot, the lawyer, secretly owns one of the five shops. He decides he wants to bring back the club. He tries to buy out the other four shop owners, so he can reopen Dirty Martini and make a fortune. Except they don't want to sell, so he gets them cursed to get them out of the building? This John Abbot was willing to kill five people over a strip club?"

"People killed for less," Jim said.

"I don't suppose there is a picture of John Abbot or an address?" I asked.

"The address is the same as the former strip club. He also could hire someone to manage one of the shops for him."

I ran through the list of shop owners in my head. "I think we can eliminate Eyang Ida and Vasil Dobrev," I said. "They were targeted."

"We can eliminate them because they were personally in danger. We can probably eliminate the chiropractor, even. I saw her face. She loves her son. But we can't discount Cole," Jim said.

"You think he could try to kill his own son?"

"People are fucked-up," Jim said.

I couldn't argue with him there. "So we have Cole, the kids from the comic book shop, and Steven. All of them seemed harmless." The kids were probably too young to be involved, but we couldn't discount them based on their appearance alone. Magic Atlanta did all sorts of fun things with people's age and looks.

"We haven't met the second kid," Jim said.

"That's true. We can go there and meet him now."

"Good idea." Jim got up. "I'll drive."

I just laughed and got my keys.

I was two blocks away from the shopping center when I saw a man running full speed down the street. He was wearing a T-shirt with a Hulk's fist smashing the ground and glasses, and he carried two identical toddlers.

Behind him two teenage boys tore down the street, their faces blanched with fear.

"Step on it," Jim said.

I pressed the gas pedal and Pooki shot forward. In two breaths we saw the building. People were running from Eleventh Planet, scattering in all directions. A crowd blocked the door of the comic book store, pounding with their fists on the door.

What in blazes was going on?

In front of us a woman stood in torn clothes, her head oddly indented. She turned to look at us. A raw, red wound gaped where the left half of her face used to be. She screeched and reached for our car with gnarled fingers.

The hair on my arms rose. Someone in Eleventh Planet was afraid of zombies.

"Not worth damaging the car," Jim said.

I stood on the brakes. Pooki screeched, slowing down. Before he rolled to a stop, Jim leaped out and pounced on the zombie. The knife flashed in his hand and the zombie woman's head rolled off her shoulders. Jim caught it. So gross. So, so gross.

The woman's body toppled.

I jumped out of Pooki. He threw the head at me. I grabbed it. Rotten magic touched my fingers and recoiled. The head melted, the skin and muscle dripping off it, turned to white ash, and disappeared.

Ha! Unclean. My magic worked on it. There were no such thing as zombies in our world, but whatever these things were, I could purge them.

Jim pulled a second knife from the sheath at the small of his back. His eyes shone with green. "Let's do this."

We walked to the crowd of zombies blocking the comic book shop. I never felt so badass and completely terrified at the same time in my whole entire life. There were so many . . . If my magic failed, they would rip me apart with their rotten teeth. For some reason the image of yellow rotting teeth stuck with me. I shivered and glanced at Jim. He just kept walking, like he had no doubt I would lay waste to the whole horde of zombies.

The zombies moaned at the comic book store, oblivious to us.

"Hey!" Jim roared, his voice deep and laced with a snarl.

They turned and looked at him.

"Fresh meat," Jim said.

The mass of undead turned and ran for us, gnashing their rotten teeth, their hands stretched for us like claws. Jim spun like a dervish, his knives out. Heads rolled.

I took a deep breath, stepped next to him, and walked into the crowd. My magic waited for my orders.

I am the White Tiger. An invisible aura flared around me.

A huge zombie with half of his guts hanging out was running straight at me.

What if it didn't work? A pang of panic shot through me.

No, can't think like that. I focused on the zombie. He was over six feet tall, arms like tree trunks.

You are an aberration. You skew the balance.

The zombie spread his arms, moaning, ready to crush me with his bulk.

I will restore the balance. I will purify this land.

He reached for me. My magic surged, the aura coating me gaining a weak, pale glow.

The zombie touched me. Foul, dark-colored fluid dripped from his fingers. He froze as if petrified, his flesh running off him in dirty rivulets. A blink and he became ash.

I could do this.

Another zombie grabbed me and melted. I held my arms out and walked right through the crowd. They fell all around me. Some bumped into me, some tried to bite me, some attempted to claw my back, but in the end all of them became liquid, then ash. Next to me Jim carved a path through bodies, each strike of his knife finding the target with deadly precision. Limbs fell as he cleaved them off, driving the knives with superhuman strength. Heads tumbled, severed clean off the rotting necks. Skulls cracked as the knives pierced the brain inside.

We kept going. It felt so right. So right. If only all fights would be like this.

The last zombie melted at my feet.

Jim straightened, splattered by gore, and winked at me.

I smiled at him and looked into the store. Three dead zombies lay on the floor, two bludgeoned and one beheaded.

Jim rapped his knuckles on the door.

Two heads popped out from behind the shelves, one blond—Brune's—and the other dark haired, probably Christian Leander's. I made a funny face and posed against the carnage next to Jim.

The two guys left their hiding spot. Leander was carrying a replica sword that looked like it belonged to some barbarian and Brune was brandishing a crowbar.

They stepped over the dead bodies and Brune carefully opened the door.

"Hi," I said, with a bright smile.

"Hi," the dark-haired guy said.

"Are you Christian?"

He nodded.

"Are you afraid of zombies?"

He nodded again.

Right.

"Have you seen your neighbor today?" Jim asked. "Steven Graham?"

"No," they said at the same time.

"What about Cole?" I asked.

"Cole and Amanda left," Brune said.

"They went down to Augusta," Christian said. "Until whatever this is blows over."

"How sure are you?" Jim asked.

"I saw them board the leyline last night," Brune said. "Amanda wouldn't get into the car after what happened yesterday, so I gave them a ride in my cart to the leypoint."

Jim glanced at me, a question in his eyes.

"No," I said. "Augusta is too far for the curse to work."

Cole wasn't our guy.

"Thank you," I said and shut the door. "Steven."

Jim's face snapped into a harsh mask. "Let's pay him a visit."

WE got Steven's address from his bodyguard at the courier shop. At first he didn't want to tell us, and then Jim asked him if he was left- or right-handed. The bodyguard asked why and Jim told him that he would break the other arm first, because he wasn't a complete bastard. The bodyguard folded.

Now I was driving through an upscale neighborhood to Steven's building. All of the houses on both sides of the road had really tall fences topped with barbed wire and at least three acres of land. Life in post-Shift Atlanta required fences and plenty of space between them and the house, so you could shoot whatever was coming at you.

"What's the deal with you?" Jim asked.

I'd been thinking about the zombie fight. "Nothing."

"I have three sisters," Jim reminded me. "I know what nothing means."

"What does it mean, Mr. Female Expert?"

"It means you're upset about something, it's been bothering you, but you don't want to bring it up because you're not sure you're up for the conversation that might follow. Sometimes it also means I am supposed to magically guess why you are upset."

I harrumphed. It seemed like a good answer.

"You know I'll never figure it out on my own," Jim said. "Don't be a chicken. Just tell me."

Come on, tiger girl. You can do this.

"I just want to be clear. This isn't a needy commitment thing."

"Okay," he said, stretching the word.

"Where is this relationship going, Jim?"

"This is the kind of question that can explode in my face," Jim said. "You're going to have to be more specific."

"I mean what happens from here?"

"We discover if Steven is responsible, beat his ass, go to your place or my place, and celebrate."

"Are you being deliberately obtuse?"

"No, I'm being very precise in my answers."

Grr. "Let's say for the sake of argument that we continue this relationship."

"I thought that was a given," he said.

I waved my hand. "Let me keep going with this, or I'll never get to the point. Where do you see us a year from now, if everything goes well and we stay together?"

"Are you asking about marriage?" he asked.

"I'm asking about mating." Mating in the shapeshifter world was a firm declaration of being in a relationship. Some couples married, some didn't, but mating cemented the relationship.

"I never liked that word," Jim said, "But yes. Mating. Marriage. This wasn't the way I wanted to approach this."

I made a conscious effort of will not to freak out because the word *marriage* came out of his mouth. This had to be said. "That would make me the alpha of the Cats."

"Yes."

Words came out of me, tumbling one over the other. "What happens when we're challenged, Jim? My purifying powers don't work against shapeshifters. The magic won't always be up. I can't always use my cursing and even if I could, they wouldn't respect me for using magic. You and I both know that they understand and respect physical prowess. They would see me as a freak. Not only that, but I would be a liability. If you stand there and protect me so I have time to write my curses, that makes our battle strategy predictable. It would anchor you to one place. I'm not a fighter, but even I understand this. We sacrifice mobility and the element of surprise. I will get you killed, Jim. I'm not an alpha. I'm a half-blind, vegetarian tiger."

There it was. It lay between us now, out in the open.

Jim opened his mouth.

"It's not that I don't want to be badass," I said. "I do. I would like nothing more than to grow giant claws and do the kick and spin and disembowel everything around me thing, but I can't."

Jim nodded and opened his mouth again.

"And it's not even the blood, because I can bite. It's just that I'm not good at fighting. I'm not vicious. I'm scared of getting hurt. I am afraid of pain. I don't want you to die because of me."

Jim looked at me.

"Aren't you going to say something?" I asked.

"Are you done?"

"Yes."

"Dali, you are a *tiger*. You're the largest cat on the planet and you weigh over seven hundred pounds in your beast form."

I took a deep breath. If he were about to chew me out because I was a tiger and I couldn't fight . . .

"Wait," Jim said. "Let me finish."

I cleared my throat. "Okay. Continue."

"You have accelerated healing even by our standards."

"That's true."

"You don't have to be a good fighter for us to make a good team. If you just sit on our attacker for a second, that's enough for me to kill them."

I opened my mouth and closed it with a click.

"You're concentrating on weakness. It's good to be aware of your weaknesses, but you need to think in terms of assets. What strengths do you have?"

I glanced at him.

"You have bulk," he said. "You have healing. You have paws the size of my head. You are majestic."

"Majestic?"

"Your fur is so white, it almost glows. You're this huge majestic creature. When I look at you in your animal form, you look otherworldly. There is almost a touch of divinity about it. The psychological effect of it is staggering. You look and think, 'How the hell do I even fight this?' I guarantee you, any attacker will hesitate. Even if they think you are weak, they will still hesitate. That hesitation is all we need. If they are unsure, if they question their judgment, psychologically we won the fight, because let me tell you, fighting me requires complete commitment. I don't play."

I tried to process what he was saying.

"You're the smartest woman I know," he said. "Think strategically and use that agile brain. Also you just drove past the house."

I brought Pooki to an abrupt halt, reversed, and parked by a large, two-story mansion. The house stood quiet.

We got out and walked to the wrought iron gate in the six-foot fence. Jim kicked the lock. The gate swung open.

"Is that what you first thought when you saw me?" I asked. "That I was majestic?"

"Yes," he said. "You asked me at Eyang Ida's house why I am with you. I'm with you because you're smart and beautiful, and you are not like anyone I know. No matter how hard things are, you throw yourself into them. During Midnight Games you walked into a cage with trained killers not knowing if your curses would work, because you knew other people were counting on you. That's what you do. You step up."

He stopped, stepping too close to me. His voice was quiet. "I watch everyone around me, waiting for a knife in my back. I can't help it. The paranoia is so deeply ingrained now, it's a part of who I am. It isn't about what they would do, it's about what they could do. I have friends, but I never forget that friendship is conditional."

"Curran wouldn't stab you in the back."

"He would if the circumstances were right."

"Jim, do you really live always expecting people to turn on you?"

He nodded. "It's like going through life holding my breath."

"That's terrible." I reached over and stroked his cheek

with my fingertips. "People are not like that. Some people are like that, but most people are honest and kind. Our friends. Curran, Derek, Kate, Doolittle, they are loyal to us."

He caught my hand and kissed it. "I love this about you."

My heart was beating too fast. "Jim . . ."

"I watch everyone, but when I watch you, all I feel is . . . that I want to be with you. You will never lie to me. And if I need help, you will be there. With you, I breathe."

I put my arms around him. I just wanted to make it better for him, to somehow shield him from that. His arms closed around me, his hard body pressing next to mine.

"Everyone has that someone who is most important to them," he said, his voice so low only a shapeshifter could've heard it. "That one person who trumps the rules. You are that to me. I would do anything for you."

The world stopped. I just stood there, shell-shocked. He did just say all that to me, right? I didn't imagine it?

"You never answered," he said quietly.

"Never answered what?"

"If you would be the cat alpha with me."

He was asking me . . . "I didn't know it was a question."

He pulled away and met my gaze. "It is."

"Yes," I said in a small voice.

Jim smiled.

We walked up to the door. Jim tried the handle. It turned in his hand. He swung the door open. We sniffed the air in unison. Steven was home. No other human smells troubled the house. What in the world did he do with his daughter? Maybe she didn't live with him?

Jim walked through the door. I followed him on soft feet, tracking the scent. The inside of the house was almost completely empty. No knickknacks. No furniture for the knick-knacks to rest on. No pictures on the walls. The house was stripped bare. Only the curtains remained, blocking out the bright light of summer.

I smelled blood and alcohol. Never a good combination.

We turned left into a vast room and stopped.

Steven Graham, completely nude, sat cross-legged in a cir-cle of salt in the corner of the room. His right foot stuck out. It looked wrong, deformed, and it took me a moment to figure out that it was missing all of its toes except for the big one. A small plate sat in front of him, next to a box of matches. On the plate, soaked in some sort of clear liquid, lay a bloody nub of flesh.

I squinted. A severed hairy toe. Ew.

He'd been cutting pieces off himself for his sacrifice. Ew. Ew. Ew.

The salt was probably a ward, a defensive spell. I tried to reach for it with my magic. Yes, a ward and a strong one.

"John Abbot?" I asked.

"I used to be John Abbot Junior," Steven said. "I changed my name to Steven Graham a long time ago."

Oh. Now this made sense. John Abbot was his father.

"What's the deal with the strip club?" Jim said.

"My old man was a lawyer," Steven said. "I worked for his firm. Most people would've made me a partner, but no, my old man made me into a junior associate. When Chad Toole got indicted, he was low on money, so he turned the strip club over to my dad. In its heyday owning that place was like printing money. Magic wiped out the Internet. All online porn was gone. Video was gone. Live girls were the only option. I wanted that club. I've always wanted one. I like women. Owning a strip club like Dirty Martini is like a fucking paradise. All that pussy and it's all yours. No strings, no guilt, just go for it and indulge."

Okay, there was something more disgusting than chopped-off toes.

"The old bastard wouldn't give it to me. Said he wasn't in the titty-bar business. I fucking hated my father. All my life he's been screwing me over. He treated me like slave labor. I worked for him and that damn law firm for almost nothing, then he'd complain I was billing too many hours.

"Then, money went missing from an escrow account. Turns out my father, the famous John Abbot, had been stealing money from his clients. Suddenly he needed someone to take the rap for him. Suddenly it was all 'son' and 'my boy' and 'will you go to prison for me.' I told him I'd take the blame for his stealing, but he had to sign the club over to me. I got it in writing. I confessed to taking the money, got disbarred, and served two years in prison."

Steven leaned forward. "I was soft. Weak. You have no

idea what that place did to me. What it was like. It was hell. I sat in that damn cage for two years, beaten, raped, abused, and I kept thinking: When I get out, I'll have my club. It kept me going. I'd live like a king once I was out. All the booze, women, and money I wanted waiting for me."

Steven gave a harsh laugh. "I come out of prison and find out my father remodeled the place and sold it off one chunk at a time. See, there was a loophole in the paperwork he signed. He couldn't sell the place completely, because I owned a chunk of it, but he could divide it into parts and sell those as long as I got one. One office. The fucker. I gave him two years of my life. I ruined my career for him and he screwed me over again."

His eyes glinted in the light. He looked deranged. He must've sat for two years behind bars and thought every day about that stupid club. It was supposed to be his big reward when he got out, and his father betrayed him. All of his hatred for his father had somehow tied into that club. Now I understood. Steven had to have it. He would do anything to own Dirty Martini. He would hurt anyone, kill anyone, just so he could walk through its doors.

"I couldn't wait for my father to die," Steven said. "I would've killed him years ago, except he had a provision in the will that if he died a violent death, I'd get nothing. So I had to go on and put my life together. I changed my name. I got this dinky little business. All the while, he was still breathing. It was torture, that's what that was. I killed him every day in my head."

Okay, he was insane. Clinically insane.

Steven pointed at the walls with a sweep of his hand. "He finally died, the bastard. I've got his 'palace.' I've sold everything he owned. There is not a trace of him left."

"I get all that," Jim said. "I don't get why you're chopping off your toes."

"They've got a new policy now," Steven ground out. "Use it or lose it. As of this year, only active establishments that pass inspection will get a liquor license. For years I've been giving them money and they had no issue with it and suddenly now they want to inspect the club. I had to get the people out or I'd miss my window. The permits and license never lapsed, the ownership of the building was never interrupted, since I still own a part of it, and I've got enough seed money to open doors in a couple of months. When it came time to renew, I'd be golden. Except those fuckers wouldn't sell to me. I offered them a fortune for their crummy little spaces and they said no."

"You're killing people to start a strip club," I said. "Doesn't that seem extreme to you?"

He looked at me. Like looking into the eyes of a chicken. There was no intelligent life there. He'd become so focused on that club, it consumed him.

"You know what your problem is?" he asked. "You don't know what your mouth is for. After I'm done with your boyfriend here, I'll fix that."

Great. "Is that how you talk to your daughter, too?"

"I would, if I had one," he said.

So he lied about that, too.

Steven struck a match and sat the toe on the plate on fire. "Let's see what the two of you are afraid of. The way this works, the one with the strongest fear wins. Good luck, lovebirds."

A darkness spun in a tight knot against the opposite wall, a twisted chaotic mess, shot through with streaks of violent red, and spat out a shapeshifter in a warrior form. He stood eight feet tall. Monstrous muscle bulged all over his frame, some of it sheathed in gold fur with black rosettes and the rest covered with dark human skin. He looked like he could rip a person in half with his hands. His shoulders were huge. His legs were like tree trunks. Claws thrust from his oversize hands. His jaws, studded with razor-sharp teeth longer than my fingers, didn't quite fit together. Long streaks of drool stretched from the gaps between his teeth, dripping to the floor.

A hot, furious scent sliced across my senses like a knife, familiar, but revolting. It was like stuffing your mouth full of copper pennies. It was the scent of rape, murder, and terror, the horrible stench of human and animal gone catastrophically wrong. My nose said, "Jim," and then it screamed, "Run!" This is what madness smelled like.

The beast opened his mouth, staring at us with glowing green eyes, and snapped his nightmarish teeth.

"Oh, this is just wonderful," Steven said. "You cost me five toes. I'll enjoy this and after it's over, I'll go get my strip club. I bet they'll sell now."

"Jim," I said. "I'm afraid of rejection. What exactly are you afraid of?"

Jim's face was grim. "Of going loup."

That's why this abomination smelled familiar. It was Jim. Except he was bigger, faster, and stronger than my Jim. Loups were more powerful than shapeshifters, shockingly so. Jim would have to fight the better version of himself and he had only me for backup. The loup Jim was a shapeshifter. None of my curses would work against him.

"Dali," my Jim said. "Focus. Help me kick his ass."

The loup Jim snarled.

My Jim went furry. One second he was there and the next his clothes ripped and a half man, half jaguar spilled out, seven feet tall, corded with muscle and ready to fight.

I had to change shape. At worst I had about a minute of disorientation, at best fifteen seconds. I didn't have fifteen seconds. Jim was in danger. I grabbed onto that thought and chanted it in my mind, trying to dedicate everything inside me to that one idea. Jim was in danger. Jim was in danger . . .

The world dissolved into a thousand bokeh, blurry, colorful points of light. They swirled and melted, chased away by a revolting scent.

. . . in danger. Jim was in danger. Jim was in danger.

There was a loup in the middle of the room. He smelled like Jim, but he wasn't Jim, because Jim was in danger. Sharp spikes of adrenaline shot through me. My legs trembled in fear. I was small and weak and I . . .

The loup lunged. He was going straight for Jim. He didn't think I was a threat.

Complete commitment. I charged and rammed the loup. My shoulder smashed into him. The loup went flying and bounced off the ward. Jim flashed by me and carved at the loup's midsection with his claws. Blood spattered on the floor. The loup spun and kicked Jim. I heard bone crunch. Jim flew past me, knocked backward.

I had to keep this thing occupied. I charged the loup again. He sidestepped me, so fast, and raked my spine, from the hackles to the tail.

Oh my gods, that hurt. That hurt so much. He'd ripped me open. I smelled my own blood.

Don't you faint. Think! Use your brain. I whipped around and roared at him so loud, the windows shook. It was the kind of challenge no cat would ignore.

The loup turned to me and roared back. Jim seized the opening and lunged at him, his claws like blades, slicing and cutting. They rolled across the floor. I chased them, trying to get in a bite or a claw, but they were moving so fast, they were almost a blur. The loup whipped around, matching Jim blow for blow, and raked its talons across Jim's chest. Blood drenched the fur. Jim roared, pissed off and hurting. I lunged for the loup's leg. He spun and kicked me in the face, right on the nose. Blood drenched my eyes, as his claws tore my skin. I still lunged, missed, and ran into a wall. Ow. Everything hurt now. My wounds were burning.

I shook my head, flinging the blood from me and willing my skin to seal, and spun around.

The loup got ahold of Jim's arm, bent it back, exposing his chest, and thrust his claws into it.

No!

I charged, roaring.

He let go of Jim and whirled to face me. I put myself between Jim and him. The loup lunged at me, sinking claws into my fur. Pain burst in me. I didn't think I could hurt that much. I snapped at him and sank my teeth into his thigh. The hot burst of blood on my tongue was the most disgusting thing I ever tasted. I locked my big teeth on his leg and flung him from me.

The loup rolled to his feet. He was hurt, but we were hurt worse. The floor in front of me was wet with blood. Everywhere. Jim was outmatched. He fought so well and tried so hard, but that thing was so big.

Jim landed next to me, bloody, his eyes glowing so bright they looked on fire. "Remember what I told you in the car?"

He told me a lot of things! I scrambled to remember. Blah blah blah, strength, weaknesses, sit on him? Sit on him? What kind of battle strategy is that?

Jim roared. It was the rolling, coughing jaguar roar. The loup was a male jaguar. He wouldn't be able to resist.

I made a move forward.

"No!" Jim barked.

What? What was he thinking? He didn't want me to help?

Jim roared again. The loup leaped across the room. They ripped and clawed at each other.

Jim wanted my help. Some men tried to do it all on their own, but Jim didn't have that kind of ego. Jim cared only about results and objectives. It had to be a diversion. What would he need a diversion for? For me to sneak up close.

I padded forward on soft paws, circling, carefully staying out of the loup's field of vision. I was getting light-headed and I couldn't even figure out if it was my body going into overdrive trying to repair me or if I was finally going to pass out from all the blood fumes that were making me sick. The memory of pain flashed through me. I was so scared to get hurt again.

None of it mattered. I couldn't allow this thing to emerge into the world. It would kill and rape and devour and it would cut a path of destruction through the city before it could be stopped.

I couldn't let Jim die. I loved him. He was my everything.

I was directly behind the loup. Jim saw me. The loup had him in a death grip, his arms around Jim, his claws digging into his back.

I braced myself.

With a roar knitted of fury and pain, Jim tore out of the loup's grip, leaving shreds of his flesh on the abomination's claws. Jim jumped and kicked the loup in the chest with both legs. The loup's body hit me, and he fell over me, landing on the floor.

I jumped on top of him and dug my claws into the wooden floorboards.

The loup strained, trying to push me off, and carved my back with its claws. It burned like fire.

I just had to hold on for a few seconds.

The loup clawed me again. It hurt. It hurt so badly. I didn't know I could hurt any worse. I was wrong.

The loup howled and bit my shoulder. My bone crunched under the pressure of his teeth.

I just had to hold on.

Jim landed next to me. His enormous jaguar jaws gaped

open, wide, wider, wider . . . His bite was twice as powerful as that of a lion. He could crack a turtle shell with his teeth.

The loup reared his head.

Jim bit down, his massive fangs piercing the temporal bones of the loup's skull, just in front of his ears. The bones crackled like eggshells. Jim's teeth sank into the loup's brain. The abomination screamed. His claws raked my back one last time and went limp. Jim squeezed harder. The head broke apart in his mouth and he spat the pieces onto the floor and crushed the sickening remains with his foot.

I crawled off the body. Every cell in me ached. Wounds gaped across Jim's frame. He was torn up all over.

Jim landed next to me, leaned over, and gently licked my bloody face with his jaguar tongue. I whined and rolled my big head against him. He kissed me again, cleaning my cuts, his touch gentle and tender. I love you, too, Jim. I love you so much. Guess what? We won. It was worth it.

"You can't get me," Steven said. His voice shook a little. "I'm in the ward."

We turned and looked at him with our glowing eyes. Silly man. We have faced our worst fear. There was nothing he could do to us now.

"We're cats," Jim said, his voice a rough growl. "We can wait hours for the mouse to leave the mouse hole. And when the magic wave ends, your mouse hole will collapse."

Steven's face turned white as a sheet.

"Squeak, little mouse," Jim said, his voice raising my hackles. "Squeak while we wait."

"DO I look okay?"

"Yes," Jim said. "You look gorgeous."

"Is my lipstick too bright?"

"No."

"I should've braided my hair."

"I like your hair."

I turned to him. We were sitting in a Pack Jeep in front of a large house. The air smelled of wood smoke, cooked meat, and people.

"Don't be a chicken," Jim said.

"What if they don't like me?"

"They will like you, but if they don't, I won't care." Jim got out of the car, walked over to the passenger door, and opened it for me. I stepped out. I was wearing a cute little dress and a sun hat. My back was a little scarred and Jim was limping and careful with his right side, but that couldn't be helped. In a month or two, even the scars would dissolve. Steven wouldn't be so lucky. The world was better without him in it.

Jim was ringing the doorbell.

Help. Help me.

"Don't say anything up front," I murmured. "We can just let them sort of come to terms with it . . ."

The door swung open. An older African-American woman stood in the doorway. She wore an apron, and she had big dark eyes, just like Jim.

"Dali, this is my mother," Jim said. "Mom, this is Dali. She's my mate."

LUCKY
CHARMS

LISA SHEARIN

The beep from the tracking chip was continuous and the dot had stopped blinking.

Yasha pulled over where Ian indicated.

McDonald's?

It was four in the morning. I was in a stolen bakery delivery truck that'd been nearly totaled by three gargoyles. In the truck with me were two hungover elves, a pair of stoned leprechauns with the munchies, a naked Russian werewolf, and a hot partner, who was actually more of a bodyguard, in a race against a goblin dark mage to retrieve a leprechaun prince with a tracking chip embedded in his left ass cheek.

The trail ended at a McDonald's in the Bronx.

This had to be weird, even by SPI standards.

It was a hell of a night for my first day on the job at Supernatural Protection and Investigations.

Six hours earlier

"How the hell did you lose five horny leprechauns in a strip club?"

I paused just outside the conference room door and mentally

filed that shouted little gem under "Questions you don't usually hear in an office setting."

Five SPI agents—three humans and two elves—stood in front of their manager, sheepish or flat-out embarrassed expressions on their faces. They looked nervous. They had every reason to be.

Their manager looked human, but his behavior—and bulging yellow eyes—suggested he might have a smidgen of ogre blood swimming around in his veins. The popular belief that ogres were dumber than a stump wasn't true. They were raging, type A overachievers, which might be good in the corporate world but was definitely bad for tolerating failure.

"But, sir, we—"

"Don't 'but, sir' me, Agent Phelps." His voice was getting deeper, more gravelly, and definitely ogreish with each word. "You had an assignment, and since all five of you are back here, that means there are five unguarded leprechaun royals out there."

A skinny elf opened his mouth to speak.

"No more excuses! Bodyguard means you *guard that body*." The manager looked out in the hall, saw me, scowled, and slammed the conference room door so hard it shook the wall around it. It didn't do much good, because every agent in every cube between here and the employee breakroom could still hear him yelling.

I just stood there. "I don't report to him, do I?"

"Oh my, no," said a petite older lady from behind me. "As the agency seer, your assignments come directly through your manager, Mr. Moreau."

Jenny from HSR (that's Human and Supernatural Resources) made it sound like a good thing, but I still wasn't entirely convinced.

My manager was a vampire, and our CEO was a dragon.

It was my first day at work. First night, actually. Full moon. Busy, all-hands-on-deck kind of busy.

My name is Makenna Fraser, a small-town Southern girl with my first job in the big city; well, at least the first one I'd be willing to write home about. I work for Supernatural Protection and Investigations, also known as SPI. They battle the supernatural bad guys of myth and legend, and those who would unleash them. Bottom line, if you were human, you called the NYPD; if you were a supernatural living in Manhattan and the outer boroughs, you called SPI.

Yep, creatures from myth and legend were real.

And for them, our world and dimension now ranked at the top of their "Best Places to Live, Work, Play, and Eat" list. Unfortunately, the "eat" part often included humans.

Why all the attention? From what I understand, it all started with two little words: indoor plumbing.

Folks usually think of creatures of myth and legend as living in fairy-tale castles, enchanted forests, and having magical this, that, and the other thing—but it's basically a medieval kind of existence. And I don't care how it sounds in books or looks in movies, that kind of life ain't pretty. It doesn't matter how highfalutin a Seelie royal you are, or how much magical mojo you've got going on, or how much gold and jewels you've got piled in your treasure room, you still gotta go. So for a Seelie royal, their chamber pot might be gold, but they're still pissing in a pot. My grandma Fraser told me that the big influx to our world was kicked off by the invention of the flushable toilet. Heck, I'd cross over for indoor plumbing.

And now that human technology had reached smartphones, tablets, and other gadgets that would have previously been called magical, there was no keeping supernaturals away. Think about it. What would you rather have: one guy singing off-key with a half-tuned lute in your great hall, or Lady Gaga, the Stones, Hank Williams, Jr., or anyone else you wanted to hear. on your phone, anytime, at your fingertips? That there's a no-brainer.

The wealthier supernaturals (Seelie Court royals and the like) or those with long life spans (or death spans, if you prefer) like dragons, vampires, and werewolves, have had time to save their pennies into hoards to be able to bankroll any lifestyle to which they wanted to become accustomed. Other less well-to-do supernaturals have come here wanting the same things as the rest of us: a good job, nice house, 2.5 kids/spawn, and a dog.

However, regardless of species—human or supernatural—there's always a small percentage that are power hungry, megalomaniacal, or just plain bat-shit crazy. As an added bonus, their powers get a boost when they come here, which in turn has an unfortunate tendency to supersize their greed. And when the treaties or bindings that may have made them behave back home don't mean squat here, you might as well put out a sign for the all-you-can-take-or-conquer buffet.

SPI's mission is twofold: keep the world safe for supernaturals and humans alike, and keep humans in the dark about things that go bump in the night. SPI has offices worldwide, and their agents are recruited from the best of the alphabet agencies, police forces, military special ops, and are supported by the sharpest scientific and academic minds.

Then there's me.

I wouldn't be doing my new job with a gun, blade, or hand-to-claw combat.

I was the only seer in the New York office, and only one of five in the entire worldwide company. A seer's job was to point out the supernatural bad guys, then step aside so SPI's badass, commando monster hunters could take them into custody—or if necessary, take them out. As a seer, any veil, ward, shield, or spell any supernatural could come up with as a disguise might as well not exist. I could see right through them. I got the satisfaction of keeping the world safe, *and* I got full medical coverage. If Bigfoot was on a rampage hurting innocent campers, I'd hunt him with a butterfly net if it meant having a decent dental plan.

I'd gotten the grand tour when I'd officially accepted SPI's offer—and after I'd signed a nondisclosure agreement. In blood. Mine. The head of HSR was a voodoo high priestess, which took contracts and company loyalty to a whole new level. I was supposed to have started a week ago, but HSR called me last week to say that they needed to push my start date. They were still paying me, so I was more than happy with a week's paid vacation before I'd even started work.

"Your office is in the main agent bull pen," Jenny was telling me as she led the way to a pair of massive steel doors. She looked human to everyone else, but I knew that she was a river hag, though "water spirit" was the more politically correct term nowadays. Though river hags mostly looked like humans anyway—that is, if you took a human, made her skin the color of the Wicked Witch of the West, and exchanged dental work with a piranha. I always thought they had to live in a body of water. Turned out any size body would do, and I'd been told that SPI had a pool in the basement for its water-dwelling employees to use during breaks. You didn't need seer vision to spot them; they left wet footprints all over the place. During my two-week orientation, SPI's hallways had always been dotted with those Warning: Wet Floor signs.

SPI's New York headquarters was located under Washington Square Park in Greenwich Village. The SPI complex was deep and wide—eight stories of deep and the entire park's worth of wide. There was a subbasement, basement, parking area, then what was called the bull pen on the main floor that was ringed with five stories of steel catwalks connecting offices, labs, and conference rooms. The bull pen was filled with desks, computers, people, and not-people. The largest shift was on duty right now—the night shift. Even supernaturals who weren't nocturnal tended to do their thing at night. Humans were essentially the same, but without the fangs, claws, and paranormally bad attitudes.

"Our seers have always been assigned the corner office," Jenny was telling me.

"Corner office" was right. My office was against the wall, in the corner.

"Our seers have preferred to be seated where they can see everyone," Jenny explained at my less-than-enthused reaction. "No one else would know the difference if one of our more physically imposing agents walked up behind them, but as a seer, you see everything all the time." The woman giggled and smiled, her perky petunia lipstick framing a mouthful of dainty fangs that were at odds with her pink sweater set and pearls. "That must be terribly exciting. How I envy you."

I stood absolutely still as a troll who had to be eight feet tall lumbered down the aisle next to mine and into the IT department's cube farm. He sat down in an office chair that shrieked in a torture of steel. Of course, everyone else saw a slight, blond, and bespectacled man in a white shirt, tie, and khakis.

I swallowed. "Yes. Terribly."

Some supernaturals who could pass for human didn't bother

with glamours most of the time. They'd just use clothing to cover their more identifying features. Coats or jackets to cover wings. Hats to cover horns or pointed ears, or sunglasses to cover larger or brighter-than-human eyes.

"The human employee breakroom is around the corner and through the first door on the right. And don't worry about human-inappropriate snacks being left on the table. We have a strict rule about food in the office. Those employees who require what might be disturbing to our human colleagues have their own breakroom. Badge entrance only."

"So . . . if there's Girl Scout cookies on the table in the human breakroom, they don't contain real Girl Scouts."

"Correct."

I'd been joking. I didn't think she was.

When a supernatural was predisposed to see you as food, you had to go the extra mile to earn their respect. It was kind of like a human being told that they'd be working with a cow. Aside from the obvious lack of intellect—cows being dumber than a bag of rocks—there was the whole working with your food thing. Not much incentive for respect and teamwork.

The politics of an inter-species and inter-dimensional workplace promised to keep me on my toes. I was more than thankful for my two weeks of orientation training where I'd learned more than I ever thought there was to know about supernaturals, up to and including the best way to avoid being swallowed by an annoyed lindworm, and the proper etiquette for greeting a Bolivian basilisk. Very carefully.

Mine was an empty, sad-looking desk. The name plate on the desk read: "Irvine Schremp." Jenny quickly picked it up with an apologetic grin.

"So what happened to Irvine?" I asked.

Jenny glanced around without moving her head. "Exsanguinated by a school of giant North American sewer leeches."

I froze. "Drained?"

"Bone dry. They even sucked out his marrow. All in less than a minute."

Breathe, Mac. Just breathe. Full medical coverage. Full medical. It's a good thing.

While my eyes started involuntarily darting around to find the nearest exit—just in case, of course—I saw that on the desk closest to mine was a collection of items I wouldn't have expected to see outside a horror movie or a psycho's happy fun-time imagination.

And a dental plan. A good one.

There were four shelves on the wall filled with everything from action figures from an assortment of fantasy and horror movies to shell casings from impossibly large guns. More than a few of the monster action figures were missing their heads, or had sharp, pointy objects sticking out of their torsos.

My confusion and concern must have been apparent.

"Desk flair," Jenny explained. "Mementos of particularly memorable missions."

The name on the desk plate read: "Ian Byrne."

"He collected all this him—"

"Oh, no. If your fellow agents deem your actions deserving, they'll give you desk flair. It's quite the honor around here."

This Ian Byrne had been a busy boy.

"Ian's really good at eradication," Jenny said.

I glanced at the nightmare-inducing trinkets. "I can see that."

I looked around at the other field agents and their desks. The only ones that had more flair belonged to vampires and werewolves.

"Ian is the highest-producing human in the company. A real go-getter. He was a detective with the NYPD for five years and was in the military the seven before that. You're in for a real treat." Jenny's green eyes sparkled with near fangirl glee. "In more ways than one." She lowered her voice. "You're the envy of every succubus and half of the incubuses in the company." She quickly held up her hands. "Though rest assured, SPI has a zero-tolerance policy in place for harassment of any kind—from sexual to trying to have a coworker for lunch." Jenny suddenly looked distracted, tilting her head to one side. "Madame Sagadraco would like to see you now."

"Are you telepathic?" River hags weren't, but I could see where it'd come in handy for attracting a human who was playing hard to get to join her for a dip.

Jenny tapped her right ear with a long, pink-lacquered nail. A really pointed, pink-lacquered nail. She smiled in her cheerful flash of pushpin teeth. "Bluetooth."

We took an elevator up to the fifth floor and the executive suite. "I'm sure Madame Sagadraco will be with you in just a moment." Jenny gave me a little finger wave and closed the door quietly behind her, leaving me completely alone in a wood-paneled waiting area that reminded me of something out of Hogwarts.

I'd been introduced to Vivienne Sagadraco, the founder and CEO of SPI, at my final interview before being hired. Maybe she met with every new employee, or perhaps being the only seer in the New York office had earned me the special treatment. The other agents referred to her as the dragon lady, but until I'd met her in person, I hadn't realized that was meant literally.

The lady in charge was a dragon.

She could morph in and out of human form; but as a seer, I got a clear view of what she really was.

To a normal person, Vivienne Sagadraco appeared to be a petite and attractive woman in her late sixties. My seer vision let me see a dragon with peacock blue and green iridescent scales, a pair of sleek wings folded like long shadows against her back. A faintly glowing aura around her told me that she was larger than I ever really wanted visual confirmation on.

The boss's voice came through the partially open office door. "You're an exceptional agent, and I believe you are also the best qualified, or I would not be asking this of you."

"How long do you anticipate this assignment lasting?" It was a man's voice, a man who was keeping his emotions firmly in check. Unhappy emotions.

Vivienne Sagadraco's British accent was cool and smooth, reminding me of Judi Dench's M about to give James Bond some really bad news. Apparently, an SPI agent was in her office and on the receiving end of some bad news right now.

Did she know I was out here? Should I close the door? Though she'd told Jenny to bring me here; and as a dragon, she had preternatural hearing. All that told me she wanted me to overhear. Though whoever she was talking to would be even less happy knowing that the newest employee had overheard him being given a crap assignment that he clearly didn't want. I hoped I liked my first assignment better than he did.

"The assignment will last as long as necessary," came

Vivienne Sagadraco's cool response. "I will inform you when you may resume your regular duties."

"Yes, ma'am. I understand." His clipped tone said he understood only too well, and he liked it a lot less.

The boss raised her voice. "Agent Fraser, if you would join us, please."

Oh shit.

I took a breath, tried for a nonthreatening, I-didn't-hear-a-thing smile, opened the door and went in.

"Agent Fraser, I'd like you to meet your new partner— Agent Ian Byrne. Agent Byrne, this is Makenna Fraser, your new assignment."

Oh *shit*.

Ian Byrne was about six foot three with a body you couldn't get in a gym, lean muscles coiled and ready for violence, cropped dark hair, cheekbones you could cut yourself on, and steel-blue eyes set on pissed and aimed at me. An instant later, pissed was replaced by professional. If I'd blinked, I'd have just seen professional. I hadn't blinked, so I'd gotten the full treatment.

I stuck out my hand without looking away from those eyes. He shook my hand with a firm grip and released it. No smile, no warmth, no welcome to the company. I'd heard what the boss had told him and his response. He knew that I'd heard. Somehow I didn't see a friendly invite to after-work drinks in my future. Ever.

This was awkward.

"Unfortunately, Agent Fraser, there is no time for further orientation or training," Vivienne Sagadraco said. "We require your presence in the field tonight. We have a politically embarrassing situation that, left unresolved, could result in the failure of the banking system of the entire supernatural world." She glanced at an elegant diamond watch. Dragons liked their sparklies. "In ten minutes there will be a briefing in the main conference room." Her sharp eyes locked on mine. "I would rather the situation not be this critical on your first mission; but unfortunately, we cannot choose the timing of our crises. I am certain our faith in your abilities has not been misplaced." The narrowing of those eyes told me loud and clear they'd better not be.

I went for a smile; it probably looked like a grimace. "I'll do my best, ma'am."

AND the awkwardness just kept on coming.

My first assignment was to locate the aforementioned "five horny leprechauns" that had vanished while in a strip club.

I recognized the five agents from the conference room, and judging by the less than friendly stares, they remembered me seeing and hearing their butts getting handed to them by their ogre manager, who had gotten a handle on his temper and was now the very picture of professional middle management, albeit with beady, yellow eyes.

Ian Byrne plus these guys equaled six SPI agents who were less than thrilled that I'd joined their ranks. I'd managed to gain half a dozen intensely resentful coworkers in less than an hour on the job, probably setting some kind of company record.

And I didn't have to jump far to land on the conclusion that the five agents resented me because not only had I witnessed their humiliation; but as a seer, I was equipped to fix on my first night on the job what had landed them in trouble. Like any corporate newbie, I wanted to prove myself; but at the same time, I didn't want to be *that* employee, the one who was followed by snide and resentful whispers wherever they went.

Vivienne Sagadraco had made it clear that failure was not an option. And being the sole employee who could see through any glamour those leprechauns could come up with, any further failure would be all mine, to have and to hold from this day forward. I wanted to keep my shiny new job. A human boss would deliver a tongue lashing, and write up an incident report for their personnel file. I wondered if vampires and dragons had a more fangs- and claws-on management style, resulting in the offending employee becoming the blue-plate special in the executive cafeteria. I knew I didn't want to find out. And key to not finding out was to not disappoint the boss—or my manager.

The main conference room at SPI headquarters resembled a scaled-down version of the Security Council Chamber at the UN. I'd taken a tour when I'd first come to town and had decided to get the tourist stuff out of the way. That way when I got a call from back home, I could say "Been there, seen that."

A massive U-shaped table dominated the room, with the light from a pair of projectors—one mounted in the ceiling, the other in the floor—coming together to form a hologram of SPI's company logo, a stylized monster eye with a slit pupil. The eye slowly spun, a placeholder for whatever visuals were going to be used in the meeting. Plush and pricey executive office chairs were spaced every few feet around the table.

The five agents who were in the doghouse were wearing suits that screamed "feds"—at least that's what they said to me based on my TV viewing. The other five agents—three men and two women, and presumably the ones tasked with cleaning up the Suits' mess, were casually dressed. This included Ian Byrne. I hadn't been sure what was considered approved SPI seer attire, so I went with slacks, blouse, blazer, nice pumps, along with a small silver crucifix and a water pistol filled with holy water—supernatural business casual.

Alain Moreau—aka my manager, the vampire—was standing preternaturally still and silent at the front of the room. In addition to being my manager, Alain Moreau was SPI's chief legal counsel, second-in-charge, and Vivienne Sagadraco's go-to guy. He wore an elegant black suit that probably cost more than my first car. His white-blond hair, pale skin, and light blue eyes reminded me of Anderson Cooper, minus the giggling and sense of humor.

After being hired and introduced to him, I'd immediately put a permanent park on any urges involving blood-sucking lawyer jokes.

Moreau quickly made the introductions. Since the Suits were in the meeting, presumably they were being given a chance to redeem themselves. That said good things about my new employer. I tried for a friendly smile at each handshake. Four of the Suits smiled back, apparently willing to let bygones be bygones. The last one decided that crushing my hand would make his ego feel better. I squeezed right back, managed not to wince, and kept right on smiling.

Asshat.

Then Moreau introduced me to the "Casuals." Two of the men and one of the women were elves, and the remaining man and woman were human. A lot of elves found their way into police and federal agency work. For some reason, they had a thing for law and order. All of these agents seemed perfectly nice; and even better, none tried to break my fingers.

The ogre stepped forward. "Some background on tonight's . . . challenge."

He said that last word in a way that would easily translate to "fiasco." Some of the Casuals were having trouble stopping smiles at the Suits' collective expense. With the exception of the Hand Crusher, the others took the ribbing with good humor.

"Normally, SPI is not in the bodyguard business, but as a favor to the local Seelie Court, we escorted a soon-to-be-married leprechaun prince and his bachelor party buddies for a night on the town." He glared briefly at the Suits. "Apparently, the prince didn't want bodyguards.

"Our agents were tasked with keeping the prince and his party where we could see them," the ogre continued. "As a refresher, a human's gaze can hold a leprechaun prisoner. However, the instant the human looks away, the leprechaun can vanish. So where was the first place the prince and his roving bachelor party wanted to go? A strip club." The ogre shot a glance at Alain Moreau. It was almost apologetic. "SPI prides itself on agents that are highly trained and disciplined." He scowled. "Obviously putting five male agents in a strip club and telling them they can't look proves that there's been a training oversight on the discipline side because the prince and his boys flew the coop before the first G-string dropped."

The Casuals couldn't hold it in any longer. Snorts and snickers filled the room. Personally, I thought the biggest mistake had been sending in five straight male agents.

Hand Crusher had a red face. "Like you would do any better." His comment was directed at a stylish red-haired woman sitting next to him.

"We can and we will," she assured him. "Sir," she said to the ogre, "never send a man to do a woman's job."

"Settle down, people." The ogre's voice went low, gravelly, vibrated the floor under my feet, and clearly meant business. "Leprechauns are masters of disguise and can make themselves look like anyone. We now have five magically disguised leprechauns running amok and unguarded through

New York's adult entertainment establishments." He leveled those yellow eyes on every agent in the room, Suits and Casuals alike. "The prince made no secret of his bachelor party plans. And in the Seelie Court, information is just as big of a commodity as gold. Even if he'd tried to keep it secret, it wouldn't have stayed that way for long. We have to find them before the opposition does."

The ogre did some click and drag, and the SPI monster eye logo was replaced by five completely average-looking human men on the screen. There was a name below each photo.

"These are our subjects' usual glamours."

"Any chance they'll still be using them?" Ian asked.

"Better than average. The agents originally assigned to the prince and his party will be deployed to the less likely but still viable clubs. They might get lucky."

"That thinking's what got them in trouble last time," Ian muttered.

"What other form can they take?" the redhead asked. "Male? Female? Animal, vegetable, mineral?"

"First two, yes. Last three, unknown."

"So we're looking for a male or female who may or may not turn into something with four legs, roots, or a rock."

That earned her some chuckles.

Alain Moreau stepped in, and the humor instantly vanished. "Apprehend them quickly and bring them here. We will keep them here until all five have been collected, at which time they will be returned to Belvedere Castle."

I couldn't have heard that right. Belvedere Castle had been built in Central Park in 1869. I'd visited during my round of doing the tourist thing. It's a combination weather station, observatory, and exhibition rooms. And every Halloween, they have a haunted house. I would have definitely noticed if there'd been fairies living there.

"The one in Central Park?" I asked.

Moreau hadn't told them where I was from, though judging from the smiles and barely hidden smirks, they'd figured it out as soon as I opened my mouth.

I'm from the mountains of North Carolina. My words have a couple of extra syllables; so sue me.

Ian Byrne hadn't said a thing when he'd first heard me

talk. And being in HSR, Jenny knew where I was from, and some of her relatives lived in the Mississippi River, so my accent wasn't big deal. She thought it was charming. Though I'd found out since moving to New York that "charming" most often translated to "redneck."

Hand Crusher smirked and muttered something under his breath. I only heard two words—"Elly May"—and they told me the gist of the rest.

Yeah, I'm from the South and the mountains. Sure, I'm a woman and a blonde, but calling me a "hillbilly"—either indirectly or right up in my face—stepped up to and over any and every line I had. But if I *was* going to channel Elly May Clampett, I'd have told him that "them there's fightin' words," put him in a headlock, and sicced my pet raccoon on him. But I wasn't going to channel anyone or dignify his comments with a response. At least not yet. However, that snide remark plus the hand crush had earned him a spot on my shit list that he'd have to work damn hard to get off of.

"Yes, Agent Fraser. It is the East Coast seat of the Seelie Court," Moreau replied. "The court exists in the same space, but in a dimension next to ours, effectively keeping it hidden from humans."

Now *that* was cool. Note to self: Check out Belvedere again, and this time pay closer attention.

"It would reflect poorly on our skills to return fewer leprechauns than we were assigned to protect," he continued smoothly. "The best outcome of this evening's shenanigans is political embarrassment. The worst would be if Prince Finnegan or his friends are captured by agents of the Unseelie Court. Leprechauns are the bankers of the Seelie Court. It could give those agents the means to send the economy of the supernatural world into a downward spiral should they gain access to the gold stores; but the security of those potential wishes is our paramount concern. The prince would have no choice but to grant his captor three wishes. And coming from a leprechaun prince, those wishes would carry world-altering power." He leveled a stare at the assembled agents. "It is critical that those wishes not be made or granted."

That explained a lot. I didn't think folks would be getting

so worked up if this was only about some leprechauns missing curfew.

"Specifically who can we expect to run into out there?" I asked.

Hand Crusher snorted, then grunted in pain as another agent kicked him under the table. Either I had a defender, or someone just didn't like bad manners. I'd take either one.

"Any number of things that call a lair—or the underside of a rock—home. But for something of this importance, our most likely opposition will be goblins."

Oh crap.

On the list of things your momma warned you about, goblins were in the same class as fast boys in faster trucks times a couple hundred. There were some things humans didn't stand a snowball's chance in hell of resisting, and goblins lounged seductively at the top of the list.

"Photos of Prince Finnegan and his party—actual and glamours—are being e-mailed to your phones," the ogre continued. "There's not much chance of the boys running around town looking like the supporting cast from *Darby O'Gill and the Little People*, but you never know. His Highness and his companions were inebriated when they were picked up, and since drunk leprechauns don't make the best decisions, their behavior for the remainder of the evening is an unknown factor. You'll also receive a list of the clubs they wanted to go to, but if they want to throw us off, they won't stick to the list. Most of the clubs on the list have surveillance cameras, though not all, as we're not exactly dealing with high-class establishments."

An agent laughed. "Just find the club where the girls are getting gold pieces instead of dollars."

"They had us run by an ATM," one of the original team muttered. "They've got cash."

Laughs were joined by snorts. I couldn't help it; I joined in.

"When a leprechaun goes out on the town or out of town, they have a bottomless money bag tied to their belts," the ogre explained. "This pouch goes straight to their personal pot of gold."

"Add muggers to the list," Ian said.

"Then that mugger would be getting back fewer fingers

than they went in with. Gold's not all that's lurking at the bottom of those bags. Flash the photos around to bouncers and bartenders. Five leprechauns on the town will definitely be making use of the bars wherever they go. Thankfully, there's one thing we know for sure—they'll be sticking together. Find one, and you'll find them all."

"Has the queen been told that they're missing?" I asked.

"Not until this agency has expended every resource available to us to locate and apprehend them. As our seer, you are our best—and potentially last—resource."

I caught a glimpse of yet another smirk from Hand Crusher. Someone wanted me to screw up even worse than he already had. Too bad I wasn't close enough to kick him myself, or I'd have taken a shot.

"We thought the agents assigned to the bodyguard duty would be more than adequate for the task." Moreau's eyes narrowed at Hand Crusher. Busted. "We were wrong. We underestimated our charges' craftiness—as well as our agents' discipline. I, as well as Madame Sagadraco, am disappointed in how the situation was allowed to deteriorate." His cold eyes lingered over the first team of agents. "Neither she nor I wish to experience that disappointment again."

Silence. The scared kind. I joined in. The first team had failed their test. Mine was just beginning.

This was the kind of assignment no corporate newbie wanted to get on their first night on the job. A race against goblin agents of the Unseelie Court while we hit New York's strip joints, and me with a partner who considered the assignment as glorified babysitting, searching for a pack of horny, shapeshifting leprechauns looking to get lucky.

A group of us took the elevator down to SPI's parking garage in silence. Moments later, a pair of steel doors slid apart in a whisper of air, opening into one of the city's many abandoned subway tunnels. In this particular tunnel, the tracks had been removed, and the ground smoothed and paved into a parking garage. Beyond, what looked like a perfectly normal street—except it was more than five stories underground—stretched into the distance; I'd seen it once on my orientation tour of the complex.

A shadow suddenly loomed in—and over—my peripheral vision.

"This is Yasha Kazakov," Ian said from beside me. "He'll be our driver and backup."

I turned in the direction Ian indicated, extended my hand, and froze.

Yasha Kazakov was a werewolf.

At least that was the aura my seer vision showed me.

Though, believe it or not, that wasn't why I was staring. I'd seen werewolves before; I'd just never seen one carrying a massive .45 in a shoulder rig, and wearing fatigues and a T-shirt that read: "Don't run, you'll only die tired."

And if that wasn't enough—and it was plenty—he was big, somewhere between six foot seven and Sasquatch. His hair was brown trying real hard to be red. Add the werewolf aura my seer vision showed me, and Yasha Kazakov was well over seven foot tall.

"In a city where there are more supernatural perps than parking spaces, having a reliable drop-off and pick-up guy's a must-have," Ian told me. "And there's no one better at turning a rampaging monster into a hood ornament."

The Russian stuck out a paw that promptly engulfed mine. "I am Yasha." His accent was almost as thick as his chest. His grip was human firm, not werewolf crushing. I was glad he'd learned to ease up before he got ahold of me.

"Makenna," I managed, my voice sounding almost as small as I felt. "Call me Mac."

The Russian gave a quick nod and a smile, and gave me my hand back with everything intact. "Mac." He looked at Ian and the smile broadened into a grin on the verge of becoming a laugh. "Which den of sin do we visit first?"

"We'll assume the leprechauns didn't go back to the club they vanished from. Regardless, the first team will stake that one out."

Yasha gave a single, booming laugh. "This time they can watch, yes?"

One of the elven agents gave Ian a wave as he, the second elf agent, and the human female agent who'd given Hand Crusher a hard time, got into one of the sedans.

"Mike, Steve, and Elana will be teaming with us," Ian told

me. "Mike knows our contacts in the clubs and can talk his way into or out of anything. Steve has enough mage skill to convince anyone that anything they saw has a perfectly normal—and non-supernatural—explanation. Comes in handy when things get too strange for civilians."

"And Elana?" I asked.

"When there are dark alleys that need investigating, she goes in first."

"Preternatural night vision?"

Ian shook his head. "Just mean."

"And I am the extractor," Yasha told me. "There is trouble, I am called."

I gave a couple of slow nods. "I can see that. Why have an entire extraction team when you really only need one?"

WE took the biggest SUV in SPI's fleet. With the huge Russian werewolf as our driver, it wasn't like we had a choice.

Yasha drove the Suburban in silence down the subterranean "street," and after about half a mile, he flipped open a panel on the dash, pushed a button inside, and a section of wall opened to our right that was just large enough to hold the SUV. Yasha pulled in, stopped, and turned off the engine. The doors closed behind us, and Yasha pressed a second button. Almost immediately, the car began to rise; the only sound the low rumble of some serious hydraulics hidden under us. The elevator stopped with a disconcerting jerk, and a pair of doors in front of us opened, revealing another parking garage.

There couldn't have been more than a few inches of clearance between the top of the Suburban and the concrete slab above it. I didn't have claustrophobia; I just didn't like the thought of heavy things squashing me, and concrete slabs certainly qualified. Yasha drove the SUV upward through the parking deck in nearly nauseating spirals until we exited the garage on a familiar section of West Third Street, a block from Washington Square Park.

Ian Byrne took a case out of his jacket pocket and handed it to me. "You'll need these."

I opened it. Inside were sunglasses, really cool and expensive sunglasses.

"These clubs will be dark," Ian began.

I grinned. "It's dark and I'm wearing sunglasses."

My stoic partner didn't get *The Blues Brothers* reference; or if he did, he wasn't amused.

"They're not sunglasses," he said. "Put them on."

I did. Suddenly I could see every detail inside and out of the Suburban as if it were broad daylight instead of o'dark thirty. "Nifty."

"Does your seer vision work with the glasses?" Ian asked.

I glanced up front at Yasha. His werewolf aura was hunched to fit in the big SUV. "Like a charm."

"Good. You'll be wearing those in the clubs."

"Gladly."

My partner gave me a quizzical glance.

"If strange men are going to see me in a strip joint, at least they won't get to see me seeing them. And it'll make it easier for me to ignore them and anything they may be . . . doing. I can guarantee you I won't be looking at anything but leprechauns."

"You won't just be looking for leprechauns," Ian said. "Any agents of the Unseelie Court will be glamoured as well; unless they're using humans, in which case we're looking for suspicious behavior."

"There're behaviors that aren't suspicious in a strip club?"

Yasha snorted from the driver's seat. "*All* behavior is suspicious in hoochy-koochy parlors."

I sat up straighter and grinned. "That's what my grandma calls 'em."

"They're probably the same age," Ian muttered.

I considered that possibility. If they kept their snouts clean and didn't go on people-eating binges, werewolves could live a long time. I studied our werewolf driver/extractor. Yasha seemed to be nice. Though as with all werewolves, I imagined that changed during "that time of the month." Mood swings, cravings, anger, and irritability—trust me, you ain't seen cranky until you've seen a werewolf trying to force down their natural inclinations during a full moon. I knew better than to ask an older woman her age, but I didn't think a werewolf would mind; at least I didn't think this particular werewolf would.

"How old *are* you?"

"Next month, I am ninety-six." The big Russian grinned in the rearview mirror at Ian. "For surprise party you are planning, hoochy-koochy parlor will be fine, but make sure is good one."

"For the last time, I'm not planning a surprise party."

Yasha glanced over at me and winked. "Your new partner is very good at keeping secrets."

I slid my Go-Go-Gadget sunglasses up on my head. "That doesn't surprise me."

"How much do you know about leprechauns?" Ian asked.

"Just what they taught in orientation," I said. "What they are, where to find them, how to catch one—and to watch out for those wishes. Usually a supernatural doesn't use a human glamour unless they have a good reason. Are leprechauns up to no good, or do they interact with humans on a daily basis?"

"Yes."

"Pardon?"

"Yes, to both," Ian said. "Leprechauns typically work in the Financial District. They have a sixth sense about which way the market's going to go. If you can get a leprechaun as a financial advisor, your investments are guaranteed to thrive. Though you should always get their commission amount agreed to in writing sealed with a blood-pricked thumbprint, drawn up by a lawyer mage. Otherwise, your leprechaun money manager will skim off the top to top off his pot of gold. Some of the commodities companies that went belly up a few years ago due to creative accounting?"

"Yeah?"

"Because there were leprechauns high up in the companies. They're great at making money—but they're even better at lining their own pockets. Vivienne Sagadraco has used leprechauns in the past at Saga Investments, but got tired of having to watch their every move. She prefers to make her own investments with the help of a team of clairvoyants."

I nodded in approval. "Nice to know the boss doesn't take risks with our 401ks."

"Our leprechaun nobles shouldn't be difficult to spot, even using human glamours. It's a bachelor party of five guys. There can't be that many of them making the rounds tonight. And when we get them cornered, remember that leprechauns will promise *anything* to gain their freedom, and their loyalties are to themselves and that's it. To trust a leprechaun for an instant means you're either a fool or suicidal."

"Is like playing Russian roulette," Yasha said. "On the upside of playing with a gun, you only lose once."

"What if the prince and his boys decide to split up?" I asked.

"Then it's going to be a long night." Ian paused and looked away from me. "Go ahead," he said.

Then I realized he was on the phone. I'd never used those little Bluetooth earphone thingies, and I wasn't about to. They made you look like you were walking around talking to yourself. Though I could see where they'd come in handy in the monster hunting/supernatural sleuthing business. If I was being chased down by something with six legs and a hankering for people sushi, I know I'd want to be hands free.

"I am from Saint Petersburg." Yasha made no effort to keep his voice down or to stop Ian from hearing his caller. Apparently the Russian was more interested in talking to me than being considerate of Ian. It sounded like someone was miffed at potentially being stiffed for a surprise party. Since Yasha was our driver *and* backup, my partner might want to rethink that.

"I'm from a little town called Weird Sisters. It's in the far western point of North Carolina."

Yasha cocked an eyebrow. "Weird Sisters?"

"It was named after the three witches in *Macbeth,* and weird does describe most of the townfolk. It's on a ley line that magnifies psychic and paranormal energies. I don't know if there's anything to that or not, but something attracts people—and non-people—to stop and stay."

"Is your family people or not-people? My pardon, but I am not a seer, so I cannot tell if you wear glamour or not."

I smiled. "That's okay. Me and my family are plain vanilla human."

"Plain vanilla?"

"Just regular folks. A lot of my family are seers who've

gone into law enforcement. As long as anyone can remember, there's been a Fraser as marshal, then sheriff. Right now, my aunt Vicki's the police chief."

There's a hesitation in Ian's phone conversation. I couldn't hear anyone speaking on the other end of the line, so it was Ian who did the pausing. Then *"Sir, are you there?"* said a tinny voice on the other end.

"Yes, I'm here. I heard what you said," Ian told the caller. "First three clubs on the list have been eliminated."

My new, and apparently curious, partner had also heard every word I had said, too.

"When I was little, I wanted to be an investigative reporter for our local paper," I continued to Yasha, talking just a wee bit louder so my partner wouldn't have to work so hard to eavesdrop. "Protect the prey from the predators in my own way, without becoming a cop. But in a town with more than its fair share of actual psychics, unsolved crimes were gonna be few and far between." I shrugged. "So I decided it was time for me to leave for good."

"Little town in mountains sounds nice. Peaceful," Yasha said almost wistfully. "Why come here?"

I shrugged again. "I wanted to use my journalism degree but all I could get was a job at a seedy tabloid called the *Informer*. You heard of it?"

The Russian chuckled. "And not in a good way."

"That's the place. Only stories like 'Donald Trump is a werewolf lovechild' had any hope of making it to the front page. If a story was the truth, great; if not, lies worked just fine. Our readership was gullible as hell and thought everything we printed was the gospel truth anyway."

Yasha snorted in derision. "No werewolf would have hair like that. Would look foolish."

"Lucky for me, one of my stories put me in Ms. Sagadraco's sights. By that point, I'd take any job that'd let me regain some self-respect. When the HSR ladies called me with an offer, I couldn't resign fast enough."

Yeah, I'd traded the scent of mountain laurel for diesel fumes, and a ley line running under the mountains for a subway line running under the city, but New York had an energy all its own. The mountains had a heartbeat, a soul. Maybe it was the ley line, running under them, maybe it was something else.

I had the same feeling when I'd arrived in New York. It was alive. The city lived and breathed. It could also devour, but so far, it'd kept its fangs and appetite to itself. I hadn't been chewed up and spit out in the general direction of the Mason-Dixon Line, so I considered my move north to be a success.

THERE it was, glowing in all its purple-neon glory over a door that was intended to look like something you'd find at one of those medieval-themed places that served dry turkey legs and cheap beer in even cheaper plastic tankards.

Fairy Tails.

Oh Lord.

"Seriously?" I asked.

"I'm afraid so," Ian replied.

The bouncer was predictably huge and surprisingly human. He was also dressed like the Jolly Green Giant complete with a club that I hoped was as plastic as the tankards inside; though when he set it down to open the door for us, it made a disturbingly solid thud on the sidewalk.

Inside was even more kitschy, if that was possible.

Ian and I were arriving first, to be followed by Mike, Steve, and Elana in a few minutes. Ian said we didn't want to attract attention by arriving in a group. I had news for my partner—in this place, no one would have noticed.

Fairy Tails looked like the set of a low-budget fantasy movie. Really low. The walls had been painted—badly—to look like castle stone. And every few feet were "torches" made of yellow bulbs and those yellow/red/orange strips of parachute fabric cut to look like flames. There was an air source coming from somewhere that made the flames flap around like the arms of those inflatable tube people you see at used car dealerships. What I assumed was the VIP section had thrones for seating. And yes, behind the bar were the expected plastic tankards and goblets. And to top off the themed experience, the bartenders were Little Red Riding Hood and the Big, Bad Wolf. The guy in the wolf suit was plenty big, but there was nothing little about what was about to pop out the top of Red's red leather corset. Those couldn't possibly be real.

I had to say it. "Maybe you should bring Yasha here for his birthday. He and Red might hit it off."

My partner didn't dignify that with a response.

We were seated by Tinker Bell.

She was made up and dressed just like the Disney version, that is if Tink was about to shoot a porno with Peter Pan and the Lost Boys. I didn't think Pete and his boys would have been quite so lost if Tink had been flitting around in what the hostess was mostly not wearing.

Moments later, our Disney parade continued when Snow White showed up to take our drink order. Her getup was the familiar Disney version except the bodice was way lower, and the skirt cut so much higher as to be virtually nonexistent. I guarantee Snow would have had a whole different relationship with those seven dwarves if she'd been sashaying around their house in that.

I don't think Snow even realized I was there. Though it was obvious she had no trouble seeing Ian, and was making it abundantly clear that drinks weren't all she was offering. I told myself right then and there that if she offered him a lap dance, leprechauns on the lam be damned, I was out of there. Though I really couldn't blame her; most of the men in this place wouldn't have been called prized bulls on their best days.

Ian ordered a beer—thankfully without a side order of Snow.

Pursing her red lips in a disappointed pout, she turned to leave.

I cleared my throat loudly. "I'll have a Coke, please."

"Will that be diet?" Snow White asked sweetly.

"No." I forced myself to smile. "Thank you." Where was an evil queen and poison apple when you needed one?

Snow flounced off, and I closed my eyes and briefly pondered the insides of my eyelids. Maybe the caffeine would help my headache, and keep me from having to prop my eyes open with those little plastic swords Fairy Tails probably used to spear the olives in their martinis, though from the looks of their clientele, they didn't get many requests for those.

Snow brought our drinks, Ian's came in a faux pewter stein, and apparently Coke warranted a goblet. Though after baring her teeth in a smile frosty enough to give the Wicked Queen a run for her money, I decided to leave that Coke right where she put it. Caffeine was overrated, and if I needed help staying alert, I'd just pinch myself occasionally.

Mike, Steve, and Elana came in a few minutes later and were seated at the table nearest to ours, but even closer to the back exit. I guess if I saw our quarry, and one or more of them tried to make a break for it, our agents' job would be to cut off their escape.

While looking around the club for our wayward leprechauns in disguise, I couldn't help but notice that more than a few of the men in the club were looking at me. Maybe I was being overly sensitive, but it seemed to me like Elana and I were getting more attention wearing clothes than the women on the stage who were one step up from starkers. You'd think they'd never seen women before, at least not any with all of their clothes on. Either that or they liked the idea of women watching other women. Pervs.

I'd put on the super spy gadget sunglasses, so at least I wouldn't have to make eye contact with them. They'd probably think I was embarrassed that my date had brought me here. While my glare would have been worthless, with or without the shades, my partner's was in perfect working order. Men looked once, found themselves on the receiving end of Ian Byrne's I-will-kick-your-ass scowl, and hurriedly looked away to find more interesting things to occupy their attention.

"If you're concerned about your safety—" Ian began.

A man that bore a disturbing resemblance to a hundred-year-old Danny DeVito scurried back to his table counting out a handful of ones. I felt my lip curl. Either the bartenders made change, or Fairy Tails had its own ATM that spit out small bills.

"I'm more worried about the contents of my stomach," I told him.

Though what I could use more than a handful of Tums were earplugs. The music was so loud it felt like the fillings were being vibrated out of my teeth, and the flashing disco lights were either going to give me a seizure or the mother of all migraines.

After my first scan of the club came up empty for leprechauns, I made myself at least glance at the dancers. Why not? I was wearing sunglasses that weren't sunglasses, and could look without anyone, including my partner, seeing me watch. It was kind of daring and dangerous when I thought of it that way.

Cinderella had traded in her glass slippers for Lucite stripper heels, and her shoes weren't all that see-through. Though after less than a minute of watching her perform moves with a pole that I wouldn't have thought physically or gravitationally possible, I realized that I was a lot less embarrassed than I thought I'd be. I mean, let's face it, the dancers had all the same boobs and bits that I had, just more of the former and were more imaginative with the landscaping and decoration of the latter.

But mainly they all looked bored. Sleeping Beauty was dancing like she was still asleep, or wished she was. And Cinderella looked like she was thinking that midnight would never get here. Their lips might have been set on smile, but their eyes said their minds were elsewhere. Maybe sorting laundry—don't wash silver pasties with that hot pink G-string again. Or the bald guy drooling at the front table made one of them remember to pick up a honeydew melon at the store tomorrow.

They were the ones with their lady bits on display, not me. If they didn't care, why should I be embarrassed? Stripping was a job, just like any other, except strippers could write off waxing on their taxes. When I thought about it like that, none of this was really that big of a deal. Speaking of taxes, SPI must have a creative accounting department to be able to slip things like strip club cover charges past the IRS as a business expense.

Did Ian think about it in a similar way or was he just that disciplined? He hadn't gotten all that desk flair from letting anything affect his focus. Or maybe he simply preferred his women with factory-original parts rather than aftermarket enhancements. I took a quick glance down at my girls. As far as I could tell they weren't anything special to look at, but at least I'd rolled off the line with them.

I glanced back up to find Ian Byrne—the senior agent at my new employment—watching me checking myself out in a strip club.

Oh, sweet Jesus.

Ignoring him—and the shadow of a smile I detected and any thoughts that may have been going on behind it—I resumed doing my job, scanning the club for leprechauns. And rogue goblins.

I saw plenty of hootin' and hollerin' men, but what I didn't see where any horny leprechauns or greedy goblins, and I was frustrated by the former, and quite frankly relieved at the latter.

I leaned toward my partner. "You said we were gonna have goblins."

"They're the most likely competition." Ian's alertness increased by ten without his moving a muscle, including his lips. Impressive. "You see any?"

"No, but I've been wondering what we're gonna do if or when they do show up."

"Unless they're standing between us and a leprechaun, we'll just keep an eye on them. It's a free country, and unless they break the law, that's all we'll do."

"And if I see a goblin with a leprechaun?"

"We will encourage the goblin to mind his or her own business."

"And if their business happens to be catching a leprechaun?"

"We'll do whatever we have to do to stop it."

Fair enough.

Fairy Tails' seats left a lot to be desired in terms of comfort. I shifted in my seat to cross my legs—at least I tried.

And I froze in complete revulsion.

The bottoms of my shoes were stuck to the floor.

Ian must have seen my horrified expression even with the sunglasses, and his right hand instinctively moved toward his gun. "What is it?"

"My shoes are stuck to the floor." Each word was higher,

squeakier, and closer to panic than the one before. I couldn't help it.

"It's spilled beer," Ian hurried to assure me.

"Beer is sticky?"

"Beer could be . . . sticky." Ian reassured me in the same tone he'd use to talk someone off a ledge.

I wasn't having it. Panic was in the driver's seat and had taken the wheel. I felt tears welling up in my eyes. "It's not beer."

These shoes were going in the garbage as soon as I got home, if not before. Maybe I could convince Ian to add new shoes to his expense report. I loved these shoes. I'd spent more money than I should've on these shoes, but no amount of money was enough to pay me to keep them after tonight. And the bottle of hand sanitizer in my purse wasn't nearly enough to wash this place off the rest of me.

I took a deep breath and tried not to think of my shoes and . . . beer.

Focus on the job, Mac. The nice job. The one you really like.

But Disney porn princesses, ATMs next to the bathrooms, fake fire, plastic goblets, even more plastic riding high in Red's corset, and sticky floors from God only knows what. This wasn't worth insurance and a 401k. Nothing was worth this.

Focus, Mac.

I glanced at my watch. It was a little before midnight. We had to find, apprehend, and deliver five leprechauns before dawn. And buy new shoes. This was New York City. There had to be all-night shoe shops. I'll bet Elana knew.

Talk, Mac. Talking will help.

"You'd think that a leprechaun prince would have more . . ."

"Taste?" Ian finished for me.

"To say the least."

Ian looked around with a dismal sigh. "Hate to burst your bubble."

I wiggled my toes in my stuck shoes. "Oh, it's long gone."

I wasn't the only one who was less than comfortable here. Mike and Steve the elves were both staring at Cinderella and Sleeping Beauty in open-mouthed disbelief. Elana had an impressive facepalm going, and her shoulders were shaking with laughter.

At a two-beat lull in the pounding music, I heard Steve say, "Can you say copyright infringement?"

Mike nodded in agreement. "Walt's doing wheelies in his urn."

Elana's shoulders shook harder.

Ian put down his beer. "They're not going to show. There's something we're missing."

"Besides leprechauns—and new shoes?" I asked hopefully.

"Yes." He stood. "We're wasting time. Let's get out of here."

That was the best idea I'd heard all night.

I thought the next two clubs had to be better.

I was wrong.

And to make it even worse, I was running out of hand sanitizer.

Three sleazy strip joints. Three strikes. Same shoes.

Unfortunately, three strikes didn't mean we were out by any stretch of the imagination, or that we could call it a night. Our night didn't end until we found those leprechauns.

Ian had been talking on his Bluetooth, checking in with the other two teams. Not only were we running out of viable clubs to check, we were running out of night. The prince and his bachelor party were due home by dawn, and we weren't any closer to getting the job done.

"Anybody else get lucky?" I asked, completely over any and all embarrassment I might have had letting a double entendre slip.

A larger problem for me than the lack of leprechauns in any of the first three clubs was the lack of a usable ladies' room in any of them. I'd assumed they all had ladies' rooms; it's just that Satan would be serving sno-cones in Hell before I would've set foot in any of them. Even the time-honored squat 'n' hover method wasn't an option. If the floors in the clubs were sticky, I didn't even want to think about what the bathrooms looked like. And I really needed a clean bathroom right now. I'd been fairly certain our waitresses in the next two clubs hadn't been trying to poison me, so I'd had more Coke than my bladder could comfortably hold. Not to mention, if Yasha hit one more pothole, I was liable to let out a burp that'd ring his windshield, right before I'd wet my pants.

"Aren't leprechauns in the Seelie Court?" I asked Ian, trying to keep my mind off the impending rupture of my bladder. "And isn't the Seelie Court the good guys?"

"When it comes to the fairy courts, there aren't good guys and bad guys," he told me. "There's just entirely too many what's-in-it-for-me guys—and gals. All goblins and Unseelie aren't evil, and all elves and Seelie aren't good. There's a whole lot of gray out there, more than black and white combined."

"If the leprechauns know they're in danger, why don't they turn themselves in?"

"Because leprechauns are adrenaline junkies."

"So they like being in danger?"

"Like it and will seek it out." Ian stopped and spat a whispered curse.

"What is it?"

"Yasha, take us to Bacchanalia."

The Russian werewolf shot Ian a sharp look in the rearview mirror. "Daredevil is one thing; suicide is another."

"That's where they've gone. And if they've been there long, we're too late. Get us there and don't spare the horses."

Tires screeched, and I was glad I was wearing my seat belt. As it was, it damned near strangled me as Yasha Kazakov spun the Suburban in a U-turn in the middle of a thankfully empty Seventh Avenue.

Ian keyed his comms. "Steve, we're going to Bacchanalia."

Silence.

"Do you read?"

A sigh from one, a "Dammit" from the other, and a heartfelt "Shit" from Elana.

Well, that made it unanimous.

"What's Bacchanalia?" I asked.

Ian answered me. Yasha was too busy trying to get us killed. "If Prince Finnegan knew he had one night on the town, he'd want to make it count and go to the most dangerous club he knew of—one owned by and crawling with goblins. He'd think that since he and his buddies would be glamoured that they'd be safe."

"Wouldn't they? Goblins can't see through glamours."

"No, they can't. So Finn would think he'd be able to live dangerously without paying the consequences."

"And . . . he would be wrong?"

"He couldn't be more wrong. Rake Danescu owns that club. He's a goblin, a dark mage, and while he can't see through glamours, he'd know when they were being used."

The depth of the leprechauns' stupidity started to dawn on me. "And the goblins know that there are five glamoured leprechauns out looking for a good time."

Ian nodded. "Rake Danescu would know exactly who they were the moment five creatures glamoured as human males set foot in his place." His mouth set in a hard line. "That little bastard Finn was going there all along. Everything he did tonight was just to throw us off."

"How's that?"

"Bacchanalia is on the other side of town from all the clubs on the list he gave us. All the clubs on the list are—"

"Sticky."

"To put it mildly. Bacchanalia is not. It's upscale and very exclusive."

"If it's that exclusive, how are we getting in?"

"My undercover alter ego has a membership."

Of course he does.

I knew how dangerous goblins could be, but that didn't stop me from giving a little silent cheer. I bet Bacchanalia had fabulous bathrooms.

Ian paused uncomfortably. "I should probably warn you that Bacchanalia isn't a strip club."

My inside voice stopped cheering. "That sounds like a good thing, but if you feel the need to warn me, then it's not." I frowned. "I thought you said it was upscale."

"It is. Bacchanalia caters to men *and* women, and bills itself as a complete adult entertainment experience."

"Complete?"

"Experience. With an emphasis on experience. People don't go to Bacchanalia simply to watch—they go to participate." He hesitated. "And the five of us will go in together. Three men and two women going to Bacchanalia isn't suspicious at all."

"Do you mean . . . ?" I made vaguely suggestive hand gestures.

"Oh yeah. It's a sex club."

And the allure vanished from my dreams of a clean bathroom.

BACCHANALIA was located in what looked like merely one brick-fronted nightclub in the city. A pair of hobgoblins, glamoured as unnecessarily huge humans, stood guard on either side of a plain door.

Ian's hand clamped down on my arm, his lips close to my ear. "Mac, this is one of the most dangerous places for humans in the entire city. Don't let your guard down for one moment. The faster you find those leprechauns, the quicker we can leave. Focus and do your job."

I swallowed and nodded.

Once inside, we had to pause to allow our eyes to adjust to the dark. My glasses had been sitting on my head. I put them on my eyes where they belonged.

Everything in Bacchanalia was black. The floor was marble, the walls black glass, and the ceiling appeared as a star-strewn night sky, far away from the lights of any city. It had to be at least two-stories high. There were constellations, stars, and even the gossamer expanse that was the Milky Way. I hadn't seen a sky this awe-inspiringly beautiful since I'd left home.

"Incredible," I breathed.

"Focus, Mac," Ian rumbled next to my ear.

Fairy Tails had a VIP section of cheap theater prop thrones. Bacchanalia had dimly lit, gauzy-curtained alcoves. Thanks to my magical mystery glasses, I could see way too clearly what was going on inside.

The only color came from the unbelievably beautiful men and women who worked there.

Inhumanly beautiful, I reminded myself.

"It's perfectly fine to stare," Ian told me. "That's your job, look around and don't miss a thing. It's your first time here, staring is expected. It's important that we do the expected. We do not want the management of this place to know who we are and what we're looking for. If they even suspect there are leprechauns here and that our goal is to get them out . . . they are able to make leaving more of a challenge than we want."

We were seated by a fairy, a female with wings as ethereal and sheer as the gown she wore. In contrast, the body clearly visible beneath . . . well, lush was the only word to describe it. The fairy might have been five foot tall, but height was difficult to judge with her hovering at least a foot from the floor, her pale and perfect face even with Ian's. She smiled in a gleam of teeth set like tiny pearls against full lips of rich pink, her violet eyes taking in Ian like the long, tall drink of water that he was. I had to agree with her. My partner was one fine-looking man.

"Mr. Phillips, it is truly a pleasure to see you again."

Then she turned those all-consuming eyes on me, and for a few pounding heartbeats, I forgot what team I batted for. And she was just the welcoming committee. Ian was right, this place was dangerous.

She showed us to a table with chairs that didn't make me feel any more secure. They were low, leather-covered stools, more of a tuffet really, with no sides or back. Anyone or anything could sneak up on me from any direction. It would also spin in a complete circle, allowing me to watch anything going on anywhere in the club. It was then I noticed that there wasn't really a stage to speak of, more like slightly raised platforms. Then it hit me—the place was like a freakin' karaoke bar, but with sex instead of bad '80s power ballads.

"All the world's a stage," Ian murmured, confirming my suspicions. "And all the men and women merely players."

I wouldn't have pegged him for a Shakespeare fan, but being impressed about it took a backseat to what I knew he meant. All of Bacchanalia was a stage, and anyone who walked in here was considered a player—and was fair game to be played or played with.

Like hell.

Any Miss or Mister Muffet—or in this place, they'd probably be called Mistress or Master Muffet—who even thought about taking me off my tuffet would pay dearly.

"What would be your pleasure this evening?" said a cool, silken voice from right behind me.

I squeaked and turned to find myself face to . . . whoa . . . with a blond god wearing a dazzling smile. That was all. The last thing I needed was more to drink, but my tongue was presently plastered to the roof of my mouth. Either that, or dry from it hanging to my knees. Blonds weren't usually my type. I was more of a brunette kind of girl, my tastes leaning hot and heavy to the tall, dark, and slightly naughty side of fun. I didn't know if it was the natural glow of his skin, or if he was actually shimmering.

"The lady will have a glass of white wine," said Ian's voice from behind me. I managed a series of mute little nods.

The waiter left as silently as he had appeared. It took every bit of control I had not to swivel around on my plush leather tuffet to see if he looked just as pretty walking away as he had standing still.

I frowned. My tuffet wouldn't turn. Ian's hand was on the leather seat next to my thigh, keeping me right where I was.

"Not. A. Leprechaun," he told me.

I whistled. "You can say that again."

"I'd rather not have to."

I snapped out of it, embarrassed. "Sorry about that."

"That's okay. It's understandable." He didn't sound happy about it. "Every creature working here was hired specifically for their abilities to bewitch and seduce humans."

Once big, buff, and blond was out of sight, he was also out of mind. And a fog lifted.

I sat up ramrod straight, my skin suddenly cold and clammy with fear that I'd been swept under that easily—and that was just from the waitstaff—and that it could happen again at any time. Then I remembered what he'd ordered for me.

"Wait a minute; why did you order white wi—"

"Bacchanalia is known for their wines. And you won't be drinking it."

"Oh, if that's the—" I stopped. "Wait, why won't I be drinking?"

"Anything served here is—or could be—drugged." Ian was speaking without moving his lips as his eyes gazed around the room with what appeared to anyone watching to be lazy appreciation. I hadn't known Ian Byrne for more than a few hours and I knew I was seeing an act, and a very convincing one it was.

"I take it Mr. Phillips is doing a little window shopping?"

"He is."

"Convincing."

"It has to be."

"Dark mages who can detect glamours?"

"And spies."

"And don't look kindly on either one."

Ian's single nod was barely detectable.

The glass tables were softly lit from beneath, providing just enough illumination to find your drink. Our drinks had been served and I hadn't seen anyone approach, and if our Adonis waiter was any indication of Bacchanalia's waitstaff—and the bounty presently on view everywhere in the club told me that he was—I would have noticed.

"Magic?" I asked Ian.

He nodded. "Pixies. Tiny and fast."

The table's soft glow sent shimmers of gold up through the delicate stem of the glass and into the wine. Pretty. And highly tempting. I remembered Ian's warning and slid my hands under my thighs, to keep them from reaching for anything gold and shiny—either a possibly drugged drink or a definitely intoxicating waiter.

I resumed scanning the club for leprechauns. "If they're here, how do we get them out?" I asked Ian, trying not to move my lips. "Do you have a plan?"

Being SPI's top agent meant you didn't walk into a goblin den without a plan, but being the control freak that I was, I wanted to know precisely what that plan was—and how it involved me.

When Ian didn't respond, I turned toward him and was hit with my partner's heated gaze.

My hand suddenly took on a life of its own and lowered my sunglasses. "Is the mostly naked hostess behind me?" I whispered.

"No." With that, Ian reached over and hauled me right off my tuffet, across his lap, and kissed me like he was diving for lost treasure.

I saw twinkly lights that didn't have a damned thing to do

with the star-strewn ceiling. Realizing I'd forgotten to breathe, I panicked and inhaled all the air in a ten-table radius through my nose.

"What the hell are you doing?"

"We're being watched," Ian held me tight, keeping me right where I was. "And listened to," he breathed against the curve of my ear.

If it'd been anyone else, I'd think he was taking advantage of the situation to get some on-the-job action. Ian must have been doing it to preserve his cover.

His lips were at my throat. "The mics have been turned on in our table."

Microphones in the tables? My karaoke analogy was closer than I'd thought.

Though the mic wasn't all that had just had its switch flipped. I'd just developed tingles in all of my favorite places. Apparently being borderline molested by a gorgeous, dangerously hot, monster-hunting secret agent was a huge turn-on for me. Who knew?

"We're being spied on?" I breathed against his earlobe, and felt him shiver in response. One point for me.

"A guest—or more than one—has apparently asked the management if you're available." His lips skimmed the side of my neck, up and down with maddening slowness. "They're trying to find out. I'm making it clear that you're with me. My job is to protect you. I'm doing my job."

And a damned fine job he was doing.

Air must have been in short supply again. I was starting to pant. "Protection? So that's what the kids are calling it now."

"As long as it's obvious you're with me, you're safe. That innocent librarian look of yours is attracting the wrong kind of attention. It's almost as hot to these people as a schoolgirl costume."

I was hot? I pulled back as much as I could, which with Ian's arms locked around me was about an inch.

"It's a challenge to every man in here." Ian's hand was sliding up my thigh, his breath hot against the hollow of my throat. "Like waving a red flag in front of a herd of bulls."

Ian Byrne was making me crazy. His lips and hands were doing more to short-circuit my brain than a baker's dozen of naked male fairies could hope to do on their best night. Either the man was one hell of an actor, or maybe he didn't mind being my partner as much as I thought.

My hormones didn't care one way or another; they stood up and cheered for the Peeping Tom who was spying on our table, whoever or whatever it was, and encouraged him to keep up the good work.

God, I loved my new job.

"Can you see them?" Ian murmured, his lips kissing their way south from my throat toward the first button on my blouse—a button that suddenly wasn't buttoned anymore.

"Uh . . . the bulls?"

Ian's mouth was making a run for the border and the hill country beyond. "Leprechauns."

If my brain and other places weren't sizzling like bacon in a skillet, I'd be able to tell him.

Ian's attention went to the bar. He swore. And worse, he stopped.

"What?"

He disengaged himself from me. "I'll be right back. Stay here."

"Where are you going?"

"I need to talk to our contact."

"I'm going with you."

"He's undercover, so am I, and you're not." He indicated Mike, Steve, and Elana's table and tuffets near ours. "Go. Stay. I'll be right back."

I grabbed my purse and scurried on over. "Psst, Elana."

"What?"

"Go to the bathroom with me."

"What?"

"I have to pee. Now. I'm not going anywhere by myself. Come with me."

Steve stood. "We're all going."

Huh? "Won't that look weird?"

The three of them just stared at me.

"Right." Weird was relative in a place where people were getting cozy in groups all over the place. "Come on, girls. Let's go."

We walked by Ian in a pack, and I mouthed "Bathroom." My partner gave me a curt nod.

That Bacchanalia had clean bathrooms was an understatement.

I could see myself even in the surfaces that weren't covered in mirrors. Mike and Steve stuck their heads in and determined that Elana and I would be the only people in here.

"We won't let anyone in," Steve assured me.

Mike glanced around nervously. "And hurry." Standing outside a bathroom in a goblin sex club was bound to make a pair of elves nervous. That made all of us.

Elana snorted. "I'll stay out here and protect your virtues," she told them.

There were five stalls, and they were huge, polished black marble, and even more mirrors. At least half a dozen people could fit in here. I ignored everything that implied and was even more motivated to take care of business in record time.

I lined the seat with more toilet paper than I knew was necessary, but considering where I was, who had probably been in here, and what he, she, or they could have been using this Stall Mahal for . . . a little paranoia equaled a whole lot of peace of mind.

Besides, it was quiet in here, and while my headache from the first club had stopped pounding in time with the music, the music was softer in here, and as a result, so was the pounding. I wondered how long I could stay in here without Ian or the others coming to look for me. Probably not nearly long enough.

I unzipped my pants and froze. If the tables were bugged, then what would they have done to a room where women got naked from the waist down? There could be a camera filming me right now and posting live to YouTube. Or what if stall number three in the Bacchanalia ladies room had its own channel on Perv-Per-View?

The door handle clicked on the stall next to mine. Holy shit, someone was in here. They must have been standing on the toilet when Steve had checked for me. I heard the click of a lighter, and two blinks later I smelled it.

I debated what to do. I had no problem with two guys sneaking off to smoke a little weed, and they obviously didn't care if I knew they were doing it or not, but it wouldn't be a good idea to come out of the ladies' room smelling like pot and sit down next to my new partner, a former NYPD detective who might still be looking for any excuse to get out of being my partner, even if it meant getting me fired from SPI.

I reached for the stall door, and the smoke really hit me.

It wasn't pot. I knew from prior experience that one whiff of pot would fling open the doors to the mother superior of all migraines.

Instead the pounding in my head stopped. Completely.

I was awake and alert.

And I felt good. Damned good.

Any hesitation I'd felt about confronting the midnight tokers vanished just as fast as my headache.

I flung open the door on the next stall.

And stared. I think my mouth fell open.

It was two tall, skinny white guys—one in jeans, the other in khakis, both in Polos—and both were glamoured leprechauns.

I've been told I should never play poker. I can't lie, and my emotions are all over my face.

The leprechauns instantly knew I knew.

I was in danger, my team was in danger, and the financial stability of the supernatural world's entire banking system was in danger—all because these leprechauns and their friends wanted to get high and get lucky.

Before I'd gotten a snootful of that smoke, I'd have yelled for help.

Now I just wanted to pound the crap out of them.

A human stare could capture them. I couldn't lock eyes with both of them at once, but there wasn't a rule that said I couldn't take them down the old-fashioned way.

They turned and scrambled for the door, but not before both of them blew smoke in my eyes, breaking my stare and burning my eyes.

Sons of bitches.

Half-blind, I launched myself toward the sound of scuffling loafers on tile, and grabbed a handful of whatever I could get—the belt of one, the waistband of the other. If they were gonna make a run for it, they'd have to drag me along with them.

I didn't think the leprechauns would want to draw attention to themselves.

I was wrong.

They started screaming for help like a pair of stoned banshees.

"Rape!" squealed the one with my fist death-gripped in the waist of his khakis.

Naturally, my Taser was in my purse hanging on the back of the stall door. What good was carrying the thing if I couldn't get to it?

The door slammed open, and Steve, Mike, and Elana charged in.

Khaki Guy was squirming like a greased pig, kicking at me until his shoes flew off. I heard the rasp of a zipper, and the next thing I knew I was left holding an empty pair of khakis. There was an "oof" and sounds of a scuffle. Once my eyes had stopped watering, though they still stung like hell, I squinted to see a pasty guy wearing only a yellow Polo, tighty-whities, and argyle socks trying to run, but mostly sliding, down the hallway with Steve and Mike in hot pursuit.

I groaned and squinted my eyes shut. I was never gonna be able to unsee that.

Steve tackled the half-naked leprechaun and I helpfully flung the khakis in his general direction. I was straddling Jeans Guy and doing my best to literally stare him into submission. Unfortunately he was the one screaming "Rape!" though at least he was still wearing his pants.

Elana was leaning against the open bathroom door teary-eyed from laughing.

A bouncer rounded the corner, took one look, and busted out laughing, but still managed to put out a hand, and snatch Tighty-Whitey Guy off his feet by the collar of his Polo.

"These the two you looking for?" he asked someone behind him.

Ian stepped into view, and didn't look the least bit surprised to see me. "These our boys?" he asked me.

I managed a nod, still gasping for smoke-free air. I hadn't found any yet.

Ian took a sniff, swore, and shook his head.

"It's not mine," I told him, keeping my eyes locked on the leprechaun.

"I know it's not."

"You do?"

"You're human. That's a recreational drug popular in the Seelie Court called clover weed. It wouldn't do you much good."

Now I was curious. "Why?"

Mike caught a whiff, blanched, and scuttled away fast.

"Sir, I—" he began to Ian.

"Get some air."

Mike fled. That was the only way to describe it.

"Steve," Ian asked, "How much did you get?"

"Not enough. I'm fine, sir."

Ian paused, not looking convinced, then muttered another curse. He keyed his comms: "Yasha, we've apprehended two of our leprechauns. More than likely the other three are in here somewhere. I need secure transport back to a holding cell at HQ." Ian paused. "And I need additional agents. *Human* agents. Steve and Mike may have been compromised." He paused for a moment, probably listening to Yasha. "Clover weed."

Yasha's booming laugh came over all of our headsets.

I wanted to see Ian's reaction, but if I looked away from Jeans Guy before we got him cuffed, in a blink he'd turn back to his leprechaun form and squirm his way into an air duct or something.

I'd only met Yasha a few hours ago, but it was long enough to know we had the same sense of humor. If the Russian werewolf nearly busted a gut laughing because of that clover weed stuff and it "compromising" Steve and Mike, then chances were good I'd get a chuckle out of it, too.

I was straddling and staring down a scrawny guy in the ladies' room of a sex club. I deserved a laugh.

"Uh. . . I'd rather not sit here all night," I told Ian. "Especially not *here* here. Can we get this guy cuffed?"

Ian grappled Jeans Guy into a pair of glowing green handcuffs.

The instant I "dismounted" and took my eyes off of his, the leprechaun reverted to his true form—and the cuffs shrank right along with him.

That didn't go over well.

The leprechaun's face twisted in rage, his green eyes went huge, and he started shrieking again, though this time it was in a language I'd never heard before, but I didn't need to know what it was to know that it was what the old-timers back home called language you didn't use around the womenfolk.

"Guard that entry," Ian told the bouncer. "No one gets in or knows we nabbed these two. And when transport gets here, we'll take these two out the back. Don't want to spook the other three if they're here."

The bouncer nodded. Looked like he worked for SPI, too.

Ian helped me to my feet. "Let's get you out front. Two down, three to go."

I about said the hunting's better in the bathroom. My headache was gone and I really didn't want it coming back.

AMAZINGLY enough, no one out in the club had seen or heard either me or the leprechauns. Maybe the music had covered the noise we'd made, and people were, um . . . focused on their own activities. The leprechauns probably could have set off a bomb in here and no one would have noticed.

The whiff of whatever I'd gotten in the ladies' room had definitely taken a big chunk out of any embarrassment I may have had left. Tonight had been my first time in a big-city club of any kind, let alone a strip or sex club. I had questions, was intensely curious, and between the clover weed and my partner's hands all over me less than a half hour before, I wasn't the least bit shy anymore about asking those questions. The little voice in my head was frantically waving for me to stop. I kicked the door shut on my little voice. Party pooper.

I half turned on my tuffet toward Ian, my right leg crossing over my left, also toward Ian. My little voice was banging on the door and screaming at me.

"Are people listening with our table anymore?" I whispered.

Ian glanced at the glowing surface. "No."

"Good. So, what is it with men and titty bars?"

Ian was only pretending to take a sip of his wine, but that didn't stop him from nearly choking. "Pardon?"

"Titty bars, or as Grandma and Yasha call 'em, hoochy-koochy parlors. You're a man, and don't think I haven't noticed," I added in a singsong voice. "And we're in a titty bar." I glanced around with even more appreciation at the scenery. "Among other nice things. If you weren't here to

hunt and hog-tie some leprechauns, why would you be here?"
I lowered my voice conspiratorially. "Come on, you can tell
me. We're partners." My voice of reason was banging on the
door in my head and screaming for me to Shut. Up.

Ian's eyes were intent on mine. Lord, but they were nice.
He was looking at something.

"What?" I swiped my tongue over my teeth. "Do I have
lipstick on my teeth?"

"No. Your pupils are enormous. Did you inhale some of
that blue smoke?"

I shrugged, the movement only made the room do a half
spin. "I've never inhaled." I gave him a goofy grin. "But a
girl's gotta breathe."

"Mac."

"They blew it in my face, okay?"

"I thought so." He took out his phone. "Can you still
function?"

I looked him up and down with a lazy, appreciative smile.
"I'm functioning just fine, darlin'." The little voice groaned
and gave up. Good. She was giving me another headache.

"I meant can you do your job?"

I had to think about that one. After pondering for a pleas-
antly dazed moment what my job was, and why I was doing it
here, the blue-smoked brain fog parted ever so briefly.

"Do you mean whether I can still see little green men?"

"That's right. Can you?"

I looked around. "Dunno. There ain't none to be seen
right now."

Ian swore under his breath and dropped his head into his
hand. "See Steve over at his table?"

"You mean Steve the elf?"

"Yes. Steve the elf. But can you *see* that he's an elf?"

"Yeah. Pointy Spock ears, clear as day."

Ian sighed in relief and put his phone away.

I didn't mention that every bit of stress had floated out of
my body. New job nerves? Gone. Awkwardness being in a sex
club with my hot new partner? Buh-bye. Giving a damn what
any man, woman, or combination thereof around me was
doing? Vamoosied.

Suddenly my partner wasn't the only badass at the table. I

was starting to feel downright invincible. I felt the urge to pull a couple of tuffets together and make myself comfortable, maybe even put my feet up on the bugged-for-sound table and really give whoever was listening to us one hell of a show.

Oh yes, I felt *much* better. And I felt myself smile, which was pretty danged impressive considering that I couldn't feel my lips anymore. Then the room spun in a slow, languorous circle.

Ian took a good look in my eyes and sighed in resignation. "Dammit, the boss didn't tell me you were part elf."

"I'm not."

"Are you feeling good?"

"Quite."

"Confident?"

"You know it."

"Absurdly relaxed to the point of doing something stupid?"

I scooted my tuffet toward my delectable partner. If Ian wanted to ensure every man here knew I was taken, I was more than willing to help spread the word. "Why don't you come over here and try me."

"If you're not an elf, clover weed shouldn't affect you, but it does. We'll deal with the why later. Right now, we need to find those other three leprechauns and get you the hell out of here."

"You're no fun."

"I never said I was."

Elana was nowhere to be seen.

"Where's Elana?" I asked.

"With Yasha and our prisoners waiting for transport from HQ."

The next dancer was slinking her way over to Mike and Steve's table. She was acting awfully friendly, and I think the boys were about to become part of the next show.

"Shit," Ian hissed in a whisper.

Their replacements hadn't arrived yet, and Ian had wanted them to just sit at their table, mind their own business, and stay out of trouble until their replacements arrived. Let's just say that due to the influence of the clover weed, the boys were getting into the spirit of the performance. Since our table was right up front, I got an all-too-close look at—and scent of— what covered Miss Congeniality's costume.

I gaped in disbelief, then giggled. "Are those Red Hots?"

Ian started to get up. I grabbed his arm and sank my nails in, my eyes wide.

Oh. My. God.

Miss Red Hots was none other than our AWOL leprechaun prince.

If I'd ever needed proof that leprechauns liked practical jokes, the proof was staring Steve right in the face—or at least his . . . uh, *her* Red Hots-spangled G-string was. She'd already tossed her top on Mike's head, and both elves looked like they were about to indulge their collective sweet tooth.

Prince Finnegan was a sex-shifting, cross-dressing leprechaun.

Well, they'd said back at headquarters that as far as shapeshifting went, leprechauns could go either way. Prince/Princess Finn looked like he was ready to go all the way.

If I hadn't now seen it all, there wasn't a damned thing left to look at.

I snuggled down beneath Ian's arm like a woman on a date with a hot guy in an even hotter club. In addition to being fun, it also gave me cover to speak.

"Found him. Our little prince is playing with fire—or at least spicy-hot candy."

Ian stiffened in realization next to me, and not in the fun way.

"You got it," I told him. "That ain't no woman."

Ian's only movement was an imperceptible upward twitch of his lip before his poker face smoothly slipped back into place. "Stare at him. When he looks at you—and he will—we've got him."

"Can't you make eye contact and get him?"

"I can't see his true form. You can."

Made sense.

"Think he knows who they are?" I asked.

"I think the probability is high. He . . . she came out from the back and made a beeline straight for them. I don't think it's a coincidence."

"Get the guys going and then change back into a leprechaun?"

Ian nodded once. "That's what I'm thinking. He's already

humiliated five SPI agents tonight. I think he's looking to add to his score—"

I snorted with laughter. "In more ways than one."

Ian ignored me. "He's also after the danger rush of turning into a leprechaun in the middle of a goblin sex club."

"And after that?"

"He'll run like hell, and I predict he'll go out the way he came in." My partner inclined his head toward the rear of the stage area.

"What are we going to do?"

Ian slowly set his drink down. "I'm going to grab and cuff the little bastard."

"And run like hell."

"Considering where we are, that would be the prudent course of action."

"I'm right behind you, partner."

I hadn't known anything about leprechaun sexuality, and I'd already learned more than I ever wanted. Ask the average person on the street to describe a leprechaun, and you'd get the little green-coated guy on the Lucky Charms box. Come to think of it, I'd never even heard of female leprechauns; but since Finnegan here was getting married tomorrow, and leprechauns had yet to become extinct, I assumed there were at least two sexes. And from what I was watching, there might be more than that.

Though from the lascivious grin Finn was wearing—with little else—you had to wonder if leprechauns had a loose interpretation of gender, or if the future princess knew what she was getting into. Even if Mike had been a seer, the prince didn't have to worry about being captured by his gaze. Mike's dazed eyes hadn't wandered north of her boobs the entire time. And at the moment, Steve's drug-addled peepers were locked and loaded on the top of Finn's G-string.

I had my eyes on Finnegan's face, but it figured that the leprechaun only had eyes for Mike and Steve and their imminent humiliation.

Mild-mannered human financial advisor or lecherous leprechaun? Which one was Finnegan gonna change back into? Ian was right. If Finnegan was going for maximum fun and thrills, he'd go leprechaun.

Prince Finnegan dropped his glamour right along with his Red Hot–covered G-string, leaving the boys ogling a three-foot-tall, naked-as-the-day-he-was-born leprechaun. Quick as a drink-delivering pixie, Finn grabbed Mike by the ears and kissed him smack-dab on the lips.

Without making eye contact with any of us. Crafty little bastard.

Then all hell broke loose.

Mike was too stunned to grab him. Ian made the dive—and the catch. Finnegan caught Ian in the forehead with the heel of one tiny foot. Unfortunately, all the bouncers manning the stage area saw was Ian's dive—and a now missing adult entertainer.

Oh crap.

Finn was unveiled and looked precisely like what he was. A leprechaun. SPI's primary mission was to keep the presence of supernaturals a secret from the general population, including overly large and testosterone-laden bouncers charged with the safety of Bacchanalia employees, especially from grabby customers.

Ian had yanked Finn off the stage and out of sight, but when Ian hit the floor, he was on top of an overly endowed dancer wearing nothing but a vindictive smile. Two bouncers grabbed Ian. Finnegan squealed, giggled, and hightailed it toward the dressing rooms, not stumbling once in the only things she was still wearing. A pair of platform, six-inch heels.

I had a moment of open-mouthed amazement. Where the hell did a leprechaun learn to run in stripper heels?

Ian might have thought of himself as my babysitter, but dammit, the boss had told me he was my partner. Partners backed each other up.

The bouncers were easily double my weight, and while I had a Taser in my purse, I'd only have one chance to use it on one of them. The other no-necks running toward the melee weren't going to stand by and tap their toes while it recharged.

Right now, the bouncers thought they had the troublemakers. The four shelves of desk flair back at the office told me that Ian could take care of himself, and if he needed help, Yasha and Elana were a hell of a lot more qualified to give it than I was. With a werewolf's hearing, he was probably already in the building. That problem was taken care of. Finn had vanished behind a curtain, presumably leading to dressing rooms. Even an exhibitionist like Finn was unlikely to run outside while starkers. He'd have to slow down to grab something.

I'd have to catch Finn myself.

The bouncers, if they'd even noticed me at all, didn't see me as any kind of a threat. And hopefully, between the liquor and the lights, any customer who saw Finnegan the naked leprechaun would talk themselves into believing they'd either had one or five drinks too many, or set up an appointment with their shrink to talk about what it meant to hallucinate a naked leprechaun in a sex club. I was sure it couldn't have been the first time a naked man had run through Bacchanalia.

I pulled back the curtain and stopped.

Talk about a needle in a haystack.

Either the staff of Bacchanalia was seriously disorganized, or a tornado had just come through here. From what little the boys and girls out front had been wearing, you'd think there couldn't be so many costumes strewn about.

Sparklies and spangles the likes of which I'd never seen in my life.

There wasn't a leprechaun to be seen—though when you're only three foot tall, hiding wouldn't be difficult in this mess.

This was a dressing room in an exclusive sex club on a Friday night. When the fight started out front, any staff still in here must have run out the back. Considering that there might be a naked leprechaun hiding among the sequins and bugle beads, they'd made the right choice.

A naked leprechaun was many things, but scary wasn't one of them.

But the man standing across the room from me was.

He wore a dark suit so well tailored it made Alain Moreau look like he shopped off the rack, with a long jacket that was more like a form-fitting frock coat.

He looked human.

But he wasn't. No human male looked that perfect.

For one, a human couldn't look that good on their best day. But mainly, it was the way he glided toward me so smoothly it was like he wasn't using his feet that clued me in.

My seer vision showed me what he really was.

A goblin.

A goblin who dropped his glamour completely as he slowly came toward me.

In a word—wow.

Goblins were mainly nocturnal. They could be out during the day, but their dark eyes were painfully sensitive to sunlight. Goblins were tall, sleek, and sexy. Combine that with darkly seductive—and light-sensitive—eyes and you had a race that took sunglasses to the heights of high fashion. Goblins were gorgeous all by their lonesome, but they took their wardrobes and accessories just as seriously as their tangled court politics. Goblin politics was a full-contact—and often fatal—sport chock-full of seduction, deception, and betrayal.

Goblin hair was dark, often worn long, and the silkiness of it would make a Pantene shampoo model kill from jealousy. Their skin was pale gray, with a silvery sheen, their eyes dark, their ears upswept to a nibbleable point.

And they sported a pair of fangs that weren't for decorative use only.

With supernaturals that had a tendency to prey on humans, I'd been taught how to act from a young age should I find myself in the presence of one. It all boiled down to one absolute rule—don't act like prey. But faced with what was quite possibly the hottest creature I'd ever seen in my life, and under the influence of a drug that had essentially evaporated my inhibitions, I suddenly found that rule increasingly difficult to follow.

"Vivienne's new seer." The goblin's voice was a whispered breath against my throat even from several feet away.

So much for being undercover.

"Uh . . . you have me at a disadvantage—"

A slow smile spread across the goblin's unwholesomely handsome face. "But at least I have you."

As he spoke, he came closer, and with a negligent flick of his long fingers, the door shut and locked behind me. Neat trick, said part of my brain; the other part was wondering what those fingers would feel like brushing against my throat, and was really hoping I'd get to find out.

"We fulfill fantasies here," he all but purred. "What is yours, little seer? If you had the chance to gain your heart's desire, what would it be?" He smiled, giving me a glimpse of fang. "And don't say finding a certain leprechaun prince. I know that is far from what you truly want." He gave me a dangerous, knowing smile, like he'd seen every dirty thought I'd ever had, flipped through them like a deck of cards, and set aside the ones he wanted us to try first.

"Sounds like we're looking for the same guy." I held my shaking hand out at hip height. "About this tall, red hair, green coat—unless he's still naked. Turn-ons are amateur-night exotic dancing. Turnoffs include SPI bodyguards and goblin stalkers."

I tried to take a step back, but my feet had other ideas. The goblin was now within arms' reach. His. He noticed me noticing, and his laugh warmed the air around me.

"I don't think he's here," I continued, "so I'll just be on my way."

The goblin's lips quirked in a smile. "But then you would miss my proposition."

Oh, I think I knew what he was proposing.

His easy smile stayed put, and I could *feel* his mind browsing through my thoughts. "I assure you, it's strictly business—at least initially. I would like it very much if you would come and work for me."

Eventually I managed to form words. "Is it the librarian outfit? Because I can assure you, no one wants to watch me strip."

"I am quite certain you have many talents where you would least expect them, but those are not the talents I am interested in." The goblin was directly in front of me, his face blocking the light—his eyes seemingly absorbing the rest. "We can save those for later exploration."

"And if I say no?" My voice sounded tiny.

"Then I will be forced to destroy you."

Just like that. Same silky, seductive voice—in one moment promising my deepest desires; and the next, my messy death.

"Isn't that a little melodramatic?"

"I assure you it is an accurate description of what would happen to your physical body should I do this." He did another negligent hand wave and vaporized a mannequin standing in the corner of the dressing room.

I swallowed. "You're right. Destroyed is a good word for that."

"Then you agree to my request." He didn't ask it as a question.

"How can I agree when you haven't told me what the job is?"

His fangs were showing, but it wasn't a smile. Like drawing a gun, he was simply showing me his weapons. And damned fine weapons they were.

"I require the same services you're presently employing on Vivienne's behalf."

"And if I refuse and you 'destroy' me, then no one gets my services and I get dead—which is my big concern as you can imagine."

"Then we are at an impasse," he murmured.

"I'm not going to help you find any leprechauns, if that's what you're getting at."

"I don't need your help finding the remaining three leprechauns. You have two in custody. The third is in this room with us; and the remaining two have panicked and are attempting to flee my place of business as I speak."

"Rake Danescu."

"You've heard of me."

"I've been told of you."

"No doubt by your new partner."

I ignored that. "If our quarry's flying the coop, looks like we're both out of luck."

"Oh, I don't believe so. My true quarry is right where I want her." His dark eyes glittered in the dim light. "Almost."

"I'm not your BOGO."

The goblin arched one flawless eyebrow.

"Buy one, get one free."

"What a charming concept." He smiled at me, showing me all of his teeth, including two alarmingly sharp fangs—all dazzling white. Looked like SPI wasn't the only supernatural organization with a good dental plan.

"I can feel the air quiver from his trembling—and yours." His black eyes gleamed as they scanned the room. I half expected a forked tongue to dart out from between his full lips and taste the air. His eyes narrowed and those lips slowly curled in a smile.

"And I can smell your fear—and arousal. Have you asked yourself why Vivienne assigned you to her most trusted agent?"

I tried to swallow with a bone-dry mouth. "To keep the newbie away from creatures like you?"

"Among many other reasons. There are things I can offer—things that you want—that Vivienne Sagadraco could never provide."

And one of them was getting entirely too close.

I swallowed hard. "Yeah, these days good insurance is hard to come by."

"When you are nearly immortal, you need not concern yourself with the injuries, sickness, and infirmities of age. Serve me well, and I could see to it that you are granted that gift."

"Package that and you'd put the insurance companies out of business." I was thinking fast, or trying to. Rake Danescu was getting closer, but my feet and—of more concern—the rest of me was making no effort to get farther away. In fact, parts of me were toying with open rebellion with my good sense.

"There are other benefits that are beyond your imagination," the goblin said.

"I can imagine quite a bit."

He gave a low laugh. "And I eagerly look forward to you telling me about each and every one."

His smile went from dangerous to downright wicked, as he slid one long arm around my waist, pulling me tight against him. I didn't know if it was a figment of my imagination or trick of the light, but I could swear the goblin's eyes were getting larger and darker. With goblins, sex was just as much about power as what you did with the parts. And from what I was feeling, he wasn't lacking in either department.

"Have you heard what happened to your predecessors?" he asked softly.

A chill ran from the top of my head to the tips of my toes. "One of them."

"Would that be the exsanguination, the fall from the Empire State Building, or the unfortunate subway accident?"

"The first one."

"You haven't been told of the others?"

"Not yet."

"Nor will you, unless you ask your new employer some very direct questions. Questions the senior management at SPI will find most uncomfortable. And an interesting fact concerning your American supernatural flora and fauna—North American sewer leeches don't live this far north."

I just stared.

"Yes, they lied to you." He smiled slowly, as he slid his other hand down the length of my spine. "Would you like to know why?"

I was officially beyond words.

"Tell me, Makenna Fraser, have you seen any demons lately?"

"Present company excluded?"

He laughed softly. "Contrary to what many in this city—human and supernatural—think, greed is not good. There is nothing wrong with acquiring possessions that are pleasing to the senses—present company included—however, I know when to stop. Others do not share my restraint. There is danger in reaching too far without acknowledging the limits of your power. Such wanton arrogance could destroy us all. Vivienne has experienced difficulty protecting her seers. Perhaps you would be safer with me."

There was a sneeze, and a pile of feather boas in the far corner poofed up in the blast of nasal air.

Rake Danescu released me and crossed the room faster than I could see, reached behind a pile of discarded costumes, and plucked out one very wanted leprechaun prince by the scruff of his scrawny neck.

"Ah, here is my little trespasser." The goblin's smile was more like a hungry hyena than anything else. And like a scared rabbit, the leprechaun couldn't stop himself from looking at the predator that'd plucked him from his burrow of feathers. Prince Finnegan was no longer a naked human woman. He was something worse—a naked leprechaun. Ick didn't even begin to cover it; and believe me, I wanted it covered.

Rake Danescu's black eyes locked on Finn's with all the warmth of a shark about to feed. What was about as bad as it could get for the prince was good for me. If Danescu wanted to keep his leprechaun prisoner, and right now, for my sake, I hoped he did, he couldn't break eye contact, or Finn would vanish faster than tips in a stripper's G-string.

And without those black eyes holding me hostage, I felt some semblance of sanity returning.

Now it was Prince Finnegan's turn to panic. However, being a leprechaun with the gift of gab, he was trying to talk his way out of the mess he'd sneezed his way into.

His words came in a gush. "In exchange for my freedom, I will gladly grant you three wishes."

Danescu smiled slowly. "Of course, you will. You will give me everything I want—including the name of who sent you here. I believe the clichéd wish is for you to give me riches, power, and my heart's desire. I already possess all three, leaving you with nothing left with which to bargain. Why are you here, leprechaun?"

Finn grinned like a used car salesman who liked a challenge and had just met his match.

"If you consider carefully and wish well," the leprechaun told the goblin, "you could accomplish what I *know* you want in only two wishes." Finn waggled his bushy, red eyebrows. "Leaving you free to use your first wish to cleanse the human and elven stain from your place of business. For no extra charge, I can include the wolf man presently lurking in your alley, after which there will be no one to prove SPI's agents were even here. Then we will be free to conduct *our* business in a civilized manner."

The goblin's expression darkened. "Be warned that my favor is not so cheaply bought—nor am I easily tempted. In fact, you may find both are priced more dearly than you're prepared to pay. You toy with those best left unmolested."

Finn jerked his head in my direction. "Yet you molest them freely."

"I can do so because I have not your shortcomings."

"The dragon uses humans as her agents. They are servants at best. They will do as they are told to avoid offending or angering our queen or your own most noble king. The balance of power is delicate now. They will not risk exposing our world to their own. We are the nobles of our peoples. We don't need the permission of the hired help to do as we wish."

"And you fail to recognize the value of 'hired help.' I never eliminate in haste that which I may need in the future."

"Then use your first wish to have me put SPI's agents to sleep for as long as would be convenient."

"That could be convenient—and most entertaining."

Rake Danescu never took his eyes off of Finn, but he didn't need to when he could run his fingers under my blouse from clear across the room.

There was a muffled explosion, and Ian stood framed in all that was left of the locked door.

"Attacking my employees in my place of business?" Danescu asked Ian, his black eyes never leaving Finn's. "And destroying my property? Vivienne's control over her favorite guard dog isn't as good as she believes. I have done nothing here. Merely giving a warm welcome to SPI's latest seer to our fair city, and giving her advice she would do well to heed."

"And kidnapping a leprechaun prince?"

"Escorting a Seelie court hooligan who is trespassing in a nonpublic area of my club. My intent is to send him on to where he deserves to be." The goblin smiled as if at a private joke. "It is my own variation of a catch-and-release program."

"You've caught him; release him. Now."

"In good time." His black eyes glittered from the shadows. "And that time will be mine; not yours."

He shot a glance at the pile of costumes Finn had been hiding in. In the next instant, that pile was flying toward me and Ian.

Then the lights went out, and a door opened and slammed.

Shouts and screams came from the guest section of the club, and what sounded like a muffled explosion came from the other side of a door with one of those emergency exit signs over it. It appeared to be the only door out of this place. Ian ran across the room and threw his hip against the door bar, his gun in his hand, held low and ready. He checked the alley, his eyes alert to any movement.

The air smelled like rotten eggs, and it was all I could do not to gag.

"Sulfur," Ian said.

"What the—"

"Leftovers from black magic. Looks like Danescu had an escape portal ready and waiting."

We ran out the back door and into the alley to the sound of screeching tires, burning rubber, and gunshots.

Elana stood at the mouth of the alley, slamming a fresh magazine into her gun, and cussing a blue streak. The leprechauns formerly known as Khaki Guy and Jeans Guy were trussed up in magic manacles and propped up against the alley wall like a pair of Thanksgiving turkeys.

The Suburban was gone.

Ian sprinted to the end of the alley. I caught up to him a couple of seconds later.

"The last two leps got past me," she growled. "Sorry, Ian."

"Don't worry; we'll get them. They took the Suburban?"

Elana gave a sharp nod and lowered her gun, but she didn't put it away. The look on her face said she really wanted to use it some more. Those leprechaun SUV-jackers better hope Elana didn't catch them first.

"Where's Yasha?" I asked.

Elana jerked her head in a vaguely skyward direction. "Up there. We've had company."

Something heavy slammed into the brick wall two stories above our heads. Then came the shower of broken brick chunks.

Ian jerked me out of the way, and we both looked up.

I had no idea what they were, but the closest thing my panicked mind could come up with was one of those flying monkey things from *The Wizard of Oz* on steroids. They'd scared the crap out of me on TV when I was a kid; and their all-too-real distant cousin had me plenty terrified right here and now.

"Danescu's club bouncers," Ian explained. "For particularly stubborn guests."

The winged monkey fell out of the sky and landed face-first and spread-eagle in the alley. Nothing landed that hard without being hurled.

Yasha leapt from the roof, shaking the now-cracked pavement under our feet when he landed. He snatched up the monkey by one ankle and slammed it repeatedly against the ground. Then he swung it a couple of times over his head and let it go. I didn't know how far that monkey flew after Yasha launched it, but the squealing went on for way longer than you'd have thought.

Yasha the werewolf looked at the spot where the Suburban had been, and let out a blood-curdling howl. Then again, those leprechauns would be better off if Elana caught up to them first. I realized that the Suburban probably wasn't the only thing of Yasha's they'd stolen.

I think they'd taken his clothes.

"RAKE Danescu took Finn," I told them.

"How?" Elana asked.

Ian smiled; it was the first real one I'd seen from him. "Portal. But when I tackled the little bastard on that stage, I tagged him in the left ass cheek with a tracking chip."

That right there went above and beyond the call of duty. Ian Byrne deserved a medal.

"Best hope that chip of yours is multi-dimensional," Elana said.

"Prince Finnegan wasn't all Danescu got," Ian continued, "he also got the identity and a look inside the mind of SPI's newest seer."

"He didn't look inside my mind," I protested.

"Did he touch you?"

Did he ever.

Elana chuckled. "From the look on your face, I'll take that as a yes."

"What does that mean?"

"Familiar with the word 'enthralled'?" she asked.

"I'm not enthralled."

"How hard did you try to escape?"

I thought about that.

Elana nodded knowingly. "Yeah, that's what I thought. Meaning that if Rake crosses your path again—"

"I'm screwed."

"And if you're lucky, it'll be literal."

"Elana," Ian said in a warning tone.

She snorted. "Any woman and half the men I know would do Rake."

Ian scowled. "It's my job to have kept that from happening."

"You had your hands full—and apparently so did Rake."

There was no denying that. My favorite lady parts got all tingly again. I mentally smacked myself. Rake Danescu was gone and the residuals were enough to . . . what if he were here, his hands running over my . . . I smacked myself for real.

Elana nodded once. "Like I said, enthralled."

"Okay, he was kind of hot. Doesn't mean I'm enthralled; I just need one really good date is all."

"New girl in town," Elana mused. "New *Southern* girl. Play up that Scarlett O'Hara of yours, and I can fix you up." She thought for a moment. "You don't mind Yankees, do you?"

"As long as they don't drink blood or eat brains."

THE goblin had Finn. We had a tracking device on Finn. Rake Danescu had flying monkeys at his command. But we had an advantage that didn't have a thing to do with minions or superior spy technology.

We had a naked Russian at the wheel—a really pissed, naked Russian.

In werewolf form, he'd have enough fur to cover the necessaries, but he wouldn't fit in the truck, let alone be able to get his hands with their five-inch claws around the steering wheel. So shapeshifting back to a naked Russian it was.

I was trying not to look. Fortunately Yasha the naked human was nearly as hairy as Yasha the werewolf. Hugh Jackman had nothing on this guy.

Those leprechauns had stolen Yasha Kazakov's tricked-out Suburban. It was his baby, his mobile office—hell, it was his partner. And his partner had been kidnapped and taken for a joyride by creatures that in their real form didn't have legs long enough to reach the gas pedal.

A couple of hours ago, I would have felt sorry for the little guys, being chased by an enraged werewolf who'd already gone wolf once tonight and had beaten one of Rake Danescu's bouncers like dirty laundry on a rock. But now? If—no, *when*—he caught up to those leprechauns, he was liable to squash them into green Play-Doh. And after all they'd put us through, I'd gladly hand Yasha the hammer.

The tracking chip Ian had planted on Finn was on the move, so we didn't have time to wait for a replacement vehicle or prisoner transport from the SPI motor pool. Ian liberated a bakery delivery truck that was parked near the end of the block.

That was the best thing that'd happened to me all night. Until I smelled those cookies, I had no idea how hungry I was. A porn crawl through New York City sure worked up an appetite.

The truck was still half loaded with cookies and pastries in all their glorious forms and flavors. Technically it was stealing, but by rescuing Finn from Danescu's clutches, we'd save the city from the effects of the goblin mage's three wishes. When you thought of it that way, we were fueling up to prevent the spread of evil. That was noble, right?

Clover weed might not have been pot, but it obviously had the same side effects, at least for the leprechauns. The two stoned leprechauns had a bad case of the munchies, and anything that would keep them quiet was good.

Though after I told Ian how the little bastard had gleefully sold us out, Finn had better hope Rake Danescu used the Hand Wave of Destruction that he'd shown me on him. As a senior agent and chief agency ass kicker, Ian had first dibs when we caught up to him. If there was anything left, I'd gladly take seconds. Finn offered to put me to sleep so Danescu could have his way with me. That pissed me off; though I didn't want to admit even to myself part of that was because I'd sleep through whatever the goblin did to me.

"I've *so* got to get a boyfriend," I muttered.

"What?"

I winced at yet another pothole Yasha found. "Nothing."

I was kneeling between the driver and passenger seats. The truck's shocks were a thing of the past and were almost as worn out as I was.

Not that I wanted to watch the Russian werewolf's kamikaze driving; in fact, I'd be happier not knowing how close we'd come to death any number of times. However, I usually called shotgun for a reason.

I was the poster child for car sickness. But with Ian literally riding shotgun, I made do the best I could and tried to convince my stomach and its contents of Coke and cookies not to leap into my throat every time Yasha found yet another pothole. I wasn't even gonna allow myself to think about the state of my bladder. I'd been in a perfectly good ladies' room, but thanks to the two leprechauns cuffed to one of the racks in the back of the delivery truck, I hadn't had a chance to use it.

We were actually getting a signal from the tracking device, meaning that wherever Rake Danescu had taken Finn through the Rotten Egg Portal of Doom, at least they were still in our dimension. While we were following the flashing dot on Ian's phone—yep, SPI had an app for tracking chips embedded in a leprechaun's butt cheek—there was no time like the present to get some answers from my partner.

I was coming down from the effects of the clover weed, so while I wasn't quite as forthright in my behavior and opinions, I felt like I was more than due some straight answers.

"When were you going to tell me I'm walking around wearing a bull's-eye?"

With that, I had my partner's full and undivided attention. I would have crossed my arms for visual effect, but they were occupied, death-gripping the cookie racks to keep me from ricocheting off the sides of the van, so I just went with a glare.

"Who tol—?" Realization hit. "Danescu. I should have known."

"*I* should have known, too. You know, the boss knows, the hot bad guy—"

"Hot?"

"Hey, I thought we'd already established that. Besides, I'll be honest if you will. I wasn't told that taking a job as a seer at SPI came with an expiration date. Danescu told me I'd been lied to, and asked if I'd like to know why. I'd like that very much—without a side order of bullshit."

Ian scowled.

"Sir," I quickly added.

He ran the hand not holding the shotgun over his face, and for a moment, I got a look at Ian Byrne, just a tired guy with too much on his plate.

"There have been accidents—" he began.

"What kind of accidents involve exsang—"

"What *at first* were thought to be accidents."

"You know differently now."

"Without a doubt."

"And I was hired to be the fourth sacrificial lamb because SPI needs a seer."

"There were no sacrificial lambs. Yes, SPI needs a seer, now more than ever. My mission is to ensure that you're alive to work for us for *many* years to come. Contrary to what Rake Danescu may have told you, and what you may now believe, Vivienne Sagadraco values each and every one of her employees. She takes the loss of any agent hard, and personally."

At that, I felt bad about implying otherwise, but not bad enough to take back anything I'd said. They'd known what had happened to my predecessors. I'd been clueless, and they'd kept me that way. I'd signed on thinking I was getting a cool job with great insurance—not a ticking time bomb to a death sentence.

"We believe a powerful supernatural entity is planning a major event," Ian said. "And they've killed three of our seers to keep it covered up. One death could be an unfortunate accident. Two is highly suspicious."

"And three means an evil plot."

Ian nodded. "That's how we're treating it, and that's why Vivienne Sagadraco assigned me as your partner."

"So you're not a babysitter for the newbie; you're a bodyguard for the next Dead Seer Walking."

"There aren't going to be any more deaths." His expression darkened. "At least not on our side."

"So I take it that 'major event' hasn't shown signs of happening yet?"

Ian hesitated. "No. It hasn't."

We both knew what that meant. As long as I worked for SPI, and as long as the unknown "they" were still weaving their evil plot, I'd still be sporting a bull's-eye.

"Rake Danescu offered me a job," I said quietly.

The only thing that little factoid got out of my partner was a raised eyebrow. "Interesting."

"Just interesting?"

"Also unexpected. Danescu doesn't work with humans. He must need a seer badly."

"He said it'd be the same work I'm doing for SPI, with an immortality bonus clause. Don't worry," I hurried to add, "I'm perfectly happy with just plain old major medical."

"Sounds like Danescu doesn't know any more about all this than we do." Ian's eyes narrowed. "But if he wants you—"

"You're preaching to the choir. My granny told me all about strange men offering candy."

Ian almost smiled. "Your grandmother sounds like a wise woman."

I shrugged. "She also said to punch 'em in the throat, not the nuts. Always lead with the unexpected."

Ian didn't have a response for that. Grandma Fraser affected a lot of people that way.

"Since Danescu wanted to hire you," Ian said, "it's unlikely that he's our culprit. And our culprit wants Danescu either taken out of the game, or watched closely enough to keep him from interfering."

"The goblin thinks Finn is in on it. Finn offered him wishes and all he wanted to know was who sent him. Why would someone send Finn to Bacchanalia?"

"To get the reaction from us that they got. What better way to force SPI to bring its new seer out of the protective confines of headquarters?"

"Wouldn't sending him to any goblin business do the same thing?"

Ian shook his head. "Rake Danescu is the Unseelie Court's most powerful and unpredictable element, which makes him especially dangerous. With either the Seelie or Unseelie Court, anything is possible. Intrigue is a full-contact sport in both. But the risk of losing a leprechaun prince's wishes to the Unseelie Court was too great for us to ignore."

"Danescu wasn't happy to find Finn there. He didn't want wishes. He wanted a name."

"The prince's bachelor party was supposed to be a week ago," Ian told me.

"When I was hired."

"Yes."

"Why did he put it off?"

"Unknown. But it correlates to when I was called to Chicago for a mission that turned out to be a false alarm."

"Someone wanted to get you out of town."

"Not provable; but again, that's what we believe."

"So Finn could be involved."

There was a commotion from the back of the truck.

"You want me to make a wish?" Mike shouted. "I'll make a wish. I wish you would shut up!"

Nerves were on edge, and any patience any of us may have had was long gone. Any creature that reduced a sweetheart like Mike to incoherent screaming deserved anything they had coming to them—or anything coming after them.

"Maybe we can trade those two for Finn." I said it loud enough to ensure they heard me.

Yasha gave a borderline evil grin. "Is good plan."

An instant later, something slammed into the side of the truck, and I was thrown across Ian's lap and against the passenger window.

Ian swore. I would've made my own contribution, but the air'd been knocked out of me.

Just what we needed, an accident at o'dark thirty in the morning.

When I caught a glimpse of what'd hit us, my eyes danged near bugged out of my head. A face was pressed against the other side of the glass, leering at me as we were going seventy miles per hour.

It wasn't a flying monkey.

It was a gargoyle.

Not that I'd ever seen a real-life, or whatever, gargoyle, but this thing filled out the checklist: all stone, freaking humongous, and uglier than homemade sin with a face only Quasimodo could love. Rake Danescu knew he was being followed and sent his minions to smash us into road paste.

I found some air. "Danescu?"

"He's never used gargoyles before."

Ian stood, pushed me behind him with one arm, and leveled the shotgun at the window. Before he could pull the trigger, a stone fist the size of my head slammed through the window, snapped open its huge hand to reveal claw-tipped fingers. The thing lunged right at me, the impact of its shoulder nearly bending the door in half. When the gargoyle couldn't reach me, it started clawing at the steel door like it was a piñata and I was the chewy candy inside.

Holy mother.

Yasha was spitting a stream of nonstop Russian. I didn't need translation to know he was cussing a blue streak.

The truck shuddered clear down to its axles when another gargoyle landed on the door, dinting the roof in a good foot. Me, Elana, and the boys hit the deck, and the leprechauns started shrieking their tiny lungs out as a fist the size of Yasha's head slammed through the weakened steel and proceeded to peel back strips of metal, shucking the roof like it was an ear of corn.

Mike and Steve were firing out the shattered back windows at something I couldn't see, and the leprechauns shrieked louder.

The gargoyle peeled off the passenger-side door in a scream of tortured metal, and Ian pulled me into the back of the truck.

Yasha retaliated by sharply jerking the steering wheel to the right and aiming the truck directly at a really solid-looking wall in what I assumed was an attempt to scrape the thing off like a cow pie off a boot.

It didn't work.

Ian wasn't so confident about the Russian's plan. "Yasha. Wall. Wall!"

"I know. Hold on. Might hurt."

Might?

The engine screamed past whatever limits it'd been designed to handle.

"Brace!"

It was all Ian yelled or needed to yell. The rest of us got the message—brace or be bounced.

The Russian werewolf continued to accelerate, surpassing any speed that was either safe or sane. The wall looked plenty solid. The truck was definitely decrepit, and I had a sinking feeling that rust was all that was holding it together.

The metal shelves looked sturdy enough and were bolted to the truck walls. Ian secured the shotgun, grabbed me with one arm and a shelf with the other. I grabbed a double handful of Ian as the right side of the truck smacked into the wall, raking the bricks, and raising a shower of sparks.

A third gargoyle landed on the rear bumper and punched out the last unbroken window in the truck.

One of the leprechauns fainted, and the other's shrieks stopped as the little guy tried to hide behind a rack of cheese Danish. The gargoyle ignored him, Elana, and the elves.

He only had glowing eyes for me.

The gargoyle had his arm through the window to his armpit, or whatever gargoyles had, and was straining to get to me, stone fingers extended and grasping, the right-rear door panel buckling under the thing's weight.

Elana pulled out a gun, the likes of which I'd never seen before, one that made Yasha's look like a peashooter. She aimed, fired, and while I knew the gargoyle and the door it was hanging onto had to be clanking and pounding its way down the thankfully empty street behind us, I couldn't hear a thing after the blast that'd come out of that gun. My eardrums felt like they'd exploded.

I guessed that was why I saw but didn't hear the blast from Ian's sawed-off shotgun that sent the gargoyle that'd grabbed at me tumbling ass over teakettle down the street after its buddy, minus its head.

Elana pointed the still-smoking muzzle up and at an angle toward where the second gargoyle had shucked enough of the roof to wedge itself through. She fired three shots in rapid succession, and after that, all I could see was empty sky.

Elana was looking around for more targets and seemed to be a mite disappointed that there weren't any more to be seen—at least for now. And I didn't miss her shooting a glance over at the two leprechauns, who during the ruckus had fainted dead away on a pile of squashed coconut-covered cream puffs.

I staggered up to where Ian was. "If Danescu didn't send those things, then who did?"

Ian kept his eyes on the sky for gargoyle reinforcements. "I think those were an upgrade from sewer leeches."

I felt the blood drain from my face. "That wouldn't have looked like an accident."

"I think our culprit has passed the point of caring."

◆ ◆ ◆

THE beep from the tracking chip was continuous and the dot had stopped blinking.

Yasha pulled over where Ian indicated.

McDonald's?

It was four in the morning. I was in a stolen bakery delivery truck that'd been nearly totaled by three gargoyles. In the truck with me were two hungover elves, a pair of stoned leprechauns with the munchies, a naked Russian werewolf, and a hot partner who was actually more of a bodyguard, in a race against a goblin dark mage to retrieve a leprechaun prince with a tracking chip embedded in his left ass cheek.

And the trail ended at a McDonald's in the Bronx.

This had to be weird, even by SPI standards.

Thankfully the parking lot was empty. I scanned the roof anyway.

"No gargoyles," I noted. "Or monkeys."

Ian and his shotgun slid smoothly from the truck. "Maybe." He held the barrel next to his leg, the stock resting against his hip. I had no doubt he could snap it up and take out any gargoyles like picking off ducks launching from a pond. I almost hoped they were hiding on the roof, just to watch him do it.

The agitated owner was pacing in the parking lot. To the guys, he was a middle-aged, balding man. I saw the hobgoblin that he really was. Ian started walking over to him; presumably to get some details and calm him down.

"Check it out," Ian called back to Mike and Steve.

"Sir."

The stolen Suburban was parked next to the door. Elana had retrieved Yasha's clothes and was transferring the two leprechauns into it from the remains of the delivery truck. Yasha was presently being reunited with his beloved SUV, murmuring what must have been Russian endearments. He started to follow us.

"I need you to stay out here," Ian told him. "We need to apprehend the leprechauns inside and take them home with all the pieces and parts they started the evening with."

"I can leave arms and legs attached."

I wasn't convinced.

"I'm sure you can, my friend, but we need them not broken, too." Ian wasn't buying it, either.

"That could be a challenge," Yasha admitted.

Mike and Steve opened the glass doors and stopped. Staring.

I walked up behind them. "They in there?"

Both agents jumped. "We'll take care of it," they said entirely too fast. "You don't need to go in."

I tensed further. "Danescu?"

"No, ma'am. Just two leprechauns, not veiled."

"Where's Finn?"

"Don't see him."

"What?" I pushed past them.

Mike was right. There were two leprechauns, and they weren't veiled. They were in the indoor PlayPlace playground.

And they were as naked as a pair of jaybirds.

McDonald's had rules about kids taking off their shoes before entering the PlayPlace. It was obvious that the leprechauns had decided to keep on going.

Thank God it was four in the morning. If it'd been an hour later, this neighborhood would be waking up and grabbing a coffee and a McWhatever to start their day. Anyone who set foot in here now would lose their appetites *and* wake up without the aid of caffeine, seeing things that were best left unseen.

One leprechaun was in the ball pit and the other was coming down the slide, his bare butt cheeks squeaking on the plastic. Neither one was Prince Finnegan.

Mike's expression was a frozen grimace of disgust. "The owner's going to need to hose down that ball pit and slide."

Steve nodded. "More like powerwash. With Clorox."

The leprechauns saw us and their eyes widened, and with a simultaneous squeak, both dove into the ball pit. Without hesitation, Mike and Steve ran across the restaurant and jumped in after them.

I came inside, letting the door close behind me. Ian would be in here any second, but in the meantime, I was going to find myself a leprechaun prince. I scanned the interior of the restaurant. The owner was still outside with Ian, and from all appearances, there wasn't another soul in here. Behind me came the sounds of thrashing and balls being thrown.

"Son of a bitch bit my ankle!" Steve spat. Then he switched from English to Elvish for a few more choice words.

I detected movement behind the counter. Thankfully, it wasn't tall enough to be Rake Danescu. Though I couldn't imagine the goblin in a Mickey D's in the Bronx with naked leprechauns. No amount of wishes could be worth that.

I peeked around the edge of the counter. Now *that* was a health code violation.

Prince Finnegan's bare butt was perched on the edge of the steel counter, head tilted back with his open mouth under the nozzle of the soft serve ice cream machine.

He saw me and sat up, but took his sweet time doing it. He smiled and wiped the chocolate ice cream from the corner of his mouth with the back of one hand, leaving a smear across his face.

Oh yeah, the prince was a real class act.

"I escaped," he said.

"Congratulations."

"You don't sound happy. We're celebrating. Join us."

"Celebrating what? That you and Rake Danescu were able to . . . let's see, how did you say it? Conduct your business in a civilized manner after you cleansed the human and elf stain from his place of business."

Finn laughed. "Mere words, love. The best way to escape a madman is to forge a connection with him, to have similar goals. A tactic, nothing more."

"Uh-huh. As one of the aforementioned stains, I don't appreciate your tactics."

The leprechaun's humor vanished as quickly as his clothes probably had. "And I don't appreciate SPI's interference. I did not ask for protection. If you hadn't come after us, the goblin wouldn't have found me. You led those goblins to us." His smile slid into a chocolate-smeared smirk. "When you look at it that way, human, this is all your doing, not mine."

I wasn't going to take the bait.

"You set us up," I said.

"Now what would be in that for me? Besides the satisfaction of making SPI look like witless fools. Which, as you must admit, didn't take any effort on my part."

"You tell me. What *was* in it for you?" I stopped merely looking at him, and locked eyes with the leprechaun. "Wish number one: Tell me who paid you to set us up."

Finn chuckled. "Hmm, perhaps not as witless as I presumed. Very well, seer. Your answer: I do not know. And if you are truly not witless, then you know that I cannot speak a lie while under wish compulsion."

Damn, he was right. "What did they give you in payment?"

"Your second wish?"

"It is."

"I received an anonymous and most generous wedding gift of one hundred bars of gold. In the Seelie Court, favors are often exchanged anonymously. The gift was given with the provision that I lose my SPI bodyguards—making SPI look incompetent, which was a fond wish of *mine*—and after that, I was to go to Bacchanalia."

"Do you make a habit of accepting gifts from people you don't know who want you to go to the most dangerous club for a leprechaun in the city?"

"Is that your third wish?"

"Nope, just a question."

"Very well. If the reward is large enough and the strings attached acceptable, then why should I not accept the gift? My friends and I didn't want mortals underfoot on our night out, and Bacchanalia is the best sex club in the city. Why wouldn't I want to go there?"

"To avoid being kidnapped and having a goblin mage rip three wishes out of you."

"An acceptable risk, far outweighed by the gift and the delights to be had in Rake Danescu's establishment." Prince Finnegan leapt down from the counter, and began walking slowly toward me. "I was getting a good show with you and Rake." His smirk slid into a leer. "I could tell that you were enjoying it." He lowered his voice to a whisper. "Tell me, seer. Had I not sneezed, how far would you have let him take you?"

Finn had endangered me, my team, and was possibly involved in the murders of three SPI seers. It was all a game to him, a game that the sicker and more twisted it got, the better.

"It's your first night with the agency, isn't it?" Finn continued. "It hasn't been the most flattering launch to your career as a seer. Leprechauns are lucky, you know." He grinned and waggled his eyebrows suggestively. "You could always rub *my* charms for good luck."

I slipped my hand into my purse. I'd been wanting to use this all night.

I Tasered Prince Finnegan smack-dab in his Chicken McNuggets.

I looked down at the leprechaun twitching on the tile floor. "Do you feel lucky *now*, punk?"

Ian stepped up beside me. "I'd say his luck just ran out."

I'D had a Coke, Egg McMuffin, two hash browns, and now there were five leprechauns in handcuffs, packaged for take-out and headed for home delivery—*and* I'd made use of the ladies' room.

A good end to a bad night's work.

I had a question for my partner. And while I really didn't want to hear the answer, I'd rather hear it now than be publically embarrassed at headquarters like the first team.

"Am I in trouble for zapping Finn?"

Senior Agent Ian Byrne grimly considered his response.

Oh great, here it comes.

"When I arrived on the scene, I witnessed a suspect in a conspiracy endangering one of my agents. She took steps to protect herself without lasting permanent injury to the suspect. I'd say the situation was resolved in the most appropriate way possible given the circumstances."

I tried not to smile. "So I did good?"

Ian's face was an expressionless mask. Almost. "I didn't say that. I said that it was appropriate given the circumstances."

To my way of thinking, that meant I'd done good. But as long as "appropriate" wasn't going to involve yelling, public humiliation, and conference room door slamming back at headquarters, I'd take it.

I didn't think the boss would necessarily see me Tasering a leprechaun prince in the Happy Meal as a good thing, but I'd be more than happy to have Ian Byrne put that in his official report.

"Will the boss tell the Seelie queen what happened?"

Ian nodded. "She would have been honest with the queen, regardless of how it'd turned out with Finnegan and his boys, but especially now that he may be involved in something bigger. And she'd definitely want the queen to have the truth, rather than the tale Finn will be spinning to make himself look like an innocent victim."

"She gonna tell the queen that her chief money handler is a disgusting little shit?"

"I'm sure Her Majesty already knows that."

"Why the hell does she put up with him?"

"He's good at what he does. You'll discover that there's a whole lot more black and gray than white in our line of work. The people and supernaturals we deal with will have motives stacked on top of schemes. Alliances are as knotted as an armful of Christmas tree lights—and about as impossible to untangle."

We walked out into the parking lot where our team waited in the Suburban. A prisoner transport vehicle had arrived— with extra guards—to take the five leprechauns home.

"What about who's behind this?" I asked.

"We picked up a few more clues tonight. He—or she— seems to want Rake Danescu out of the picture, meaning Danescu has them worried."

"Meanwhile Danescu wants his own personal seer to get to the bottom of this on his own."

"Probably to see if it's interesting enough to want a piece of."

"Finn said he escaped from Danescu."

"I heard."

I blinked. "You heard?"

"I listened to your entire exchange. I knew Finn would tell you things he'd never admit to me or in an SPI interrogation room."

I nodded. "The word of the new SPI agent against a Seelie prince." I growled. "Can I zap him again?"

"*Twice* would not be appropriate."

"Too bad," I muttered. "Why would Rake Danescu let him go?"

"Because I imagine we're not the only ones tracking Finn. The identity of who's pulling the prince's strings might just be worth more to Danescu than three wishes from a leprechaun royal."

"Three murdered seers and one goblin dark mage willing to give up three wishes from a leprechaun prince. That's something ugly."

"And big."

A chill went through me. "Something a very powerful someone thinks they need to kill me to keep secret."

"Danescu wants to hire you and keep you alive because his rival wants you dead. Goblins do like to piss each other off. Of more concern to me is how Danescu and his rival knew you had been dispatched from headquarters."

"We have a spy at SPI?"

Ian's expression darkened. "I hope not."

BELVEDERE Castle in Central Park was wreathed in magic, gauzy tendrils covering the stone like the ivy did during the daylight hours. The fabric between dimensions was thinner in the moments of twilight and daybreak. Seelie guards in intricate armor—both male and female—patrolled the battlements.

We'd seen a few of NYPD's mounted police on patrol. All of them near Belvedere Castle had been elves. Like I'd said, elves had a thing for law and order.

Yasha parked next to the prisoner transport, and as close to the castle's doors as he could get. We got out and were hit with an overwhelming scent of flowers, like a hedge of gardenias. Normally I liked gardenias, but only a few at a time. This was like being smothered by a maze hedge of the things. Yeah, the veil between dimensions was thin, all right.

A limo pulled up moments later. Alain Moreau got out, turned back, and offered a gallant hand to Vivienne Sagadraco. Earlier in the evening, the five leprechauns were clients who needed protection. Now, they were being brought home wearing magical manacles riding in the back of a prisoner transport van. While they weren't prisoners in the literal sense, more like clients who needed protecting from themselves, SPI/Seelie court relations demanded an explanation.

Ian and I were standing next to the Suburban.

"Surely the Seelie folks won't be surprised to see their boys being brought home in a paddy wagon," I said.

"I'm sure it's happened before."

I had an unpleasant thought. "Do you think the boss knows I zapped Finn?"

I detected a hint of a smile. "She knows."

"And I still have a job?"

"You do."

I sensed his eyes on me. I looked up at him, but his face was mostly hidden in darkness.

"Is it a job you still want?" he asked quietly.

I took a breath. "I kind of came into this thinking that most of the time, I'd be hunting for the supernatural equivalent of jaywalkers. I knew there'd be Big Bad Guys, but I kinda thought those would be the exception. Or did I just have a bad first night?"

"Yes . . . and no."

"You could've stopped with the 'yes.' I'd have been perfectly happy."

"But it wouldn't have been the truth."

"So now I'm due the truth?"

"You are."

"Does the boss know that?"

"She will. I'll tell her."

I looked out over the lights shimmering on the surface of Turtle Pond. Peaceful. Quiet. Not like anything I'd encountered tonight.

"Thank you," I told Ian.

"For what?"

"For honesty—and for being there for me tonight."

"You're my partner."

"And you're my *reluctant* partner. I heard you and Ms. Sagadraco talking in her office."

"I know."

We grew some silence between us. It wasn't entirely uncomfortable, but at the same time, it didn't exactly fill me with the warm and fuzzies.

"I am reluctant," he admitted.

"More honesty is good." What wasn't good was the knot that'd just formed in the pit of my stomach.

"But I'm not reluctant in the way that you think," he said. "I simply don't want to involve another seer in this."

"But you said yourself that it'll take a seer to get to the bottom of it."

"Correct."

"So there's no way around my being involved."

"You wouldn't be involved if you didn't work for SPI. Do you want to stay?"

The knot grew larger. "I'm not a good enough seer?"

"I didn't say that. Vivienne Sagadraco didn't hire you without looking into your background—all of your background. Your family is well-known in supernatural law enforcement. She's confident in your abilities." I could see his eyes now. The sky was getting lighter; the sun would be up soon. "You're good enough."

"Thank you—again."

"There's nothing to thank me for. Merely giving my professional opinion."

I smiled a little as I watched Alain Moreau and Vivienne Sagadraco talking with two very tall and impossibly beautiful courtiers. At least I assumed that was what they were.

"You still haven't answered my question," Ian said. "Do you want to stay?"

"Something big is brewing."

"It is."

"It sounds like tonight was just another round in what could be a long fight. Probably the smartest thing I could do is turn tail and run home for the hills."

"The file we have on you says you don't always to the smartest thing."

I felt one side of my mouth twitch upward. "Yeah, it's a failing of mine."

"I heard you telling Yasha earlier that you felt called to protect the prey from the predators."

I smiled. "So I wasn't the only one eavesdropping tonight."

"A good agent always keeps their ears and eyes open."

"And their mouth shut?"

"Sometimes that's a good idea, too."

"That's another failing of mine."

"I noticed."

I nodded slowly, more to myself than anything else. "I'd like to stay. If you don't think I'd screw this thing up six ways from Sunday."

"I can't predict any screwups, but I think that given the right training and discipline, you could do a lot of good." He hesitated. "Can you live with being a target for a while? And having me be your shadow?"

"If I quit and the city went down the crapper, I'd feel like it was my fault. If I stay and do a good job, I could help stop it." I looked up at him. "Though I'm gonna need a lot of help. I'm new at this."

Ian Byrne held out his hand and I took it. "That's what I'm here for, partner."

THE BEAST OF
BLACKMOOR

MILLA VANE

PROLOGUE

Victory made gods of men.

So had claimed the first man who'd hired Kavik's sword. At the end of the day, the man's gold had filled Kavik's purse and the blood of his enemies had stained his armor, but Kavik knew little about gods and couldn't imagine what it must be to feel like one. After years of swinging his blade to no avail, however, he finally knew what it was to defeat rather than be defeated.

By midnight, victory tasted of too much ale and ached of the urgent need to piss.

Stomach roiling, he stumbled out of the inn and into the courtyard. The heat of this kingdom fed on a man's sweat even at night. He wiped his brow and turned away from the noises of rutting coming from the shadows. Two other warriors celebrated their victory with more than ale, and he couldn't stop the sour bile from rising into his mouth as the sounds resurrected memories that he'd buried again and again.

Blindly he walked until the warriors' grunts no longer echoed in his head. The streets twisted through the city like Blackmoor's maze of stone. He retraced his path. Nothing was familiar. The courtyard that he thought sat in front of the inn was overlooked by a tower of white marble instead. Runes marked the door.

A temple to the moon goddess, Vela. Kavik had never seen one before. All temples in Blackmoor had been destroyed before he was born. In this land, they must have been, too. This temple had been newly built. The marble still shone like polished ivory.

As he stared, dim recollections crowded his throbbing head. Whispered tales of warriors who earned the goddess's protection and great reward. They only had to complete a dangerous task in her name.

Kavik had a task to complete. He'd dedicated half his life to it—only to know failure each time.

But today he'd finally known victory. He would soon know it again.

The temple doors were unlocked. He staggered through them and into a dark rounded chamber. No torches or candles burned. The only light shone through the temple walls, where the phases of the moon had been carved through the marble. The carvings circled the chamber, a full turn of the moon, from a thin crescent to full and then waning.

A silver offering bowl sat on a pedestal in the light of the full moon. Kavik started toward it and tripped over an unseen stair. His steel helm slipped out of his hand, dropping onto the stone floor. The loud clatter broke the reverent quiet.

"You are drunk, boy."

A woman's voice. A priestess. Through the darkness, he made out the shape of a chair beneath the carving of the new moon.

Boy. She couldn't know how young he was. Though he'd only seen fifteen winters, Kavik had already grown larger than most men. He stepped into the light shining around the offering bowl so that she could see him better.

"Not a boy. A warrior." He tossed a coin into the bowl. "With gold earned by my sword."

His first coins. When he had enough, he would have an army. But he wouldn't need an army with a goddess by his side.

The priestess's voice came from the darkness again. "Have you come to pray that you will survive your next battle, then?"

"I want a quest."

"A quest?" The woman stood, a slim shadow in long black robes. "That is a dangerous thing to ask for, young warrior. No quest comes without great pain. And if you fail, you will wear Vela's Mark."

Kavik already had scars. Some on his flesh, some deeper. And some wounds that weren't scars yet, but still raw and dripping agony from his heart like blood. "The goddess must send me to Blackmoor to defeat the warlord Barin."

The priestess's light laughter sounded through the chamber. "You do not dictate what your task will be. Vela will determine what needs to be done and will work through you. You can ask for a reward, though it does not always take the form you expect."

"I will do anything she requires of me. In return, I want the power to defeat him. If not strength, then the knowledge. He cannot be touched by blade or fire."

The priestess's head tilted, as if considering his words as she came closer. She was small, not even of height with his shoulders. A black veil concealed her hair and face.

When she spoke again, her voice was no longer as light and as amused as it had been. "Is he a demon, young warrior?"

"Only a man," Kavik said. "Though a demon who was freed by the Destroyer also plagues our land. If the goddess has power, she will know what to do."

"*If?*" the priestess echoed. He could feel her studying him through the veil. Finally she said, "Vela has no quest for you."

No quest? How could she refuse? His fists clenched. "My people need help. Too many have died. More still suffer."

"That is true everywhere, young warrior."

"Why is it true? You say to me 'if.' " He spat the word back at her. "*If* your goddess truly had power, she would have stopped the Destroyer. She would have stopped Barin. So many need not have died."

"You blame her for what *they* do?"

"I blame her if she had enough strength to destroy them and didn't." Sudden desperation joined frustration. What would persuade her? Gods and priests wanted worshipers. Kavik would crawl on his knees if it would help. "You can prove she has that power. Send me on this quest. When I hold Barin's bloodied head in my hand, I'll believe in her."

Her laugh was light and amused again. Turning away from him, she said, "Vela does not seek the belief of one angry boy and she does not give quests to those with no real faith. Your only task is to leave this place in peace."

Jaw clenched, Kavik stared at her retreating back, then retrieved his coin from the offering bowl. He would need the gold for his army. Better to leave an offering suited to charlatans who promised help and sat on their asses, instead.

Swaying, he pushed down the front of his brocs and took his cock in hand. The ache intensified, then released in a liquid rush onto the silver plate.

In the center of the chamber, the priestess froze mid-step. Slowly her veiled head turned.

Kavik stared back at her defiantly. *This* was victory. Now he felt like a god, because he had no power to stop this even if he'd wanted to.

The black veil fluttered as her whisper floated through. *"Vela. Look upon this."*

A pale glow at the woman's side drew Kavik's gaze. The priestess's hand. Though her skin was as dark as his, light shone through it as if viewing the moon through finely woven cloth.

All at once, a blast of icy air tightened his flesh. His breath billowed in a steaming cloud. His balls shriveled, and the seemingly endless stream of piss reduced to drips. Pulling up the waist of his brocs, he spun toward the door.

The priestess stood in front of him. Her hand shot up and gripped his throat.

As if he weighed no more than a boy, she lifted him off his feet. The glow through the veil almost blinded him, yet he could see her clearly, the shining skin and the eyes filled with cold moonlight.

"You little beast," the priestess said, but now her voice was as clear and as cold as the ring of steel against stone. Each word echoed in his bones. "Even a dog knows better than to do that within his mistress's home."

Wheezing, Kavik tried to pry her frigid fingers away from his neck. They might as well have been made of iron. Terror splintered through his racing heart.

He could not die now. He hadn't yet killed Barin.

"Heed this, Kavik of Blackmoor." Her grip tightened,

cutting off his air. "You have suffered, but you have suffered no more than any other that the Destroyer has touched, and many have suffered worse. I help those I can, and who ask it of me, but you will know what it means to have no help at all. Leave this temple. Buy your army. Do all that you can to save your people. And at the moment when you have lost everything, I will come to you again to twist the knife. Wait for the woman in red. When she arrives, you will know that the end is near, and that you will soon be on your knees again."

She released him and flicked her finger against his armored chest. The blow hit him like a charging tusker, lifting him off his feet and sending him flying through the temple doors. He landed hard in the stone courtyard, back slamming into the ground, and he lay there, ears ringing, his lungs caught in an agonizing vise.

Pain still circled his throat, as if her cold hand was still upon it. Like a collar.

He rolled onto his side and retched. His eyes closed, but he could still see hers. He was suddenly certain he would dream of those cold eyes forever.

But when he finally fell into restless sleep that night, Kavik of Blackmoor dreamed of another woman, instead.

CHAPTER 1

—————

A ragged cloth hung between the tall stone pillars at the head of the bridge. The frayed edges flapped in the spring wind, the snap almost drowned by the rush of the swollen river below. Whatever message that had once been written across its fluttering length was lost; the ink—or blood, more likely—had long since faded. Only a trace of the runes remained.

It mattered not. Mala could guess what the sign had said. She only had to look beyond the bridge and the message was clear. *Turn around, fool. Death lies in Blackmoor.* Or perhaps, *Beware the beast!*

Bones littered the roadside beyond the river. Rags still clung to rib cages, the limbs rived from their torsos and scattered by animals. Wagons lay in splintered ruins—but only on that side of the bridge, as if the travelers had been attacked as soon as they'd crossed over . . . or, if they'd started out from Blackmoor, attacked before they could escape the cursed land.

But if the beast that Mala had been sent here to tame had slaughtered these people, it hadn't been recently. No flesh remained on the bones. The splintered wood from the wagons was pale and weathered. Surely the beast didn't wait on the other side—and surely Mala's quest wouldn't end so quickly. Of all goddesses, Vela was the most generous, but she wasn't the most kind. Those who completed their sacred quests and received Vela's gifts usually endured far more pain than Mala had on her journey thus far.

So that pain still awaited her. When Mala crossed the river, it would soon find her.

She was ready to meet it.

Her companion didn't seem as eager. Stamping the ground with one massive hoof, Shim tossed his head and snorted, the sound heavy with discontent—obviously unhappy with their destination now that he'd seen it. The bones wouldn't disturb him. The big Hanani stallion had killed more than a few men during their travels, and he cared little for humans in general. More likely, the stallion's disgruntlement sprouted from his stomach. Lush spring grass blanketed the valley behind them. A barren waste lay ahead.

Mala rolled her weight back in the saddle and loosened her posture, so that if Shim decided to buck her off and be done with her, she wouldn't hit the ground so hard. "If you don't like the look of it, you can stay here while I press forward."

She couldn't mistake the derision in his snorted response, as if his opinion of her brains had plummeted when she'd uttered the suggestion. Grinning, she patted his muscular neck. Her fingers came away covered in coarse hairs. His heavy winter coat had been sloughing off in patches since they'd trekked out of the mountains, leaving reddish brown clumps along their trail. He needed a thorough grooming, she needed a flagon of dark ale, and neither of them would get what they needed while tarrying here.

As if Shim had come to the same conclusion, he started forward. On the bridge, Mala kept a wary eye on the river and her right hand on the pommel of her sword. Even if the beast she sought didn't lurk in the rushing water, many other creatures made their lairs beneath the surfaces of rivers and lakes. She bore scars from encounters with several.

If any beasts with stinging tentacles or poisoned jaws waited here now, however, they weren't hungry. Nothing stirred as the clap of Shim's hooves crossed the stone bridge and became a rhythmic thud against the hardened ground. Safely across. Still, Mala kept her sword arm ready.

A more somber land she'd never seen. If the valley behind them had been scooped out by a loving hand and seeded by a gentle breath of wind, the terrain ahead had been clawed out between sullen hills and stamped flat beneath an angry boot. Leaden clouds piled overhead. A chill breeze scraped across slabs of protruding stones and skimmed the back of her neck. With a shiver, Mala drew the hood of her heavy red cloak forward. Only this morning she'd considered shedding her winter leggings, but this land seemed to shun the sun. She would be wearing her furs a while longer.

The silent road stretched south through the barren flats. By midday a drizzle began to fall, and she hadn't seen another living being aside from a crow and the biting gnats that plagued bare skin.

At least the rain chased away the gnats. Pushing back her hood, she asked Shim to stop. Better to eat now than before the drizzle worsened.

The jawbones hanging from her belt rattled when she dismounted. Chewing a strip of dried venison, she studied their route while Shim devoured a sack of grain. Ahead, the shadowed hills to the east and west converged, their faces abruptly changing from shrouded swells to bleak cliffs. The road led to a deep crevice between them, the entrance to Vela's Labyrinth—a maze of canyons dug out by the goddess's fingernails as she'd writhed in the agony of labor and gave birth to the twins, Justice and Law. This gaunt landscape had been their first cradle. It seemed better suited to a grave.

The labyrinth would not be Mala's grave. She scratched Shim's withers. The Hanani stallion could follow a scent as well as a wolf. Any travelers who had passed through the maze might have left markings to indicate the route, but even if they hadn't, Shim should be able to guide her through.

She poured watered mead into her cupped hand and let him quench his thirst before taking her own swig from the wineskin. Despite the rain, this land was as dry as it was gray. Since leaving the river, not even a stream had trickled across their path.

But there would be plenty to drink when they reached the city beyond the maze, which still lay five sprints distant. She swung up into her saddle again, but before Shim had taken a step, his body tensed beneath her.

A rider on a gray horse emerged from the crevice ahead. An oxen-drawn wagon followed, then several more. A caravan—obviously headed for the bridge and the lush valley behind them, because unless they planned to settle on this barren waste, there was nowhere else to go.

Eyes narrowed, Mala studied the train. The law of the road demanded courtesy between travelers. Most of the people she'd encountered followed that code. The eyeteeth of those who hadn't decorated her belt like pointed beads.

She probably wouldn't be adding more today. The arrangement of the wagons suggested that they were driven by families who had banded together for safety. Almost all of the horses were pulling wagons and carts. Packs burdened both humans and animals. A few dozen people walked behind on foot, some of them children.

And perhaps one hired soldier. A mercenary, maybe, or a roaming warrior who earned his coin as he traveled. A dark figure mounted on a gray horse, he halted on the side of the road, as if studying her as Mala studied him. He would see no more detail across the distance than she did—Mala would be a red-cloaked figure atop a brown horse—but the color of her cloak would tell him enough. Only those who quested for Vela wore such garments.

For good or ill, the cloak always drew notice. The goddess favored and protected those who served her, and seeing Mala inspired in some strangers the hope that the terrors wrought by Anumith the Destroyer were coming to an end. But Mala had also encountered those who had challenged Vela's protection, most of them determined to prove that the goddess was weaker than the demons and demigods they worshiped.

Mala wore those challengers' teeth, too. She hadn't even needed to call upon the goddess to defeat them. When she'd faced groups of more than three or four, Shim had come to her aid, instead.

Now she told him, "Be easy, friend."

The appearance of these strangers was an unexpected

boon. Shim would have a fresh trail to follow through the maze, and if they weren't averse to talking, Mala could learn more about the beast she'd come to find.

As the stallion started forward again, Mala's attention returned to the mounted warrior. He'd ridden to the tail of the caravan, waiting near the crevice as the last of the travelers emerged. Mala frowned. Instead of walking at a steady pace, now they rushed ahead. The caravan had stopped, the train breaking apart as wagons and carts drove off the sides of the road and clustered into a group.

Circling, she realized. Creating a defensive wall. Against what?

The warrior's gray horse pranced uneasily. Steel glinted at its side. His rider had drawn a sword, and he backed his mount away from the crevice.

Shim suddenly pitched to a halt, ears laid flat against his head and nostrils flaring. Mala's thighs gripped his sides, her body swaying with the abrupt motion. Furtive movement drew her gaze to the cliffs surrounding the maze's entrance. Shadows crept across the bleak stone face.

Dread filled her stomach. *Revenants.*

The creatures would rip the humans apart.

"Shim!" she cried, crouching low over his neck and gripping his thick mane in her left hand.

The stallion surged forward. The beat of his hooves quickened, each powerful stride cleaving the distance. The wind and rain blasted Mala's cheeks and whipped tears from her eyes, but she kept her gaze on the slinking shadows. While unmoving, they had only appeared as crags on the rock face, but their hunt betrayed their positions. Almost three dozen of the creatures. Once, they might have been goats or dogs or ponies. Befouled by demons, revenants only faintly resembled the animals they'd once been—and most animals couldn't have traversed that sheer cliff face, yet they slithered across it like sinuous spiders.

Still four sprints away. Each sprint measured the distance that a good horse could race without flagging, yet Shim was still gaining speed. Few mounts could have matched his swiftness or endurance.

But they wouldn't be swift enough. The revenants were gathering high above the warrior's head, beyond the reach of his sword or spear. If they charged him one at a time, he might stand a chance. But that wasn't how revenants fought. They would strike all at once to overwhelm the strongest foe, then individually pick off the weaker prey. Only when the slaughter was finished would they return to devour their kill.

Hold them off, warrior. Unslinging her bow, Mala didn't tear her gaze from the man who faced his oncoming death with his sword held firm. *Stay alive as long as you can. I am coming.*

The warrior continued backing his mount farther from the cliff, gaining more distance and more time to prepare for the creatures' inevitable attack. Behind him, other men and women abandoned their attempts to corral panicking live-stock behind the safety of the wagons. It didn't matter. Whether running free or tied to a cart, the animals would find no protection after the humans fell, and their barricade would not stop the revenants.

Perhaps the travelers' arrows would. Three figures had clambered atop the wagons with bows in hand. Others stood with pitchforks and scythes. The mounted warrior raised his sword high in the air. The archers aimed at the squirming mass of gathered revenants and drew back their strings.

The warrior swept his blade forward. The archers loosed their arrows.

Like pus from a lanced boil, the revenants burst away from the cliff and poured down its stone face in a dark flood of teeth and claws.

Mala's heart bolted against her ribs. "By Temra's fist, Shim—*faster!*"

Flying couldn't be faster, yet Shim's huge body surged ever harder as the wave of demon-fouled creatures swamped the warrior. The gray horse reared, forelegs striking. For an instant, its rider was raised above the swarming mass. His sword flashed in powerful strokes.

He was still swinging his blade when the revenants over-whelmed his horse and pulled him under.

Teeth clenched, Mala held back her shout of rage. Silver-fingered Rani would soon carry that man into Temra's arms—and the revenants' blood would soon spill in a river over Mala's feet.

Only two sprints remaining. Still too far for her arrows.

A revenant slipped from the writhing pile atop the fallen warrior and streaked toward the wagons. Another followed. Another.

Screams pierced the distance. Terrified women, men, children. The revenants' skin-crawling shrieks and howls joined in. As if to escape the horrifying cacophony, a frenzied ox fought against its harness, whipping its hooked horns from side to side. The wagon behind it jolted forward. Suddenly unbalanced, an archer standing on the driver's bench toppled to the ground and scrambled underneath a nearby cart. A revenant followed him. More of the creatures climbed over the sides of the barricade and slipped beneath the wagons.

Pulse pounding in her ears, Mala counted the beats as Shim's swift strides carried them nearer to her arrows' range. Only a few more breaths.

A revenant bounded from the left side of the barricade, dragging a small child by the arm. A screaming woman ran after him, her shoulder stained with blood. The boy was still moving, toes and knees digging at the ground as if trying to find purchase on the rain-slicked earth.

Swiftly, Mala sat up. Her wet bowstring released with a taut *flict*, spitting rainwater over her wrist. The arrow fell short of the revenant—and the next would only fall shorter as the foul thing raced toward the cliff.

She crouched over Shim's neck again. "Carry me to the caravan!" she shouted into the wind. "Then save the child if you can!"

At a full gallop he approached the wagons. Arrow notched, Mala searched for a target, but the barricade blocked her view of the people and revenants within the circle, and she dared not loose her arrows on the creatures fighting the humans atop the wagons. While riding at this speed, her aim was not so true, and she might hit the travelers, instead.

Her blade would not miss. Slinging her bow, she reached for her sword and fixed her gaze on the nearest wagon. "That one!" she cried.

Without slowing, Shim struck a course that would take her

past it. A yellow-haired youth crouched atop the sacks of grain stacked high on the wagon's bed. With a small knife, he slashed wildly in the direction of a revenant stalking him from a nearby cart, as if to keep it at bay. At his back, another revenant scaled the side of the wagon in a single leap. Once, it might have been a long-toothed snow cat. Now nothing remained of its thick white fur, and its blood-blackened hide hung loosely over emaciated flesh. Jute sacks ripped open beneath the creature's talons as it clawed its way closer to the boy. Alerted by the noise, the youth spun to confront it, his eyes wide and his mouth a pink rictus of terror. His blade was shorter than the revenant's canine teeth.

Mala's blade wasn't—and she was only a breath away. The revenant abruptly froze, its ragged ears flicking backward, as if the creature suddenly recognized the danger thundering closer.

Gathering her legs beneath her, Mala vaulted from the saddle. The revenant whipped around as she flew toward it, propelled by Shim's speed. Teeth like daggers, the creature lunged. Grunting, she swung her blade with enough force to spin her body in mid-air, red cloak flaring open. Her weapon razed its emaciated neck, steel slicing through the gristle and slinging its stinking blood in a wide arc.

She landed hard halfway up the piled sacks of grain. Seeds spilled over her boots like sand. The revenant's head rolled past her feet. Atop the stack, the youth stared down at her with the creature's rancid blood splattered in a crimson path across his chest.

Mala leapt over the long-tooth's headless corpse and scrambled up the pile. "Get down, boy!"

As if suddenly remembering the revenant stalking him from the cart, he paled and spun to face it, brandishing his small knife. *Not* getting down, as she'd told him to.

Curse it all. She snatched up a grain sack and flung it at the backs of his knees. His legs collapsed at the same moment the revenant pounced at his head. Mala braced her feet and greeted the creature, instead. Her blade rammed into its chest. Fetid breath gushed from its snapping mouth, only a handbreadth from her face. She ripped the steel through its heart.

With her foot, she shoved the creature's convulsing body off her sword and stole a glance toward the cliffs. Shim had caught up to the revenant dragging the child. Most of the creatures still swarmed over the warrior and his horse—as if in the shrieking chaos of their numbers, they didn't realize their opponent had already fallen. Mala didn't know whether she had the rot in the revenants' brains or the goddess Vela to thank for their confusion, but it meant that the caravan wasn't yet overwhelmed by the creatures, and she could more easily cut down the handful of revenants attacking the travelers. When Shim returned, together they would slaughter the ravenous swarm, but the people within the barricade needed her help first.

On the ground, a gray-haired woman clutched a pitchfork in her wizened hands. Her shoulders butting up against the wagon's side, the crone desperately held off a wulfen revenant, stabbing the tines at its slobbering jaws. Two shouting men clubbed a befouled spitting lizard, smashing the spines circling its leathery neck, though it was too late to save the woman pinned beneath its claws. Children screamed and scrambled and hid. A frantic horse pitched and bucked, striking a revenant in the throat, then a glancing blow to a fleeing woman's hip, sending her sprawling to the ground. Everywhere Mala looked there was blood, and the air was filled with cries of terror and the stench of death.

No more. Gripping the hilt of her sword in two hands, she took a flying leap off the wagon and into the fray. A single blow cleaved the wulfen revenant's spine. Rain pelted her face as she charged the next, meeting razored fangs with hard-edged steel, and the creature's hot blood sprayed over her hands.

Each breath, each step, another swing of her blade. No slowing, no stopping. Too late, the revenants within the barricade understood that they'd pursued their individual prey too quickly, that they should have mobbed this new foe, but by the time the creatures began attacking her in twos and threes, they were the last—and two or three would *never* defeat her.

Sweat mingled with the rain and blood by the time she kicked away the final stinking corpse and faced the wagons nearest the cliffs. Around her, the travelers cried out in relief, but Mala could not join them. This wasn't finished; the second wave of creatures should be coming. Yet no new revenants were storming over the barricade.

Did they still swarm over the fallen warrior? She couldn't hear their shrieking now. Over the travelers' din, all else was quiet.

Carefully, she slipped between two loaded wagons and glanced out. A revenant's head flew past her shoulder and *thunk*ed against a buckboard. Astonishment pulled her up short.

The warrior still lived. Knee-deep in slaughtered revenants, his blade gory and his body soaked by the carnage. He chopped through the neck of the last and swung toward her, his face a mask of blood and the unseeing madness of battle still burning in his eyes.

And she was a stranger. Mala immediately spread her hands, the haft of her sword dangling from her loosened fingers, trying to present as little threat as possible.

"It is finished, warrior!"

Weapon raised, he stared at her, his body frozen in place but for the heaving of his broad chest. Studded leather bracers guarded his forearms, but the corded muscles of his upper arms were bare. The revenants' claws had scored ragged furrows in his flesh.

Not just blinded by the frenzy of battle, she realized, but by pain. Viscous crimson matted his dark hair and lay thick over his clothes and skin. She couldn't tell how much of the blood was his, but he hadn't fought through the swarm of revenants and emerged unscathed.

Vela, help him. And Mala, too. She had defeated men of his size before—men who had been so certain of victory when they'd faced her, simply because of their great heights and the strength in their thickly muscled arms. She had defeated men more heavily armored than this one. But when battle-madness possessed warriors, it bestowed upon them a wholly different kind of strength, one that did not falter with injury. Pain fed the bloodlust and rage, and they couldn't be stopped except by death.

The bloodlust had probably saved his life. Even Mala could not have survived so many revenants. Not alone—unless the madness of battle had possessed her, too. But if he came for her now, one of them would die by it.

Mala didn't want to die. And she didn't want to kill the man who had stood firm and risked everything to protect the people in the caravan. Such warriors were far too rare in these cursed lands.

"It is finished," she repeated, more quietly this time. "Your sword has feasted on the flesh of every revenant at your feet, and those that made it over the barricade have been slain—"

"You have come." His harsh interruption startled her to silence. "Finally come."

He dropped his sword. Mala's heart jumped against her ribs, and she started forward, thinking that she would have to catch him before he collapsed into the pile of corpses, but he began to wade through the carnage, instead.

Wading toward *her*—and the bloodlust in his eyes had been joined by fierce hunger.

"I waited for you, little dragon," he said roughly. "Every night, I dreamed of you. And now I will have you."

CHAPTER 2

No. Mala would *not* be had like this.

"Warrior, do not come closer," she warned. "You've waited for nothing."

"Nothing? No." Triumphant laughter filled the warrior's eyes and voice. "You have come and it is not the end."

Easily Mala spun the haft in her palm and gripped her sword properly. "It will be."

He grinned, his teeth white in that face of red. Bits of flesh and blood dripped in a trail behind him. "You know me, little dragon."

Little dragon. He spoke the name as if to a loved one. Did he even see her, or did he see someone else? Was the madness putting a false vision behind his eyes?

Curse it all. Mala didn't want to kill him. Yet if he took a few more steps, she would rip open his throat. It didn't matter that he was unarmed. He was tall, towering over her, and his shoulders were twice the breadth of hers. Combined with the bloodlust, his strength and size made him as dangerous as ten men with swords.

She raised her blade and hoped either the sight of her weapon or the steel in her voice would pierce his senses before it was too late. "I don't know you, warrior. But if you come closer, I'll be on intimate terms with your still-beating heart."

His grin faltered—as did his step. Hoarsely, he asked, "You don't know me?"

So he had heard her. "I don't," she said.

He halted. Confusion darkened his laughter into a frown, then sudden awareness flared across his face in a painful spasm. Abruptly his fists clenched at his sides and he closed his eyes, as if shutting out the sight of her. His heaving breaths became slow and controlled.

The madness was passing, she realized—and he must be feeling his injuries. Mala's tension eased, but although she lowered her blade, she didn't glance away from him and didn't drop her guard.

Finally she asked, "Are you yourself again?"

Mala didn't know who that was, but she suspected it was not the man who had come for her with that wild and ecstatic grin. That suspicion was confirmed when he looked at her, and instead of laughter there was only the hardness of stone.

When he spoke again, his voice was as rough as the side of a mountain and as bleak as the cliffs. "How many?"

He did not ask how many revenants, Mala understood. This was every honorable warrior's curse—to never remember the number of lives saved, and to never forget how many he hadn't. The sounds of relief coming from within the barricade had given way to the grieving wails of the living and the agonized cries of the wounded. Now that the bloodlust was fading, he must hear them.

"Three," she said softly. "Two men and one woman. Two others will only survive the night with Nemek's blessing. There are a few who might lose a limb, or who might not rise from their sleep until many days have passed, but they will live. Some livestock will have to be put down before the revenants' poison transforms them."

Hoofbeats neared. Shim. Mala glanced at the stallion. Sweat lathered his flanks and crimson spattered his legs. Nearer to the cliffs, a revenant lay pulped on the ground, and the woman with the bloodied shoulder was carrying the sobbing child back toward the caravan.

She looked to the warrior again. He was watching her with

an unwavering gaze, the whites of his eyes a piercing contrast to the red masking his face. A thick and tangled beard hung to his chest and dripped blood onto his molded leather breastplate. If he wore a crest upon his armor, the gore concealed it.

The blood couldn't conceal the rips in his woven tunic and slashes in the winter furs belted over his loose brocs. What hadn't been protected by armor had been shredded by the revenants' teeth and claws. Though she couldn't see the flesh beneath his clothing, the muscles of his legs and back must have been gashed as badly as his arms.

That might be why he hadn't yet taken a step since the madness had passed. He had to be in agony. "Have you anyone in this caravan who will see to your wounds, warrior?"

He abruptly looked away from her. "No. I only ride alongside them."

As a hired man. But she'd already guessed as much. Though a few travelers had peered over the wagons, none had called to him with concern. They'd only been making certain that the revenants were dead.

So she would tend to him, warrior to warrior. Not yet. He still hadn't moved—probably because he didn't know if his next step would bring him to his knees. Mala's pride would have pinned her in place, too. If he had to fall, best to give him privacy to do it.

She turned away. "I'll see to the livestock."

No response from the warrior. Instead his penetrating gaze returned to her face, and he silently watched as she gestured Shim closer and retrieved the single-bladed axe lashed to her saddle. She pushed the handle into her belt, then dragged the tack from Shim's sweating back.

"Scout the entrance to the maze to make certain that no other revenants are lying in wait," she told the stallion. "Then take your ease. I'll rub you down when we've finished here."

With a nicker and a soft butt of his head into her chest, he trotted off. Glad to be away from the stinking pile of revenants, most likely. Probably glad to be away from the wailing humans, too.

She glanced at the warrior. Shadowed by heavy black brows, his dark gaze followed the stallion before he suddenly turned his head, searching the ground. He stilled again when his gaze lit upon the heap of corpses, and all expression wiped from his face, as if a cold wind had scraped across a bare rock.

His horse, Mala realized. His mount's body lay beneath the carnage. Perhaps he'd been attached to the animal, and perhaps it had only been useful to him—but a hired warrior was only worth as much as his steed, and if his mount died, often several seasons passed before he could earn enough to buy another. Sometimes years.

Mala only had to look at this warrior's face to know the gray horse's death was a devastating loss . . . and to know that he would not welcome her sympathy.

Her chest tight, she strode around the wagons, the red cloak sweeping out behind her. Ahead, two men squabbled over a limping ox. A gray-hair held a butcher's blade. The younger barred his way. They both fell silent when Mala pushed past them, and she ended the argument with a swing of her axe. Another valuable animal dead—but this one not a complete loss.

She pointed to the teeth marks on the ox's flank. "Cut away the poisoned flesh. The remaining meat can be saved."

Without waiting for a response, she sought the next infected ox. The old butcher followed her—his knife sheathed now, and his gaze on Mala, not the animal. "It has been many years since anyone wearing the questing cloak has passed through Blackmoor."

Probably not since Anumith the Destroyer had razed Vela's temples and slaughtered her oracles. A full generation. Mala did not say that in her homeland of Krimathe, old men such as he were just as rare. The Destroyer hadn't left any young men alive, so there were none to grow old.

She only said, "I am not passing through—and don't eat this one." Teeth clenched, she silenced a bloodied and bleating goat. The animal's eyes had already begun to redden; the poison had infected its brain. "What fouled these creatures?"

"A tusker," the old man said.

Her breath stopped in her chest. A long-haired mountain of an animal, tuskers were strong and aggressive, with enormous jaws guarded by long, razored tusks. A *beast*, if ever there was one. "Possessed by a demon?"

"It is."

Then unlike the revenants, the tusker wasn't poisoned. A demon's evil inhabited the beast's flesh, instead, giving it terrible strength beyond its own. Because a demon had great power, but like a god, it needed flesh to use that power. Unlike gods, however, the demon didn't work through the living or the willing; demons possessed dead flesh, which could give no consent—and could not withdraw it. After a demon inhabited a body, its corruption fouled all that it touched. The possessed creature could only be stopped if its magical protections were breached and the demon within slain, or if a sorcerer released it from the flesh.

For the first time since visiting Vela's new temple and receiving her quest, real unease stalked Mala's heart. She expected pain. She expected to be driven to the edge of her endurance. But she'd also expected to find an animal in Blackmoor, not an abomination.

Why hadn't the goddess asked her to *slay* the demon? Such a dangerous and laborious task was well worthy of any quest. But to *tame* a demon? It would be easier to tame one of the thunder lizards in the southern jungles—if such a thing was possible at all.

But it must be, or Vela wouldn't have sent her here. The goddess wouldn't have given her a task that couldn't be completed. Only those who doubted her or who proved unworthy failed their quests.

Mala wouldn't fail. If she had to tame a demon, then she would tame a demon. "How long has it plagued these lands?"

"It is said that the demon was imprisoned beneath the fiery mountains to the north until the Destroyer released it from that prison and helped it possess the tusker's flesh."

Many evils were said to be the Destroyer's doing. Often, it was truth. But that sorcerer was not responsible for every evil laid at his feet. " 'It is said'? You don't remember?"

The lines in the old butcher's face deepened, and his voice hollowed. "When so many evils come to your home at once, where they hailed from ceases to matter. It only matters when they leave."

The demon tusker hadn't left. But if Mala tamed it, perhaps she could send it away.

With renewed determination, she continued past the

caravan, to where a brown horse lay thrashing on the wet earth. Another swing of her axe finished the grisly task. The rain was subsiding when she returned to the wagons. Those travelers who were not grieving or tending the wounded had begun to restore order to the train, and she felt their gazes upon her. Some appeared curious. Most were wary and wore an air of resignation—as if they wouldn't have been surprised if Mala had only helped save them from the revenants so that she could destroy the caravan herself.

As if they had learned never to trust those with strength, or those who were supposed to protect them.

Including the warrior who had risked his life for theirs? But at least one person seemed to trust him. Mala paused at the edge of the barricade. Still on his feet, he was wading through the heap of revenants, a gore-covered saddle slung over his shoulder. So he'd gone in after his horse—and his sword. With a blue scarf now covering her yellow hair and a sling supporting her arm, the woman who had chased after the boy was offering him a large wineskin, but the warrior didn't take it.

The woman thrust it toward him again. Her voice rose with frustration. "You will soon need this more than we will, Kavik."

Kavik. He knew Mala stood watching; he'd spotted her the moment she'd come around the wagon. His gaze rested on her face for an instant before he shook his head and responded to the woman. Mala could hear the deep gravel of his voice, but couldn't make out his reply.

But he'd clearly refused the wineskin again. When the warrior walked stiffly past the woman, striding across the thickening pools of blood toward the wagons, she determinedly stalked after him. "What harm will come to me? Lord Barin's reach doesn't extend past the river."

This time he was close enough for Mala to hear his answer. "And your family? Your husband's family? Even after you have gone, they will still reside in this land."

All at once, the fight seemed to leave the woman. Despair and helplessness darkened her expression as she turned her face away, her jaw working as if she could taste the words she wanted to say, but knew uttering them wouldn't make any difference.

The warrior looked to Mala again, but he came no nearer. With a heavy sigh, the woman brushed past him. Tears glittered in her eyes when she stopped in front of Mala and bowed her covered head.

"I am Telani, and I stand forever in your debt." Her voice was thick. "My boy only lives because you helped us."

All of these people lived only because of the man behind her, but Mala would not be so quick to reject the woman's offering.

"My mount needs to quench his thirst," she said, then gestured to the wineskin. "What do you carry?"

"Water." With renewed irritation, the woman shot a glance at the warrior, whose dark gaze had not left Mala's face. As a stranger to them, she expected to be watched. Unlike the travelers, however, Kavik didn't appear wary. Instead he looked at her with an expression both haunted and fervid, as if he saw his death approaching, yet could not bear to glance away from it.

"Water will do." And she wanted to know why this woman had told the warrior that he would soon need it, but only asked, "How fares the boy?"

"We will know when the fever passes." With dirty fingers, Telani touched her injured shoulder. "Several of us will."

Though humans couldn't be transformed into revenants, the creatures' poison produced a dangerous fever. There were remedies for it, but Mala supposed that few of Nemek's healers journeyed to Blackmoor to sell their wares—or if they had, their bones were littered beside the river. Fortunately she had encountered several during her travels.

"Go and tend to him, then," Mala told her. "I will see to my horse and this man, then come to you with a salve to draw out the venom."

The woman's renewed gratitude sat uneasily on Mala's shoulders. If Mala was to tame a demon, and if the salve was not readily available in Blackmoor, she might soon be in dire need of it. But Vela never offered the easy path. If giving the salve to these travelers meant that Mala would soon suffer a revenant's fever, then she would suffer it—and trust that her own strength and the goddess's generosity would see her through it.

Wineskin in hand, she retrieved the salve and an oiled

cloth from her saddlebag. The warrior didn't look away as she approached him, but his big body seemed to stiffen with her every step.

Mala stopped an arm's length away and extended her hand. "Your sword."

His grip tightened on the weapon. Roughly he said, "I won't harm you."

"I didn't fear you would," she told him. "Your blade needs to be wiped clean, and you've been standing with a saddle on your shoulder for so long that the blood has begun to dry. I suspect that you remain still to avoid tearing open one of your injuries. So give the sword to me, and I'll see it cleaned."

His mouth flattened. Without a word, he reached for the saddle and lifted it from his broad shoulder. His gaze never left hers as he held the heavy tack out to his side for one breath, two—then deliberately dropped it.

Stupid, stubborn man. But Mala couldn't say that her reaction would have been any different, so she offered him the oiled cloth.

He abruptly crouched and slammed his sword hilt-deep into the ground, as if driving in a stake. The muscles in his arms bulged as he ripped the blade to the side through the dirt, then hauled it out again. Aside from a ring of blood and mud near the hilt, the weapon had been scraped clean.

His jaw was tight when he stood again. "It is done."

She looked to his arms. The gashes *were* bleeding again, and he stank of revenant. With a sigh, she opened the small pot of salve.

He shook his head. "Don't tend to me."

"You will be fevered, warrior."

"I've lived through a revenants' attack before."

That was not all he'd lived through. Closer now, she could see the ridged scars that marked his skin. A wide slash on his left cheek, as if from a blade. The pucker of an arrow in his upper biceps. A ragged half moon from some animal's teeth lay above his elbow—and there were probably far more scars that she couldn't see beneath the blood, his beard, and his clothing.

She dipped her fingers into the cool salve. "This time you will live through it more easily."

"No." His big hand shot out, covering the pot, his bloodied

fingers trapping hers. "Do *not* tend to me. You will pay for your kindness."

It wasn't just kindness; it was a warrior's honor and duty to care for another's injuries. Even in Blackmoor, it must be. But she only asked, "Why?"

When he didn't answer, she studied him for a long moment. He wasn't much to look at—just a huge bloody mess of matted hair and gore. He reeked like a putrid corpse, too, but his eyes were the warm brown of a good beer. That would be reason enough to like him, but Mala appreciated warriors who used their strength well even more than she appreciated her ale.

And she was more aware of his hand on hers than she'd ever been of any man's touch. Usually she was prying their fingers away or chopping them off. She didn't mind his.

He must have run afoul of someone, though, if he believed she would regret helping him.

"Are you ill-favored by a god?" she wondered.

"No," he said bleakly. "Just forsaken."

If he had been truly forsaken, it might be his own fault—or it might be undeserved, if he suffered from a god's caprice. It mattered not. Mala was not a god, and she was not in the habit of forsaking warriors who had stood against dozens of revenants in the hope of saving a small group of travelers.

Travelers who were apparently escaping the reach of one man, though their families had been left behind. What name had Telani spoken earlier?

"Should I fear Lord Barin?" When his chest lifted on a sharp breath and his gaze hardened, her guess was confirmed. "What have you done to offend him, that he would punish anyone who helps you?"

Anger tightened his face. But he didn't offer a reason. He only said, "Don't risk it."

"Why? Who will tell him?" She smiled and looked up into the gray sky. "The birds? Or will he read the truth in the revenants' bones? Or perhaps I will tell him myself, because I have no wish to hide it. I don't wear this cloak lightly, warrior—and I won't risk Vela's wrath by ignoring someone in need."

She wouldn't have ignored him even if she hadn't been wearing the cloak, but he might be less likely to refuse her if he believed it would inspire a goddess's anger. But old scars were sometimes more sensitive than new wounds, and whatever his reason for denying her—and denying the other woman's simple gift of water—the pain of his injuries must have paled in comparison to whatever retaliation he thought the kindness would bring.

He shook his head and released her, his fingers skimming the back of her hand. "Give the salve to me, then. I'll see to the wounds myself."

That would have to be enough for now. She poured water into a clay bowl, left the wineskin at his feet, and called for Shim. Mala kept her back to Kavik as she rubbed down the stallion's legs. Shim would watch for any danger from behind, but she didn't think that the warrior would pose any threat now. Turning her back gave him privacy to feel his pain. By the heaviness of his breath and the long catches between, she suspected that the agony of removing his armor and tending to his wounds had all but immobilized him.

Yet the rest of the caravan seemed to be preparing to move again. Not right away—there was still much to be done—but no one was setting up camp. "How far do you intend to journey today, warrior?"

"To the river." The response emerged on a grunt, then he hissed before adding, "Beyond that, they travel alone."

Then he would return to Blackmoor? But the question died on her tongue when she looked behind her.

Though Kavik had refused her help, he apparently wasn't such a stubborn fool that he would haphazardly slap the salve over his injuries rather than properly attend to them. To better reach the wounds, he'd removed his breastplate, tunic, and loose brocs, leaving only the winter furs belted around his hips to cover his loins, and the leather-wrapped boots hugging his strong calves. With one arm crooked behind his head, he slicked the cream down a slash alongside his ribs, glistening fingers smoothing over taut muscle.

Her own fingers curled against her palms. She'd known he was strong. She hadn't known that seeing the evidence of his battle upon his flesh would call to hers so forcefully, but her pulse pounded anew.

Hanan be merciful—but that god rarely was. He'd sprayed

his seed throughout the world and rocked the earth with his fuckings. Under his influence, she would be rolling in the blood and mud with this warrior.

She thought that Kavik would roll with her. His head suddenly lifted, and his body stilled as his gaze met hers. No pain in his eyes now. Only the same hunger as before, and no madness with it.

Little dragon.

A fire burned in her now. Not for the first time since she'd earned her sword, Mala wished that she wasn't bound by the obligations of her rank and could seek the same pleasures that her fellow warriors and friends often did.

Still holding her gaze, Kavik covered the pot of salve. "It is finished," he said gruffly.

No, it wasn't. "Do not move, warrior."

She walked slowly toward him, her gaze following the trail of blood over his rippling stomach. His belt hung low on his hips, the line of it bisecting the ridges of muscle that defined his pelvis and the flat plane of his lower abdomen. He'd rubbed salve into a gash on his heavy thigh, smearing the blood around it. He'd had to spread so much on his arms that his skin appeared oiled. His sides had not been spared the revenants' teeth and claws; only his chest, which the breastplate had guarded.

"Do not move," she said again. She was close enough to touch him now, and his hands were clenching as if he stopped himself from reaching for her.

She slipped around his broad shoulder—and sighed. Just as she'd thought. He wouldn't let anyone attend to him, but he couldn't reach his own back.

Mala held out her hand. "The salve," she said.

He began to turn. "Don't risk—"

She jammed her thumb into his torn flesh—a bite wound, already swollen and red. Every muscle in his back went rigid. His breath hissed.

"I am not tending to you," she said. "If your Lord Barin sees this, then it will be said that I am torturing you. Can you withstand it?"

Mala knew he could, because the evidence on his back told her he'd withstood far worse. Not just the revenants' claws and teeth, but more old battle wounds, and the pale stripes of a whip. Had he been enslaved? If so, he must have been young. The edges of the scars had softened with age.

From what she could see, it was the only part of him that had softened. The rest was hard. So very hard. "The salve," she repeated.

Jaw clenched, he lifted the pot over his shoulder, as if to pass it to her.

"Hold it there for me," she said and dipped her fingers in. His back stiffened again as she smoothed the cream over the bite.

A frown darkened his blood-masked face as he looked over his shoulder. "That is not torture."

She hadn't said it would be painful. Her hand slicked forward around his side, her fingers skimming the skin at the edge of his belt. His big body tightened all at once, thick muscles straining. A laugh rumbled from him, cut short by a groan, then he hung his head and was silent.

Mala grinned and soothed salve across parallel slashes low on his back, then slipped her hand beneath the furs to test the hardness of his ass.

Like glorious steel.

"If you didn't stink of revenant, I'd taste you all over," she told him.

A rough sound reverberated through his chest, like another laugh that was strangled before it emerged. Hoarsely he asked, "Will you have me? Will you destroy me completely?"

"I cannot," she said with real regret.

"Then your touch is torture enough." A shudder ripped through him, then he stilled again. "Will you give me your name, red one?"

"Mala." High Daughter of the House of Krima, second in line to the Ivory Throne, and one of Vela's Chosen. "And yours is Kavik."

"Only to those who've known me longest."

"And what does someone call you if she's known you a day?"

His hesitation told her that he took no pride in his current name. "I would have you call me Kavik."

So she would. "Why do you only escort them as far as the river?"

"The revenants attack anyone leaving this land, but they don't follow any travelers beyond the bridge."

"You expected to fight them."

"Yes. But never so many before."

"How many times before?" She recalled the bones and shattered wagons littering the sides of the road—and how they'd been weathered and old. "When did you begin?"

"I returned to Blackmoor five summers ago. Since then, those people who want to leave this land come to me."

Most of those bones had been there longer than five years. So Kavik had stopped the revenants from slaughtering the travelers. Yet the creatures still continued to attack—and though other people risked their lives to leave Blackmoor, he had come back.

But Kavik didn't give her a chance to ask why he had returned. He slowly tensed again, but not by her touch—instead he was frowning at Shim. "Your mount was bitten."

Mala had already seen to the shallow wound on the stallion's chest. But that likely wasn't what concerned the warrior. "He won't become a revenant."

Disbelief filled his voice. "He's one of the Hanani?"

A descendant of the god Hanan, who had not only speared his cock into humans but had also fucked every animal he encountered, no matter how big or small. Those born of his seed were often gifted with abilities beyond the natural. Shim was far stronger and smarter than any other horse she'd ever encountered—but most Hanani animals didn't associate with humans. Shim's herd had resided in the highlands west of Krimathe.

"He is," Mala said.

"He allows you to ride him?" Slowly he turned to face her, his shadowed eyes searching her features. "You must be favored by the gods."

"No. I am only favored by one horse." And only because Mala was patient and stubborn, and she'd promised Shim that he would stomp on many men's heads during their travels.

"And a goddess." His gaze fell to her cloak. "You are a Narae warrior?"

One of the wandering women who served Vela and enforced her laws. Those warriors wore dark crimson cloaks—and most traveling women who claimed to be Narae were not, but simply used the cloak to protect themselves from assault. A bandit couldn't risk being mistaken, because any man who attacked the wrong woman wearing a crimson cloak was a dead man.

But this man knew Mala wasn't a false warrior. "No. I travel on my sacred quest."

"From Vela?" The words were rough. When she nodded, his eyes closed. "Did she send the quest to you in dreams?"

"No, warrior. She speaks to some that way. Not to me. I visited a priestess, instead."

Her reply seemed to open some torment within him, and for an instant the agony in his gaze was deeper than any wound he'd received. Then his face hardened, as did his voice, though the grittiness remained. "And she sent you here?"

"Apparently I am to find the demon tusker."

The scar in his cheek whitened. "She sent you to die?"

"I hope not." Mala trusted the goddess hadn't. "Have you faced it?"

"Yes."

"And lived?" Perhaps it wouldn't be as difficult a task as Mala feared.

"Barely. Many of the men I fought with did not." His gaze searched her face again, his jaw clenched and his nostrils flared, and Mala realized that he was stopping himself from forbidding her to go. He must have realized that she would, anyway. "Keep away from it, if you can. No blade or arrow can breach its hide and I've seen warriors cut in half by a blow from its tusks. Find some way to kill it from a distance."

Mala didn't intend to kill it, only to tame it. But she wouldn't explain now. "Where will I find it?"

"It usually comes down from the mountains when the goddess turns her back."

During the new moon—and the next was almost a full turn away. "Then it seems I will be in Blackmoor for a while. Perhaps I'll see you again, warrior." She hoped to. "Who should I ask for if I wish to find you?"

Eyes like stone, he took a full step back from her. "You would do best to say you have never spoken to or helped me."

Perhaps. But she didn't like that he retreated from her now, so she *would* see him again. "I don't always do what is best. I only do what must be done."

Kavik didn't immediately respond. Instead he looked to the wagons when a hail came from that direction—the caravan was preparing to leave, and Mala still needed to give the salve to Telani and her injured boy.

He drew back another step, his gaze still on her. "Don't drink or bathe in any of the rivers and lakes beyond the maze—they've been fouled by the demon. You'll only find safe water in the wells dug in the city and villages."

So that was why he would need the wineskin full of it. Mala didn't. She would not always be in the city or villages if the beast was in the mountains, but she didn't travel without protection. "Whilst I quest, Vela will bless and cleanse it for me."

Though only if Mala asked. And if she was foolish enough to drink without asking, then she would get what she deserved.

Eyes like stone, Kavik shook his head. "The goddess has abandoned this land."

"I am here, warrior."

"That only means it is almost the end," he said, and his voice was that of a man who did not dare to hope anymore. He only braced himself for worse. "Try to avoid the notice of the warlord."

Lord Barin? Mala would not be able to do that, either. "Why?"

"You're strong." His dark gaze lingered on her features. "He'll want you—or he'll want to break you."

The man standing before her was strong, too. But she wouldn't ask now how Barin had tried to break him. They'd meet again, and perhaps Kavik would tell her. "He can want all he likes. Only I choose who will have me. But I thank you for the warning."

He nodded and, after a final look at her face, turned away.

Curse it all. She called after him, "Are there markings to guide me through the maze?"

It didn't matter if there were. Shim could follow the path.

But she wanted the warrior to look at her like that again, with that strange combination of hunger and bleak torment—because she might understand *why* he looked at her that way if she could hold onto his image a little longer.

"You don't need markings." He bent to his saddle and slung the bloodied tack over his broad shoulder. "Just follow the bones."

CHAPTER 3

Mala could follow the bones all the way to Lord Barin's citadel.

Beyond the maze, the bones no longer littered the ground, but they stood in the people on the road to Perca who watched her with wary eyes. They stood in the fallow fields and the sagging walls of the crofters' huts. They stood in the thousands of bowls and vases set out to catch the rain, and in the desperate faces of the children who quickly backed into the shadows and alleys as Shim carried her into the city.

This was a land stripped bare, with hope carved away. Mala's mother had once told her that Krimathe was the same in those months after the Destroyer had passed through their lands. But Mala's home had recovered. Blackmoor had not, though it had obviously once been strong. Mala could see those bones once she reached Perca, too—in the high walls surrounding the city, the wide roads, and the heavy stone of the city's fortress. They had all been built to last, by careful planning and knowledgeable hands. Now the flesh was gone, and the skin stretched over those durable bones was thin.

Guards were lighting torches at the citadel's gate when Mala rode through. None attempted to stop her or to question her presence there, as if Barin did not fear anyone who might enter his fortress.

She dismounted in the courtyard. Beside her, Shim raised his head, sniffing out the horses tied in front of the garrison on the eastern wall. Saddled, they stood with their backs to the rain and heads down. Two of the mounts responded to his whinny, but all moved uneasily against their tethers, as if they'd caught wind of the revenant blood still staining his legs and Mala's cloak.

The musty scent of peat smoke hung in the air. Two servants crossed the yard, heading for the garrison and carrying a heavy soup cauldron between them. She had apparently come during the guards' supper. Mala pulled up her hood, marking the remaining guards' positions. The courtyard was large—too large for the scarce number standing watch. Most of those who weren't eating waited near the keep's entrance, and a few others walked the battlements.

No vessels stood atop the walls to catch the rain. The people within the citadel must have no trouble procuring water. That couldn't be true for everyone within the city. How desperate must that make them?

Her gaze fell upon the pillories standing in the courtyard's northwestern corner. A dozen of the devices stood silhouetted in the torchlight. She'd never known any city to need so many. Half were in use, the prisoners bent over with their heads and wrists trapped between slabs of darkwood, their pale faces and hands visible through the gloom. Two more guards watched over them, and—

Mala's step faltered. It could not be. Yet she could hear the pained cries from one of the prisoners now.

Her blood seemed to thicken. Pulse pounding in her ears, she turned toward the pillories. Shim kept pace beside her, yet she barely heard the clop of his hooves. One guard watched as the other rutted behind an imprisoned man. He spared her a glance as she approached, but must have thought that she was there to pelt the prisoners with offal or to stand as another spectator. His gaze returned to the rutting pig. It was the last thing he saw.

The scrape of her blade across the bottom of his helm went unnoticed by the grunting pig, but the pilloried woman closest to Mala shrieked when the guard's helmeted head dropped in front of her.

The other guard looked up. He stumbled back one step, brocs falling to his ankles before Mala reached him. She struck twice, and the pig only had a blink to realize that his cock had been separated from his balls before his head joined it on the muddied ground.

Shouts echoed across the courtyard. With rage boiling in her veins, Mala shattered the pillory lock with the butt of her axe. Whatever this man's crime, he'd been punished as no one ever should be and had served sentence enough.

All of these prisoners had. Sick fury rose from her gut as her gaze raced over their soiled clothes, the bruises and stains. She stalked to the first pillory and kicked the guard's head away from the imprisoned woman's feet. Teeth clenched with every bone-jarring swing, she moved down the row, destroying each lock.

"Halt!"

A handful of guards marched toward her. Mala gave them no note beyond a glance. Like any other horse, Shim stood with his head down and his back against the rain, yet his hooves would bash in the guards' helms if they came too close. She continued to the last pillory, where a slam of her boot sent the blackwood slab flying open on the hinge. As if the prisoner's legs were too weak to hold her, the woman dropped into the mud.

Chest heaving, her heart like ice, Mala tossed back her hood and stood waiting in the torchlight, sword and axe in hand. A brute of a woman with greasy lips and a ragged scar over her pale left eye led the guards.

Mala punted the rutting pig's head to her. "Are you captain of these men?"

The gore-stained helm landed at the woman's boots. Shock and anger painted her cheeks red. She reached for her weapon.

"Stay your hand!" Mala snapped. "Are you captain of these men? Heed the cloak I wear and answer well, or I'll spill your lump-weeded brain into the mud with them."

Lips pinched, the woman gripped her sword. Mala grinned. So this guard wouldn't heed the warning. Good. Near the pillories, a bowl of grease and a rod strapped to a belt had told Mala that not only the male guards had been raping the prisoners. By Vela's moon-glazed blade, she would enjoy gutting every one of these bum-birthed scuts.

A guard behind the woman caught her forearm. *"She is Vela's,"* he hissed.

Unease slipped over the woman's anger and she hesitated. Curse it all. Mala would have preferred that these pigs were among those who didn't fear the goddess and attempted to challenge her power, instead.

But if they defied her laws and forced themselves on these prisoners, they obviously didn't fear her enough. Before Mala left this land, they would.

The guard's hand fell away from her weapon. "The captain is at his supper."

"His name?"

"Heddiq."

"Then this will be Captain Heddiq's last easy meal. You will announce me to Lord Barin, then you will visit the garrison and tell your captain to begin running as far from Blackmoor as he can, because if ever I see him, I will not stay my weapon. Perhaps your next captain will know better than to risk Vela's wrath by allowing his guards to violate the prisoners under his charge." She pointed her axe at the other guards. "You three will help these men and women to the citadel gates and release them. One more bruise on any of them and I come for your heads."

Shim would keep watch outside and let her know if she needed to.

The guards exchanged uncertain glances. "But our Lord Barin—"

Mala interrupted them. "Will allow it."

And if possible, would suffer the same fate as the guards. The captain wasn't the only one who should have prevented the guards from raping these prisoners, but Mala wouldn't make threats that she couldn't be sure of carrying out. Earlier that day, when she had returned to the caravan to give Telani the salve, she'd learned from the other woman that Barin had ruled over Blackmoor since the days of the Destroyer—and that the warlord couldn't be killed, though many had tried.

That couldn't be true; even gods could die. But Mala wouldn't test her blade against his neck today.

The guards hastily backed out of her way when she started toward the keep. Solidly built, the towers rose like spears against the night sky. The greasy-lipped guard rushed ahead—most likely to warn Lord Barin and to report what Mala had done at the pillories.

Mala gave the woman time and followed at a slower pace. As she passed through the inner gate, a chill raced down her spine. The rain? By Temra's fist, she hoped it was. But the cold weight in her belly and the sudden urge to draw her sword warned her that this trepidation was nothing so simple.

She'd sensed magic before. Never had such an icy dread accompanied it, but she'd heard this reaction described by her mother, upon first seeing Anumith the Destroyer.

He wasn't here. But either his sorcery was still at work, or someone here abused the same foul magics.

Perhaps it was someone who couldn't be killed.

The lilting notes of a hornflute and the distinctive mossy fragrance of roasted constrictor greeted Mala at the entrance to the great stone hall. So the warlord was at his supper, too.

She paused between the stone columns at the head of the chamber. The hornflute player danced in the center, the silver threads in his embroidered tunic catching the firelight from the torches. On either side of the room, two darkwood tables ran the length of the walls, each heavily laden with platters of sugar-dusted fruit, steaming soups, and a portion of the roasted snake. The benches were filled—by courtiers, she judged. Intricately woven garments in bright colors adorned many of the men and women, and even those who were dressed more simply wore finer cloth than any Mala had seen outside the citadel.

At the far end of the chamber, thirteen men ate at a shorter table atop a stone dais. Lord Barin sat in the center upon a tall, carved chair—but even if he hadn't chosen to raise himself above the others or wrap himself in yellow robes edged in gold, his position would have been impossible to mistake. The fanged head of the giant constrictor gaped open near his left hand, and the first portion of its roasted body stretched to the end of the table. The longest portions fed the courtiers at the other two tables, but the tail ended at the warlord's right hand, as if the snake's body had circled the room. The message was clear: even the very food these people consumed began and ended with Lord Barin.

Though he had ruled this land for almost thirty years, the warlord didn't appear much older than Mala. No gray threaded his brown braids or his short beard, and his tanned skin appeared smooth and unlined, marked only by the sun tattooed around his right eye.

The cold dread in her stomach sharpened. That tattoo marked the sun god's disciples. The Destroyer had been one, too—before claiming that he *was* Enam, freed from his fiery prison in the heavens and reborn. Not all who wore that mark believed it. But many did.

At the east wall, the greasy-lipped guard was speaking to a tall, wiry man dressed in simple robes. The marshal, perhaps, who would relay the guard's news to Barin. Smug anticipation lit the guard's face as she spoke, and her gaze upon Mala was that of a child's tattling to an elder and hoping to watch the inevitable punishment.

Mala didn't fear it. She strode past the columns. The sound of a sharp breath to her left made her glance in that direction. A dozen people sat naked and leashed, each one wearing a thick leather collar.

Hot fury exploded through the icy dread, but she forced herself to continue on. She didn't know what purpose or punishment those people served. But she would find out.

Silence fell over the hall. His pale gaze upon her, Barin had raised his hand for quiet. For a long moment, there was only the light sound of her footsteps, the rustle of cloth as the courtiers shifted to better see her, and the faint crackle of the torches. The marshal bent his head to Barin's ear.

She reached the dais. After a nod from Barin, the marshal straightened. His deep voice sounded through the hall. "Our glorious liege welcomes the High Daughter of Krimathe to Blackmoor!"

Mala hadn't told them who she was, yet she wasn't surprised that he knew. Rumors traveled the roads even faster than Shim did. "You were expecting me, my lord?"

He leaned forward slightly, his glacial eyes arrested on her face. His angular features were handsome, almost beautiful, yet she preferred the fanged grin of the roasted snake near his elbow to the small smile upon his lips. "It is said that a red-cloaked daughter of Krimathe has journeyed across the mountains on a quest, and that as she travels, she has been renewing alliances that have long lain fallow. When I heard of you, I hoped that your quest would lead you through Black-moor. Do you intend to form an alliance with me, as well?"

Not in a thousand years, not as long as this man ruled this country. Alliances had only foundered because the Destroyer had corrupted so many royal houses, or killed them and replaced their heads with his own men—and because it had taken a full generation for Krimathe to gain the strength to look outside of its own borders again.

But Mala only said, "It is true that your predecessor, Karn of Blackmoor, was once a strong ally, and I hope that we might once again renew ties with your people. But I have also come for another purpose."

"Your quest? And what is it?" His brows arched with amusement. "To kill more of my guards?"

"If necessary."

"You must believe it is." Indolently he leaned back in his chair. His golden robe fell open, revealing a smoothly mus-cled chest. More runes had been tattooed down his throat and across his pectorals, but Mala recognized none of the sym-bols. "As a daughter of Krimathe, you must be especially sen-sitive to such punishments."

Because after the Destroyer had killed every man and boy that he hadn't already enslaved for his armies, he had set his soldiers upon every remaining woman. But although Barin's careless reference to the most horrific assault her people had ever endured steamed Mala's blood, she would *not* be baited.

"I administer Vela's justice," she said. "And before we ever speak of an alliance, I must first know if I must administer it again."

"Upon me?" Barin's grin seemed to crawl up her spine and was answered by a few uneasy titters from the listening court-iers. "For what offense?"

Probably more than the one she was about to name. "You have men and women leashed in this chamber."

"And you wonder if they are enslaved? Let me set your avenging mind at ease, Krimathean. To pay their debts, they have chosen to serve me in this manner." He rapped upon the table. "Come up, Gepali. Your deliverer has arrived to rescue you from your labors."

Oh, she would not draw her sword. *She would not draw her sword.* No matter how she wanted to.

Unlike the other tables, Barin's had been covered by a long blue cloth that concealed everything beneath. Mala had thought the man sitting two seats to the warlord's left had been drunk—his eyes were glazed and his skin flushed, and he'd only seemed to be half listening while she spoke to Barin. But when a collared woman emerged from beneath the cloth, her mouth red and her lined face a portrait of humiliation and misery, Mala could only imagine taking her blade to every single courtier in this chamber.

Gripping her leash, Barin tugged the woman closer. "Tell us, Gepali—tell all who are here—is it by choice that you serve me and my court?"

The old woman had to draw two long, shuddering breaths before the answer came. "Yes, my lord."

"And do you enjoy performing with my guests?"

Her tortured gaze flicked up to meet Mala's. "It is my honor to please them and to repay his lordship's generosity to my family."

Generosity. Mala wondered what threat Barin had made toward her family that this woman—that all of these leashed people—had chosen this, instead. If he'd threatened their lives, there would be no difference between choice and force.

But merely asking this woman whether that was true might endanger her family, too. And remembering Kavik's warning that any kindness might earn Barin's retaliation, she dared not offer Gepali encouraging words, either. Mala would have vowed to her that she wouldn't leave this land without seeing Lord Barin dead.

She silently made the vow to Vela, instead, knowing the goddess would hear her and hold her accountable.

"So you see that I have spoken truth, chosen one," Barin said and pulled on Gepali's leash again. The old woman sank to her knees, unresisting. "Now tell me why you so urgently seek alliances from our neighbors. Perhaps you have also heard the rumors that the Destroyer is returning from across the western ocean?"

No reason to lie. "We have."

"It is no rumor. He comes." Those pale eyes seemed to glitter with amusement, as if Barin could sense the shiver that raced over Mala's skin. "So it would be best for you and your people to form that alliance with me, because there will be no standing against him. He is the storm, and the wind, and the sun."

Then Mala and her people would be mountains. They didn't need to stand forever—only long enough. "Then we will speak of alliances after I have completed my quest. I have been told that a demon tusker haunts the mountains to the north."

Barin abruptly stilled, his gaze intense on hers. "You seek to destroy the demon?"

Did he not want her to? Watching his reaction just as intently, she said, "Vela has sent me to tame the beast of Blackmoor."

Utter silence. As he stared at her, the warlord's expression loosened into stunned disbelief—then he snorted, and laughter erupted throughout the great hall, rising like thunder as courtiers slapped their knees and the tables, reaching a hysterical pitch. But although everyone laughed, not everyone meant it, and Mala saw the grief and confusion that passed over the faces of some. The marshal, who looked to the floor; Gepali, who looked to the heavens. A few of the courtiers wore grins that seemed like a rictus of death, and their chests hitched as if they'd rather be sobbing than laughing.

"Hold, hold!" Barin stood, calling for quiet, his amusement still shaking through every word. His glittering gaze fell upon Mala again. "I have longed to see that beast tamed again. This is the brightest news that my court and I have received in some time."

Again? "Vela must believe I can achieve that which you have only longed for, my lord."

"Not if you search for the beast in the mountains. You should wait for him in the Weeping Forest, instead—or at the maze, as he should be returning through it shortly. And you will need this." Quickly he pulled Gepali up by her graying hair and unbuckled the collar. "If you bring the beast back

here, tamed, I would not have much use for this one any longer. I would consider her debts paid in full if you return with
him on her leash. I will consider *all* of my servants' debts
paid, and remove the collars of every one, for the beast on a
leash is worth more than a dozen others."

Jaw set, Gepali stared back at Mala with wild eyes—as if
silently begging her to *refuse* the offer. With ice filling her
stomach again, Mala strode forward to accept the collar.

"My lord," she said, "I know of a man who will shortly be
returning through the maze. Do I seek the one called Kavik?"

At the mention of his name, silence again—but Mala
imagined the click of Barin's teeth as he grinned, and she saw
more runes tattooed into his palms as he held out the coiled
leash and collar. That familiar cold dread scraped down the
back of her neck, and she lifted the leather from his grasp
without touching his skin.

"That is he." Barin sat back again, softly petting Gepali's
head. "You have met?"

"We have." With a thin smile, Mala bowed. "I will return
when my quest is finished, Lord Barin."

He nodded, still so pleased, and though her hand itched for
her weapon, Mala didn't try to take his head with her sword.
Clutching the leash and collar, she strode between the courtiers' tables, ignoring their shouts of encouragement. Her gaze
fixed upon the group of leashed debtors. Though she held
their freedom in her hand, there was little hope to be seen in
their faces when they looked at her. Their spirits seemed to
resemble this land, barren and gaunt.

And though there had to be others who stood against
Barin, Kavik was the only one she'd seen fighting for any of
Blackmoor's people. Now she would bring him here with a
collar on his neck?

She made it past the columns before sour bile shot up her
throat. Forcibly she swallowed it down. Vela could be cruel,
but this could not be what the goddess meant by taming. And
it wasn't how Mala would have tamed any being—beast
or man.

But no doubt this was what Kavik would think she
intended to do to him. *Again*, if Barin was to be believed.

Outside, the rain had returned in full force. Shim met her

near the inner gates. She wrapped her arms around his neck and buried her face in his mane.

This could not be what Vela intended. It could not be. Mala simply had to trust in that.

But her voice was still thick when she said, "It is never the easy path, is it?"

And there was nothing to do but follow it.

KAVIK finally dreamed of her again.

After two years without seeing her while he'd slept, her return was more torturous than the absence had been— because this was not a vision sent to him, but a memory. This time he didn't watch her from a distance, as a stranger. This time he knew the warmth of her touch. He knew the huskiness of her voice. He finally knew what to call her.

Mala.

He met the gray dawn with her name on his tongue and need hardening his flesh. But the torture wasn't over. Because she'd finally come. The woman who hadn't been much younger than Kavik the first time he'd seen her, a stripling Krimathean with a long brown braid and a wild edge to her grin. He'd watched her train with sword and axe and fist, just one of many young women and men—and he'd watched her practice alone by moonlight until her arms shook from exhaustion. He'd watched her fight; he'd seen her face ground into the dirt by her opponents and he'd seen her win. He'd watched her scream with laughter after diving into icy mountain streams and dance in the firelight until her body glistened with sweat, and as she knelt with tears dripping over the unmoving figure on her mother's bed.

That death was the last time he'd dreamed of her. And though Kavik knew Mala's face better than his own, he'd never imagined the woman in his dreams would be the woman in red. He'd never seen her wear the color before. But now she was here—and she was the woman who heralded his end.

So it was time to meet it.

Stiffly, Kavik rose from the bed he'd made on the ground, with his brocs laid out beneath him and his saddle pillowing his head. His breath steamed in the morning air and the cold ached through to his bones. The previous night, darkness had forced him to stop at the head of the labyrinth. A fire would have drawn the leather-winged raptors that hunted these canyons and the sun wouldn't climb above the maze's high walls until midday. If he wanted warmth, he needed to start moving.

His brocs were crusted with dried blood and dirt, but he dragged them on, then slung the saddle over his shoulder. Pain tugged at his wounds, but it wasn't the agony he'd expected. Mala's salve had not only drawn out the revenants' poison and kept the fever at bay; his injuries were healing faster, too.

Many charlatans claimed to sell potions blessed by Nemek, yet in all of his travels, Kavik had never met a divine healer. Mala had come across one, though. She must truly be favored by the goddess.

Vela's favor wouldn't help her defeat the demon tusker. The goddess protected those who quested for her, but they had to complete their tasks without Vela's assistance.

With every step through the maze, Kavik debated whether to offer his. If Mala coming to Blackmoor meant his end, then he could think of few better deaths than while fighting beside her against the demon. That creature had plagued his people too long. And all the while, he'd pray to Hanan that she would torture him with another touch, and burn him with the heat in her eyes.

Another good way to die.

But she would pay for his help when Barin took notice of it, and if Kavik was dead, he wouldn't be able to stand with her against the warlord. He could help her . . . but doing so might hurt her worse than the demon could. Which meant the choice would have to be Mala's, not his.

And throughout these long years, Vela hadn't abandoned him. Instead the goddess had remained nearby, sliding her blade so slowly into his heart that he hadn't even known she'd pierced his flesh. She'd promised to return when he'd lost everything. And what had he left? No family. No home. Not even a horse. So Vela only had to twist the blade through his heart—and somehow, she would use Mala to do it.

At least he would see her again. And it wouldn't be a dream.

KAVIK passed through Perca's gates just before the guards closed them for the night. Familiar rage clutched at his throat when he glanced up and saw the torches burning in the citadel towers, so he kept his head down through the streets. Better not to think of Barin.

Instead he would think of how to find a horse. A full day had been lost walking through the maze and across the moors—and Kavik couldn't hunt the demon on foot. But escorting the caravan had only earned him enough gold to buy a few meals, not a new mount. And although hunger gnawed an ache into his gut, better to save the coins for those days when not even a lizard could be found in the fens.

Except he probably didn't have many more days remaining.

So he would buy a meal. He was already headed to the Croaking Frog, where Telani's sister was innkeeper. He'd promised to let Selaq know whether the caravan had made it across the river, and he had no doubt that Telani had encouraged Mala to stay at her sister's inn. Kavik might find her there.

Along with a dozen of Barin's soldiers. Kavik set his jaw when he spotted their horses in the alley leading to the inn's stables. The Croaking Frog lay near the eastern gate and in the shadow of the city wall, so Selaq served more ale to Barin's men than to travelers needing a bed. Usually Kavik came during the day, when soldiers and guards were less likely to have settled in. There'd be no avoiding them this night.

But no matter how enjoyable cracking their heads would be, Kavik would stay his fists. Selaq didn't need the trouble he would bring.

The inn's thick clay walls trapped the heat from the hearth and the warmth instantly soaked through his wet tunic and brocs. Quiet fell in the common room when Kavik entered, as it always did. Then voices rose again, but he ignored the soldiers' taunts about collars and leashes. He'd heard it all before. His gaze searched the tables. Mala wasn't here.

He fought the heavy disappointment. Her absence didn't mean she hadn't come to the inn. She might have taken a room and preferred privacy to the company of soldiers. He'd learn more from Selaq.

The innkeeper was already almost on him. Though petite, she always moved with the determined stride of a man twice her size, but her step faltered a few paces away. She blinked rapidly, then seemed to steel herself and approached him with tightened lips.

"There's clean water and soap in the basin out in the brewery." Rag in hand, she swatted him in that direction. "Use it."

To bathe in. Kavik shook his head. "Don't—"

"I'm not helping you, fool. Your stench will empty out this room in a breath."

The revenants' blood. Not all of it had washed off in the rain. Kavik hardly noticed the stink anymore—but nearby patrons were covering their faces. "Considering who's here, I should stay as I am."

She snorted and swatted him again. "I don't want them taking their coin elsewhere. Go on." More quietly, she said, "I'll join you shortly."

With a nod, he started across the common room. Best to wash, anyway. Mala had talked of tasting him if not for the stench—even though she hadn't smelled much better at the time.

By Hanan's shaft, it mattered not. He'd have tasted her even if she'd been dipped in dung.

And here was the gods' answer to that. He just had to think of dung and one of the soldiers rose from his table and pushed into his path. Kavik stopped only when another step would have pressed their noses together. He knew this measle. A brute, Delan was one of the few men who stood level with him. But like all of Barin's soldiers, he took Kavik's unyielding gaze as a gesture of disrespect.

They were right. It was disrespect, mixed with the same hatred and rage he felt for their warlord. Fueled by it, Kavik had stared down Delan before. Doing it again would be no effort. He could stand here all night.

But Delan had been distracted by the burden on Kavik's shoulder, and he called out, "Look at this! She's already saddled him."

A burst of raucous laughter came from the soldiers. Someone shouted, "Then we'll all ride the beast!" and then abruptly fell silent when Kavik glanced in that direction.

No one would *ever* ride him again.

And he *would* stay his fists. Maybe. He looked back to Delan and saw the sudden unease in the measle's shifting eyes.

"Now move aside, little pony, so I can take this piss in my

belly outside." Delan's overloud command rang through the room. "Or continue standing in my way so I can piss on you."

Unsmiling, Kavik waited. A span of breaths passed. Finally, Delan muttered and shoved past him.

Shaking his head, Kavik moved on. Pissing on him? Hardly a threat. Kavik couldn't smell worse than he already did.

He couldn't be wetter, either. The rain was to thank for that, and for the basin of wash water. As a brewer whose inn was favored by Barin's soldiers, Selaq had freer access to the city's wells than most citizens did, yet even she didn't waste a drop. The downpour of the past few days offered a few luxuries, however.

Four basins would be needed just to clean his blood-encrusted hair and beard, so he took care of the matted strands with a few sweeps of his blade. Stripping down to skin, he lathered up and rinsed, careful to catch the runoff in an empty bucket. His brocs and tunic went into the rinse water to soak before their scrubbing. Furs, boots, and breastplate wiped clean with a damp rag.

His belt and furs went back around his hips, leaving his torso and legs bare. He hung the linens to drip from the ceiling beams near the ovens and was cleaning his saddle leathers when Selaq finally joined him.

He kept his gaze on his saddle and tried not to sound like an eager boy. "Is the Krimathean woman staying here? The one who wears the questing cloak."

"Yes," Selaq said, but the response seemed hollow. When he glanced over, her normally bright eyes were shadowed in the firelight. "And I pray you will forgive me."

Kavik frowned. "Forgive you?"

"I should have turned her away." Arms crossed beneath her breasts, she averted her gaze from his. "But you know I could not."

All public houses had to follow the law of the road. Long ago, Selaq's own parents had taken in Kavik and his father for the same reason. No innkeeper could turn away someone in need of a bed and with money to pay, even if it meant putting them in the stables.

Yet why would she have turned Mala away? Even if the other woman hadn't helped protect the caravan, Mala was Vela's Chosen—and there were few in Blackmoor more devoted to the goddess than Selaq. As a girl, she'd wanted to be a Narae warrior. Later, she'd hoped to become a priestess and rebuild the city's temples. But when Barin had forbidden any temples but Enam's, establishing an inn and adhering to Vela's rules of hospitality was as close as she'd come . . . until Mala had arrived. If someone had told him Selaq had paid Mala to take a room here, simply to ask the other woman about her journeys, he'd have believed it.

Now Selaq wanted to refuse her lodging? "Did she not tell you that Telani sent her here?"

Confusion filled her voice. "Telani did?"

So Mala hadn't said anything of it. He gestured to the raw wounds on his arms and thighs. "We were set upon by revenants. The Krimathean saved your sister's boy." And many others. "Then she gave her a healer's potion to spare them the fever."

Selaq's face paled and she whispered, "She didn't tell me."

"She shouldn't have had to." And none of this made sense. Frowning, he slowly rose. "What are *you* not saying?"

Swallowing hard, she turned her face away. "Do you know who she is?"

Of course he did. In dreams, he'd seen the palace where she'd eaten and slept. He'd watched her don a hauberk of glittering green dragon scales, and stand in front of a cheering crowd before bowing her head beneath her mother's sword. "She is the High Daughter—and second to her sister."

"Second to her cousin," Selaq corrected softly, and still she wouldn't look at him. "And she is here to form an alliance with Barin."

Ice filled his gut. "No."

"Yes."

"You've seen her cloak," he said. "She's on a quest."

Now she met his gaze, and at the sight of the moisture pooling in her eyes, the ice began to spread into his chest, cold and heavy. "And did she tell you what it was?"

"To slay the demon tusk—"

"No. Oh, Kavik. No." She shook her head, drew a shuddering breath. "She's here to tame the beast of Blackmoor."

There was nothing inside him. Nothing for a long, endless beat. Then a single word, and though it screamed within him, it emerged so quietly. "No."

"It is truth." With arms folded around her middle, Selaq seemed to squeeze herself tight. "Osof was in the citadel's great hall when she arrived. Barin gave to her a collar and leash. She is to bring you back to him."

Osof. The warlord's marshal, who'd once served under Kavik's father. He was one of the few good men remaining in the citadel, and one of the few men whose word could be trusted. Anyone else might have twisted the story and spread a lie. But not Osof.

And so Kavik was to be tamed.

Tamed.

Pain ripped through his heart—the goddess, twisting her dagger. As forceful as a dream, sudden memories crowded his mind. The choking collar on his neck. The soldiers behind. His bleeding knees. Barin's laughter and his father's unseeing stare.

And Vela would put him there again? *Mala* would?

Temra's fist, he could not bear it.

Selaq made a small distressed sound. She stared at him, with eyes wide and fingers twisting. "Kavik?"

Afraid. Of him. As if she could see his rage and agony and knew he was at the edge of warrior's madness, though no revenant or blade had bitten into his skin.

But he *would* control this. If not the anger, then at least his flesh. "Go," he said roughly. "I'll be out."

She edged to the door. "Are you staying?"

"I'll buy a supper."

"I can give—"

"Don't."

She fled. Jaw clenched, Kavik stared after her, wishing that Delan would come back for a piss now. He'd pound the man into a bloodied pulp. And the soldiers who would ride him? His blade would taste their flesh, and he would roast their tongues before they ever joked of whips and collars again.

But, no. That wasn't who he wished to see. He wanted Mala. Vela's Chosen. He would hear it from her own mouth. He would see the truth confirmed by her eyes.

She thought to tame him? Better to die first.

And he would *never* be on his knees again.

CHAPTER 4

By the hushed anticipation that fell over the soldiers when she entered the Croaking Frog, Mala knew that Kavik must have come. Still, she didn't immediately see him, until her gaze searched the darkened corner of the common room. He sat at the end of a long table, apart from the other patrons and facing the door where she stood. His black hair only touched his shoulders now and his beard was shortened and cleaned. If not for the healing gashes on his arms and the width of his shoulders, she might not have recognized him.

Focused on his plate, he didn't glance up as she crossed the room. He ripped away a piece of bread with stiff fingers. Oh, Vela. She hadn't expected that this would be easy. She'd expected his anger. But what she saw in him now was different—the cold, sharp edge of rage. Her own blood and temper were hot, but she knew that ice well. He didn't ignore her out of petulance or bad humor. He ignored her because looking at her might snap his control.

And this was the man who needed to be tamed? He had himself well in hand.

With a sigh, she pushed back the hood of her cloak and slipped onto the bench opposite him. His body tensed only for a moment before he resumed eating, his gaze cast firmly on his roasted meat. He'd bathed. And though she couldn't be certain without glancing under the table, she thought he only wore his belt and furs, along with a leather baldric that crossed over his chest and sheathed the sword at his back.

"So you have a face under the revenants' blood," she said softly. And a fine face it was. Wide cheekbones, a strong nose, firm lips. But she still liked his eyes the best, though they hadn't yet met hers this evening.

His voice like gravel, Kavik told her, "Go home"—then slipped another piece of bread into his mouth, as if she were nothing but a fly to be swatted between bites.

Her chest tightened. "You know I cannot."

"You won't die if you give up your quest."

No. If Mala gave it up, she would be marked by Vela, forsaken and shunned. She would lose her place among her people. But she didn't pursue her quest because she was afraid of failing. She needed to succeed.

"I won't die," she agreed. "But my people might. The Destroyer is returning. We're ready to fight, but our numbers are so few. I've asked Vela to help me find the strength of ten thousand more warriors."

"Make alliances. Pay the rest."

"Do you think we haven't tried? But no one is interested in coming to the aid of another country when their own people are in danger. They make vague promises at best."

"Even Barin?"

He spoke the warlord's name in the same way a wolf ripped a chunk of flesh from a haunch. So it was not just her quest that enraged him. He'd heard of her meeting in the citadel.

"He can promise what he likes," she said quietly. "None of it will come to fruition, because I have vowed to see him dead."

Kavik barked out a hard laugh and glanced up for the first time. The back of Mala's neck tensed as alarm shot through her, yet she stayed her hand instead of reaching for her sword. Never had anyone looked at her with such hatred and anger— but he was still cold. Still controlled.

A sharp smile touched his mouth. "That sounds like a lie you would tell a man you meant to win over. To *tame*."

Sickness balled in her stomach. "That doesn't mean what you believe it does."

"What does it mean, then?"

"I don't know." From all that Mala could see, Kavik was no more savage or feral than she was. So it must be something she couldn't see yet—and so she needed to know him better. "I suppose I must discover what it means."

He shook his head and resumed eating. Not believing her.

Then she would make sure to stay with him until he did. "Though it is not my quest, I still intend to slay the demon tusker while I am here. I would hire your services."

No response.

"I've purchased a mount for your use." Along with two additional pack horses, over which Shim was currently playing lord of the herd. "We could leave for the mountains tomorrow."

Only silence.

That would not break her. Still, she was grateful when Selaq approached their table with two flagons of ale. Setting them down, the innkeeper quickly looked from Kavik's face to Mala's again. "Will you be having supper, too?"

"I will, thank you."

Selaq hesitated. The woman had been abrupt and resentful when Mala had arrived at the inn, and during every following encounter. Now she seemed torn between that resentment and guilt.

Her next words revealed why. "Kavik told me you saved my sister's boy."

"My horse did." Mala pushed one flagon in front of Kavik and picked up her own. "And he enjoys a warm grain mash."

"I'll see that he gets one." But the innkeeper still did not move away, and the twist of her hands revealed that anxiety had joined the guilt. In a rush, she admitted, "I spit in your ale at the midday meal."

"I knew," Mala said easily and took a swig.

Selaq looked at her in astonishment. "But you still drank it."

Of course Mala had. She wouldn't waste good ale because of a little spit. "Have you never kissed someone? It is the same—mouth to mouth and spit to spit. So a drop in that ale was no different than a kiss from you. I considered it my welcome to Blackmoor."

And she'd had kisses thrown behind her feet all day. Word

of her encounter with Barin in the citadel had already traveled through the city. No matter that they called Kavik a beast, not everyone Mala met had approved of her quest, and their reaction told her what she'd already guessed: many of these people cared for Kavik, even though he didn't want them to show it. Yet they cared enough to risk both Vela's and Barin's anger by spitting on the path she walked.

"A poor welcome," Selaq said.

Mala shrugged. A welcome mattered not at all. Only the man across from her did.

His gaze had risen from his plate again, but not to look at Mala. Instead he frowned up at Selaq. The color rose in the innkeeper's cheeks.

"I shouldn't have," the woman said, as if in reply to a silent admonishment.

Had she read disappointment in his expression? Mala searched his face, but she didn't know it as well as the innkeeper did. She could see nothing at all but his frown, then even that was gone when he began eating again.

Oh, but that small exchange gave her hope. The woman had admitted to spitting in Mala's drink, yet he hadn't enjoyed hearing it. For all of his hatred and anger—justifiable anger, if what Mala had guessed of his history with Barin was true—he hadn't taken pleasure in Selaq's insult. Mala suspected that, in his place, every single soldier in the common room would have mocked her or tried to make her feel shame for having sipped a little spit.

He was an angry man. But unless Mala had completely misread the reason for his frown, he wasn't a cruel one.

And there was one way to be certain. One that might put them on a more level understanding.

But she waited, gathering her courage. Mala expected pain on this quest—but she believed it wouldn't come at Kavik's hands. Still, she feared being wrong about him more than she feared what he might do.

Quietly she ate the meal Selaq brought her, and after Kavik refused to touch the ale she'd bought for him, she took it back and drank it herself. When he cleaned his plate, every last crumb of bread and shred of meat and drop of gravy, she couldn't wait any longer.

Without a word, she brought the coiled leash and collar from beneath her cloak, and placed it on the table between them.

And Temra forgive her, because *this* was cruel. For an instant, there was not just rage and hatred when he looked at her, but an agony so deep she didn't know how he'd survived it. An agony she'd seen before, on the faces of some older women at home—as if they'd been subjected to a torture that simply wouldn't end.

She forced herself to speak past the constriction in her throat. "This isn't what it means to tame you."

Jaw like steel, his gaze a cold blade, he only watched her.

"What do *you* think it means?" Mala hoped to understand him better. "Whatever you believe I would do to you—do to me, instead."

His eyes narrowed. "You want me to show you? To *tame* you?"

"Yes," she said simply, but when his gaze went to her neck, she prayed to Vela for strength and courage, because she didn't know how she would bear the collar around it.

And he seemed more enraged now than he'd been. No longer cold but hot, with a pulse pounding in his temple and a flush over his skin. He reached for the collar. His voice was hard. "Come here, then."

First she placed her sword on the table, followed by the daggers from her thighs. Her heart thudded in her ears. Dimly aware of the sudden quiet in the common room, she rose. The jawbones swinging from her belt clicked together as she moved to his side. He stood, so tall, and his gaze locked on her throat. His knuckles were white. The thick leather of the collar had folded under the pressure of his fingers.

His bare chest lifted on a ragged breath. "Put your hands together."

Why? But she didn't ask; she simply obeyed. Kavik moved closer, then relief and hope lifted through her when he wrapped the collar around her wrists, instead. He was angry, so angry. But he wouldn't do to her what was done to him.

Maybe.

Abruptly he yanked on the leash. Her body slammed against his, her armor hard against his chest and her arms trapped between them. His left hand fisted tightly in her hair, tilting her face up. He lowered his and spoke through gritted teeth.

"Now I bend you over this table and fuck you, before I give you to every soldier here. You want me to show you *that*?"

Perhaps the first part, one day. But it should not be today. "In a half turn," she said.

His black eyebrows lowered in a heavy frown. "What?"

"On the full moon." Lifting her chin farther, she bared her throat to him. "Do you see? No scar. I've not yet had my moon night."

And man or woman, a virgin's blood belonged to Vela, and only could be offered when she looked fully upon them.

He shoved the band of her cloak aside, searching beneath the thick material fastened across the hollow of her throat where the ritual scar was usually placed. "Krimatheans don't prize virginity."

"No." Most enjoyed fucking, and enjoyed it often. "But other houses do, and I am High Daughter. It might come to pass that an alliance depends upon a marriage and my acceptability to the person I wed."

"Yet you'll take my cock in a half turn? What of that alliance?"

It had never been certain, anyway. She'd only abstained because of the possibility—and this was just as important. "This is my quest," she said simply. "If you believe that being tamed means being fucked, then I will submit to you. Only to you. But I prefer to honor the goddess when I do." When he didn't immediately respond, but only looked at her as if to determine whether she spoke true, her gaze fell to his strong throat. "You are not marked, either."

His body stiffened. "My moon blood scars are on the back of my neck."

Scars. Not one, but many. And Mala suspected that not one of them counted. Blood by rape was not an offering; it was an offense of the worst sort, to the human who suffered it and the goddess who witnessed it. But this time Mala was the one who was silent, because his rage had turned cold again, and now he would decide—to honor her preference, or not. To bend her over this table, or not. But no matter what he did to her, it would not be the same as had been done to him. Because this submission would be her choice. No one forced her.

His gaze like ice, he gathered up the long leash and tossed it up over a ceiling beam. He hauled back on the leather, dragging Mala's arms up over her head, until she was pulled up onto her toes. The sleeves of her cloak slipped down over her leather bracers, bunching at her elbows. He tied off the leash at her bound wrists.

"Now stay," he said softly and sat at the table again.

Like a dog. Or a horse. Mala almost laughed, but hearing the same reaction coming from the soldiers kept her quiet. With her back to the common room, she hung from the ceiling beam, suspended with most of her weight on her arms and the rest supported by her toes. Uncomfortable, though not terribly. As punishment, it wasn't the worst she'd ever suffered.

She glanced down at Kavik. Pewter scraped over wood as he dragged her flagon to his side of the table and drank. Cooling his anger, perhaps. She still couldn't see how he needed to be tamed.

And she liked him just as well as she had while tending to him after the revenants' attack. Even better now. She'd taken him for an honorable warrior when he'd stood his ground against the creatures, despite the overwhelming risk. Nothing he'd done since had dissuaded her of that opinion. Instead he'd only cemented it.

She would not regret spending her moon night beneath him. There would be no mere submitting to his attentions. She looked forward to them and fully intended to take her pleasure.

Mala hoped to give him pleasure, too. It would be no hardship. His hair was thick and dark, and his mouth so fine. She liked his teeth, so even and white, and imagining their bite sent a hot shiver racing through her. He no longer smelled like death, but soap and smoke, and she wondered if the taut skin of his neck would taste the same as the skin over his sinewy thigh. Soon she would find out, and trace every rigid muscle with her tongue.

She had always loved strength. All her life, she had fought to increase her own. She wasn't like her cousin Laina, the first

High Daughter and heir to the Ivory Throne, whose line had been blessed by Hanan's seed and who could defeat a dozen warriors with barely an effort. Mala could never equal that—and if the worst happened, if Mala ever had to take Laina's place, she would never be as strong. But she had trained and practiced, so that ever if it did occur, she would have as much strength to offer her people as possible.

Now she recognized the same dedication within Kavik, who had not defeated the revenants because his ancestor had been fucked by a god but because he constantly fought to keep himself strong. To protect others. Perhaps to protect himself, too. His path had obviously not been an easy one.

Whatever came of this quest, Mala hoped it made his path less painful to walk. As he tipped his head back to drain the last of the ale, she wondered, "So this is what a taming consists of? I merely have to make you wait for me to finish a meal."

"No." Gaze unfocused, he stared down into the empty vessel. "If your task was to make me wait for you, your quest would already be done."

She frowned her confusion, then recalled that he'd said something similar while struck by the battle madness. *I waited for you, little dragon. Every night, I dreamed of you. And now I will have you.*

Perhaps it had not been madness. "How long did you wait?"

Face hardening, he shook his head. "You are tamed. You should remain silent."

"Holding one's tongue is not what it means to be tamed," she said. "If it were, my quest would have been completed during our supper, when you barely spoke a word. Now, will you signal Selaq for another flagon? I grow thirsty."

His gaze flicked up to her bound wrists. "How will you drink it?"

"I have many talents, warrior. One is that I can carry an ale to my mouth with my feet," she said, and the corners of his mouth twitched before his lips set in a firm line. There. Still angry. But not unreasonable. "I am surprised you do not have me on my knees."

His humor vanished. "What?"

"Were you not showing me what you believe taming

means? You started with a promise to fuck me. Now I only hang here. And although you wait until my moon night, fucking is not all I can do."

The vein throbbed in his temple again. "You want to service me on your knees? In front of *them*?"

The soldiers. Mala didn't even look in that direction. "I care nothing of what they think or say."

Only of what Kavik thought and said. But he said nothing now, and she couldn't read his face, except to know that his expression was like cold steel again.

Mala sighed. "I imagine it is too dangerous for you. Who needs leather and a collar? A man's leash grows between his legs. I would only have to tug on it a few times to make you mine."

"Then a woman's leash must be much shorter."

She laughed. "So it is. And harder to find."

His hand shot out and snagged her belt. Surprise stopped her laugh when he dragged her toward him, the leash twisting as it rolled along the ceiling beam. Her thighs hit the edge of the table, but he continued pulling. Suddenly breathless, Mala swung her feet up and planted them beside his flagon.

Kavik shoved aside her sword and knives. Strong fingers gripping her hips, he settled her in front of him—with Mala sitting on her heels, and her arms still stretched overhead, but almost all of her weight on the balls of her feet.

He swept her cloak open. The red fabric pooled on the table around her. Her breath stopped when he pushed her knees wide.

"How many tugs?" he asked softly, but his voice held the edge of a blade. "How many tugs until you're mine?"

Her heart thundered. "I don't know. No one has had me."

"I will." His long fingers untied the sides of her molded leather cuirass. "And I will *not* be the one who is tamed."

He would. Perhaps not today. But she would not fail in her quest.

Until then, she would take her pleasure in being with him. Her breasts felt tight and heavy when her armor loosened. He couldn't remove the cuirass, not with her arms bound over her head, but he didn't need to. At her waist, his hands slipped beneath the armor and linen undercloth that protected her from chafing. Warm callused palms scraped over her ribs, drawing a shudder of breath from her lips. Her skin seemed afire beneath his.

And by the gods, his face was the finest sight. There was no ice now. Only heat, as arousal joined the anger. His gaze followed the path of his hands, as if he could see her skin and his fingers beneath the armor.

But although her nipples ached for his touch, he could go no higher without ripping the cuirass apart. Perhaps that was for the best. The sharpest ache centered lower.

His burning gaze rose to hers as his hands slowly journeyed to her belt. Panting softly through parted lips, she didn't look away from his face as he whisked away her furs. Cooler air kissed the skin of her inner thighs. Though her knees were spread wide, the soft loincloth tied around her waist hung between her legs and concealed her from his sight.

But not from his fingers. His hand slipped beneath the cloth and found slick, bare flesh. Oh, sweet gods. Her head fell back, and she couldn't stop her moan—didn't want to stop it. By Vela's blood, she wished it were the full moon.

A roughened growl penetrated her bliss. "You're already drenched."

Disbelief filled his voice. With a breathless laugh, she looked to him again. "What did you expect? I have wanted you since the maze, warrior."

His eyes closed, as if in sudden pain. "Since the maze," he echoed hoarsely. "I've wanted you since I first saw you."

"Then I don't know why you've stopped," she said, and his eyes flew open again.

"I won't." He dragged her closer and bent his head. "Not even if you beg."

He swept aside the loincloth. Her body trembled, and she forced her muscles to steel. Then his strong teeth nipped the inside of her thigh, her hips jerked forward, and she would beg, she would beg if he didn't bite her again.

But he didn't bite. He gripped her hips and tilted her forward and licked. And licked again as she cried out and pulled against the leash, bucking against his mouth and thanking the goddess for sending her to find this man. This beast who growled and held her still as he devoured her.

Abruptly his head shot up and he stared past her with jutted jaw, glistening lips, and the promise of death in his eyes. But even as she realized that someone had approached the table, they must have retreated, because he dragged her closer again.

So he wouldn't hurt her . . . and he wouldn't share her, either. Chest heaving, she whispered, "Kavik," and he looked up at her through thick black eyelashes as his mouth gently closed over her clitoris—and softly tugged. He tugged again, and this time she screamed his name, then begged, but not for him to stop. Never to stop, and to give her more, and harder. He licked and tugged again, and again, pushing her closer and closer to the edge. She suddenly froze, her body straining, then shattered all at once when he followed another lick by thrusting his longest finger deep into her sheath.

The orgasm ripped another scream from her, her body writhing and her inner muscles clamping down on him. His satisfied groan buzzed through her flesh. Her spine arched, because now it was too much, she'd begged for more and he'd given her more than she'd been ready for.

His licks softened and slowed. His finger slid from inside her, and though he still held her knees open his touch had changed. The kisses that moved up the length of her thigh weren't hungry, but almost reverent.

Then a soldier shouted, "If your head's down there, little pony, she's got you tamed already!" and Kavik shoved her off the table.

Her blood still roaring, she swung from the beam before her toes found the floor again. Her legs were as steady as pudding. Over the soldiers' raucous laughter, she heard Kavik call for another ale.

She grinned down at him. "I didn't count how many tugs that was, warrior. You might have to do it a second time."

He shook his head. His skin had flushed with anger again—at her, at himself, or at the soldiers, she didn't know. He downed the ale in a few great gulps, then without looking at her, reached past her thigh and slipped his broad thumb into her swollen sheath.

Mala gasped, her muscles tightening around him. She canted her hips to allow him deeper access, but he was already withdrawing his hand and rising from his seat.

Holding her gaze, Kavik brought his thumb to his lips and sucked her wetness from his skin. "I'll wait until I can fuck it."

He abruptly strode past her, abandoning the table. Mala bowed her head, biting her lips against her laughter. She didn't know if he was leaving her to hang or just going outside to jerk the stiffness from his cock, but either way, this quest had started out *very* well—and Kavik was not as cold toward her now as he'd been when she'd first stepped into the inn.

Light steps approached. Mala looked over her shoulder to meet Selaq's concerned gaze.

"Do you need to be helped down?" the innkeeper asked.

"Is Kavik returning?"

"I don't know. He is through the back chamber, gathering his clothes."

So he might be returning. "I'll wait. With another ale, if you'll bring one."

But the next steps that neared weren't Selaq's or Kavik's. Mala swung around to face one of the soldiers, a drunken brute with greedy eyes and his erection making a tentpole beneath his brocs.

His gaze rose to her bound wrists before sliding down her body. "Your beast ran off to his den. But it sounded like he warmed you up good."

Mala recognized this one's voice. *Little pony.* "He did. Now walk away from me. He had my permission. You don't."

The soldier scratched his bristled chin. "Problem is, you warmed up me and my men good, too. And we're thinking it won't be long until you're screaming and squirming on our pricks, and liking it just as much."

She stared at him in disbelief before glancing at the others. They didn't look as eager to fuck as they did entertained. They would enjoy her encounter with this brute no matter the outcome. "Do you not know what I'll do to you?"

"We've heard what you did to the citadel guards." He tilted his big head to the left and eyed her wrists. "Don't know how you'll manage that now."

Easily. "I warn you, soldier. You'll lose any hand that touches me."

Behind him, Selaq came into the common room, carrying

Mala's flagon of ale. Her eyes widened in alarm. "You soused lout, Delan! Get away from her before she takes your fool head!"

Her warning only made him more determined. His lewd sneer turned ugly. "We'll see."

He reached for Mala's loincloth. By Vela, she would not even give him a chance to touch her.

Gripping the leash, she hauled herself up and snapped her booted foot into his balls. He folded over, retching. Swiftly she spun toward the table. Kavik had shoved her sword farther down its length than she could reach, but one of her knives lay close enough. She trapped the hilt between her feet and flipped upward, bringing the blade to her hands. Before her legs swung back to the ground, she'd sliced through the leash.

With an enraged roar, Delan came at her like a charging ox. The idiot. Her hands were still bound but she held a leash and a blade.

Choosing her weapon, she whipped the length of leather around his throat, leapt up onto the table and vaulted past him, yanking the leash. His feet kept going; his upper body didn't. His legs flew out from beneath him and he landed hard on his back, choking and ripping at the leather circling his neck. Mala jumped heavily onto his chest and stomped his cock again. It wasn't so hard now.

She glanced up. Kavik hadn't run off to a den; he'd apparently only been donning his clothes and gathering his belongings. Arms crossed over his now-armored chest, he stood at the nearest table, watching without expression. Selaq waited behind him, her mouth agape.

Good. Mala had worked up a thirst even before this scut had attempted to touch her.

"The ale?" she asked, and gratefully took the flagon the innkeeper brought to her. Beneath her feet, a purple-faced Delan tried to heave her away. She ground the toe of her boot into his throat and didn't step off until his eyes rolled back and his struggles ceased. Not dead. Just beaten soundly.

As if suddenly uneasy, the other soldiers looked away from her and quietly resumed their drinking. Since they weren't going to display the same stupidity or avenge their comrade, Mala approached Kavik and held out her bound hands.

"Are you still showing me what it means to be tamed? We'll need a new leash."

"No." He unfastened the collar from her wrists with a few sharp pulls. "I'll return for you here when the moon is full."

"I'm supposed to wait?"

"You will."

The warrior hadn't tugged her leash *that* well. But she said nothing and watched him go. There was still much to learn about Kavik the Beast; it could not all be done now. He had more to learn about her, too—such as how patient and stubborn she could be.

He would soon find out.

CHAPTER 5

The woman in red followed Kavik across the moors. Riding her stallion and leading three other horses, she'd appeared behind him as the midday sun slipped behind gray clouds. As the rolling hills flattened into a dank marsh, she dismounted and trailed him on foot. When evening fell, she stopped to tend to the animals and to lay out a camp. By night, she was only a small flickering fire in the distance. Though hungry and tired, he continued on until the shadows of the Weeping Forest swallowed his trail.

By midmorning she was behind him again.

And no longer at a distance. If she had been, the thick forest would have concealed her presence. Yet she followed close enough that he could hear the clomp of the horses' hooves over the noise of the rain and the dripping leaves. Her voice floated among the occasional nicker and whinny—and at times her laugh. That night she didn't stop to camp before he did, and set up hers so near that the glow of her fire was indistinguishable from his. Over the flames he roasted the red-crowned hopper taken with his bow in the morning. The wingless bird's meat was tough and stringy, and he watched her skin a fat opossum while he ate. She glanced over at him once, holding up half the animal—offering it. Kavik shook his head and made his bed on the wet ground.

Though Kavik would have liked to smash the other man's teeth for it, the measle Delan had spoken truth. It hadn't mattered that Mala had been the one bound by the collar and leash; Kavik had been the one being tamed from the moment he'd tasted her—and by the time she'd screamed his name, he'd forgotten his rage. Instead he could only reverently kiss her sleek thigh. He'd have done anything for her, this woman he'd loved even before knowing her name. Who'd been drenched in her need even before he'd touched her.

He'd been led so easily. He'd gone exactly where she'd wanted him to go.

Never again.

But Kavik couldn't summon more rage. Instead he went to bed with a heavy ache in his chest, and it still remained when he woke. He'd known an ache like this before, following his father's death. Now Mala stalked his path and heralded his own.

Vela had been clever. She'd sent the one person in the world Kavik couldn't fight. But he could stand firm. And he would have to until Mala abandoned this quest. He might lose everything. He might die. But he wouldn't face the end tamed and on his knees.

In the morning she came to him, leading a sturdy black gelding. Her eyes were still heavy with sleep and her dark hair newly braided. The rain dripping from the trees overhead beaded on the shoulders of her red cloak before soaking in.

"This mount is yours, if you wish," she said. "He's sound and even-tempered."

And of a similar build to his gray horse, as if she'd noted the size of his saddle and chosen a horse it would fit. With a nod, Kavik asked her, "Do you still want to hunt the demon tusker?"

Her lips parted and she stared at him for a long moment—she hadn't likely expected any answer. But he couldn't stand firm while running away.

"I do," she finally said.

He took the gelding's reins. "Then we will go."

◆ ◆ ◆

THE density of the trees prevented Mala from riding along-side Kavik, so she continued following him to the forest's edge. Though the rain had ceased, the leaves still dripped, and she studied him from beneath her shadowed hood. He'd hardened himself again. Not with icy rage, this time. Instead he seemed filled with iron determination.

She preferred his anger. Fire could be doused. Ice could melt. But iron wasn't so easy to bend.

Mala knew it well. Her own will and stubbornness was crafted from iron just as strong. So they would be as two hammers, striking away at each other. Neither one would break.

But if Mala's task were simple, the reward would not be so great.

When they emerged from the forest, her gaze immediately sought the jagged peaks to the north. The demon tusker reportedly haunted those mountains, but that wasn't why the sight drew her so powerfully. Two nights before, when she'd bedded down in the marshes, an orange glow had lit the dark clouds shrouding those peaks—the same glow that had lit the southern sky outside the window of her bedchamber at home. The Flaming Mountains of Astal. They were all that stood between Krimathe and Blackmoor. But there were no passes that allowed travelers across those treacherous, burning peaks; instead they had to trek far east or west before finding a path over the Astal range.

Mala had taken the fastest, most dangerous route, yet it had still been a two years' journey to this land. When her quest had finished, it would be two more years before her return—and with her she would carry Vela's promise that, when Mala most needed it, the strength of ten thousand warriors would be added to Krimathe's own.

She had begun to hope Kavik would be one of those warriors.

Though she couldn't imagine that he would leave Blackmoor as it was. Not as long as Lord Barin still sat on his corrupted throne and the demon tusker still fouled the waters.

Mala frowned and looked westward. This land had dark, rich soil. With so much rain, at this time of year the earth should have been bursting with growth. Instead thin, dried grasses wove a scraggly carpet across the moors. Game was scarce. She'd seen no animals grazing—only those protected behind the city and village walls. Yet Shim hadn't given her any indication of danger near.

Scratching the stallion's neck, she asked him, "Have you scented any revenants?" When he responded with a shake of his head, she urged him to catch up with Kavik's mount. "Warrior, do you slay all of the revenants at the maze each time you escort a caravan through?"

His gaze searched her face, as if he wondered what had prompted her question. "I do. A few have escaped my sword. Not many."

"So when more animals are corrupted, the new revenants congregate at that same location and wait for the next travelers?" Mala shook her head. "That is unlike anything I've ever heard. After forming packs, they usually roam."

A humorless smile touched his mouth. "It is whispered that Barin has tamed them, and that he has ordered them to prevent anyone from escaping his rule. They also say the same of the demon tusker."

Fear made people whisper many things. "Do you believe they're under his control?"

"I believe they could be."

So did Mala. Foul magic surrounded the warlord and his citadel. "Telani told me Barin couldn't be killed."

"Perhaps he can." Jaw suddenly tight, Kavik looked ahead. "But I haven't found a way to do it yet."

"You've tried?"

"Countless times."

Her mouth dropped open. Even Shim snorted his astonishment, his ears swiveling back as if to better listen. Kavik glanced at the stallion, then back to Mala as she asked, "What did you try?"

"Blades forged of every metal, axes and spearheads made from every stone. Knives of bone and ivory. Catapults launching boulders that required a dozen oxen to move. Fire, arrows, and poisons. At sunrise and as it sets, at midnight and midday, during the full moon and new moon and every turn in between." The litany stopped, then he added with a faint smile, "I even tried using a charm I bought from a peddler who told me it would make Barin's eyes boil in his head. It smelled like tusker dung."

Mala grinned. "It probably was."

"I attempted it anyway."

She couldn't imagine him being cheated by a peddler now. "How old were you?"

"It was during my eighth winter when I took my first sword to the citadel. It was my fourteenth when I left Blackmoor. I haven't made any attempts since my return."

And he'd returned five years ago. Since then, he'd helped people leave this land—saving them from the man he couldn't kill.

"Why did Barin allow it?"

"I amused him. And with my every failure, those who opposed him lost heart. Everyone knew a blade didn't cut his skin, boiling oil didn't burn him, and that he could drink poison by the barrel."

"When I saw the debtors leashed in his hall, I vowed upon my blood to see him dead."

A dry laugh broke from him. "You shouldn't have been so hasty."

Perhaps not. But she couldn't regret it. Instead she tried to imagine a young boy marching into that hall each day, determined to destroy a warlord who only viewed his attempts as entertainment.

And failing each time. "You lost heart, too?"

"No. I realized that I couldn't succeed alone. So I left Blackmoor and hired out my sword until I'd earned enough to pay for my own soldiers. I returned with them five years ago."

She'd known he was an honorable warrior. Now her admiration knew no end. "Where are your men?"

Grim memory hardened his eyes when he looked to her again. "We came upon the demon tusker. Those who weren't killed then were later killed by Barin."

"But not you."

"I still amuse him."

That couldn't be the only reason. Men like Barin never took offenses against them lightly. No matter how Kavik had amused him as a boy, hiring an army of mercenaries to challenge his rule should have ended in Kavik's torture or death.

Instead the warlord hurt anyone who helped Kavik—and although that must be torture of a sort for Kavik, why did Barin bother?

"But why does it amuse him to hurt you? He doesn't even hurt *you*, he hurts others. You wouldn't even take water from Telani. And I didn't expect you to take the gelding."

Though now that she thought of it, a sharp pang struck her chest. She wasn't afraid of the warlord, but Kavik's refusing her help and warning her away from Barin had mattered. Did he not care anymore whether Barin tried to hurt her?

His expression had iced over again. "You're on a quest to bring me to him on a leash. You're the last person he would harm now."

The ache in her chest eased. So he'd accepted the gelding because he thought she was safe. "But why *you*? Even if he was amused by a boy, why single you out in such a way?"

Mouth flat, he looked to her, then to Shim. "Tell me how you tamed him."

Caught unawares by the change of topic, she only stared stupidly back at him—until Shim seemed to realize Kavik was talking about him. The stallion's head shot up, and he reared toward the warrior, trumpeting an outraged neigh. The black gelding balked and shied. Kavik rode out his mount's fright smoothly, the heavy muscles of his thighs tightening on the horse's sides, his big hands easy on the reins.

"Shim *isn't* tamed," Mala snapped. She smoothed her palm down the stallion's tense neck. Shim was snorting air like a bellows. "He's my friend and my companion."

"You ride him."

And now he trembled with rage beneath her. Was Kavik *trying* to anger Shim so much that the stallion would attack him? Even now, Shim probably only held back because he might injure the gelding. Fortunately, Mala had traveled with the stallion long enough to know exactly how to deflect his anger. She leaned over to scratch his shoulder, just where she knew he liked it, and fondly teased him, "Because he's weak-minded and easily led by his stomach."

Laughing, she rode through the stiff-legged hop and buck that was the stallion's response.

Kavik tensed and reached for her, then seemed to realize

she wasn't going to be tossed. He frowned at Shim, then his gaze went to Mala's hands when she let go of the stallion's mane. "No bridle or reins?"

"Of course not." Mala didn't know if Shim would kill her if she ever tried to put a bit in his mouth, but he'd certainly see it as a betrayal. Losing his trust could never be worth having the security of reins. She scratched his neck again. "We came across each other in the highlands west of Krimathe shortly after I set out on my quest. I told him he was beautiful, and that I thought he would enjoy traveling with me, because there'd be bandits to kill. I assumed that he disliked humans, just as so many others born of Hanan's seed do."

Shim snorted again, as if to say that "disliked" wasn't a strong enough word.

Kavik smiled faintly. "But not you?"

"He did then. He blew air at me and walked on."

"What did you do?"

She bit her lip, but still couldn't stop her grin. "I followed him through the highlands until he gave in."

Kavik said flatly, "I did not give in."

"I know." Instead he'd filled himself with iron. "I didn't even ride him at first—I had another horse. But we were fording a river and a paddle-serpent stung my leg." She pushed down the top of her boot to show Kavik the veiny scar that burst like a pale star against her brown skin. "I thought Shim would abandon me then, but he carried me to the nearest village, and we found a healer there. After that, he let me ride him, but only because he realized how much faster we travel when I do. No other mount matches his speed."

He nodded. "You came upon us at the maze faster than any other I've seen."

"That is Shim's gift." She rubbed his neck. "So you see he is not tamed. Not as other horses are—and not as humans think of it. If he ever was, I would fight to the end of my life to free him."

His hard gaze found hers again. "Even if Vela had made your task breaking him to a bridle and bit, instead?"

In truth, she didn't know. Because it didn't have to be force; if so much depended on his taking a bit, Shim might willingly submit.

But it mattered not. "It isn't the same, warrior. The taming is not what you think. There will be no collars or leashes. I would never be so cruel to anyone. So I have faith that Vela won't ask it of me."

Kavik didn't look as convinced.

MALA'S stomach was grumbling when they stopped for the night in the shadow of the mountains.

"I'll cook," she told Kavik, and was glad when he didn't argue. They'd only caught a few snakes and lizards that day, and she suspected by the meager amount of his possessions that he typically shoved a blade through their stomachs and roasted them.

Though no longer raining, the ground was sodden and the horses soaked. Mala tended to the animals while Kavik built the fire, then wished she hadn't sent them to graze so quickly when a fat crescent moon shone through thin clouds, shedding weak light over the valley below and the ribbon of muddied road winding through it.

"Is that a village?" A ring of shadows lay in the distance—if she wasn't mistaken, that was a village wall. "Should I have Shim herd the horses back this way? Perhaps we can find an inn."

"We can't."

She glanced back. Their tinder was dry and had started well, but the peat he'd added to the flames was slightly damp. The fuel smoldered, the thick smoke obscuring Kavik's face, but she couldn't mistake the bleakness of his reply.

"You patronized an inn in Perca. An innkeeper has to take you in. Surely Barin doesn't punish them for it?"

"He already did. All of them. There's no village there anymore. He razed it to the ground."

Stomach tightening, she looked across the distance again. "Why?"

"We aren't far from where my men and I fought the demon tusker. Most of us were injured. The villagers took us in. They tended to us. And they all died for it."

The tension in her gut rolled into a sick ball. He didn't glance up when she crouched next to him, his gaze fixed on the tiny, flickering flames beneath the heavy peat. She studied his strong profile, remembering the matted tangle of his hair, his long beard. That hadn't just been because he'd been doused with revenant blood. Unable to abandon the people in this cursed land, and unable to reside among them, he'd chosen to live like this instead. Not just while on the road, as Mala did. But all the time, except for when he escorted others to the bridge.

"So you became the beast of Blackmoor," she said. And she'd been sent to tame him.

As if reminded by the name, he finally glanced at her. "I did."

Determination had hardened his expression again. She met his gaze with iron in her own.

"We *will* see Barin dead."

"You're favored by the goddess. Perhaps you'll find a way that I could not." Abruptly he stood. "But it is too late for them."

Mala knew that well. Even if she completed her quest, Vela's help would come a generation too late for thousands of Krimatheans. "We help those we can, warrior."

He only shook his head and retrieved the lizards lashed to his saddle. With a sigh, she concentrated on encouraging the fire. The weight of hope for her people couldn't compare to the burden of death that he bore. But Mala would know that burden if she failed her quest.

It would not be completed tonight, however, so she focused on what *could* be done. Such as skinning lizards. She was too hungry to wait for a stew, so she stuffed them with yellow peppers and sweetroot before laying them in a clay pot, filling the remaining space with ale, and setting the pot in the fire. It would be a hearty meal, especially after adding tender slices of the opossum she'd smoked throughout the previous night. She would do the same for the snakes this evening—they were better eating on the road.

Then there was nothing to do but wait. Kavik had already gathered their sleeping furs and saddles, and he joined her by the fire. He glanced into the crackling flames. Fragrant steam was slipping from the pot. He leaned over and breathed deep before settling down beside her.

She passed him the wineskin of ale. "I hope that you are weak-minded and easily led by your stomach."

His grin seemed to increase the heat from the fire. She watched his throat as he drank, slipping her fingers down the length of her own. Mala wouldn't touch him now, not without permission. Oh, but she could imagine so well.

She needed a deep drink when he returned the ale, aware that Kavik watched her mouth, and of the slide of his gaze down her body.

It came to a rest at her hips. "You wear your mother's trophies."

The jawbones suspended from her belt. An outdated tradition, but one that Mala was glad to carry on. At least for these.

"I do." She took another drink, regarding him curiously. He'd spoken as certainly about their origin as if he'd seen her mother wearing them. "How did you know they were hers?"

He looked into the fire. "They're old. And I think you would be wearing many more."

So she did. Many more eyeteeth studded her belt. But she only said, "One is my father's."

His eyes met hers again. "They were the Destroyer's men?"

"Yes." She tilted her head back, looked up at the moon. Her mother had told her it had been full that night. Vela had seen it all, but there had been no help for Krimathe. "I'm fortunate that most of my traits resemble my mother's, because they must have been the stupidest of soldiers. They turned their backs on her when they'd finished."

Kavik didn't respond. But this time, only because there was no response to make. Mala passed him the wineskin, then untied the jawbone hanging from the middle of her belt.

"I think my father must have been this one," she said and held the bone up to her own jaw. "It's the same shape, don't you think?"

And in this short time with him, love must have been coming upon her. Because when Kavik choked and spit ale into the fire, she didn't think about what a waste it was. Instead she watched him laugh, and the deep sound of it made her heart seem stuffed full. Then he looked at her, and his laughter quieted, and she hoped he felt the same.

If he didn't, she would see that he did. "I hope you still intend to lie with me on my moon night."

Fire filled his eyes even before he looked away from her and into the flames. "If you are so willing to take my cock, then I am still willing to fuck you."

"I'm not only willing, warrior. I am *eager*. But I should warn you that once I have you, I will not share you."

His hands clenched. He stared into the fire, his broad chest rising on a series of deep breaths. Finally he looked to her again. Hard determination had covered the heat.

Slowly he stood. "Come here, then."

Her heart pounded as she rose. With each step, her breasts seemed to grow heavier, her nipples teased by soft linen behind stiff armor. Her gaze locked on his, she moved close enough to touch. His face a mask of tension, Kavik reached for her, his big hand cupping her jaw before sliding back to fist her braids.

"Down." His voice was harsh. "Take my cock now."

And taste him. Finally taste him. Anticipation sliced through her, hot and sharp. She sank to the ground, her knees cushioned by the folds of her cloak bunched beneath them. Her hands gripped his thighs, her palms sliding over the threadbare brocs and thick, steely muscle.

Oh, sweet gods. So strong.

"Now." His fingers tangled deeper into her hair. "If you are so eager for it, take it all now. Tug as hard as you can."

Her gaze shot to his face. A grimace had pulled his mouth taut, as if he lifted a weight beyond his might. Strain made sharp lines of the sinewy strength in his arms as he reached beneath his furs and shoved down the front of his brocs. His stance widened, powerful legs braced apart.

Because she was about to yank his leash, and he was apparently determined not to be moved by it.

Mala didn't care if he moved. This wasn't about taming him. She just wanted her tongue on his skin, and to give him pleasure. So if Kavik wanted the satisfaction of resisting what he felt for her, and if he needed it hard, and now, that was how she would give it.

Wetting her lips, she pushed aside the furs hanging from his belt. Oh, generous goddess of creation. There was so much for her to taste. Already his cock stood so tall for her, thick and heavy, with ruddy shaft and substantial crown.

"Thank you, Mother Temra," she breathed against the broad tip, and after a swift lick to catch his flavor—*like precious salt*—she swallowed him down.

With a grunt, his body stiffened as if he'd been kicked in

the gut. His hand tightened in her hair. She heard his sharp inhalation, followed by a long, slow release that was cut short when she drew back and took him as deep as she could.

It wasn't deep enough. Surrounded by his scent, like rain, like leather and a long hard ride, she sucked hard upon him and worked his thick length to the back of her throat—then was forced to release him, coughing and afire with frustration.

Temra had been too generous, perhaps. "I can't take all of you, warrior."

"You will," he said hoarsely, then guided her lips back to his shaft, the head still glistening from the wet heat of her mouth. "Your moon night and every night after."

All of this inside her. She groaned and swallowed his cock to her limit again, and every hard draw upon his length stoked her hunger. His left hand joined his right, his fingers clenching and unclenching in her braids, the rest of his body like stone.

"Your hands." The ragged words seemed ripped from him. "Stroke what you can't suck."

Her fingers were already slick from tending to her own need. She gripped his shaft tight and looked up to see his gritted teeth and his nostrils flaring, his eyes as fierce as when he'd first seen her and his gaze had been filled with the madness of battle.

I waited for you, little dragon.

Her warrior did not have to wait much longer. Her eyes locked on his face, she pulled him to the back of her throat and pushed her hand between her legs, gathering the wetness there. His shaft throbbed against her tongue. His breath shuddered with each stroke of her fingers down his length, but the rest of him didn't move at all, except for his grip growing tighter and tighter in her hair.

Abruptly he stopped the movement of her head and pulled her from his cock. Mala glanced up. Oh, how he fought. His eyes were closed, his face contorted as if in agony. But there was never any stopping this.

Huskily she said, "Give to me your seed, warrior," and with a savage thrust he filled her mouth, first with his heavy cock and then his salty release, and she took all of that though she still couldn't take the rest of him.

Not yet.

Softly she licked away the remaining seed and thought she knew why he'd placed such reverent kisses upon her thigh. It was so easy to give pain and to become hardened to it. To give pleasure instead—and to know it was accepted—was a real gift. Mala had never felt so gently toward anyone as she did at that moment.

"No more." Fingers rough in her hair, Kavik pushed her away from his cock and held her there. "I've finished."

With his iron determination in place again, along with satisfaction—as if he'd passed a test of his own making.

So he would not show her any tenderness, as if tenderness meant he was tamed. Very well. In all her life, Mala hadn't known much softness. She didn't need any now.

And the dull ache in her stomach was just hunger.

With a nod, she licked her fingers and turned to the fire. The juices in the clay pot steamed and bubbled around the edge of the lid. "The supper is ready, warrior, and at just the right moment. Your cock isn't as filling as it appears."

A sudden tug at the base of her throat pulled her back—Kavik had grabbed the hood of her cloak. Mala suppressed her instinct to fight and let him take her. Dragging her against his hard chest, he wrapped his fingers around her neck.

"Make your bed with mine this night." The soft gravel of his voice rasped against her ear. "You won't go to sleep hungry."

She nodded and shivered as his callused thumb scraped over her racing pulse. "I'll lie with you."

Kavik let her go, and with shadowed eyes he watched her prepare the rest of their meal. But this one did not pass in silence, for she asked him about his travels as a sword for hire, and he told her of a mad king who'd paid a thousand soldiers to escort him to the southern jungles, only to sacrifice himself to the jaws of a great thunder lizard. He spoke of creeping vines that would wrap around a sleeping man like a constrictor, and continue holding on until the rotting body had been drained of its fertilizing juices. He'd seen the Salt Sea's beaches stacked high with giant bones, and he'd hunted wraiths at the feet of the monoliths of Par, said to have been built by the gods themselves.

Belly full, limbs warmed by ale, Mala listened in wonder.

He had been farther than any other person she'd known. "Have you ever traveled north? Have you seen Krimathe?"

He looked into the fire for a long moment before shaking his head. "I've never been north of these mountains."

Mala had never been south before her quest. "Have you seen any place untouched by the Destroyer's hand?"

"No," he said softly, and they fell quiet then. Finally she rose to prepare the snakes for smoking.

Kavik laid out their bed. When she'd watched him the previous night, he'd only removed his armor. Now he stripped down to his brocs and boots before laying his sword by his saddle, where he would rest his head. The glow of the fire bathed his skin in orange light, and even the fiery sky above could not draw her gaze away.

She laid her sword beside his. Only their exposed position prevented her from removing her tunic and loincloth, and sliding in next to him skin to skin. If bandits came upon them, best to be wearing more than her boots and cloak.

His body was as hot as the fire. She tried to turn toward him, but he pulled her back against his chest, lying on their sides with her head pillowed on his right biceps. His rigid cock nestled into the cleft of her ass.

Frustration bit deep. "Warrior—"

His heavy thigh pushed between hers and lifted, separating her legs. His left hand swept down the curve of her ass and delved through her slick folds from behind. Gasping, Mala arched her spine, pushing closer. His biceps flexed as he pulled her up higher against his shoulder and wrapped his arm across her chest, holding her tight against him. His fingertips teased her entrance.

Oh, no. No teasing. She reached back and gripped his thick hair. "*Now.*"

He thrust into her. Oh, Vela. She cried the goddess's name, because even though her sheath was soaked by her need there was pain as he filled her with two broad fingers instead of one.

Kavik froze behind her. "Mala?"

"Don't stop." With a breathless moan, she rocked her hips back and forced him deeper. "Take me hard, warrior."

A groan rumbled through his chest, and she felt the sharp bite of his teeth on the lobe of her ear before he abruptly rolled her onto her stomach and followed her over, his weight pinning her torso to the furs and his cock heavy against her hip. His fingers pushed into her again—slowly, so slowly. Mala screamed and tried to come up on her knees, to force him to a deeper angle. His foot against her ankle shoved her legs wide, denying her leverage. Leisurely he stroked into her, again and again. Cheek pressed into the furs, crying out with each deliciously torturous thrust, she desperately worked her hand beneath her stomach and down to her clitoris. Trapped beneath the weight of her pelvis, she could barely do more than wriggle her fingers, but it was enough, and the painful tension began to spiral more quickly toward the end.

Kavik's slick fingers glided past hers and paused. She was discovered. Mala stilled, grinning into the furs, her body a taut, throbbing ache.

A chuckle sounded above her. "Now, little dragon?"

"Yes," she breathed.

He set his teeth against her shoulder and drove his fingers deep. Oh, sweet gods—like this. Mala cried his name and Kavik struck a brutal pace, the heel of his palm pounding her ass with each thrust of his hand. Pinned with her legs wide-spread, she couldn't move, could only take every rough stroke. Orgasm roared upon her like a charging beast. Screaming, she came in a hard rush, her slick channel constricting tighter around him with each convulsion that jolted through her flesh.

Then she lay limp, with his chest a heaving bellows against her sweating back. She groaned when his thick fingers slipped from inside her, until he pulled her against him again.

"Every night I will sheathe myself within you," he said roughly and pushed his thigh between hers, so that her slick, heated flesh rode against heavy muscle. "After your moon night, it won't be my fingers but my cock, and each day I will have you until my seed overflows your well and runs in a river down your thighs."

"I hope that is a vow." With a yawn of sheer exhaustion, Mala snuggled closer and closed her eyes. Her voice was thick with sleep as she said, "Happy dreams, warrior."

His arms tightened around her. "I do not need them."

CHAPTER 6

He did not need happy dreams and, in the nights following, he did not receive happy ones. Kavik held her in his arms but in his dreams Mala was walking away, and no matter how he raced he could not catch up to her. But these dreams meant nothing, because upon waking he would have her again. He gave her pleasure and took his whenever and however he wanted.

He was not tamed. Even if his heart was not his own. Even if he could never have enough of her touch or her laugh. Even if he never wanted to face a dawn without her.

He stood firm. For although she believed his taming would not be cruel, Kavik knew it must be. Vela had sent Mala to bring him to his knees again.

So even when she lay so softly against him, her face flushed with sleep, Kavik did not kiss her awake as he wanted to. He watched her, his chest filled with an ever-deepening ache. He stood firm. But for how long? He would do anything for her. If she knew how his heart lay in her hand, soon he might be putting the collar on himself.

But hiding his heart would not be enough. He needed to persuade her beyond any doubt that he would never give in.

He needed to push her away, because he weakened with her every touch.

It would not be today, though. Today they would reach the dark river that tumbled down the nearby mountains. Tomorrow they would cross the fouled waters, and Kavik would continue leading her farther away from the demon tusker's den. He had seen too many men killed by that evil, and he would not see Mala hurt by it, too.

Even if it meant his life, Kavik would *never* see her hurt.

She stirred against him, lashes fluttering and a soft smile on her lips. He remained still as she turned in his arms. After so many mornings, he didn't need to tell her what he wanted; his body spoke for him. But as she skimmed lower, her mouth brushed his shoulder, then his chest, and she repeatedly touched her lips to his skin as she moved down his rigid stomach.

Each kiss was a sweet knife. He couldn't bear it.

Roughly he gripped her hair. "Take my cock," he commanded hoarsely. "Now."

She did. So hot. So hard. She gave him what he wanted, needed. He controlled this. He was not tamed. *She* was.

And it mattered not that he thought he might die without her.

THE sun had finally come to Blackmoor, but the cursed land looked no happier for its warmth. Along the great river, blackwood trees lay twisted and dry. Bones strewed the rocky banks, animal and human, as if those who had drank directly from the waters had immediately fallen dead.

Though it was long before sunset, they stopped to camp within an arrow's flight of the river. A stone bridge lay farther south, but it was gated, and Barin's soldiers only allowed travelers to pass through while the sun was up. Kavik had told her it was better to sleep at least a half day's ride away and cross at midday, because bandits were never as much trouble under cover of darkness as the bored soldiers at the bridge garrison were.

Although Mala might have enjoyed a fight, she would enjoy an undisturbed night with Kavik more—and a bath. Her last had been at the Croaking Frog, and for a quarter turn she'd made do with wiping herself down with a damp rag. So as he built the fire, she retrieved a small packet of soap and a cloth from her packs.

"See that the others stay away from the waters," Mala said to Shim, who had taken to watching over the horses when they weren't traveling. "I will let you know when it is safe."

Small bones cracked between her bare feet and the rounded stones at the edge of the river. It was unfortunate that she and Kavik couldn't cross at this spot instead of requiring a bridge. But the recent rains had swelled the waters, and although they flowed placidly near the banks, the current at the middle appeared deep and swift.

After unbraiding her hair, she shed her clothes and stood before the lapping waters, wearing only a knife strapped to her thigh. There was no ritual required for this. Only honesty. "Vela, most gracious of goddesses," she prayed softly. "I am your servant, awed and humbled by your protection. I need it now, for these waters are fouled, and only your power can cleanse them. Take my body as your vessel and my faith as your due."

Soap in hand, Mala stepped in. Braced for icy cold, she was pleased to find it merely cool. Bliss. She waded out to her waist, where the current was still only a constant, gentle push against her legs.

She didn't feel Vela move through her; she never did. Some priestesses said they were filled with ice, others described it like fire. But however the goddess worked through Mala, it was quiet, like a breath.

Holding hers, she dunked her head.

Kavik's shout met her ears when she came up. Bellowing her name, he raced toward her, his powerful stride tearing across the distance. Alarmed, she unsheathed her knife and scanned the water's surface. Had some monster survived the poisonous waters?

Slowly, so as not to attract any creature's attention, she started back toward the river's edge.

Eyes feral, Kavik charged directly toward her across the rocks and splashed into the river. "Out of the water, Mala!" Desperation hoarsened his voice as he reached for her. "*Out!*"

Heart thundering, she searched the water again. "What is—"

Kavik's fingers snagged her wrist. Dragging her against him, he hooked his arm beneath her legs and forged toward the shoreline. At the rocks, he dropped to his knees beside her clothes and began scrubbing her wet skin with her cloak. Lips white, his face was a mask of anguish. "Did you drink any?"

Understanding swept over her. The fouled water. He must have been certain she would be poisoned. That she would be dead within a few breaths.

Yet he'd charged into the same water after her.

Mala cupped his face in her hands, forced him to look at her, and could barely stand the devastation in his eyes. "I told you that Vela would protect me," she said softly. "That she would cleanse any water I need."

"A wineskin," he said harshly. "She cannot cleanse a fouled river."

"She can, warrior. She *did*. It will be safe from the head-waters to the end." She stroked her fingers along his bristled jaw. "Now come and bathe with me."

Chest heaving, he shook his head. With a sigh, she rose from his arms. She hadn't taken a step before he caught her hand, frowning up at her.

"You are not going back in?"

"Of course I am. I haven't properly washed, and the water holds no danger now."

Anger hardened his face. "You could not have known that when you first stepped in. It was a fool's risk."

"That is faith, warrior. It wouldn't be very strong if I required proof before I believed in her power. But Vela *does* want us to believe in her, because she must work through us—and we would have no reason to allow it if she didn't keep her promises. She only asks that I keep mine." Still holding his hand, she took another step toward the water. "Perhaps you don't trust the goddess. Trust me instead."

Tension coiled in her chest as she waited, then constricted painfully when he let go of her fingers. Blindly she turned to the water. So he didn't trust her. It mattered not. One day he would, because she was patient and stubborn, and never would she give him any reason to believe she might betray him. She would keep her promises, too.

But her eyes still stung, so she bathed her face in the cool water, then went under completely so that the ache in her heart could be blamed on her lungs.

Kavik was wading naked into the river when she emerged, his fierce gaze fixed on her face. "Either you are right," he said roughly, "or I will die with you."

Reaching for her, his fingers delved into her wet hair. But no command followed this time. No *down*. No *now*.

Instead his mouth descended upon hers. A kiss. Like sweet fire, he singed her lips with a possessive taste that slowly gentled as he lingered over her mouth, returning to it again and again. Mala clung to him, loving his strength, loving this tenderness.

When he finally lifted his head, she told him, "We will not die," and her voice was thick. "But if we do, our corpses will smell better than they would have before we bathed."

His grin loosened every painful ache inside her. Easily he lifted her against him, wrapping her legs around his waist before moving deeper into the water. "We must not smell as bad as revenant yet. You have tasted me many times these past days."

"Much better than revenant." Mala lay her head on his shoulder and held him close. "But I would have you anyway, warrior."

MALA washed his hair, and Kavik thought there could be no greater pleasure until he took the soap and lathered every stretch of her beautiful skin. Touching her was the greater pleasure. Kissing her was. He followed each spot that she rinsed with a tender press of his lips.

He should not. Kavik knew he should not let himself touch her like this. But after seeing her in the water, he knew how it might feel to lose her—and that when he pushed her away, it would tear his heart from his chest. It mattered not if he began his torture early. This was all he would have of her until the end.

She slipped her strong arms around his neck, the movement lifting her small breasts. The water lapped her erect nipples. Suddenly ravenous for a taste, Kavik bent his head.

Mala stiffened against him. "Wait."

He looked up. She had not denied him. Instead her gaze had fixed farther down the riverbank, where Shim and the other horses had been splashing through the shallows, nipping and kicking at each other. Playing, Mala had said, and Kavik had ignored their whinnies and squeals. But now the stallion let loose a more strident neigh as he faced the west, nose in the air and snorting.

"Revenants?" Mala called.

The stallion shook his head, then with nips to their hindquarters began herding the others toward camp.

Frowning, Mala glanced up at Kavik before starting for the shore. "The demon tusker?"

Shim whinnied impatiently and shook his head again.

"Humans?"

A stamp of his hoof answered her.

"Humans," Mala said to Kavik and swept her cloak over her shoulders before collecting her clothes from the shoreline. "Maybe bandits, maybe travelers. Do you see them?"

Fastening his belt and furs, Kavik scanned the western horizon. The rolling landscape that led down to the river was not in their favor. "Not yet."

But it did not take long after they'd returned to the camp to recognize a squad of Barin's soldiers, the sun glinting off their polished helms. Riding quickly, they headed directly toward the camp.

"From the bridge garrison?" Mala asked him, tightening her armor. Her dark hair hung long and wet over her shoulders.

"No." Kavik had spotted the dogs running ahead of the soldiers. "They've tracked us."

Her full lips twisted with irritation. "Sent by Barin?"

"We'll find out."

Not by waiting at camp for them to arrive—their position would be too much of a disadvantage. Mounted, they rode out to meet the soldiers. Only a dozen of them. If Barin meant to kill Kavik and Mala, he'd have sent more.

The company leader slowed at their approach and Kavik recognized the captain of the citadel guard. Red-faced and sweating, Heddiq was more accustomed to sitting for meals in the citadel garrison than hard riding.

At two hundred paces, Heddiq rose his fist and shouted across the distance, "Halt! We have a message for the questing one."

For Mala. When Kavik looked to her, she was regarding the soldiers with pursed lips. Finally she murmured something to Shim, who slowed to a walk. Kavik reined in his gelding.

She slid him an amused glance. "It seems that whatever the message is, they do not want to be too near us when they deliver it." Lifting her voice, she called out, "What is this message?"

"It is of two parts, and from our glorious Lord Barin!" Heddiq shouted. "He wishes you to know that a cleansed river will only bring the demon tusker from his den more often! You do not help anyone, and many will likely die when the demon emerges!"

Her expression flattened. "And the second part?"

Heddiq's horse pranced uneasily and backed up, as if the man's hands were hard and nervous on the bit. "Our glorious lord grows weary of waiting! You must bring the tamed beast to his hall by the new moon."

"And if I do not?"

"He will kill the son of Karn and you will fail your quest!"

Her brow furrowed in confusion. She glanced to Kavik. "The king's son still lives? Why would his death affect my quest?"

His heart a burning weight, he could only return her gaze. Her lips suddenly parted and she sucked in a sharp breath. Abruptly Shim reared and pivoted. Mala's red cloak flared open over his back, and Kavik had never seen anything so fierce and beautiful as when she faced the soldiers again.

"Return this message!" she shouted. "The goddess Vela guides my blade, and when her hand is upon my sword, it will cut even a sorcerer's neck from his shoulders! And to make sure the message is delivered properly, piss on him as you speak it! Now, *run*!"

The captain of the guard only hesitated a moment before giving the signal. With a thunder of hooves, the company started south. Mala stared after them with clenched jaw.

"Heddiq won't piss on Barin," Kavik said. The guard

would probably be too afraid to relay her message at all. "But he likely just pissed on himself."

"Heddiq?" She whirled to face him. "That was the captain of the citadel guard?"

"He is."

Rare indecision warred upon her features. "I had never seen him. But I warned those raping pig guards that if ever I did, I would kill him." She looked to Kavik. "Barin must have known that when he sent him. It can't be usual for a guard to ride with mounted soldiers."

"It's not."

"More of Barin's amusements, perhaps," she said softly. "He must have expected me to kill him. But I will not be yanked by a leash any more than you will. So Heddiq has a reprieve. Now that I know his face, however, he will not have one again." She looked to the river. "Is it true what he said of the demon tusker—that it will emerge early to foul the waters again?"

"It might be." Kavik nudged his mount back toward camp. "Or Barin might hope to stop you from cleansing them again. His concern is not for the people, but how to control them—though I don't know how he knew to send the message when you cleansed the river only today."

"Shortly after I began following you, I cleansed the river just north of Perca," she said. "Shim was thirsty."

Kavik frowned. "Did you tell anyone?"

She shook her head. "It would do more harm than good if people knew and began to use the waters, then they were befouled again. I would not have said anything of it until we slew the demon tusker. We need to return to the city. If Barin spoke true, then the demon will soon come to that river."

"Or this one."

But even as he said it, Kavik knew there was little choice. If Barin spoke truth, then many villages north of Perca would be in the demon's path. Far fewer people lived near this river. So instead of leading her away from the demon tusker, Kavik would ride with her toward it.

"We will have to gamble," she said, then suddenly grinned. "I prefer the city, because we will be more likely to find a soft bed to pass my moon night in."

Kavik's chest tightened. And he would be more likely to find the help he needed to persuade her that he could not be tamed. She might not abandon her quest, but if she did not touch him, he could continue standing firm.

Her grin faded when she glanced at his face. "Kavik?"

He forced himself to nod, his voice rough. "I agree. A soft bed."

She watched him a moment longer. "You are truly Karn's son?"

"I am."

"And so that is why Barin amused himself with you." With a sigh, she looked ahead. "My mother spoke well of your father. They met once when she was young. Before the Destroyer. Was that who killed him?"

"No." Kavik stared at the river, seeing nothing. "Barin came to Blackmoor ahead of the Destroyer. He was instructed to persuade my father to give him the location of a passageway beneath the mountains. My ancestors had trapped the demon there during the time of the ancients. Barin said the Destroyer wanted to use the demon's power, and such an alliance might save Blackmoor, but my father refused. At first."

"He was tortured?" Mala's dark gaze was solemn upon his face. "But that is not all Barin does to those he wants to hurt."

Of course she understood. Though the details were not always the same, this story was a common one from during the time of the Destroyer. "I had brothers, a mother. Barin gave them to his soldiers. My father revealed the passageway's location, hoping to save them."

"Did he?"

His throat burning, Kavik shook his head. "She had been heavy with child—with me. I was all that Barin returned to him. Then he let us go."

"Because it amused him," Mala said flatly.

"It did."

"Where did you go?"

"The Weeping Forest. Not as I live there now. There was an inn at the edge of the forest. My father still had gold, a few servants. But Barin had taken most of his fingers and he couldn't hold a sword. So I held it for him the first time I returned to the citadel."

Jaw clenched, she looked ahead again, but held her tongue.

He knew what she would say. His father must have been mad. Kavik had only seen eight winters then.

"He *was* mad," Kavik said softly. "But the hope of freeing Blackmoor from Barin's reign was all that he had. And I knew nothing else. Nothing but trying to discover a way to kill him."

"Until your fourteenth winter, you said. What happened then?"

"We tried an ivory blade under a full moon. It failed, but before we left, Barin decided that would be my moon night. My father died trying to stop them from putting the collar on me. His heart gave out. And I left Blackmoor to earn gold for my army."

Eyes glistening, she looked away from him again. Kavik had no tears left for his father, or for the boy he had been. All that remained was the icy ache in his chest.

Her throat worked before she spoke. "I vow to you that it will never be a collar," she said, and the hoarse catch in her breath scraped over his heart. "And Vela will not ask it of me."

"I pissed in her temple."

Mala's shocked gaze flew to meet his. "You did *what*?"

"I pissed in her offering bowl. Do you think Vela would put me on my knees in front of Barin for it?"

The goddess possessed cruelty enough to punish him that way. Mala knew it. Uncertainty flashed over her face.

His throat seemed full of grit. "If you will not have me in a collar, take off the robe. Abandon your quest."

"I cannot." Breath shuddering, she shook her head. "And the taming will *not* be that. I have to believe it won't be. I know you don't trust her. But trust in me, warrior. Please."

He couldn't answer. Nudging his mount's sides, he rode ahead. But as soon as he dismounted, she came to stand before him. Rising onto her toes, she captured his face between her hands, her gaze fixed on his lips.

He caught her hair. "Down."

"Kavik—"

"Now," he said. "I have no need for your mouth except on my cock."

Fire lit behind her eyes. Holding his gaze, she slid down. His shaft hadn't been hard when he'd given the command, but the touch of her fingers started a brutal ache in his flesh. She raised his stiffening length to her lips.

And kissed him, so gently. Kavik froze. Again, a reverent press of her mouth. Releasing her hair, he ripped himself away from her touch. His chest was heaving, each breath tearing raggedly from his lungs.

Still on her knees, she looked up at him. Her dark eyes were haunted. "Do you have no need for any part of me, warrior?"

He could not stop his harsh laugh. She was everything he needed. All of her.

But he turned away from her. "Not if I can't fuck it. I'll wait for your moon night."

And wait for his end.

IT was three days' hard journey back to Perca. Mala wasn't surprised when Kavik retreated into silence again. He didn't share her bed. Instead she was left alone with her thoughts and the growing ache of the distance between them.

Mala had known this quest would be painful. But she'd thought it would be her body that suffered, not her heart.

But the pain made her hopeful that she was on the right path. If this had been easy, it wouldn't be a quest, and she could think of few more difficult tasks than winning Kavik's trust—which made her wonder if the answer to his taming had lain before her almost from the very beginning. She had befriended another beast who hadn't been easy to win over. And although she didn't consider Shim tamed, many others would. Just as some thought a collar meant its wearer was tamed, and Mala called it cruelty, instead.

It only mattered what Vela intended the taming to mean. If Mala was right, then she only had to be patient. She had to be stubborn. And she had to remember Kavik's anguish as he'd charged into the water to save her. She had to remember his tenderness as he'd kissed her.

He hadn't covered his heart in iron to hurt her, but to protect himself. She'd seen his pain after she'd refused to abandon her quest, and knew that he expected more agony to come. If it did, the agony would not come from her hand, and she would help him fight its cause. Though he could be hard, and the distance between them painful, Mala trusted that he wouldn't deliberately hurt her; she could wait until he trusted her in return.

And she hoped the single night remaining before the full moon passed quickly. Though Kavik had been quiet these past days, his ravenous hunger for her still burned in his shadowed gaze. Taking him would not be easy, either. But she didn't care if he was rough, or tried to persuade himself that he hadn't softened toward her. Mala would find her pleasure in every merciless touch, in each brutal thrust.

She was just as hungry as he was.

Until the full moon came, however, she suspected that her only need to be sated would be her thirst. The sun had been warm, their ale had run dry two days before, and watered mead never satisfied as well. She was glad to see the Croaking Frog's familiar banner with its lucky lily pad. Dally birds squawked in the stable yard behind the inn, bald pink heads bobbing, and their scraggly gray and white feathers floating everywhere. The ugliest birds that Temra had ever created—but also the most delicious.

As soon as she removed Shim's saddle, the stallion trotted into the yard and began to snort at the swirling feathers. She glanced over to find that Kavik was already seeing to the packhorses. The furs he'd worn over his shoulders had been shed days before, leaving his steely arms bare. Her bottom lip between her teeth, she watched the sinews flex in his strong forearms as his long fingers tugged at the leather ties.

Without looking up, he said gruffly, "Will you go and see if there's a private bed available for us?"

Swift joy rose through her. "Will we be sharing it tonight, then?"

"We will." He came nearer, his gaze hot on hers. "And add this."

He pressed a thin gold coin into her palm. She glanced up curiously.

Kavik turned to the horses again. "Ask Selaq to join us in the bed tonight."

Did he think his fingers and tongue weren't enough? Mala grinned at his back. "I prefer your touch, warrior. Not hers."

"I want her there for me."

Her brows rose. "Do you not realize she prefers women?"

Easily he lifted the heavy grain baskets balanced over the animal's withers. "But she will lie with men for extra coin. I'm desperate for your sheath, but there's no need to wait. I can fuck another tonight."

No, he could not. "Why would you say this to me, warrior?"

"Because one sheath is the same as any other."

The edges of the coin bit into her fingers. "I told you that I would not share you after I had you."

"I've not had you yet. That is why my cock aches for waiting." His gaze was shuttered when he looked up. "And that is why I will have another tonight."

"Do you believe that we've not already had each other just because my moon night hasn't come? We've had each other over and over these past days, warrior. We had each other when you kissed me. When you rode by my side. When you slept by me and held me close." She didn't mistake the sharp agony in his gaze before he looked away. "Do you *intend* to hurt me or are you simply being a stubborn fool? Because I promise you, this will injure me."

It would shred her heart more quickly than a pack of revenants.

Determination hardened his expression again. Catching her wrist, he took back the coin and started for the inn. "I will pay her myself, then."

She stared at his retreating back. Her face seemed hot and numb all at once, as if repeatedly slapped. He'd been devastated when he'd thought she'd been poisoned at the river. And yet . . . this.

Maybe he would truly do it, maybe he wouldn't. It mattered not. She'd told him this would hurt her and he intended to carry on anyway.

She'd been wrong about him. So wrong. Swallowing hard, she said after him, "If you give her that coin, you will not touch me again."

For an instant, his step faltered. His fists clenched. But he continued on.

And she had not expected agony like this. Never had she imagined Kavik would slip a blade between her ribs and leave her bleeding. Throat burning, she blindly turned toward the packs, vision wavering with hot tears.

Vela. I need your strength now. Help me, please.

But the pain did not ease.

HIS legs barely seemed able to carry the crushing weight in his chest. It was done. She would not touch him. He would never touch her again. Even if she continued her quest and followed him until the end of his days, he would stand firm.

Except he could barely stand now. The heat from the ovens in the inn's brewing chambers seemed like a demon's breath on his face. As soon as he moved out of sight of the stables, he leaned back against the support of the walls.

"Kavik? Are you unwell?"

Selaq, with a blue cloth covering her yellow hair and a wooden tub propped on her hip. Her appearance made the coin in his hand seem heavier than any boulder. He would never give it to the innkeeper. Mala never needed to know.

Whatever her injuries, they couldn't be deep. Her pride had been damaged. Not her heart. She hadn't known him well enough or long enough to feel more.

Except that she felt everything deeply. He'd never seen anyone possess such ferocity and passion. Who was so quick to grin—or to make him laugh.

His throat a knot, he said, "I would ask for your help."

Eyes widening, Selaq stared at him. "*You* would ask? Has the sun risen in the west? Or has the *truly* impossible happened, and Barin is dead?"

Kavik could never joke about Barin's death. "I need you to let Mala believe I have paid you to come to my bed tonight."

"Oh, no." She hefted the tub up onto a table. "She'll kill me."

"No. It would not be you that she hurt." And Kavik would take any punishment she gave him. Had already given him. *You will not touch me again.* "She would never hurt anyone who didn't deserve it."

"You don't deserve a collar."

The coin seemed to burn in his palm. "She has vowed never to put one on me."

And she wouldn't. Kavik knew she wouldn't. She'd felt deeply then, too, when he'd told her of his father. Of his moon night and what Barin and his soldiers had done.

Selaq scoffed and lifted a ball of brown dough from the tub. "Even if Vela demands it?"

"She believes the goddess wouldn't ask it of her." The image of cold silver eyes flashed through his memory. "I do not believe the same."

"Do you think she would defy the goddess? Abandon her quest?"

"She will have to." Because Kavik would never give in. "Or never complete it."

Her brow furrowed. "You say that very easily. When I heard of the taming, I wished her no success. But I would still never wish what would come upon her if she abandoned it."

"She will be marked. But she has no vanity. And she wears other scars." Almost as many as Kavik did.

Selaq's kneading hands stilled, and she stared at him. "Kavik, you fool. You utter fool."

Tension gripped his chest. *A stubborn fool.* "Why?"

"A quest is a promise made to Vela. Do you think she accepts a broken vow lightly? Mala will be forsaken. Shunned. Never allowed to return home. Never allowed to stay in any one place because anyone who offers her shelter or aid will risk Vela's wrath. Any village she enters, they will drive her away with dogs and stones. You think Barin plagues you? It is *nothing* to what the goddess will do to her."

Ice splintered through his veins. And he had shoved her away? Sworn never to give in? He would crawl into the citadel with a bit between his teeth if it pleased Vela.

And beg Mala to forgive him.

His legs found their strength again but as soon as they carried him into the stable yard, a vise seized his heart. Mala was sorting through the packs, adding items to the pouches on Shim's saddle, her head bowed and her movements slow. Leaving.

Her head shot up when the stallion gave his nicker of warning. She wiped her cheeks.

The tightness in Kavik's throat became a burning knot. "Mala—"

"You can keep the black gelding and the other two horses. They will only slow me down." Without looking at him, she opened a jute sack and began dividing the contents. "They will be compensation for your assistance in searching for the demon tusker."

"Don't, Mala. Please." Voice broken, he reached for her.

She whirled on him, her hand flying to her sword. Her blade pressed against his throat.

Kavik stilled. It was not the weapon that stopped him. Her dark eyes swam with tears, but the expression in them was a spear through his chest. Not just pain. Devastation that matched his own.

"You have no permission to touch me now," she said through gritted teeth.

With desperate hope, he opened his hand. Though it had weighed so much moments before, the gold in his palm seemed like nothing now. A boy's trinket. Yet he had risked her life and her quest with this worthless thing. "I would not have given it to her," he rasped. "I never would have."

"That matters?" Her hollow laugh told him it mattered not at all. Tears slipped over her cheeks. "I thought I finally knew what Vela wanted. I wouldn't call Shim tamed, because he is free. But others would call him that, simply because I ride him. Even you said he was."

Kavik had. And he would still say it. But he couldn't speak past the pain in his throat.

Her fingers trembled as she continued. "I began to believe that was what Vela meant. Not a collar, but trust. Shim and I ride together. One day, though, I know we will part ways. He will return to his herd. But I thought . . . I thought if that was what it meant to tame you, then we might have so much longer."

If that was taming, then Kavik would give anything to be tamed. "We will."

"No." Her simple response shattered his hope. On a sobbing breath, her hand dropped to her side, her blade falling away from his throat. "When I first began to ride him, he would throw me. He never meant to hurt me—he was just unused to the weight on his back. Sometimes I surprised him, or treated him like any other horse, and he needed to remind me that he was free, not just another animal to be tamed. But never did he turn on me. He never bit at me. He never kicked at me. He *did* hurt me, but he never meant to."

And she had warned Kavik that he was hurting her. No wound from a blade could have matched the agony of the emptiness spreading through him now.

"He was never deliberately cruel," she continued softly. "If he had been, I would have left him behind—because how could I have trusted him at my side if he might turn and kick me in the chest? So it is not that you might have touched another woman, because I knew you might try to throw me. I knew you didn't want to soften toward me. But you meant to hurt me tonight."

No. He hadn't known it truly would. But it mattered not, because she'd warned him—and he'd been so determined to stand firm that he hadn't listened. Hadn't seen.

He'd had everything. She'd told him that, too. Her kiss. Her warmth at his side. Her heart. Now he had nothing.

Except he could make certain she wasn't hurt again. "What of your quest? You have my trust. I will ride at your side."

Or behind her. Anywhere she went. Even if she never spoke to him again, he would follow her until the end.

"You no longer have *my* trust, warrior. I'm not traveling that path anymore. So I pray that I was wrong, and that was not what Vela meant, because you are not worth the pain you would do to me." Her eyes were dull as she turned away. Sheathing her sword, she picked up Shim's saddle and moved out to the stable yard. "And there is another kind of tamed, one I didn't begin to consider until I learned you were Karn's son. It simply means to bring something wild into a home, and that wild thing takes a place within the household. Perhaps my task is to return you to your place in the citadel. I would need to kill Barin—and I have already made a vow to see him dead, so I was on that path. Or perhaps I am meant to tame the demon. That was what I first believed when I came to Blackmoor. Perhaps *that* was the road I was supposed to take."

Both roads so dangerous that they'd already taken too many people Kavik had known. New determination filled him. "I will help you."

She set the saddle upon Shim's back. "You will not be able to keep up with me."

Maybe not. His mount couldn't match the stallion's speed. But he could follow. Blood pounding, he raced back into the stables for the black gelding.

He was cinching the saddle when Selaq came into the stables. "I'm leaving these other horses with you." They would slow him down, too, and he'd survived for most of his life with nothing more than a horse and his sword. "Do whatever you like with them."

"Mala is leaving?" The innkeeper whispered the goddess's name on a long sigh as Kavik led the gelding past her. *"Then this is the moment you've lost everything."*

Ice seized Kavik's gut. That had not been his friend's voice. Those were not Selaq's eyes, orbs pale as a milk moon against a blue sky.

Her frigid hand closed over Kavik's arm and iron seemed to fill his legs, locking them in place. "Stand firm, beast. Stand firm while I twist the knife."

He had already stood firm for too long. "There is nothing to twist it into," he said hoarsely. "I've destroyed my own heart. You cannot do worse than I have already done."

"No?" Her smile was a scythe. With rigid forefinger, she tapped the armor over his chest. Abruptly his lungs constricted, cutting off his breath. "But Mala was right. She *did* understand what the taming meant. It was never a collar. And you had her heart, warrior."

So she *could* twist the knife. There could be more agony. It joined the desolating emptiness as the last of his air escaped his lips.

"Oh, that is not the knife, beast," she answered as if his thoughts had been spoken. Her icy finger slid down his throat. "This is the knife. Because she abandoned the path that I'd chosen for her."

No. Understanding cut through him. His gaze shot to the stable doors, but he couldn't move, couldn't call out. Wildly he fought the heaviness of his legs, the choking airless grip on his voice.

But his strength was nothing, and Kavik was nothing when Mala's scream ripped through the air, followed by a cry of limitless pain and despair. His empty lungs convulsed on her name. His body stood rigid. Blinded by agony, he looked to Vela. She had to let him go to her.

"Go to her? You want to see what is happening? I will show you, as I've shown her to you so many times before."

Mala sobbing on her knees amid swirling feathers. Still wearing her cloak, but it was black now, as if all the red had bled into her face, into the ragged disfiguring scars that raked from jaw to hairline as if slashed by a dragon's claws. Blood and her tears rained into her cupped hands.

Shim nudged her shoulder. All at once she scrambled away from the stallion, her hand fisted against her chest as if holding closed a wound that threatened to spill her innards onto the ground.

"The path is ended for us, my friend. I will not see you forsaken, too."

The stallion shook his head.

"You must shun me!" she cried. *"You must!"*

Snorting, the stallion pranced an uneasy circle.

"Please, Shim," she added brokenly. *"Please. Return to your herd. I cannot see you hurt, too."*

The horse blew a long breath and pushed his muzzle into her shoulder again. She stroked his nose once before letting her hand fall to her side.

"Be safe, my friend," she said. Her tears ran a jagged path over the ruined lines of her face as he continued past her. Head hanging, she slipped to her knees again, and her sobs were silent.

Vela's voice filled Kavik's ears. "Look at you, honorable warrior. Look how firmly you stand when she needs kindness more than she ever has."

He would go to her. He would hold her. But his chest convulsed again, wracking spasms that ripped down into his gut, up through his head. Darkness filled his vision of Mala, then brightened on a pair of milk moon eyes. Vela studied him for a long moment.

"I don't know why you cry, beast," she finally told him. "Her mouth is still hot and you said her cunt is the same as any other."

No. Mala was unlike any other.

"Of course she is. She is my chosen." Cold fingers pried his hand open. "I will have this coin. It is not worth as much as the one you stole from my temple, but I will consider it a proper offering—and perhaps I will piss in your mouth while you sleep. Happy dreams, beast."

She tapped his head and all was gone.

SELAQ'S eyes were her own again when Kavik opened his, and found her looking down at him in concern. The dirt floor of the stable was hard beneath his back. The sky was dark.

Mala would be far ahead of him.

His body a solid ache, he rose to his feet and stumbled toward the gelding. Someone had removed his tack.

"Do you know which gate Mala used?" His voice was hoarse with grit, but he could speak again.

"East," Selaq said softly. "But she turned north after she was outside the city."

Kavik nodded, then stilled. He looked to her again.

A watery smile touched the innkeeper's lips. "She left something in me."

Something that let her see beyond the walls of the city. "Are you all right?"

"I am." Her gaze narrowed. "You're a fool."

He picked up the gelding's saddle. "I don't need a goddess's vision to know that."

CHAPTER 7.

Hood shadowing her face, Mala rode across the empty moors. Unlike Shim, the dun mare would not be punished by Vela. The mare had no understanding of what it meant to be forsaken. The Hanani stallion did.

The mark burned. Her face didn't feel like her own, but a heavy and swollen mask. But that was only skin and flesh. It was nothing compared to the shattered wound in her heart—and Vela must have been her breath. Because now that she'd been forsaken, Mala seemed to have none left, and every time she tried to draw a new one it never eased the drowning ache in her chest.

She had failed Krimathe. Mala would make no alliances now. No warriors would answer the call of a woman who wore Vela's Mark. And two years would pass before the House of Krima would know of her failure and attempt to send someone else.

If ever she returned to Krimathe at all. She had failed her quest, but she would not abandon her vows—and before she left this cursed land of Blackmoor, she would see Barin dead.

Though she did not know how to do it. While she'd been wearing the red cloak, Vela might have guided her. Mala could not expect help from the goddess now.

Mala could ask for help from no one else, either. Not even the man who'd tried so many ways to kill Barin before.

Kavik.

As soon as he slipped into her thoughts she desperately tried to shove them away. But it was too late. The shattered ache erupted through her chest and doubled her over into helpless tears. Vela forgive her. She should have been more patient. She should have been more stubborn.

She should have let him stab her over and over.

But, no. No. Her tears passed, leaving only the hot agony of the salt burning in her marked cheeks. She could not believe that was Vela's intention. The goddess could be cruel. But Mala had believed Vela would not make the taming a cruel one—and it made no sense that she would not be cruel to Kavik, but would be cruel to Mala. She couldn't believe that the goddess had meant her to love a man, and then ask her to endure as he shredded her heart whenever his fears threatened him.

He'd thoughtlessly, deliberately hurt her. She was not sorry for walking away.

And she had not abandoned her quest. She had *not*. She had only stepped on the wrong path.

She would find it again.

Pushing her hood back, she looked up. The moon shone fat and bright. Tomorrow Vela would look fully upon all of them, but Mala rode by her light now. Not completely forsaken. And with so much to be grateful for.

"Thank you," Mala called to the sky, and the next breath she drew was an easier one. "You sent me to him. What you put into my path would have been so much more than I expected. I didn't come to find love. Only strength. But you chose well for my heart. I wish Kavik had taken the same care with it."

There was no reply. Mala hadn't expected one. She was still forsaken.

She looked to the path ahead again just as the mare shifted nervously beneath her. Tension gripped Mala's neck. Her gaze scanned the barren hills.

A piercing whinny split the night air.

Shim.

No. Oh, no. The mare answered and wheeled toward the

call. Mala tried to rein her in. The mare slowed, then fought the bit when Shim trumpeted again. Curse it all. Mala would not saw at this horse's mouth.

Swinging her leg over the saddle, she slid from the horse's back to the ground. The mare galloped away and into the dark.

"Do not follow me, Shim!" she shouted.

He did. Within minutes he strode behind her, nose nudging her back with each step. The mare walked alongside him, and every time Mala tried to mount her again, Shim nipped at the mare's hindquarters and her wild bucking sent Mala flying to the ground again. As if it were a game.

Her heart would not stop aching. "Do you not know what this mark means, you god-swived scut of a horse? You will be forsaken, too. Danger will come into your path. Your fortunes will turn."

He blew air at the back of her neck and shook his head.

Oh, Temra. Why had that goddess not given this horse sense? She couldn't bear to see him hurt. But she didn't know how to send him away without hurting him herself.

Shim's sudden snort had her reaching for her sword again. His ears pricked forward, he faced the darkness behind them.

"What is it?" Gripping his mane, Mala prepared to haul herself onto his back. Not riding together again—she would defend him. Then when the danger had passed, she would make him go.

A rider crested the low hill. Mala's heart constricted. At this distance, he was nothing but shadow, but she couldn't mistake him. Kavik.

He'd pushed her away. Why come after her now?

But it mattered not. "Shim," she whispered. "Let me mount the mare. Please."

He only lifted his head and whinnied loudly. Kavik's horse answered. All part of Shim's little herd.

Heart racing, Mala drew up her hood and swiftly struck out north again. Dead grass crackled under her boots. Shim and the mare plodded along behind. And the pounding of the gelding's hooves was growing ever louder.

Abruptly the gelding slowed. She heard Kavik dismount. Moments later, the crunch of grass under his boots caught up with her own.

"You must go away from me." She did not shift her gaze from the path ahead. "I am forsaken."

"So am I," Kavik said softly.

No. Not like this. "Danger will come into your path. Your fortunes will turn."

"Danger has always come into my path. And how could my fortunes be worse, little dragon?"

"They will be." Pain swelled in her chest. He had no more sense than a horse. "Please, Kavik. I could not bear being the one responsible for the hurt this will bring you. How can you not understand this? To protect your people from Barin, you haven't allowed them to help *you*."

"If I choose to stay, then *I* am the one responsible for any hurt this brings me. Not you." His voice roughened. "You once helped me despite my warnings. You called the sweetest touch torture. I would torture you the same way, if you believe it would save me from Vela's wrath."

With his fingers sliding beneath her belt. With his hands gripping her ass. Then telling her how much he wanted to taste her.

She stared ahead without answering. A heavy cloud passed in front of the moon and the moors darkened. Kavik was only a shadow beside her.

"Now she won't see me walking with you and know to punish me," he said. "You could touch me without fear."

"I don't wish to touch you."

"Then why do you care what Vela will do? Already I suffer punishment beyond bearing."

Her breath hitched. "Why have you come? It is still not my moon night—and there are many sheaths in the city."

"But I do not love any of the women who possess them," he said gruffly. "I only love you."

"And what of it?" Teeth clenched, she looked into the sky, at the silver-laced clouds with the moon lit behind. Why could she not breathe again? "You think I am so desperate for your heart that I would let you stab mine?"

"What I did wasn't meant to hurt you. I was a stubborn fool."

Just as she had already told him. So she said nothing.

"I dreamed of you," he said. "For so many years. Every night, Vela sent me visions. I didn't know your name, but I knew who you were. My little dragon, the High Daughter in a hauberk of green scales. I was earning coin to build my army, and fought amongst giants, yet I measured every warrior I met against you because I loved you even then. And I wanted to come for you. But how could you love a man who'd abandoned his people in favor of his heart? So I built my army, and planned to go to you after I killed Barin. But Vela sent you to me first."

To tame him. Mala could not halt her laugh. "She *can* be cruel."

"I believed it was cruelty, too. When I pissed in her offering bowl, she told me that I had to wait for the woman in red. That when that woman came, I would be on my knees, and it would be the end."

Mala's heart clenched. She stopped walking and her gaze flew to his face, but the darkness hid him from her. "*Your* end?"

"It must be mine" was his bleak reply. "At the labyrinth, when I saw your red cloak at a distance, I knew it must be coming. I didn't know the woman in red would be my dragon. I had not dreamed of you since your mother's death."

Shards of remembered pain pierced her chest. "That was when I took up my quest."

"Then that is why my dreams ended. I would have seen you wearing the red. I would have been prepared. Instead I learned when I met you that the woman I love would be my end."

Mala wouldn't be his end. But it might not be her choice. "Perhaps because you walk with me when I am forsaken, warrior. She *will* be cruel."

"Not in this." His response sounded raw and thick, as if he'd choked down sand. "She sent you here. I had you, even if only a short time. She is more generous than I knew. If simply walking beside you is all that I will ever have, I will thank her for every moment, no matter how painful it might become, and no matter how it might hasten my death."

Mala glanced into the sky. Not so very long ago, she'd thanked Vela for the same. But it was too late. "I would not have you beside me."

"I vow on my life that I would never hurt you again."

"How could I trust that?"

"I'm not asking you to have faith in me. I'm not a god, but sometimes a foolish man, and you'll be able to trust me because I'll prove that you *can* trust me. Every day, I will prove it. Every breath. Not a single word or touch will ever be made with the intention of giving you pain."

Tears burning in her eyes, she looked to the sky again. Where was Vela and her guidance now? There was none.

And she wanted to believe in him. Wanted to believe so much.

But it was impossible. "Even if I did trust, it cannot be. You can't abandon your people. I can't abandon mine—even if I can no longer live among them."

"Then we will use Stranik's passageway. It is only a week's distance between Blackmoor and Krimathe through the tunnel. If ever your people needed help, you could quickly go to them."

Mala knew of the passageway. It was said that during the creation of the earth, the snake god had fallen asleep, and the pounding of Temra's fist had built the Flaming Mountains of Astal around him. When Stranik had finally woken and slithered on, the tunnel in the shape of his body remained. "That is only legend, warrior."

"No." There was certainty in his voice. "It had only fallen out of use when the demon was trapped there by the ancients. The Destroyer opened the passageway again and released the demon—and the demon tusker uses it as a lair."

It could not be true. And yet it was not legend but fact that when the Destroyer had attacked Krimathe, he and his army had suddenly appeared in the mountains to the south, as if brought there by his sorcerer's magic. At the time, the latest reports had placed him at least two years away, and Krimathe had still been preparing their defenses.

But it had not been magic. "So he didn't want the demon's power, as he told your father," she said softly. "He wanted a fast route to the north."

"Or both. My father believed Barin was left behind to protect the demon tusker from anyone who would destroy it, and that the demon's power protected him in return. Neither can be hurt by blade or fire. Many of the weapons we used against Barin were those that are often used by demon hunters. When I returned with my army, we had many more—and yet my warriors still fell before it."

"Then how do you propose we use the passageway if the

demon can't be killed?" A week's travel to Krimathe. Incredible. Determination and excitement filled her just thinking of it.

"It was trapped before. We could do it again. But not in Stranik's passage."

Which would defeat the purpose. "Where?"

"The labyrinth? I know not." His deep laugh suddenly rolled through the dark. "But we should discover a place quickly. If danger will come at me simply for being near you, then the demon will probably be upon us soon."

Her excitement burst like a rotted eggfruit. How could she have imagined for one moment that this was possible? Perhaps the demon could be killed or trapped, but Kavik could not remain by her side.

"You won't be near me, warrior."

Already challenging her, he moved closer. Not touching her. But walking so near that her cloak swept against his leg with every step.

"I will," he said, and iron hardened his voice. "We are both forsaken. We must both remain separate from our people. So we'll live together in the Weeping Forest, and when Krimathe needs your help, we'll go to them. When Blackmoor needs us, we'll be here for them. And every morning I will kiss you awake—"

"No," she whispered.

"—and every night I'll hold you as you fall asleep."

The longing that had pierced her with his every word was unbearable now. "Stop this, warrior."

"Wherever you go, I will ride beside you," he said, and added when a sharp snort sounded behind them, "and Shim."

"You can't risk this!"

"And whenever you wish, you can ride *me*."

All at once, agony and frustration hacked through her control like an axe. No more. Mala whirled on his shadowed form. She slammed her palms into his armored chest and shoved. "Go!"

He didn't move.

With a scream, she set her feet and threw her shoulder against his breastplate. Pain shot down her arm. A soft grunt escaped him, but he stood firm.

Eyes burning, she pushed harder. There were so many

ways to defeat him. To make him go. To make sure he couldn't follow. But all would hurt him more than he deserved.

"Use your sword, Mala." The suggestion was soft. "I will not defend myself against it."

And she could not use it against him. Not now. But did he know?

Salty tears scalded her ravaged skin as she backed away. In the darkness, her polished blade was only a dull slice of smothered moonlight. "Is it truly worth your life to have me?"

"Merely the chance to have you is worth far more than my life." His massive shadow came nearer, then sank before her. Hoarsely he said, "But my life is worth nothing at all if *you* will not have *me*."

Her breath wouldn't come. It wouldn't come, though she dragged it in, over and over, trembling as she looked down at him. His head was bowed, she thought, but wasn't certain until she searched for his face in the dark. Her fingers slipped over his hair before sliding down to cup his jaw. He shook, and a ragged groan burst from him before he turned his cheek against her palm.

"Mala." His mouth pressed against her inner wrist in a hot, shuddering kiss, and the jagged pain in her chest eased. "Can you see? I am on my knees before you. I am tamed. For as long as I draw breath, I will walk by your side and do it willingly. I will *fight* to walk by your side."

Not tamed. Still strong. Still free. And just as stubborn as she.

But he could call it whatever he chose.

"You cannot walk by my side on your knees, warrior." She sheathed her sword. "You'll fall behind."

Or he would carry her forward, because as he surged to his feet Kavik lifted her from the ground. His mouth found hers, so sweet and rough, and her tears would not stop falling.

Abruptly he tore his lips from hers and stepped back, fingers lightly brushing her shoulders, then her arms, as if he couldn't bear to let her go but was afraid to touch her. "Your tears, Mala." His voice was agony. "I forgot your mark. Did I hurt you?"

She had forgotten it, too. And there was no pain at all, as if the burning, swollen mask had peeled away.

But she had no time to wonder over it. From behind her came Shim's urgent whinny, and a moment later, a thunderous roar echoed across the moors. Kavik stiffened against her.

Dread settled in her stomach. "You know that sound?" she asked, and could barely make out his nod through the dark.

"The demon tusker," he said.

WITH Mala beside him, Kavik raced to the top of the next hill and looked north. Her path from Perca hadn't lain along the roads, yet he knew this land, and a village didn't lay far distant. If the demon tusker passed it by, he and Mala might not have such a dangerous fight on their hands.

Dread filled his chest when he saw the flames flickering in the distance. "It's at the village," he said.

"Then we will be, too. Shim!"

His heart clenched. He wanted to tell her to let him go alone to help the village, but knew she would not remain here any more than he would.

The gelding waited down the hill. Kavik started toward it, but halted as heavy hoofbeats drew alongside him.

"Kavik!" Mala called from atop Shim. The hood hid her face, but the light of the distant fire made her into a dim silhouette, her hand extended toward him. "Shim is strong enough to carry us both, and he's faster. On your gelding, it will be over before you arrive."

He only hesitated long enough to glance at Shim. "You agree?"

The stallion snorted and Kavik swung onto his back as lightly as he could without a saddle. As soon as he settled behind her, Mala's small form crouched over the stallion's neck.

"Go!"

The stallion surged ahead. Only Kavik's light grasp on Mala's hips saved him from tumbling over the horse's rump. He leaned forward until his chest pressed against her strong back. The sides of her cloak flared out like wings as they raced across the hills, Shim's hooves like rolling thunder. Her hood flew back.

"Mala!" he shouted into the wind.

By the slight turn her of head, he knew she listened.

"If this is the end, it's not because I was with you! It's because of the demon and because I pissed in her offering bowl!"

The vehement shake of her head whipped her braids against his face. "It's not the end," she shouted back at him. "Because if I'm the one to herald it, then *I* want to be the one to end you!"

Grinning, he squeezed her waist. "Don't try to fight the demon! Just guide the villagers to safety, if you can! If they can't reach the southern gate in the wall, make them climb over it. Then they need to run out over the hills, away from the demon's sight!"

The demon rarely followed. It only attacked what was in its path. Her nod told him she understood.

"There will be revenants!"

She tensed against him and nodded again just as the demon bellowed, a deafening roar that drowned out the drumbeat of Shim's pounding hooves. The stallion carried them over the next hill.

The village lay directly ahead. Its northern wall had been destroyed, the mortared stones lying in shattered heaps. Houses nearby burned, the thatched roofs blazing. Indistinct figures darted through the dense smoke that choked the northern half of the village and had begun billowing south along the road. Human screams mingled with the revenants' shrieks.

"People will be hiding in the houses!" Kavik shouted. Almost a hundred and fifty lived in this village. "They think they'll be safe if the demon doesn't destroy their building. But the revenants will hunt them down."

"Can we draw the revenants?" Mala called back to him.

So she was already thinking the same as he. The creatures might be searching individually for prey now, but they would converge upon a stronger foe.

"Take me to the northern wall!" The demon tusker had already broken through—moving south. The demon likely wouldn't turn around, but the revenants would still come for Kavik. "I'll draw the revenants. You *stay* on Shim! You can move through the village and help any people you can, but if the demon comes at you, let Shim run! You can ride back around to help them from another direction!"

She nodded, and her hand reached back to grip his thigh. "My heart is yours, Kavik!"

Fierce love grabbed hold of his chest. But before he could reply, her fingers abruptly clenched. A gust of wind blew through the billowing smoke and revealed the demon tusker.

Given a choice, Kavik wouldn't want to face a tusker even if the animal hadn't been possessed by a demon. With legs like thick tree trunks, a hulking back, and heavily domed head, the bulls were aggressive and territorial—and big, often growing as tall as the mammoths that roamed the far southern steppes. Unlike mammoths, however, a tusker didn't wear a pair of long tusks beside its prehensile snout. A tusker's snout and the tusks that flanked it were shorter. The primary tusks jutted straight out from beneath the jaw like a pair of flat blades. The animals used them to slash through thick branches and vegetation as it foraged, and as defense. He'd seen a tusker cut a hunter's horse from beneath him by swinging those tusks like a scythe.

The demon's possession transformed an already-dangerous animal into a monstrous terror. The tusker's long red hairs had been shed from its hide. Bloated white skin stretched tightly over its enormous frame, as if the burning evil inhabiting the creature expanded its body to an ever-greater size to contain the demon inside it. Each of its tusks had elongated and sharpened, and its jaw could unhinge to reveal jagged teeth unlike any natural tusker's.

And unlike a tusker, the demon didn't lumber. It stalked the ground swiftly, silent when it wasn't roaring. Now it slipped through the smoke like a wraith and vanished from their sight again.

Through the dark, he spotted a handful of villagers scrambling over the eastern wall. No one had yet fled through the southern gate as Shim raced north around the village. "Check the southern gate first! Revenants might be blocking escape!"

Nodding, she squeezed his thigh and released him. Throat tight, Kavik pressed his face against the back of her neck and breathed deep. *Mala.* No longer in red. But he'd been on his knees. Now there was only the end.

He would still fight to his last breath against it. Never would he leave her alone, forsaken. He would never leave her side.

Shim rounded the northern wall. Fire raged in the nearest houses, throwing wavering orange light through the wall's shattered remains. With his sword, Kavik pointed to the breach. "There!"

The horse slowed as he passed it. The shrieking howls of nearby revenants sounded as Kavik swung to the ground, landing amid the broken stones. Without stopping, Shim continued on, and Kavik stole a last look. His gaze met Mala's. She'd glanced back over her shoulder, her face lit by the burning houses behind him.

Her unmarked face.

Shock jarred him forward a step, but the stallion's speed had already carried her past the breach and into the darkness beyond. Kavik stared after her for a breath. His heart pounded as he crossed the shattered remnants of the wall.

He'd been on his knees. That didn't just mean the end. Kavik had told her something else—that he was tamed.

Now her mark was gone. No longer forsaken. Her task accomplished.

The beast of Blackmoor was tamed.

Wild elation whipped through him and he answered the revenants' shrieks with a howl of his own, banging the flat of his sword against stone. "Come for me, then!" he shouted. "I am leashed! An easy kill!"

A red-eyed shadow raced toward him. A wulfen revenant, jaws slobbering. Kavik cleaved through its neck with a mighty swing, then set his boot against the neck stump and ripped the creature open from gullet to stomach. Hot blood poured out, steaming on the ground, stinking.

The stench of a revenant's blood always drew more—as if its scent told the others that their blood had been spilled, so there was a foe to defeat.

Within moments, he'd killed two more, then charged forward to protect a white-faced woman who emerged from the smoke screaming. He slaughtered the revenants chasing behind her, then sent her over the breached wall.

They did not stop after that. Revenants by twos and threes. A family who scrambled gratefully past him in the dark, a bleeding old woman that he couldn't help over the broken wall until he'd put down the five revenants that came at him. The demon's roars were followed by the crashing of stone, more flames.

Rapid hoofbeats pounded through the smoke. Mala.

Her sword cleaved the neck of a revenant snapping at Shim's hindquarters, her blade already dripping with gore. Her grin was wide as she approached him and took in his pile of corpses. "We ran!" she shouted on a laugh. "We're heading back around! The south gate is open now!"

So she'd encountered the demon and fled. "Your mark!" he called as Shim swept past him. "I'm tamed!"

With a heaving snort, Shim abruptly wheeled around. Mala clung to his back, her expression a mask of disbelief and astonishment. She touched her cheek.

Suddenly she laughed and looked to the sky. "Vela!" she shouted. "I would appreciate those ten thousand warriors now!"

Kavik grinned but couldn't respond. Another revenant was upon him—what had once been a cow. Grunting, he swung through its thick neck, and the next was already lunging. He greeted it by shoving the point of his blade through its eye.

He glanced back. Mala had crouched over Shim's neck again. They were gone.

A chorus of shrieks and howls warned him before he saw the pack of revenants coming. His grip firm upon the handle of his weapon, he moved closer to the wall, made sure the stone was at his back.

As much sweat as blood dripped into his eyes when he could pause for breath again. Where was the demon? He hadn't heard its roar since Mala had come through. If it had passed through the village, then there were only revenants left. And no more of the creatures had come for him yet—the slaughtered pack had been the last, and he'd taken at least fifteen breaths since.

Was it done?

Kavik listened. The only roar was from the nearby fires, the loud rumble of roofs and walls collapsing, the snap and crack of heated stone. Animals bleated outside the walls—probably those that had escaped through the south gate and were running loose. A distant shout.

He started in that direction as another sound carried across the distance—Shim's enraged, trumpeting neigh.

Kavik bolted toward it. Smoke burned his eyes and throat. The thick clouds obscured everything past the reach of his sword. Obstacles appeared almost the same moment he was upon them. He vaulted over a cart abandoned in the road and landed on the lump of a body. A revenant. Mala's work.

Icy dread filled his chest, squeezed at his lungs. She was another strong foe.

But she was on Shim, fast and mobile. By the time any revenants were drawn to the others she'd slain, Mala would already have been gone.

Unless she'd come upon a pack, too. One might have slowed her down.

Heart pounding, he raced south through the village, faster than he'd ever run. The smoke thinned. The roaring of the fires dimmed. And he could hear them now, the shrieks and howls. He followed the noise through a courtyard and abruptly saw her.

They'd swarmed her. Four or five dozen of them. With Mala still astride him, Shim had backed up against the stone wall of a cottage, and they fought together as if one. Mala's blade and axe protected their sides, and Shim's tearing teeth and striking hooves guarded their front. Every revenant that leapt at them was driven back or slain. Given much longer, or a single miss, they might have been overwhelmed—but not yet. And not now.

Kavik didn't howl to announce his presence this time. The revenants did not know what was coming behind them. Mala saw him, and he saw her fierce grin.

Then he saw his end.

Vela had not said it would be his death. But it mattered not. This was the same.

An oxen revenant charged through the pack. Mala's axe fell upon its skull but couldn't stop the thrust of the heavy body behind it. The creature slammed into Shim's shoulder at the same moment the stallion reared to strike at a revenant. The impact whipped the stallion around, hind legs swept from under him. Mala flew from his back and into the middle of the swarm of revenants. She disappeared beneath them.

Red filled his vision. Kavik roared, charging the swarm,

and his heart was a shredded thing, the agony growing with every beat. Shouting her name, he began hacking a path toward her through the mass of revenants. The nearest creatures turned toward him then, but he didn't see them anymore, his gaze fixed on the spot where she'd vanished. She was still fighting. Through the swarm, he saw the flash of her sword. The fall of her axe.

And the demon tusker silently coming from around the cottage behind her.

"Mala!" Desperately Kavik tried to reach her, his sword swinging, but the mass of revenants pushed him back. He couldn't get to her.

But she must have sensed the huge demon, or realized the revenants behind her had scattered, or felt its hot breath. She spun to face it.

The demon swung its head. The blades of its tusks swept into her like a scythe.

"Mala!" He screamed her name, then there was nothing, nothing but the blood and agony and the fall of his sword. He had to reach her.

With a final swing, abruptly he was through the mass of revenants, and he knew the madness of battle was upon him. Or simply the same madness that had befallen his father after he'd lost his queen and his sons.

Ahead, Mala was still standing. Feet braced, her jaw tight with effort, she held the edge of the tusks away from her stomach, as if she'd instinctively caught the ivory blades and tried to stop them from cutting her in half.

The demon screeched. Rage filled that shriek, and its own powerful legs were braced. A spasm shook its head.

Not a spasm, Kavik realized. It was trying to shake her off. To move her.

He wasn't mad. She had captured the tusks in an unbreakable grip. An *immovable* grip, as if she weighed more than the demon tusker could lift.

Kavik had felt an unbreakable grip before. But no silver light filled her eyes. Her skin didn't shine.

This was Mala. Only Mala.

A revenant slashed at him from behind. Still staring, Kavik swung his sword in that direction, and still didn't look away even when the stamp of hooves sounded beside him and the revenant's brains splattered his boots.

The demon roared, its terrible jaws opening wide. Nose wrinkling, Mala closed her eyes and turned her face away.

"By Temra's fist," she breathed. "It smells worse than revenant."

Kavik's wild laugh broke from him. She laughed, too, then shook her head.

Determination set her face. "I still don't know if we can kill it. But perhaps I can make it easier to try."

Adjusting her grip on the tusks, she looked back at the demon. Slowly, she began to twist. The demon screamed, its head turning to the side.

A crack split the night. Not the demon's neck. The tusks. Gritting her teeth, Mala drew back her fist and swung it down hard against the flat blades. Those tusks had rammed through stone, had withstood sharpened steel.

They didn't survive the hammering of Mala's fist.

All at once they snapped, the long blades coming away in her grip—and releasing her hold on the demon tusker. Kavik shouted and rushed at her. With a roar of pain, the demon charged. Stumbling back, she desperately swung the long bladed tusks.

The ivory cleaved through its neck even as Kavik slammed into her, yanking her out of the demon's path. Its charging body tripped over its own head and fell, plowing into the ground. Still moving.

Mala pulled out of Kavik's arms. With a ringing battle cry, she stalked forward and shoved the blades through the demon's chest, through its heart.

The body tried to get to its feet. She stared at it, chest heaving.

Suddenly laughing again, Kavik suggested, "The head?"

Shaking hers, she stalked toward the body and slammed her foot against the end of the bladed tusks. The ivory splintered. She ripped one away, a shard as long as a sword, and stabbed it through the demon's eye.

It fell quiet.

They waited, watching. Still nothing. Mala murmured, "It wasn't ten thousand warriors."

Kavik looked to her and she met his eyes, hers wide and disbelieving.

"It wasn't ten thousand warriors," she said. "That's not what she promised me. I assumed it would be. But it was the *strength* of ten thousand warriors." She looked at her hands. "The durability, too. Those blades should have cut through my hands."

"And the weight," Kavik said. "It couldn't move you."

She glanced up. "You moved me. But can I—"

Striding forward, she tried to lift him. Then again, wrapping her arms around his waist and grunting with the effort. When she made a sound of frustration and stepped back, Kavik gripped her waist and lifted her easily, bringing her up to his mouth.

Smiling, Mala slipped her arms around his neck. "She also said 'when you most need it.' I apparently don't need it against you. Or the revenants."

When she'd been thrown from Shim's back. Kavik could still see the revenants swarming over her. "No," he said roughly.

Her hands cupped his jaw. Softly she kissed him, then slid back to the ground. She turned toward Shim. "You're all right?"

The horse responded with a stamp of his foot. Yes.

"He's limping," Kavik said and the stallion pinned his ears back and bared his teeth at him.

Mala stroked the stallion's neck, soothing him. "Can you call the other horses? We should stay through the night and make certain all of the revenants are dead."

Through the night. Sudden overwhelming emotion filled Kavik's chest, and he turned away, staring at the demon's body. He'd thought this would be the end. But there would be a tonight. A tomorrow.

It hadn't been the end. At least, not *his* end.

And what Mala had assumed Vela meant wasn't what she'd received at all.

His gaze moved to the ivory shard embedded in the demon's eye. In that temple so many years ago, when he'd sought Vela's help, he'd asked for the strength to defeat Barin—or the knowledge to do it.

Mala had received strength. And Kavik had been a fool about many things. He would not be a fool about this.

◆ ◆ ◆

VELA looked fully upon them when Mala rode with Kavik to
the citadel gates. Unlike the first time she'd come here, the
gates were closed—but Selaq had already told them they
would be. With eyes closed, the innkeeper had looked beyond
the fortress's walls and told them the citadel guards waited in
the courtyard, two hundred strong.

When Barin had learned the demon was dead, the warlord
should have hired ten thousand.

She dismounted. Of heavy blackwood and reinforced with
iron, the gates were a formidable barrier, built to withstand
battering rams and armies mounted on tamed tuskers and
three-toed beasts. But she thought that a demon tusker could
have probably broken through it alone. And so could she.

Raising her foot, she slammed her boot into the gates.

The barrier exploded open with a shriek of iron and rain of
splinters. Mala strode through with axe and sword in hand
and met the stunned, fearful faces of the citadel guard.

"If you know what is good for you," she shouted, "you will
move aside and create a path!"

The guards shifted uneasily, looking to each other. Mala
spotted Heddiq mounted on a horse at the opposite end of the
courtyard. With a grunt, she whipped around and threw her axe.

The heavy weapon flew end over end, spinning above the
heads of two hundred guards and smashing through Heddiq's
face. With a *thunk*, the blade embedded in the stone wall
behind him—with Heddiq's helm pinned between. His body
toppled from his horse.

Two hundred guards moved aside.

There was only silence as Kavik joined her, and together they
walked to the keep. Mala opened the doors with another kick.

More dedicated guards waited inside. Kavik met them
with his sword, and Mala didn't need her strength now. She
fought beside him until the last guard fell to the floor, and
walked with him to the great hall.

Mala didn't have to smash those doors. A tall, wiry man
stood outside them, keys in hand and tears in his eyes. The
marshal, she remembered.

She strode into the great hall and called, "I have brought my beast, Lord Barin!"

In his robes of yellow and gold, the warlord stood at the center of the hall. No courtiers sat at the tables now. More guards waited—but Barin held his hand up to them, and his smile was still amused.

"Did you think killing the demon tusker would be the end of me?" He laughed and looked to Kavik. "Come and see. There is still no sword that can harm me."

Mala glanced at her warrior. When she had first encountered him at Selaq's inn, just after he'd learned of his taming, Mala had thought she'd never seen such cold hatred and rage directed at her.

She had never seen him look at Barin. Vela had gifted her with the strength of ten thousand warriors, yet if ever Kavik had looked at her like that she would have fled for her life. He was death itself, not silver-fingered Rani come to gently carry a warrior into Temra's arms, but ragged screaming death, contained within sheer muscle and bleeding from his savage stare.

Yet Barin did not flee. Not as Kavik stalked toward him, his steps fluid and strong, his sword held loosely in his grip. The warlord even spread his arms wide, robes falling open and baring his tattooed chest.

When Kavik set his blade against the side of the man's neck, Barin looked into his eyes, grinning. He didn't look down to see the ivory shard in Kavik's left hand—until blood spilled from his mouth. Then he glanced down to see it embedded in his heart.

Cruel. But Mala thought Barin deserved it.

The warlord looked up, and she thought that now he saw what Kavik was. His end. His death. It was the last he saw. Kavik yanked the shard from his chest and shoved it through his eye.

Barin slid to the floor. Unmoving, Kavik stood over him with head bowed, and when Mala went to him he was staring at the man's dead body, his chest heaving with harsh, ragged breaths. She touched his arm and he caught her against him, burying his face in her hair.

"It is done," he said hoarsely. "It is finally done."

Mala held him tight. Around them, chaos was exploding.

Some of the guards shouted with fear, others with joy. Near the entrance to the great hall, the teary-eyed marshal was unfastening the collars of men and women tied by their leashes. Someone spoke a word, and soon it was repeated, louder and louder.

King.

So he was. She drew back and looked up at him. "Your work has only begun, warrior."

CHAPTER 8

———

Later that night, her warrior followed her. When she'd left the chaos of the citadel below and climbed the stairs of the northern tower, Mala had known that he would.

She didn't want to be inside, not this night. Instead she cleared the guards from the northern tower's battlements and laid out a soft bed atop the stone. When Kavik found her, Mala stood at the parapet wall, looking over the city below. Barin's fall was still being celebrated and fought over within the citadel and beyond its walls. Yet there was no one who argued with the name they were calling him now. Kavik, the king of Blackmoor.

He was still her beast.

His arms circled her waist from behind, and she leaned back against a chest as strong as these stone walls. "There is still much corruption to root out," she said and shivered as his warm lips found her neck. "And Stranik's passage is likely full of revenants."

"We will root those out, too." His gentle hand cupped her throat, holding her still as his fingers untied the side of her cuirass. "And I will return with you to your home, which will soon have far more than your strength available when they need it. Change will come to both our lands when others hear of this pass through the mountains. Everyone will be traveling this route—including more warriors. Perhaps even ten thousand of them."

Bringing trade, riches, and trouble to both sides. Mala looked forward to it all.

But she only needed one warrior.

Unsheathing her knife, she turned in his arms and pressed the tip to the hollow of this throat. "The full moon still shines overhead. Do you intend to have me?"

His hunger lay stark upon his face. "I do."

With a flick of her wrist, she carved a shallow crescent into his skin. Not a flinch passed through his body, but a question lay in the arch of his dark brow when blood began to slide down his chest.

"The scars upon the back of your neck are not moon blood scars, Kavik. Those cannot be offered by force. Your moon night is here with me." As his gaze turned fiery, she flipped the knife in her hand, offering it. "Will you mark me?"

"I will." His voice was guttural as he took the blade.

She tilted her chin back, exposing her throat to him. The sting at her neck was nothing, and yet it was everything. Hope for her future filled these drops of blood—a future with this man, blessed by the goddess who had brought them together.

Taking the knife, she let it clatter to the stone. "Vela has been given the blood that she wants. Now I will have what I want. Down, warrior."

His grin was instant and fierce. Down he went, taking the long path. He stripped away her armor, and cold air caressed her skin. His lips followed the trickle of her moon blood, then journeyed over the swells of her breasts. Their stiffened peaks ached even before his mouth reached them, and when he had finished his heated assault upon their tips, her nipples throbbed from the suckling and her whole body was aflame. Only then did he continue down, pushing her back against the parapet wall and feasting upon her yielding flesh until she screamed.

Her hands fisted in his thick hair. *"Now."*

With a growl, he lifted her against him and carried her to the soft bedding. Laying her upon it, he stepped back and removed his armor. Mala watched him undress with pleasure, stroking between her thighs as the torchlight flickered across his bared chest. His ravenous gaze fell upon her fingers. Grinning, she widened the spread of her legs.

"Do not be easy with me, warrior."

He was not. With a rough grip, he caught her wrist and brought her fingers to his mouth to suck the wetness from her skin, then pinned her hands over her head. He pushed her legs wider before his weight settled between her thighs.

But he did not fill her. Instead he took his cock in hand and slicked the broad tip through her lush cleft, testing her entrance with gentle pressure. Again and again he did this, sliding up to tease her clitoris with his cockhead before returning to gently nudge her center again. Crying out in frustration, Mala arched beneath him, trying to force him in.

"Now, Kavik!"

"I have waited long, little dragon," he replied through gritted teeth. "You will wait until I have seen you take all of me. I will not pound into you before I know how much you can bear."

"I can bear everything you give to me, warrior."

Abruptly he pressed harder. Mala gasped and stilled as her sensitive flesh stretched to accept his immense crown. Oh, but Temra had been generous to him. So generous.

Kavik paused, rigid above her. "Mala?"

"More." With a rock of her hips, she urged him deeper. "If you will take me, take me hard."

Bending his head, he claimed her mouth with his—but though his kiss was hard and deep, the invasion of her sheath was slow. So slow. Mala cried out as he retreated slightly before advancing again. He filled her, and filled her, and even as she wondered whether there would be an end, his loins finally settled heavily against hers.

"Do you see?" Mala panted, looking down between them. Her clitoris was nestled against the dark hair growing at the base of his cock. The delicate gates of her sheath embraced the root of his shaft. They were the only delicate part of her, and even they were strong enough to take him. "I can sheathe you, though your sword is so massive."

"And you are tighter than a blademaster's fist."

Body shaking with strain, his eyes locked on her face, he rocked against her. She cried out, and her thighs came up to grip his hips.

·   Teeth clenched, he rocked again. "Is this pleasure, Mala?"

"It is." Slicing through her, deeper and deeper. "The path is never easy."

He stopped with his cock buried to the hilt. Mala bucked under him in desperate frustration. His gaze hot, Kavik licked his fingertips before sliding his hand between them. She shuddered as he brushed her clitoris—then screamed when he gently tugged with slick fingers. Heat rushed up under her skin. Kavik groaned and tugged again. Mala sobbed his name and her thighs fell away from his hips. Her sheath clenched around his shaft with each soft caress, as if trying to pull him deeper.

"This," he ground out. "Better?"

So much. She arched beneath him. "Hard, now. Hard."

He drew back, and his cock was drenched in her need, the heavy shaft glistening. Slowly he thrust into her again, with no resistance, no invasion, just a long sweet stroke that stoked fire through her veins. Helplessly she moaned and tilted her hips to take him deeper.

Withdrawing his fingers from between them, Kavik braced his elbow beside her shoulder. Letting go of her wrists, he fisted his fingers in her hair. Laughing, Mala took hold of his.

"Now," he said hoarsely.

His cock drove deep. Her scream was cut short by another savage thrust, and she cried out again before setting her teeth against steely muscle. Kavik groaned, grinding hard between her thighs. The brutal pressure against her clitoris burst into stars behind her eyes.

Ruthlessly, he pushed her left knee up to her shoulder and fucked deeper.

Mala couldn't get enough, couldn't get close enough. With open-mouthed kisses, she tasted the saltiness of his chest and the bleeding mark on his throat. Her hands dragged down his flexing back. His cock surged into her, each heavy thrust striking harder, winding her body tighter.

"I love you," she whispered against his skin.

Abruptly he pulled away from her, leaving her empty. His cock stood reddened and thick. His gaze was feral.

Mala licked her lips and reached for him. Kavik trapped her wrists and flipped her onto her stomach. His big hand pinned the back of her neck. He dragged her up to her knees and mounted her like a beast, his rigid length spearing deep.

The bedding muffled her scream. He slammed into her again and orgasm crashed through her, writhing along her spine and jerking her hips even as he pounded harder into her convulsing sheath. She sobbed his name, fingers clenching.

Then he slowed, slowed. Reverent kisses trailed across her shoulders.

With a blissful sigh, Mala stretched beneath him, widening her knees. So sweet, this fucking. Sweet and tender and slow, and when the shattering pleasure splintered through her again, she needed to know this pleasure was his, too.

"Come into me, warrior," she urged. "Fill me with a river of your seed."

A primitive groan sounded behind her. Hard fingers bit into her hips and his cock stroked deeper, faster, before his body abruptly stilled. His shaft throbbed the release of his seed and her sheath clenched around him, stealing her breath with the unexpected ecstasy of it. Moaning, she turned her face against the bed.

His breath a hot shudder against her ear, he withdrew and rolled her over atop him. She went bonelessly, muscles still quivering. The full moon gazed down on them, and she thanked the goddesses for giving her a strong heart and a resilient sheath.

"Ale?" Mala asked when she could catch her breath. When Kavik grunted, she reached for the wineskin she'd put beside the bed. He sat up and drank with her, then pulled her over his lap, her thighs straddling his.

He kissed her, and it warmed her better than any drink. She slipped her arms around his neck. Already his cock stood hard again.

She grinned and tasted his mouth. "Was I worth the wait?"

"Worth waiting forever," he said gruffly.

"Instead you'll have me that long," she said and rose over his straining shaft. "Now we'll ride together."

His hands caught her waist, holding her in place. Concern deepened his voice. "Are you raw?"

A little. She didn't care. Biting her lip, she sank onto him, her head falling back as he filled her.